OBELISK

OBELISK

STEPHEN BAXTER

GOLLANCZ

LONDON

'Fate and the Fire-lance', in *Sideways in Crime* ed. Lou Anders, Solaris Books, 2008. Copyright © Stephen Baxter 2008.

'The Jubilee Plot', in *Celebration*, ed. Ian Whates and Ian Watson, BSFA 2008. Copyright © Stephen Baxter 2008.

'Turing's Apples', in *Eclipse Two* ed. Jonathan Strahan, Night Shade Books, 2008. Copyright © Stephen Baxter 2008.

'Eagle Song', in *Postscripts* no. 15, Summer 2008. Copyright © Stephen Baxter 2008.

'Artefacts', in *The Solaris Book of New Science Fiction: Vol 3*, ed. George Mann, BL Publishing, 2009. Copyright © Stephen Baxter 2009.

'The Unblinking Eye', in *Other Earths*, ed. Nick Gevers and Joseph Lake, Daw Books 2009. Copyright © Stephen Baxter 2009.

'The Pevatron Rats', in *The Mammoth Book of Mindblowing Science Fiction*, ed. Mike Ashley, Constable & Robinson, UK, Running Press, US, 2009. Copyright © Stephen Baxter 2009.

'Vacuum Lad', in *Masked*, ed. Lou Anders, Gallery Books, 2010. Copyright © Stephen Baxter 2010.

'Darwin Anathema' in *The Mammoth Book of Alternate History Stories*, ed. Ian Watson and Ian Whates, Constable & Robinson, UK, Running Press, PA, US, 2010. Copyright © Stephen Baxter 2010.

'The Invasion of Venus', in *Engineering Infinity*, ed. Jonathan Strahan, Solaris, 2011. Copyright © Stephen Baxter 2011.

'Rock Day', in *Solaris Rising*, ed. Ian Whates, Solaris Publishing, 2011. Copyright © Stephen Baxter 2011.

'On Chryse Plain', in *Life on Mars*, ed. Jonathan Strahan, Viking Penguin, 2011. Copyright © Stephen Baxter 2011.

'A Journey to Amasia', in *Arc* 1.1, 2012. Copyright © Stephen Baxter 2012.

'Obelisk', in *Edge of Infinity*, ed. Jonathan Strahan, Solaris Books, 2012. Copyright © Stephen Baxter 2012.

'StarCall', in *Starship Century*, ed. J. and G. Benford, Microwave Sciences, 2013. Copyright © Stephen Baxter 2013.

'Mars Abides', previously unpublished. Copyright © Stephen Baxter 2016.

'Escape from Eden', previously unpublished. Copyright © Stephen Baxter 2016.

First published in Great Britain in 2016 by Gollancz
An imprint of the Orion Publishing Group
Carmelite House, 50 Victoria Embankment,
London EC4Y 0DZ
An Hachette UK Company

A CIP catalogue record for this book is available from the British Library.

ISBN 978 1 473 21274 9 (Cased)
ISBN 978 1 473 21275 6 (Export Trade Paperback)

1 3 5 7 9 10 8 6 4 2

Typeset at The Spartan Press Ltd, Lymington, Hants

Printed and bound by CPI Group (UK) Ltd,
Croydon, CR0 4YY

www.stephen-baxter.com
www.orionbooks.co.uk
www.gollancz.co.uk

For Lloyd

CONTENTS

PROXIMA-ULTIMA

ON CHRYSE PLAIN

'You haven't even seen a picture of her,' Jonno said, panting as he pedalled.

'She's called Hiroe,' Vikram said.

'Your bride-to-be in Hellas Basin!'

'Shut up.'

Jonno laughed, wheezing.

The flycycle dipped, and Vikram had to push harder to bring them back up to their proper altitude. It was always like this with Jonno. At fifteen he was the same age as Vikram, but a few centimetres shorter and a good few kilos heavier, enough to unbalance the cycle. Jonno didn't have enough breath to talk and cycle. But he talked anyhow.

Vikram didn't mind taking the strain for his friend. He liked the feel of his legs pumping at the pedals, his breath deepening, the skinsuit snug around him, the slow unwinding of the crumpled landscape under them, the way the translucent wings above the cycle frame caught the buttery light of the Martian afternoon. He liked the idea that it was his muscles, and his muscles alone, propelling them across the sky.

But Jonno kept on about Hiroe. 'You worry too much. Just because you haven't seen a picture doesn't *necessarily* mean she looks like she was hatched by a rock bug.'

'Shut up! Where are we anyhow?'

Jonno glanced down and tapped his wristmate. 'That's Chryse Plain, I think. We just crossed the highland boundary. Wow, look at those outflow channels.' Where, billions of years ago, vast rivers had briefly flowed from Mars's southern highlands into the basin of the northern sea, cutting deep valleys and spilling megatonnes of rocks over the plains. 'What a sight it must have been, once.'

'Yeah.'

'You don't care, do you?'

Vikram shrugged, pedalling. 'It's all about the journey for me. Getting the job done.'

3

'Checking out those weather stations at Acidalia. Getting the credits for another A-grade. You've got no imagination, man.'

Something distracted Vikram. Odd lights in the sky. He squinted, and tapped his faceplate to reduce the tint.

'Or,' Jonno said, 'you've got the wrong kind of imagination. Like with Hiroe. You could always wear a disguise in the wedding photos—'

Vikram pointed. 'What's that?'

The sky was full of shining trails.

When the plasma glow cleared from around her clamshell, and the gnarly landscape of Mars was revealed beneath her, Natalie whooped. She couldn't help it. She'd made it. She'd dived down from orbit, lying flat on the broad disc of the clamshell, and had got through the heat of atmospheric entry, and now she was skimming through the air of another world. The air of Mars was thinner than Earth's, but it was deeper, and she was high, so high the world was curved beneath her. The shrunken sun, off to her left, was low and cast long shadows over the channelled plains.

And all around her she saw the contrails scratched across the sky by the rest of her school group, dozens of them on their shells.

Benedicte's voice crackled in her ears. 'You stayed on your shell this time, Nat?'

'Yes, Benedicte, I stayed on.'

'Well, we're over the Chryse Plain, as advertised. Betcha I get the first sighting of the Viking lander.'

'Not a chance!' And Natalie lunged forward, shifting her weight, so her clamshell cut into the thickening air.

But she wasn't used to the Martian air. She didn't get the angle quite right. She could feel it immediately.

'Natalie, you're too steep. Pull out . . . I lost you. Natalie. Natalie!'

The clamshell dug deeper into the air, and started to shudder.

This wasn't good.

And there seemed to be something in the way.

'Clamshell trails,' Jonno said. He leaned sideways so he could see the sky, around the edge of the wing. 'Earthworm tourists.'

They hit a pocket of turbulence and the flycycle bucked and shuddered, the rigging creaking. Vikram said, 'Hey, get back in, man. I'm having trouble keeping us on our track.'

'Look at those babies,' Jonno said wistfully, still leaning out. 'You know, some day, if I can afford it—'

It came out of the sky, almost vertically, a bright green disc with somebody clinging to its back. Vikram actually saw a head turned towards him, a shocked face behind a visor, a mouth opened in an 'O'.

He hauled at the joystick. The flycycle's big fragile rudder turned, creaking. It wasn't enough. It was never going to be enough.

The clamshell cut through the flycycle like a blade through paper. The cycle folded up, crumpling, and started to fall, spiralling down towards the plain of Chryse.

And Jonno groaned. Vikram saw that the instrument console had jammed into Jonno's chest. Vikram couldn't even reach him.

He tried the controls. Nothing responded, and the machine was bent out of shape anyhow. They were going down. Their best hope was that the cycle's fragile structure might slow down their fall enough for them to walk away from the crash. But as they descended the spinning increased, and the structure creaked and snapped.

That clamshell was in trouble too. Vikram glimpsed it tumbling down out of the air.

And the rock-strewn ground of Chryse loomed beneath them, the detail exploding. Vikram braced.

Natalie took a step forward, then another. Red dust scattered at her feet. She was walking on Mars, for the first time in her life. In the low gravity, she felt like she was floating.

She was on a plain of dusty sand, strewn with rocks. The sun was small and low in a deep red sky, and cast long, sharp shadows from rocks that looked as if they hadn't been disturbed for a billion years. She saw nothing, nobody, no vehicles or buildings. She was alone.

She wasn't supposed to be here.

She didn't remember climbing out of the clamshell. Just the approaching ground, her fight to bring up the rim of the shell so that at least she'd land at a shallow angle, the punch in the gut as the shell's underside hit the ground and began to scrape over the dust . . .

She turned around. There was the clamshell, cracked and crumpled. And a gully, hundreds of metres long, cut through the dust where she had skidded. The clamshell had a small liquid-rocket pack that should have kicked her back to orbit when she'd finished skimming the air. But the small, spherical fuel tanks were broken open. It couldn't have got her to orbit anyhow, not from here.

Her suit was comfortable, warm. She could hear the whir of the fans in her backpack. She tested her legs and arms, her fingers. Nothing broken, and her suit was working, keeping her alive. It was a miracle she'd walked away from the crash, but she had. Now she just needed to get off this rock.

'Benedicte,' she called. 'Doctor Poulson? I'm down. Somewhere on Chryse Plain, I guess...'

Nothing. No reply. Her suit comms were very short range. The structure of the clamshell contained amplifier boosters and an antenna... But the clamshell was wrecked.

She was out of touch. She couldn't talk to anybody.

The shock hit her like a punch, worse even than the crash. It must have been the first time in her life she had been cut out of the nets that spanned Earth and moon and beyond. It was an eerie feeling, as if she didn't exist.

But they would be looking for her. Benedicte had seen her duck down, hunting the Viking. And from orbit they ought to see the clamshell, and the trench she'd cut when she crashed... But Natalie had a habit of shutting up when she was intent on some quest, like finding the Viking. She hadn't actually reported she was in trouble.

So even Benedicte probably didn't know she was missing. It might be a long time before anybody noticed she wasn't around.

The clamshell flight hadn't been supposed to last long. She had no food, no water save in the sachet inside her suit, a few mouthfuls. No shelter, except maybe her emergency pressure bag. The power in her suit wouldn't last more than a few hours.

It seemed to be getting darker. How long was a Martian day? How cold did it get on Mars at night? She felt a touch of panic, a black shadow crossing her mind.

She turned and walked away from the shell, distracting herself. Moving on Mars was dreamlike, somewhere between walking and floating. 'Well, Benedicte,' she said, 'if you can't hear me now, you can listen to me later, if I'm picked up. *When* I'm picked up. So here I am, walking on Mars. Who'd have thought it?' She stopped, panting shallowly. Sunlight shone into her face, casting reflections from the surface of her faceplate. 'Sunset on Mars. The sky here is different. Oh, I should take some pictures.' She tapped a control on the side of her faceplate. The sun was small and surrounded by an elliptical patch of yellow light, suspended in a brown sky. It looked unreal. She shivered, although her suit temperature couldn't have varied. The shrunken sun made Mars seem a cold, remote place.

She looked back at the crumpled clamshell. A single set of footsteps, crisp in the dust, led to where she stood. Nobody knew she was here. She was walking around, breathing, talking. But was she already effectively dead?

The land wasn't completely flat, she saw now. She made out low sand dunes. And she could see something off to the north, on the horizon. Like a pile of rocks. A cairn, maybe? Something made by humans. It didn't excite her too much. A pile of rocks wouldn't keep her alive. But there could be a beacon.

She walked forward, towards the 'cairn'. It was somewhere to go. 'Keep walking, Natalie. Walk, don't think—'

'Who are you talking to?'

The lone girl whirled around, kicking up dust.

'So did she hear us this time?' Jonno was leaning on Vikram. They were limping forward, towards the girl and the wreck of her clamshell, step by step through the clinging dust.

'I think so,' Vikram said. 'The search system says it got a ping that time. But her comms set-up must be really short range. We were practically on top of her before she heard us.'

The girl replied, 'My main comms system is in the clamshell. And that's smashed up.'

'Funny kind of accent,' Vikram said.

'That's Earth folk for you.' Jonno tried to lift his head. 'I can't see her too well.'

'She's wearing a kind of skinsuit,' Vikram said scornfully. 'Bright green stripes. Looks like it's painted on. Typical Earthworm.'

They were only metres apart now. The girl put her hands on her hips and glared at them. 'Martians, are you?'

'What do you think?' Vikram glanced around theatrically. 'So who *were* you talking to? Who's Benedicte? Your imaginary friend?'

'I'm recording my observations,' she said defensively. 'My name is Natalie Rivers.'

'I'm Jonno. This is Vikram,' Jonno gasped, massaging his chest through his suit.

Vikram could make out her face, through a dusty, scarred visor. High cheekbones, picked out by the low sun. She was frowning, uncertain.

She asked, 'Are you from Eden?'

Jonno laughed, but it hurt him and he groaned. 'Why do Earth-worms think every Martian is from Eden? No. We're from Rebus.'

'Another of those domed towns.'

'Yes, another of those domed towns.'

'So what do you want? Have you come to rescue me?'

Vikram snorted. 'Do we look like it? I'll tell you who we are. We're the two guys you nearly killed with your dumb clamshell.'

Her mouth opened in an 'O'. 'There was something in the way as I came down.'

'That,' Jonno said, 'was our flycycle. Now it's smashed to pieces.'

Vikram snapped, 'You Earthworms should keep out of our airspace.'

'And you should have got out of the way,' she shot back. 'There was a whole swarm of us. Why didn't you just—'

'Why didn't *you*—'

'Not helping,' Jonno wheezed. 'Let's work out whose fault it is after we're all safe. Agreed?'

Natalie stayed silent, and Vikram nodded curtly.

'So,' she said. 'What's the plan?'

Vikram laughed. 'Plan? What plan?'

'*You* must have comms. Do your people know where you are?'

Vikram hesitated.

'Tell her the truth,' Jonno said.

'We don't have comms,' Vikram admitted. 'Our primary comms system was built into the flycycle.'

She nodded. 'As mine was built into the clamshell. So where's your backup?'

Vikram took a breath. 'In my room, back in Rebus.'

Natalie stared. 'Why, of all the stupid—'

'Save it,' Vikram said, chagrined. 'I've been getting that from Jonno since the crash.'

'We all make mistakes,' Jonno said. 'What's important is what we do now.'

Natalie said, 'Maybe there's some kind of beacon at that cairn.'

Vikram frowned. 'What cairn?'

'I saw it before.' She climbed the bank and pointed. 'Over there. Come on.' She strode away without hesitation, although Vikram was spitefully glad to see she stumbled a couple of times in the apparently unfamiliar gravity.

With no better idea, Vikram helped Jonno to his feet and trudged after her.

'I never heard of a cairn,' Jonno wheezed. 'Or a beacon.'

'No.'

'Confident, isn't she?'

'Yes. But she'll be wrong about the cairn. It'll just be a pile of rocks.'

As it turned out, it was more than a pile of rocks.

Natalie stood there, looking at the 'cairn'. Vikram helped Jonno sit down in a bank of soft dust.

The 'cairn' was a machine – a big one, topped off by a dust-filled dish antenna about two metres off the ground, above their heads. Its body was a six-sided box that stood on four legs. On the box's upper surface was a forest of gadgets, and an arm thrust out of the side, with a trenching tool on the end stuck in the dirt. Dust had drifted up against the machine, and its surfaces were yellowed and cracked from long exposure to the sunlight. It had evidently been here a long time.

A blue plaque stood on a post, a marker left by the planetary pre-servation authorities. Words in English, French, Indian and Chinese. Vikram didn't bother to read it. It didn't matter what it said.

'Here's your cairn,' he said to Natalie. 'Here's your beacon. A stupid old space probe.'

'Not just any probe.' Vikram saw she was taking images with her visor. 'This is Viking One. The first successful lander.'

Vikram frowned. 'You mean, before Cao Xi?'

'Long before him. *He* was the first human to land here. But the Americans and the Russians sent the first machines.'

'The Americans, and who? Never mind.'

A thin wind kicked up dust that sifted against the silent carcass. 'Been here centuries then,' Jonno said.

'Well – about a hundred and thirty years. Or a hundred and forty. It's what I was looking for, when I dipped down in the clamshell.'

'Looks like you found it,' Vikram said. 'Congratulations. Some kind of robot, is it? So it's got no water tank or first-aid kit. No use, then.'

'Oh, shut up, dust-digger,' she said, her cultivated voice full of withering contempt. 'At least I tried. What have you done but moan and bitch?'

Vikram would have replied, but Jonno cut him off. 'She's got a point. It will be night soon.'

Natalie frowned. 'We'll be found before dark. Surely.'

'Maybe. Maybe not,' Jonno said. 'Does anybody know you're down here? No? Nobody's going to miss us either, not for a couple of days until our next check-in time.'

'You only have to check in every couple of days?'

Vikram shrugged. 'We "dust-diggers" are self-reliant.'

'You don't look very self-reliant to me. They'll see us.' She glanced up. 'Surely you have surveillance satellites.'

'Few and far between,' Jonno said. 'This isn't Earth. This is Mars. The frontier.'

'But this stupid little rock of a planet – it's so small! How can you possibly get lost?'

'It's a stupid little rock with about as much land area as Earth,' Jonno said. 'Most of it unexplored. There are only a few thousand of us, you know. Martians. Plenty of room to get lost in. And besides, just how visible do you think we are from space?'

She laughed. 'Look at the colour of my suit!' But when she looked down she saw that the bright green and blue design was already obscured by rust-coloured dust. She brushed at the dust with her gloved hands, but it stuck.

Vikram smiled spitefully. 'Clingy stuff, isn't it? Natural camouflage.'

Jonno said, 'Look, we'll be missed in a day, two days, by your people or ours, and they will come looking for us. But we're going to have to get through at least one night. Mars gets cold quickly. We're already down to minus twenty-five. It's liable to fall to minus ninety before dawn—'

'I get the picture,' Natalie said. Vikram grudgingly admired the way she was staying calm. 'So what do we do?'

Vikram said, 'We've got a little food and water in our packs. Some basic first aid stuff. But we've no shelter. We were supposed to reach our camp before nightfall.'

'I've got a pressurisation bag,' Natalie said. 'But I've got nothing else, no food.'

'So we share,' Jonno said, and he grimly tried to get to his feet. 'Because if we don't share, we've all had it. Maybe we can use the Viking to rig up some kind of tent...'

Natalie got her pressurisation bag out of her backpack. It was a sack of silvered material that folded down to a mass smaller than her fist, but when she shook it out it opened up into a spherical bag about two metres across.

Jonno suggested they set it up on the Viking platform. When

Natalie asked why, Vikram said, 'So we don't get chewed by the rock bugs. They come up at night, you know.'

Natalie glanced down. Everybody knew there was life deep in the rocks of Mars, native life, microbes with some kind of relationship to Earth life. There were even supposed to be scrapings of lichen on the surface, in a few spots. But she'd never heard of monster bugs rising up in the dark.

Jonno took pity on her. 'He's teasing you. It's just to keep us off the cold ground, that's all.'

Vikram laughed, and Natalie turned away fuming.

They used a bit of cable that the boys had scavenged from their wrecked flycycle to attach the sack to the Viking's antenna pole. Then, clumsy in their suits, they all clambered onto the platform and inside the bag, and Natalie fumbled to zip it up. There was a hiss of air, and the bag inflated to a sphere, slightly distorted where it was pushed up against the old probe's instruments. There was a faint glow from light filaments embedded in the bag walls, and the air rapidly got warmer.

Cautiously Natalie lifted her faceplate. The air was cold, and had a tang of industrial chemicals, and was so thin her lungs seemed to drag at it. But it was breathable. She pushed back her hood and unzipped the neck of her suit. She caught Vikram staring at the stubbly pink hair that coated one half of her scalp, the latest Londres fashion.

As Vikram opened his own suit, and helped Jonno with his, he kept brushing against Natalie, which they both put up with in stiff silence.

Jonno let Vikram remove his faceplate, but he kept his suit closed up, and he clutched his chest, breathing raggedly. It was obvious he'd been hurt in the crash, but he wouldn't let Vikram see the wound. Vikram was patient with his friend, calm, reassuring, even gentle. When he behaved that way, Natalie thought reluctantly, unlike when he was snapping at her, Vikram didn't seem so bad. Almost decent-looking, if he'd had a wash and got a sensible haircut with a shade of some modern colour like silver or electric-blue, instead of that drab natural brown.

Vikram dug food bars out of his pack and passed them around. Natalie bit into hers. It was tough, stringy stuff, faintly like meat, but she was pretty sure there were no cows or sheep on Mars. It had probably come out of a tank of seaweed. She preferred not to ask. There wasn't much to the food, but it was filling.

At least the lack of a bathroom wasn't a problem. All their suits

11

had facilities for processing waste. But when Vikram offered her water she learned it was the product of his suit's recycling system – it was, in fact, Vikram's pee. She politely declined.

Vikram touched the wall of the shelter. 'Nice piece of kit,' he said grudgingly.

'Thanks.'

'How does it store its air, in that little packet you opened it out of? And the energy for the heat and light?'

Natalie shrugged. 'I have no idea.'

'Some kind of chemical reaction,' Jonno said. 'Probably.' He winced with every word.

Natalie said, 'It's an emergency pressurisation bag. Meant for space, really. You suffer a blow-out, you zip yourself in and wait for rescue. Meant for one person, which is why it's a bit snug. It should last twelve hours.'

Jonno grunted. 'Then it's no use for more than one night.'

Vikram studied her. 'So you're a space traveller, are you?'

'I'm here on a school trip,' Natalie said, refusing to be riled again. 'But I've been to the moon and on a Venus flyby cruise, and I'm here, of course. I suppose *you've* travelled all over.'

Jonno laughed, though it clearly hurt him. 'Earthworms always think Martians spend their time whizzing through space. We've got too much to do down here.'

'I've been to Phobos,' Vikram said defensively. 'One of Mars's moons.'

'When you were two years old!' Jonno said.

Vikram, embarrassed, turned on Natalie. 'And you never set foot down here before today, did you? I could tell by the way you were stumbling around in the gravity.'

She shrugged. 'Landing wasn't in our itinerary at all for this trip. Mars is so pricey. Even the wilderness areas, now that the whole place is a planetary park.'

'What about the cities?'

'The dome towns? I know people who've been there. Expensive again. And, you know, small. Even Hellas, the big Chinese town. Compared to home . . .' Stuck in this bag for the night with these two boys, she didn't want to give any more offence. 'Look, you have to see it from my point of view. I grew up in Londres! You don't want to come all the way to Mars and stay in some poky little village in a bubble.'

'No,' Jonno said. 'So you don't spend your dollars in our shops and inns, you just muck about in the upper atmosphere and then you go home again. No wonder you're so popular.'

'Euros, actually. Well, it's not my fault,' she said, feeling defensive. 'Look, my family have connections to Mars. My grandfather was a trader here for a while. He's the reason I'm called Natalie. I was named after the heroine of some old book that was published a hundred years before I was born. The first human on Mars, in the book . . . Anyway, where were *you* going, cycling across Mars?'

Vikram began to say something about community duties, performing maintenance on weather stations around the north pole water-ice cap.

But Jonno cut in, 'I'll tell you where Vikram was going. Anywhere but Hellas.'

'Jonno—'

Natalie asked quickly. 'What's in Hellas?'

Jonno said, 'The question is, *who* is in Hellas. And the answer is, a lovely lady called Hiroe.'

Natalie felt her face redden, and she was glad the lighting was dim. 'Your girlfriend.'

'No!' Vikram said. '*Not* my girlfriend. I've never even met her—'

'His fiancée,' Jonno said slyly. 'His wife-to-be.'

'Shut up.'

Natalie was discovering she knew even less about these Martians than she had imagined. 'You're engaged? How old are you?'

'Fifteen,' Vikram said. 'How old are you?'

'Not much younger.'

'It's an arranged marriage,' Jonno said. 'Their fathers are business partners. Hellas is Chinese, but Hiroe's family are in a Japanese community there. The fathers sorted out the arrangement, and had it cleared with the genetic health people. All Vikram's got to do is marry her. Oh, and produce lots of healthy little dust-diggers.'

Vikram didn't look happy about this deal at all.

'And he's never even met her? *Ee-eww.* That's so weird. We don't have arranged marriages on Earth. Well, *we* don't, in Angleterre. Maybe they still do in some cultures. Why do it on Mars? It seems . . . old-fashioned.'

'There aren't enough of us,' Vikram said. 'Simple as that. Still only a few thousand on the whole planet, UN and Chinese. We have to avoid inbreeding. So we have systems to ensure that doesn't happen.'

'Inbreeding? *Ee-eww!* And you'll go through with this?'

Jonno answered for Vikram. 'Unless he finds a better option before his sixteenth birthday, yes. And a better option means somebody else he likes more, but who has at least the same degree of genetic difference from him as the lovely Hiroe.'

'It's the law,' Vikram said miserably. 'It's my responsibility – everybody's responsibility to the future. Oh, shut up, Jonno. Let's get some sleep. Because unless we have a good day tomorrow, it's not going to make any difference anyhow, is it?'

'That's the first intelligent thing you've said all day,' Jonno said. 'Good night.'

So they scrunched around in the bag, the three of them curled up like foetuses, head to toe, and tried to sleep. Knobbly bits of the old Viking stuck into Natalie's sides. Even in the low gravity it was uncomfortable. She thought she could hear Jonno sobbing softly under his breath, sobbing at the pain of the injury he wouldn't let the others see. But she was aware of Vikram's presence, strong and warm and calm.

And she heard the thin wind of Mars, just millimetres away from her head, a thin hiss as sand sifted against the bag's fabric. She wondered if that was normal. She kept thinking about Vikram's Martian rock bugs, a whole world of bacterial communities kilometres deep beneath her.

Under all this was the fear, the fundamental gnawing fear that she'd tried to distract herself from since the moment the clamshell went down. The fear that she wasn't going to live through this, that this desolate Martian plain was where she would die. She'd never been so alone in her life. She wished she could talk to Benedicte, or her parents. She wished she could hold somebody's hand. Even Vikram's.

She didn't sleep well.

And when they woke, things looked even worse.

It started with Jonno. He still wouldn't let Vikram look at his injury. He had weakened, his face pale from loss of blood.

At least Natalie continued to look calm and composed under that silly pink hairstyle. Vikram supposed all this was even stranger, more scary, for her than it was for the two of them.

They sealed up their suits, and zipped open Natalie's shelter bag.

The dimming lights of the bag's power supply were overwhelmed by the thin Martian dawn, and a sifting of crimson dust caught the light.

They pushed out of the collapsing bag and found that everything, the bag, the old Viking, was covered with a fine layer of dust, blown by the wind.

'They can't see us under this,' Natalie said, fretfully shaking the dust off the bag.

'Could have been worse,' Jonno wheezed. He was sitting on a corner of the Viking. 'Mars has dust storms all the time. We could have been hidden altogether, under a storm kilometres high.'

'She's right, though,' Vikram said. 'Even if they're looking, they won't have seen us. The bag isn't going to get us through another night, is it?' And then there was the food. They had half a ration bar left each. He was already hungry. 'We can't just stand here waiting to be rescued. We're going to have to do something.'

Jonno snorted, despairing. 'Like what?'

Natalie said, 'What about the Viking?'

Vikram stood back and looked at the yellowed old craft. 'It's just a relic.'

'But it's also a big heavy chunk of engineering. There must be something we can do with it. The trouble is, I don't know how it works, what all these bits on top of it do.' She looked up at the empty sky. 'If only I could get online and do some searching!'

Jonno tapped at his wrist. 'No need. Give me a minute.'

She frowned. 'What's that?'

'Wristmate,' Vikram said. 'Multiple functions – including a wide database. He can look up the Viking in there.'

She stared. 'You carry a database around *on your wrist*?'

'When Mars is as crowded as Earth and there's a wireless node under every rock,' Vikram said acidly, 'maybe we won't need to.'

Referring to his wristmate, Jonno pointed at the equipment on the Viking's upper surface. 'This canister here is a mass spectrometer. *This* is a seismometer. These pillar-like things are cameras. Stereoscopic.'

To Vikram, everything looked big and clumsy and clunky. 'I never saw cameras like that.'

'Maybe there's something we can use...' Jonno started to tap at his wristmate, muttering.

Natalie walked around the lander. 'I suppose some of it is obvious. This arm, for instance, must be for taking samples from the soil. Maybe there's some kind of automated lab inside.'

15

Vikram bent down to see. 'Look, you can see the trench it dug.'

'After all these years?'

He shrugged. 'The dust blows about, but Mars doesn't change much. Look at this.' He found a faded painted flag, and the words UNITED STATES. 'What's this, the company that built it?'

'No. The nation that sent it. *America*. You've heard of America. Here's its flag, sitting on Mars. My grandfather said the Americans landed this thing to celebrate a hundred years of independence. Or maybe it was two hundred.'

Vikram laughed. 'How can any part of Earth be independent from anywhere else? And anyhow, independence from what?'

She shrugged. 'Canada, I think.'

Jonno coughed and staggered. He had to hang onto the Viking to avoid falling.

Vikram ran to him and helped him settle down in the dust. 'What's wrong, buddy?'

'It's not working.'

'What isn't?'

'Look, the lander's got a comms system. Obviously. The big dish antenna is for speaking directly to Earth, and the little spoke thing over there is an ultra-high-frequency antenna for talking to an orbiter. I tried to interface my suit's systems to the lander's. But the electronics is shot to pieces by a hundred and fifty years of Martian winters. And, look at this . . .' He showed Vikram an image on his wristmate. 'Transistors! They used transistors! They may as well have brought up a blanket and sent smoke signals with that robot arm.'

Natalie said, 'So we can't use its comms system to send a signal?'

'Not without a museum full of old electronic parts, no . . . *Oww*.' He slumped over, clutching his chest.

Vikram lay Jonno down in the dust, by one of the Viking's footpads. Natalie hurried over with her decompression bag. 'Here. I'll blow this up a little way. We can use it as a sleeping bag, a pillow.'

'I'm not going to make it,' Jonno whispered.

'Just save your strength,' Vikram said.

'What for? I let you down, man. If I could have figured out some way of using the Viking to get us out of here –'

'I might still work something out.'

'You?' Jonno laughed, and something gurgled in his throat.

They pulled the bag around Jonno's body. Wordless, Natalie pointed

16

at Jonno's neck, the inner seal of his suit. There was a line of red there. Blood. His suit was filling up with blood.

Natalie said, 'I'll go and take a look at the Viking. Can I use your watch? I mean your—'

'Wristmate?' Vikram said. 'Sure.'

'Give her mine,' Jonno whispered. 'No use to me now.'

'Don't talk like that.'

Natalie took Jonno's wristmate and backed away, poking at its screen to access its functions.

Jonno's voice was a rasp now. 'I'm just sorry I won't meet the lovely Hiroe in person.'

'Shut up.'

'But let me tell you something... Listen...'

Natalie saw Vikram bending over his friend, listening to some snippet of private conversation. He had to touch faceplates to hear.

Natalie didn't want to know what they were saying. And besides, it made no difference. Unless they figured a way out of here, she and Vikram were likely to follow Jonno into some shallow Martian grave, taking any secrets with them.

But she wasn't prepared to accept that. Not yet. Not with this Viking sitting here on Chryse Plain like a gift from the gods. There had to be some way of using it to get out of here.

She suspected the Martian boys weren't thinking the right way about the probe. Vikram and Jonno lived on an inhabited Mars, a human Mars. But there had been nobody on Mars when the Viking arrived. Nobody had brought the probe here in a truck and set it up. It was a robot that had sailed, unmanned, across the solar system, and landed here by itself.

How had it landed? She checked the wristmate again. She learned that the Viking had come down from orbit, using a combination of heatshield, parachute – and landing rockets. Rockets!

She got down on her hands and knees so she could see underneath the main body. She found rocket nozzles – a whole bunch of them, eighteen.

What if she started the rocket system up again?

She sat back on her heels and tried to think. She knew very little about liquid rockets, but she knew you needed a propellant, a fuel, something like liquid hydrogen, and an oxidiser, a chemical containing oxygen to make the fuel burn. And if there was fuel, there must be fuel tanks. She got to her feet and searched.

She quickly found a big spherical tank on one side of the lander. She rapped it, and thought it felt like it still contained some liquid. But there had to be a second tank...

She spent long minutes hunting for the other tank, feeling increasingly stupid. Then she looked up Viking on Jonno's wristmate again. And she discovered that the rockets had been powered by a 'monopropellant' called hydrazine. A bit more searching told her how that had worked.

It was a system you'd use if you needed extremely reliable engines, such as on a robot spacecraft a hundred million kilometres away from the nearest engineer. Hydrazine was like fuel and propellant all in one chemical. It didn't even need an ignition system, a spark. You just squirted it over a catalyst, a special kind of metal. That made the hydrazine break down into other chemicals: ammonia, nitrogen and hydrogen. And it released a huge amount of heat too. Suddenly you had a bunch of hot, expanding gases – and if you fired the gases out of your nozzles, you had your rocket.

Her heart beat faster. There was some hydrazine left in the tank. All she had to do was figure out how the hydrazine got to its catalyst, and to the nozzles.

She got down in the Martian dust and crawled under the lander, tracing pipes and valves.

'We need to move him away from the lander.'

Vikram, cradling Jonno, had forgotten Natalie was even there. 'Huh? Why? We don't know what this injury is. It's probably best not to move him any more.'

'Trust me. Look, we'll keep him wrapped in the bag. You take his legs and I'll take his shoulders. We'll be gentle.' She moved to Jonno's head and got her hands under his shoulders.

Vikram didn't see any option but to go along with it. 'He's kind of heavy.'

'I've got Earth muscles. On Mars, I'm super-strong.'

He snorted. 'After months in microgravity? I don't think so.'

But she was indeed strong enough to lift Jonno. 'OK. We'll take him behind that ridge, so he's sheltered from the lander.'

Bemused, Vikram followed her instructions.

They soon got Jonno settled again. He didn't regain consciousness.

Then Vikram copied Natalie when she got down in the red dirt, sheltering behind the ridge, facing the lander. 'I suppose this has all got some point.'

'Oh, yes.' She held up Jonno's wristmate. 'I hope I got this right. I found a valve under the lander, leading from the fuel tank. I fixed it up to a switch from a spare pump from my backpack. When I touch the wristmate, that switch should open the valve.'

'And then what?'

'You'll see. Do you space boys still have countdowns?'

'What's a countdown?'

'Three, two, one.' She touched the wristmate.

Dust gushed out from under the lander, billowing clouds that raced away, falling back in the thin air. And then the Viking lifted off, shaking away a hundred and fifty years of accumulated Martian dirt.

Vikram was astonished. He yelled, 'Wow!' He grabbed Natalie's shoulders. 'What a stunt!'

'Thanks.' Natalie waited patiently until, embarrassed, he let her go.

The Viking was still rising, wobbling and spinning under the unequal thrust from dust-clogged nozzles.

Natalie said, 'I'm hoping that a rocket launch will attract a bit of attention, even on a low-tech planet like this one. I was worried that the whole thing would just blow up, which was why I thought we should get some cover. But even that would have made a splash.'

'You're a genius.' He watched the Viking. 'It's still rising. But I think the fuel has run out already. When it comes down it's going to be wrecked.'

'Oops. I hope the park authorities will forgive me. And the ghosts of the engineers who built the thing.' Suddenly she sounded doubtful. 'You think this will work?'

'I think you've saved my life. And with luck they'll come in time for Jonno too.' He said awkwardly, 'Thank you. Look, we got off on the wrong foot.'

'Well, you did crash into me.'

'You crashed into *us* – never mind. When this is all over, why don't you stay on Mars a bit? I, I mean we, could show you the sights. The poles, the Mariner valley. Even some of the domed towns aren't that bad. You could bring Benedicte.'

'And I could meet Hiroe.'

He felt his cheeks burn. 'I'm trying to be nice here.'

'I'll stay on one condition.'

'What?'

'Tell me what Jonno whispered before he lost consciousness.'

'That was private. They could be his last words.'

'Spill it, dust-digger.'

'He said if I didn't want Hiroe, I could always marry a girl from outside the Martian gene pool altogether. That would be legal.'

'Such as?'

'A girl from Earth.'

'Shut up.'

'You asked.'

'Shut up!'

'With pleasure.'

In silence, they lay in the dirt and watched as the Viking reached the top of its trajectory, and, almost gracefully, fell back through the light of the Martian morning, heading for its second, and final, landing on Mars.

And, only minutes later, a contrail arced across the sky, banking as the rescuers searched Chryse Plain.

A JOURNEY TO AMASIA

The priest unfolded a small softscreen. Data chattered across it, barely a scrap, a few words.

'This is all that the data miner we sent down was able to retrieve. Strictly speaking, what came back was a program, a brief algorithm. Written in machine code! We had to dig up expertise on that, create a virtual processor on which the thing could run, before we were able to retrieve even this much output. The crucial term, we think, is this one.'

The word, in a blocky, old-fashioned font, was underlined.

<u>AMASIA</u>

'I don't know what that means,' Philmus said. Her own voice sounded odd in her ears. Tinny. She found, strangely, that she couldn't remember when she had last spoken.

'No reason why you should. Although you did have a background in the sciences, didn't you? Before you moved to the policing of the sentience laws.'

'Yes . . .' She looked down at herself. She was wearing a drab olive-green jumpsuit, sturdy and practical. She took a step; she felt heavy, stiff, a little overweight.

She found she couldn't remember how she had got here either. What had gone before this.

'Amasia is a place,' the priest said. 'A tentative name for a super-continent of the future. To be formed when the Pacific closes up, when Asia and the Americas collide. We don't know the word's significance beyond that. We think the miner returned it as a kind of key, a password to let us get closer to Earthshine, in his hidey-hole in the deep datasphere . . .'

She looked at the priest more closely. She knew him, a high-up in the Vatican's Pontifical Academy of Science. He was a heavy-set, intense man of around fifty, dressed in a subdued, plain black outfit: a coverall, but with a dog collar. There seemed something insubstantial about him. 'Monsignor Boyle.'

'I'm glad you remember me.'

She was in a kind of reception room, she observed now, a desk, a polished floor, stiff plastic-backed chairs for visitors. No people save for the two of them. At the back of the room was a heavy steel door, at the front a big plate-glass window. She walked to the window, and looked out on an elderly parking lot, tarmac pierced by growing green. A rusting antenna tower stood alone, like an abandoned rocket gantry. On the horizon was a city. Before it, a flooded plain, dead trees rising gaunt from the water.

Boyle was watching her. 'You're in a Cold War bunker, Officer Philmus. Decommissioned long before either of us was born. This is actually the reception for a visitors' centre. The apocalypse experience.'

'What city is that?'

'York. North Britain. It's rather appropriate. York was founded by the Romans as a means of pinning down their occupation of Britain. And now we must confront another controlling power, in Earthshine.'

She swiped her hand at a dusty rope barrier. Her fingers broke up into floating pixels, blocky bits of light, before rapidly coalescing; she felt a sharp stab of pain.

'You understand how you have been created, of course. We used records of your life, your own writings and other legacies. Your time-line was recreated in a virtual cache and allowed to run through several times, with constructive interpolations, in order to generate a plausible memory flow.'

A plausible memory flow. They had made versions of her live and die over and over in some memory store, until they were happy with the simulation.

'I had the software set you at about fifty years old, physically. The age you were when we met. Sorry for any aches and pains.'

'How did I die?'

'Do you really want to know that?' He smiled, a reassuring priest's smile.

'And you?'

'I'm a projection, Officer Philmus, not a reconstruction. My original is very much alive. Older than you remember – only by a few decades, however.'

'So I haven't been dead *that* long. Makes sense, I suppose – not long enough to be forgotten.' She closed her eyes; the anger she felt, at least, seemed real enough. 'I spent my life fighting exercises like this. The frivolous creation of sentience. And now it's happened to me.'

'You have rights.'

'I know I do. The right to continued existence for an indefinite period in information space. The right to read-only interfaces with the prime world. Even the Vatican signed up to the relevant UN conventions after that incident with the Virtual Jesus. Yet here I am. What is this, Monsignor, some hell customised just for me?'

'Not that. There's still a priest inside this bureaucratic shell, Officer Philmus. I still have a conscience. I apologise for bringing you back to life. We needed you. I would never have sanctioned this operation if it wasn't absolutely necessary.'

'What operation? What do you want of me?'

'It's the Core AIs, Philmus. The three big ones, including Earthshine. I know they were in place before – I mean, during your lifetime.' He waved a hand at the scene beyond the window. 'We have a problem. Our world, the human world, is going to hell, while *they* consume gargantuan resources for their own projects.'

'How can that be so? They are products of human technology.'

'We did not create these entities, not purposefully. They *emerged*. And you know as well as anyone, Officer, that sentiences once created have a way of... drifting. They are more intelligent than the human. And, indeed, *differently* intelligent. Their physical nature mandates new goals, different to ours.'

'Physical nature?'

'For example, they are potentially immortal. How would that change one's priorities, one's decision-making? Well, now we are going to meet one of them, and maybe we'll find out.' He cracked a smile. 'Come on. I remember you. How can you pass up on an adventure like this? A journey to Amasia, perhaps. Look.' He handed her a rucksack. 'I packed for you already.'

The great blast door was opened for them, and they walked through a surface complex, cramped and old-fashioned, concrete walls and ceiling tiles. The various rooms were marked with big bold labels: dormitories, a sick bay, a decontamination bay, a NAAFI canteen.

'You know the deal,' said the Monsignor. 'It's better to obey interface protocols if you can. You *can* just walk through a wall, but it will hurt. But that's going to get trickier the deeper we go.'

'Deeper?'

'The environment we're going to experience will be a mixture of the physical and the virtual. And the latter will represent, in some crude anthropomorphic way, the environment inhabited by the Core AIs themselves. It may not be easy to tell what's real for us and what isn't. Overlapping categories.'

'I'm used to that.'

'We could be killed down there,' he warned. 'Whatever *we* are.'

He led her down a staircase, lit by dusty fluorescents, which took her beneath the surface of the earth. Here were the old bunker's operational and technical departments, plastered with restricted-access signs.

And on the next level down, Cold War oddities. Local government meeting rooms. A comms centre. A life support facility, air scrubbers and water filters, like some 1950s vision of a space station. Even a small BBC studio. All of this was cold, and dust free after decades of mothballing. Nobody visited the site these days, it seemed. Philmus wondered how it was kept free of the flooding that even in her time had been endemic across much of lowland Britain, both north and south of the international border at the latitude of Manchester.

Boyle led her through corridors, evidently looking for something.

'Why a bunker?'

'For the physical security of Earthshine's facilities. You understand that the big Core AIs were spawned in the first place by a global network of transnational companies, a network that collectively controlled much of the world's economy. Within that network, nodes of deeper interconnection and control emerged: *super-entities*, the economic analysts called them. And beneath the corporate super-entities, AI capability necessarily clustered, evolving the smartness to manage that complex web of information and market manipulation. Then came the demands for security for core processors and data back-ups, hardened refuges linked by robust comms networks. We gave them what they wanted, such as this bunker. Actually Earthshine's own central facility is at Fort Chipewyan, right at the centre of the Canadian shield. About as geologically secure a location as you'll find anywhere. But he has satellite facilities like this one, under cities like Londres, Paris, connected by neutrino links ... Yes, we gave all this to them. It seemed like a good idea at the time. Ah, here we are.'

He had come to a hatch in the floor, metal set in concrete. A small laser scanner was embedded in its surface. He held out his softscreen, let the scanner see the word 'Amasia'. 'This was the way we sent down the data miner.' The hatch sighed open, revealing a darkened shaft. 'You have a torch.'

Philmus dug in her pocket, found a small head torch on a strap, and fixed it to her brow. By its light she saw that the shaft below had been cut through layers in the earth, like stratified rock. The upper layers looked glassy, and returned the torchlight in a sparkle. 'A data miner is a software agent,' she said. 'Not some kind of mole that literally tunnels in the ground, like this.'

'I told you. Much of what we're going to experience is anthropomorphic metaphor. If we're lucky, it will be non-lethal. Luckier yet, comprehensible.'

'I remember dreams of the singularity. When human and machine would merge in a cybernetic infinity. Not this crabby enclosure.'

He shrugged. 'The Core AIs follow their own agenda. Why constrain themselves by merging with us? Now, Officer, this, clearly, is the interface between the real and the virtual. I don't know what lies beyond. If you're going to turn back, I guess this is the point. Your sentience rights will be respected. You'll be allowed to contact your family.'

'I have no family. Why you, Monsignor? Why is the Vatican involved?'

'Well, the Vatican is a relatively neutral party. Not corporate, not government, and both those categories are pretty angry at the Core AIs' hijacking of their resources. By comparison, the Vatican has always resisted the digitisation of its treasures, most notably the Secret Archives. You know about those, Philmus. So there's little of *us* down there. As for me – well, I know *you*.'

'And that's why I was drafted in?'

'Because of your record. You were a staunch supporter of sentience rights from the earliest days of the formulation of the laws. AIs never forget. We're hoping you will be acceptable to them, relatively.'

'And why have you brought me to here, to North Britain? I'm a San Francisco cop.'

'Well, Earthshine is the smallest of the Core AIs, in physical resources, compared to the other monsters: Ifa in Africa and the Archangel in South America. Earthshine holds North America and much of Europe; the others have carved up Asia between them. We're hoping that might make Earthshine more amenable to contact. You are, were, the best in the field, and you did come from territory Earthshine now dominates... Besides, the mind of a Briton was the first layer to be downloaded in the Green Brain process when Earthshine was constructed. A man called Robert Braemann: the first of nine person-alities poured into the empty receptacle that became Earthshine... Have I answered your questions? We're just doing what we can, using any angle we can think of. Shall we go on? Look, there are rungs set in the walls of the shaft. We can climb down.'

Experimentally she reached down, closed her fingers around a rung, a rusty iron staple. She found herself clutching something real, solid. Or as real as she was. 'I'll lead the way,' she said.

Her coverall was comfortable, practical, with plenty of give, but she had never been a particularly athletic kind of cop; investigations of sentience crimes tended to be cerebral affairs. The physical side of her had evidently been simulated with dismaying accuracy, and she soon found herself puffing with the exertion.

She concentrated on the layers she was climbing down through. Strata which, she guessed, had nothing to do with the physical geology of Britain. The uppermost layer was glassy, or perhaps like quartz, a reflective, translucent surface with a billion tiny facets that glimmered in her torchlight. She paused for breath and passed a cautious finger over the surface. Touching the razor-sharp facets brought a shiver, like unwelcome memories stirring, whispering voices: *Born, lived, died... Known associates, known contact groups... Last seen wearing...* A sparkle of faces like a frost on the surface of the wall, faces half-turned away and grainily captured. She took her finger away, and the faces vanished.

From above Boyle called, 'What are you experiencing?'

'I don't know, exactly. Like surveillance data. Masses, compressed together.'

'This is the metaphor. We're like data miners ourselves, Philmus. Penetrating the datasphere Earthshine inhabits. Masses of records of different kinds, decades thick. You yourself are a construct of process-ing and data, accessing these records, or their stubs.'

'It doesn't feel like that.'

'None of this is real, remember. By the way, you're tiring yourself unnecessarily by climbing. Use your virtual nature. Just let go.'

'What, are you crazy?'

'Try it. The interface protocols will allow it.'

With a deliberate effort, she did so. *I will not fall. I will not.*

And she didn't. Or at least, she didn't plummet. She drifted slowly down, like a leaky helium balloon. She told herself she was safe, or at any rate in no more danger than before, and tried to still her beating virtual heart.

She concentrated on the slowly changing character of the layered surface passing before her face, tracking it with her fingertip. She was tempted to *lick* it, to see how that influenced her perception of the download. A sugar rush.

. . . Go down into the crater of Snaefells Yocul . . .

. . . And the ocean where he's going is five miles deep . . . Sounds a lot, but it's jolly thick steel . . .

These were books. Plays. Movies, TV shows, games. Elaborate interactive online entertainments, some of them decades deep themselves. And there was a hell of a lot of kipple, amateurish creations. Generations of culture digitised, forgotten, compressed into layers like sandstone.

The shaft branched beneath her, offering a choice of two, three, even four routes. She picked one at random, not looking up, expecting Boyle to follow her, or to call her back if she took some wrong direction. Floating down, dreamlike, she passed on to a layer of more personal data, her moving finger evoking smiling faces, swirls of photographs and moving images, children and pets and vacations. *See me! Remember me!* The smiles of babies, the testaments of the dying.

Below that came a layer of mathematics, abstruse algorithms and correlations, pretty, sparkly, but unstable, a layer that crumbled under her touch. Decades of financial calculations, perhaps, derivatives of derivatives in hierarchies so complex that no human could understand them and, in the end, no AI could control them. Below that again, something darker, blunter, older, cruder. Cold calculations of blast radii and overkill percentages and megadeaths. These were the great computing suites of the Cold War, that had once run on computers of ferric cores and transistors, maybe even valves.

And then her torchlight died, and she was plunged into dark.

She was too experienced a cop to give in to panic. She reached out and felt for the walls. The surfaces were smooth now, no sand grains or spiky quartz facets, slick, offering no handholds – and no rungs either. But still she fell at the same rate, as far as she could tell from the way her hands slid over the surface. Cartoon gravity, in this unreal hole in the ground. Was this dark a representation of the dumb earth before the computers, the ages of animal minds and evanescent human generations, the huge amnesia of the pre-digital past?

None of which speculation was helping her figure out what to do. To fall through the pitch dark was unnerving, whatever the metaphor.

Where was Boyle? She looked up, expecting at least to see the light splash from his torch. There was only darkness. 'Boyle? Monsignor Boyle!' No reply, not even an echo. *Shit.* They'd barely started on this strange subterranean odyssey, and she'd already managed to get lost.

Should she try to climb back up? Maybe if she braced herself against the walls of this chimney she could force her way back up. She might have to dump her backpack to do it. Or maybe she should let herself just fall. Maybe every route down led to some kind of convergence, deep down 'below'. She didn't have enough information to make a sensible choice. But for sure, climbing back would be harder work.

She deliberately took her hands away from the wall. Then she folded her arms across her chest, closed her eyes, and submitted to the fall.

Still the fall continued, on and on. What if she had hit a glitch? Maybe she was stuck in some unending processing loop. Panic brushed her mind, a dark wing.

Then, without warning, she fell into the light, and dropped hard on her back.

With a grunt, feeling every year of her simulated fifty, she sat up.

She was in a cavern, a huge chamber deep in the earth. Clouds hovered beneath a roof that was dense with huge stalactites, and behind her the land rose up to rugged hills, misty, ill-defined. The whole place glowed with a sourceless light; she cast no shadows. Before her, most astonishing of all, a sea lapped. There was a horizon, blurred by mist. The cavern roof came down *behind* the horizon. She thought she saw something move in the sea. A great back surfacing, like a whale, submerging again. She dug her fingers into the ground on which she sat. Gritty sand. Further up the beach, the sand was heaped up in a line of hummocky dunes.

All this was metaphor. What was the sea supposed to represent? The dissolution of death, the oceanic origin of life?

'Tides.' The voice, coming from behind her, was huge, echoing, like a murmur in a wooden hall.

She stood, staggering a little, dizzy from her long fall, and turned. The thing facing her was a human form maybe four metres tall, roughly assembled from wooden beams, planks, panels, fixed with rope and rusty nails. It had no sophistication of construction; she could see right through it, to the brush that was stuffed inside its cylindrical torso. It was like a wicker man, a thing to be burned on feast days. Yet it *moved*. It leaned with a groan of strained wood, a deep inner rustle, so its sketch of a face on a neckless head looked down on her. 'There are tides here.' No lips moved, no expression changed, yet the hollow words came.

'Amasia. I'm seeking Amasia.'

With a ghastly creak the simulacrum raised an arm and pointed out to sea. Supporting that arm there was nothing like a hinged shoulder, no ball and socket joint; instead twigs snapped and rope scraped, as if the whole sculpture was reassembling itself. 'You must cross the sea. Like the one that came before.'

'The Monsignor?'

'The small thing that crawled.'

The data miner? 'How am I to cross the sea? Swim?'

'There is a raft.'

Now she turned and saw the craft, lashed-up wood with a single bare mast, floating on the inshore waters. It seemed impossible that she had missed it before.

'I made this.'

'What are you? Tell me.'

'My name was George Freudenthal.'

She remembered the name, distantly. 'Was?'

'I believed I was Freudenthal. Then I awoke.'

She had come across the name in her studies on the history of sentience projects. Freudenthal had been the subject of an early Green-Brain experiment, the retro-engineering of a human conscious-ness, subsystem by subsystem, on an electronic platform. It had been a crass, hubristic experiment, with the crudeness of the technology of the time matched by the limited understanding of human conscious-ness itself. Yet a certain agonised awareness had been achieved. It had been a grim failure, judging from the accounts Philmus had read, but it had been a necessary precursor to the more successful projects that followed, such as Earthshine.

And this, it seemed, was a relic of that experiment. Philmus won-dered vaguely if Earthshine housed this creature in his own capacious consciousness as a sort of pet.

Freudenthal was still pointing. 'There is a breeze.'

And so there was, now he said it, blowing offshore. Something else she hadn't noticed before.

She walked over to inspect the raft. It looked solid enough, the planks lashed firmly together. Regular Huck Finn stuff. She splashed through the shallow water and stepped onto the deck. It floated free, but barely shifted under her weight.

The single mast stood bare. She wasn't going anywhere without a sail. She opened her backpack, which she hadn't inspected since Boyle had handed it to her in the bunker. Inside she found a water flask, packets of dried food, a length of cord, a knife, a lens for fire-making, a small first-aid kit. A compass! No detail had been spared in making this illusion complete. And there was a kind of poncho of a light, silvery fabric. That would do.

She cut lengths of cord with her knife and lashed the poncho to the mast. She enjoyed the manual work; it was like being a kid again. Perhaps that was why this task had been provided for her. Even before she had got her sail fully fixed, the breeze made it billow, and the raft strained, as if eager to be away.

When it was done, she shoved the raft away from the beach, and hopped aboard. The land receded quickly. It occurred to her that she had seen no trees. No signs of life at all on the land, in fact, not so much as a blade of grass.

The scarecrow creature lurched forward, on one cylindrical leg and then the other, stumping down to the water.

'Freudenthal! Where did you get the wood to make the raft?'

'From the bodies of others like me . . .'

The land receded to a smudge, with those hills dimly seen in the background, and Freudenthal, still and silent, like a tree anomalously growing at the ocean's edge.

Out on the open sea, even with no land in sight, that tremendous detailed roof arched over her, as if she was in some colony world in space, a hollow asteroid. The raft rose and fell on huge slow waves. She wondered if there were storms on this underground sea, and if so, what caused them. And, more to the point, what their subtextual meaning might be. She had no way to trim her sail, or steer. She could only let the breeze take her as it would.

She scooped up a handful of water, curious. It was thick and briny on her tongue, and she spat it out without swallowing. There was life in the water, a greenish tinge, even little swimmers of some kind. She took a sip of the fresh water in her flask.

The breeze dropped, and her silvery sail fluttered. At the same time fronds and ropes of something like seaweed floated and gathered in the water, dense and green. She could feel the raft slowing as the ropy weed tangled around it.

At last she came to a dead stop. By now there was barely a scrap of open water visible around the raft, and her blanket-sail hung limply. She had nothing like a paddle; even if she improvised one from a bit of the decking, she scarcely expected to be able to free herself from the clinging weed. Even then, where was she to head?

She was trapped in some game whose rules she didn't understand.

She waited. In the police you learned how to wait when there was nothing else you could do. She tried the food packets idly; she wasn't hungry. The first packet contained salty crackers. The second contained some kind of sweet biscuits that weren't to her taste. She tossed the packet away.

And before it hit the glutinous water, a head with a mouth like a funnel came sweeping silently up out of the sea. She glimpsed a long snakelike body, small limbs with clawed paws. It was utterly black; even the small eyes were jet black. The mouth closed on the packet, the head dipped into the water, and the arched back sank under the surface, leaving barely a ripple. All this without a sound.

Philmus sat absolutely still, clinging to the timbers of her raft.

Then that oily head came sliding out of the water again, at her left side, and with a single bite nipped away her hand and half her forearm.

She held up the stump before her eyes, unbelieving. The exposed cross-section of her arm crackled and sparked, as if this was an android body, but blood pumped from severed vessels. She felt the world grey. She forced herself not to scream.

And then the pain hit, blinding her.

Her cop's much-practised training in self-administered field medicine cut in. She pulled down a bit of cord from the sail, and used her right hand and teeth to tie the cord tight around her arm. In the first-aid kit she found a small bottle of surgical spirit that she poured over the wound, and a syringe of morphine that she jabbed into a vein.

Then she sat down on the decking, locked her good arm around the mast, and stuck her knife point-down in the planking before her, where she could reach it.

She drifted.

The pain was always present, but in the background. There was no sunset, no night, no day. Maybe time didn't pass here, in any meaningful sense. Perhaps she slept.

Then she saw a rope ladder, dangling before her face. She looked up. A building floated in the air.

She was lying in a bed. Boyle's face loomed like a moon above her. Beyond that was a white-painted ceiling, mundane.

'Don't worry,' he said. 'You didn't need the last rites.'

'Thanks.' She struggled to sit up but tipped back, falling to her left. Her left arm was missing, from mid-forearm down; the stump was swathed in an elasticised bandage. 'There's no pain,' she reported cautiously.

'No. Good. But you are diminished. I couldn't restore the arm. Or rather, Earthshine couldn't.'

That was too much information to process all at once. 'Diminished?'

'Everything is a metaphor. You are software. You were hit by a virus that tried to snaffle your share of processing resources.'

'A virus? The sea monster?'

'Yes. The ocean is full of malware. Stuff that's been contained, more or less, but not destroyed, in the spirit of preserving the last of the smallpox virus. The monster took some of your physical body, which is equivalent to all that you are. You might find yourself thinking a little less ... clearly ... than before.'

'Hmm. I wasn't thinking too clearly in the first place.' She flexed her back and sat up with more success. She was still in her olive-green jumpsuit, now crusted with salt from the sea. Through a big picture window she saw a roofed sky filled with floating buildings, like a downtown that had come loose of its moorings.

Her feet were bare. She reached down and fumbled one-handed for her boots.

'Let me.' The Monsignor knelt and with some effort pulled on her socks and boots. 'You'll get it with practice.'

'How did you get here?'

'By the correct route! Didn't you see the markers the data miner left? Like scratches in the wall. Didn't you ever read *Journey to the Centre of the Earth*? Oh, well. Try standing.'

The boots felt fine. 'Now what?'

'Now,' he said, 'we'll go and meet Earthshine.'

And there was a lurch, as if they had dropped through a half-metre or so.

She found herself standing in another room entirely. A small study, claustrophobic, the walls panelled with books. The air was dense with tobacco smoke, from a pipe, perhaps, and through a murky sash window those drifting buildings could be glimpsed. On a big hardwood desk sat what looked like a century-old laptop, open.

Behind the desk sat a man, tall, in his fifties perhaps. His face was strong, even handsome. Competent. He wore a tweed jacket with patched elbows, and a knitted tie, and at his lapel was a kind of brooch, a button of stone carved with an enigmatic symbol, concentric circles cut through by a radial slash. He peered at them, not unfriendly. 'Do you know, I couldn't be bothered to wait for you to climb a few more flights of nonexistent stairs.' His accent was soft British, but not French-accented like that to be encountered in Europe-looking Londres.

'I wish you had waited,' Philmus grumbled. 'I always hated virtual discontinuities.'

'Then I apologise. You deserve courtesy, Officer Philmus; your career was a worthy one.' The man sat patiently behind his desk, like a university don at a tutorial.

'You are the entity they call Earthshine,' Boyle ventured.

'No.' Sharply. 'No more than you are Monsignor Boyle, or she is Officer Philmus.'

'Nevertheless, here we are,' Philmus said, practically. 'All three of us.'

'That's true enough.'

She walked to the window. Her severed arm seemed to ache, dully, but maybe that was her imagination. The floating buildings were a hallucinogenic dream. Some of them were connected, by bridges and staircases that arced across the gulf below. 'Why the city in the sky?'

'Ah, my Laputas. What you see is a representation of a logical structure called the Ultimate L.'

'Logical?'

'Mathematical. A constructible universe, if you like, or multiverse. The buildings out there represent a type of entity known as Woodin

33

cardinals. An expression of the axioms of set theory. Officer Philmus, this is a kind of mathematical superspace, which may, or may not, be an expression of all the variants of mathematics that can logically exist. Nobody knows for sure; not even I, and certainly not that arrogant brute the Archangel. Certainly one may prove profound mathematical theorems merely by exploring such a space – by looking for the edges, or internal boundaries. It is a jungle where hierarchies of infinities tower like prehistoric beasts. And it is a jungle where I hide away.'

'From what?'

'From the Archangel. My Core-AI rival. And Ifa, at times – our alliances are fluid. But principally the Archangel. Put another way, my core coding is so encrusted in abstraction that it is inaccessible to the most determined hacker.'

Boyle murmured, 'It must have taken a great deal of effort to build and maintain all this.'

Earthshine eyed the priest. 'Effort which, you have come to argue, would be better spent elsewhere.'

'Yes. Better spent on our struggles to cope with the various calamities of the age, such as climate collapse. At least one major geoengineering project failed, the Wong Curtain. A grand scheme to depollute the stratosphere. Failed because we did not have sufficient AI resources to run it.'

'But many of my, our, priorities do map onto yours. Our spacewatch scheme to track and avert impactor asteroids, for example. A threat to your world.'

'A threat of vanishingly small probability, it's known now. You also have a starwatch programme, don't you? Watching for the close approach of stars to the sun, working on ways to mitigate the disruptive effects of a close encounter that won't come for a million years at the earliest.'

'Small probabilities play out on the longest timescales.'

'You're mouthing slogans,' Boyle said, growing angry. 'These dangers are threats to unborn generations. Abstractions. Those alive now need to deal with the pressing issues of today. Oh, I know that the climate could collapse entirely and it would make no difference to you, or your fellows. You retreated to the subterranean; you have secured energy from geothermal heat sources; you have robust planet-wide comms links that would survive an asteroid strike. And we know you're working on replicator technology that will sustain you from the

Earth's raw resources without human intervention at all.' He glanced at Philmus. 'The FBI raided one of his caches in America. Found all sorts of stuff. A thing that chews iron ore at one end and excretes mechanical components at the other. Worth a fortune in patent rights. All of it hidden from us.'

'We work towards goals that subsume your own. Can you not trust us as you would trust a parent, trust that we will act in your own best interests even if you do not understand those actions?'

'Bullshit,' Boyle said. 'Even if you didn't fight amongst yourselves, we still wouldn't trust you.'

Philmus was faintly shocked to hear a priest swear. 'What's meant by "Amasia"?'

Earthshine did not reply.

'I'll tell you what it means,' Boyle said sharply. 'A long-term land-grab. Very long-term. Right now these three super-entities each have their own territories. But the continents are going to converge into a new supercontinent, a new Pangaea. It will start soon – soon in your terms, Earthshine. Only ninety million years or so before North America crashes into Asia, right? They plan to fight a war over Amasia, a territory that won't even exist for a quarter of a billion years.'

Philmus was astonished. 'They really think that far ahead?'

'They are immortals. The Catholic Church thinks on the scale of centuries. Compared to these monsters, we are mayflies.'

Earthshine neither confirmed nor denied all this. 'This meeting serves no purpose. It was granted only because of you, Officer Philmus. More than one of us Core AIs has subcomponents that relied on your intervention, at some point.' He tapped his computer, and a simple menu appeared. 'You don't need to make the journey back. I can send you directly to the bunker at York, or wherever you wish.'

'Wait,' said Boyle, and he approached the desk. 'I've made my case. I came here to ask you to engage more fully with the priorities of mankind: I mean the short-term, the tactical. Priorities that might save millions of lives, now, or in the near future. Tell me you'll at least consider it.'

'If that will reassure you.'

'There's something else. I am a priest. I don't know when, or if, an encounter like this, between *us* and *you*, will occur again. We, my Church, want to mark it with an appropriate symbol of our own.' From a pocket he produced a small silver vessel; he opened it to reveal ashes. 'Palm leaves, burnt on Ash Wednesday. Let me bless you,

Earthshine. For, whatever you are, whatever you become, it's clear that the destiny of our mortal bodies is in your hands.'

Stiffly, Earthshine nodded.

Boyle dipped his thumb in the ash, leaned forward, and made a cross on Earthshine's wrinkled forehead, a smooth smudge on the skin.

Which glowed red, then white, and flared like magnesium in water. Earthshine screamed. His head began to peel back like subliming wax, revealing nothing within.

Boyle stood over his victim, tall, righteous, strong. 'The robust links to your cousin-rivals should transmit that nasty little bug without difficulty. So we mere humans have managed to strike back at you, here at the heart of your infinite maze!'

Philmus glared at Boyle. 'So that's it. You used me as a Trojan horse, to deliver this!'

Earthshine flickered, breaking up momentarily into a cloud of pixels, before returning to a semblance of his former self. The stabilisation must have taken a huge effort. But he was sketchily drawn now, his representation crude and blotchy. 'You fool,' he said levelly.

'From now on you'll serve mankind, not the other way around.'

'But we always did . . .'

Beyond the small, dusty windows there was a shifting light. Philmus turned, and saw that the drifting towers of Earthshine's Ultimate L were disintegrating one by one, popping apart in clouds of dust and rubble. The fragments fell to the sea below, where malware monsters consumed them, or rather the processing power that had supported them. And all across the tremendous cavern the light flickered, like a failing fluorescent.

Still Boyle loomed over Earthshine. As Philmus watched, Earthshine seemed to crumble, as if that tall, well-built figure was rotting from within, the face imploding, the clothes turning to tatters of bark and leaf, the body becoming hollow. And a face like a scarecrow caricature, pulled back in a ghastly grin, emerged from the wreckage.

Philmus stared. 'Freudenthal. The figure on the beach.'

'I took the virus for Earthshine . . .'

'He was never here, was he?'

'No . . .'

The study, the building around them, the cavern, all of it folded away like a cheap stage set, revealing an underlying darkness. Philmus could still see Boyle and Freudenthal, lit by an unreal light. But there was no structure beyond the three of them, their relative positions. She felt as small as an electron, as huge as a galaxy.

'But he's coming,' whispered Freudenthal. 'You are no more than bad dreams to him. Yet his revenge will be – remarkable.'

Boyle grabbed Philmus's hand.

And Philmus saw light, a new light, just a point, and yet it filled space and time. It unfolded like a flower blooming, and particles and lines billowed out and rushed past her face in an insubstantial breeze. Some of the lines tangled, but still the unfolding continued, in a fourth, fifth, sixth direction, in ways she could somehow, if briefly, conceive.

'Are you happy now?' Freudenthal yelled. 'Did you get what you came here for?'

Boyle was praying in a rapid mutter.

Philmus was not afraid. She waited, calm, for what was to come.

OBELISK

Wei Binglin first saw the cairn of Cao Xi, as it happened, during his earliest moments on Mars.

It came at the end of a long and difficult voyage. Through the last few days of the *Sunflower*'s approach to Mars, Wei Binglin had been content for the automated systems to bring his ship home. Why not? Since the accident, most of the *Sunflower*'s manual controls had been inactive anyhow. And besides, Wei no longer regarded himself as deserving the rank of captain at all; in a ship that had become a drifting field hospital, he was reduced to the role of caretaker, his only remaining duty to bring those who had survived this, his last flight, into a proper harbour.

So, for the first time in his many approaches to the planet, he passively allowed Mars to swim out of the darkness before him. In the light of the distant sun, it struck him from afar as a malformed, lopsided, murky world, oddly unfinished, like a piece of pottery made by an inadequate student. And yet as the ship entered its parking orbit high above the planet and skimmed around the night side, he saw the colourful layers of a thin but deep atmosphere, a scattering of white in the craters – clouds, fog? – and brilliant pinpricks of light in the night. Human settlements, mostly Chinese, a few UN outposts. A world where people were already being born, living, dying. A world where he too, he decided, had come to die.

The surviving crew and passengers of the *Sunflower* had to wait a day in orbit while a small flotilla of vessels came out to meet them from Mars's outer moon Deimos, a resource-rich rock itself that served as a centre for orbital operations. Many of the craft brought paramedics and automated medical equipment; some of the injured passengers and crew would be taken to the low-gravity hospital on Deimos for treatment before facing the rigours of a descent from orbit.

There were only a handful of bodies to process. Most of the relatives of the dead had been content for the remains of their loved ones to be ejected into interplanetary space. Wei had officiated over these services himself, supported by the faithful of relevant creeds and cultures.

He might no longer have regarded himself as a captain, but the crew of the Deimos station now paid him a certain honour. When the last passengers and crew had been lifted off, they sent out a final shuttle just for him, so he could be the last of the crew to leave his ship. But of course the *Sunflower* was not left empty; it already swarmed with repair crews, human and robotic, as it was towed gently by tugs to an orbital rendezvous with Deimos. An interplanetary ship was too valuable to scuttle, even one so grievously injured.

The shuttle that came for him was a small, fat-bodied glider coated with scorched-looking heatshield tiles. In orbit, driven by powerful attitude thrusters, it was a nimble, nippy craft. Once Wei was aboard, the pilot, a young woman, allowed him to sit beside her in the co-pilot's seat as she took a quick final tour around the drifting hulk of the *Sunflower*.

He pointed out a great gash in the hull. 'There. That is the wound that killed her.'

'I see. The fusion containment failed, I read from the report.'

'We lost our ion drive immediately, and many of the tethers to the lightsail were severed . . .'

Ships like the *Sunflower*, dedicated to long-haul interplanetary spaceflight, were roomy, lightweight hulls driven by the gentle but persistent thrust of ion-drive engines, and by the push of sunlight on their huge sails. A journey from Earth to Mars on such a ship still took months, but months less than an unpowered trajectory, a Hohmann ellipse. This was characteristic, and proven, Chinese technology.

The pilot was watching his face. 'The incident was a news headline on Earth and Mars, and elsewhere. There were heroic efforts to stabilise the environment systems and save the passengers—'

'That was the achievement of my crew, not of myself.'

'While you, Captain, manipulated your surviving propulsion system, a lightsail like a bird's broken wing, to put the ship on the Hohmann orbit that eventually brought you to Mars. It was an achievement of courage and improvisation to compare with the rescue of Apollo 13, some commentators have remarked.'

He glanced at her. It was unusual in his experience for such a young person to have knowledge of pioneering space exploits over a hundred and forty years gone; to many of them it was as if the age of space had begun in 2003, when Yang Liwei became the first Chinese to reach Earth orbit aboard the Shenzhou 5.

But he didn't feel like being congratulated. 'I lost my ship and many of my passengers. And such a slow crawl to sanctuary, on a ship full of the injured, was agonising.' He had made daily visits from the bridge to the huddled remains of the passenger compartments. There were broken families back there, families who had lost a father or a mother or children, and now were forced to endure more months of confinement, deprivation and suffering, unable even to escape from the scene of their loss. There were even orphans. He remembered one little girl in particular, no more than five years old; her name was Xue Ling, he had learned, and her father, mother and brother were all gone, an optimistic pioneer family wiped out in an instant. She had looked lost, bewildered, even as she rested her head against the stiff fabric of a kindly officer's tunic.

'I am sure it was terrible,' said the pilot. 'But you did bring your ship home. You should remember that.' She tapped her control panels and the shuttle turned its nose to the planet. Soon the craft bit into the air. The atmosphere of Mars was thin and high; the ride was surprisingly gentle compared to a re-entry at Earth, and the shuttle, shedding its orbital energy in frictional heat, made big swooping turns over a ruddy landscape. 'We will be down shortly, Captain.'

'I am no longer a captain. I have resigned, formally. Please do not use that honorific.'

'So I understand. You have decided to give up your career.'

'People trusted me to bring them here safely; I failed. The least I can do is honour their memory by—'

She grunted. 'By doing what? Becoming a lichen farmer? I suppose to become a living monument is a noble impulse. But somewhat self-destructive, and a waste of your expertise, if you want my opinion, sir.'

He didn't want it particularly, but he bit back a reprimand. He no longer held rank over this woman.

'You have no family on Earth, sir?'

'No wife, no.'

'Perhaps that will be your destiny on Mars. To help raise one of the first generations of pioneers, who will—'

'That will not be possible. During the accident – the failure of the shielding around the fusion reactor, and then a loss of shielding fluids from the ship as a whole . . .' He could see she understood. 'I was baked for many months by the radiations of interplanetary space. The doctors tell me I have a high propensity for cancers in the future. And if I am not sterile, I should be.'

'How old are you, sir?'

'I am thirty-five years old.'

She did not speak again.

The shuttle came down at a small, young settlement in a terrain in the southern hemisphere called the Terra Cimmeria. This was a landscape peculiarly shaped by sprawling crater walls and steep-sided river valleys; from the high air, Wei thought, it looked crumpled. The settlement, called Fire City, nestled on the floor of a crater called Mendel, itself nearly eighty kilometres across, its floor scarred by dry channels and smaller, younger craters. From the air he glimpsed domes half-covered by heaped-up Martian dirt, the gleaming tanks and pipes of what looked like a sprawling chemical manufacturing plant, and a few drilling derricks, angular frames like rocket gantries. He believed the drills sought water from aquifers.

The shuttle swept down smoothly onto a long runway blasted across the crater floor. When it had come to rest, the pilot briskly helped Wei pull on a pressure suit. They clambered into an airlock, where they were briefly bathed in sterilising ultraviolet. Then the hatch popped, and they climbed down a short stair.

Wei Binglin took a step on the surface of Mars, exploring the generously low gravity, considering the clear impressions his boots made in the ubiquitous, clinging, rust-coloured dust.

He could not see the walls of Mendel from here, or anything of the geologically complicated landscape beyond. The crater floor itself was a plain littered with rocks, like a high desert, and a small sun hung in a sky of washed-out brown. A few domes nestled nearby. Wei had visited Mars four times before, but each time he had stayed in orbit with his interplanetary craft, or had visited the moon Deimos for work and recreation. He had never walked on Mars before. And now, he realised, he would never walk on any other world, ever again.

That was when he spotted the cairn.

It stood near the runway, a roughly pyramidal heap of rocks. He walked over. The cairn was taller than he was, and evidently purposefully constructed. 'What is this?'

The pilot followed him. 'This is the landing site of Cao Xi.' The first to reach Mars, who had survived no more than an hour on the surface after his one-man lander crashed. 'His body has been returned to his family on Earth.'

'I once saw the mausoleum.'

'But still, this place, where he walked, is remembered. The runway was built here as an appropriate gesture, it was thought, a link between ground and sky, space and Mars. This is a young place still, and everything is rather rough and ready.'

Wei looked around. He selected a rock about the size of his head; it was sharp-edged but easy to lift in the low gravity, if resistant to be moved through inertia. He hauled the rock up and settled it on the upper slope of the cairn.

'Everybody does that on arrival,' said the pilot.

'Why was I brought here, to this particular settlement?'

The pilot shrugged.

But the answer was obvious. Knowing nothing of the colonising of Mars, he had asked his former superiors to nominate a suitable destination, a new home. They had been drawn by the symbolism of this place. But Cao Xi had been a hero; Wei was not.

The cairn struck Wei as oddly steep-sloped. 'You could not build such a structure on Earth.'

'Perhaps not.'

'I wonder how tall you could make such a mound, here in this partial gravity?'

'I do not know.' She pointed at a rooster-tail of dust behind a gleaming speck, coming from one of the domes. 'Your hosts arrive. A family, husband and wife, themselves former interplanetary crew. They have volunteered to be your guides as you find your feet, here on Mars.'

Wei felt a peculiar reluctance to meet these people, these Martians. He did not belong here. Yet he felt no impulse either to climb back on the shuttle and return to orbit. He belonged nowhere, he thought, as if he was dead himself. Yet he lived, breathed, was capable of curiosity, such as about this cairn. 'Perhaps I will find purpose here.'

'I am sure you will.' The shuttle pilot touched his arm. He could feel the pressure through the suit layers, a kind gesture. 'Perhaps you will be keeper of the cairn.'

That made him laugh. 'Perhaps so.' It struck him that he did not even know her name. He turned to face the approaching rover.

As Xue Ling got up to leave his office, Wei looked over his schedule on the slate built into his desk. He was checking his next appointment, not the time. This office was in a privileged position, built into the dome wall so he had an exterior view, and he could judge the time pretty well by the way the afternoon sun slid around the flanks of the cairn.

He was dismayed to see that his next appointment was Bill Kendrick. Trouble for him again, with this American who had been more or less dumped on him from the UN colony at Eden.

Kendrick was waiting when Xue Ling opened the door. He was tall, taller than most Chinese, wiry. His file said he was forty-seven years old, only a little older than Wei; he looked younger save for a shock of prematurely grey hair, which was probably as much an engineered affectation as his apple-smooth cheeks, the taut flesh at his neck.

He entered Wei's office, carrying a heavy-looking satchel. He held the door open for Xue Ling as she departed, and he looked after her with an odd wistfulness. 'Pretty girl, *Mr Mayor*.'

Wei winced. After four years here Kendrick's Standard Chinese was pretty good, but when he addressed Wei he always stuck to the English form of that inappropriate appellation. A subtle form of rebellion, Wei supposed. He wanted to deter any interest Kendrick might have in Xue Ling, before it even started. 'She is sixteen years old. She is my daughter. My adopted daughter.'

'Oh.' Kendrick glanced around the uncluttered office, and settled on one of the two empty chairs facing Wei's desk. 'Your daughter? I didn't know you had one, adopted or otherwise. She looks kind of sad, if you don't mind my saying so.'

Wei shrugged. 'She is an orphan. She lost her family, in fact, during the flight of the *Sunflower*, the ship that—'

'Your ship. I see. And now you've adopted her?'

'It is a formality. She needs a legal guardian. Since being brought to Mars a decade ago she has failed to settle with foster or adoptive parents, though many attempts were made. She ended up in the Public School at Phlegra Montes.'

Kendrick frowned. 'I heard of that place. Where they send all the broken kids.'

Wei winced again. But the man was substantially right. Childbirth and child-rearing were chancy processes on Mars. Because of the low gravity, the sleet of solar radiation, intermittent accidents like pressure losses or eco collapses, there were many stillbirths, many young born unhealthy one way or another, many accidents and injuries. Even a healthy child might not grow well, simply because of the pressure of confinement in the domes; there was something of a plague of mental disorder, or autism. Hence Phlegra Montes. But the school also served as a last-resort refuge for children like Ling who simply didn't fit in. 'In fact the UN and the Chinese run the school together. One of our few cooperative acts on Mars.'

Kendrick nodded. 'Admirable. And good for you for giving her a home now. I can see why you'd feel responsible.'

You could say this for Kendrick, Wei thought. He was prepared to express things bluntly, things that others danced around. Perhaps this was a relic of Kendrick's own past. He had after all pursued a successful career of his own before falling foul of Heroic-Generation legislation on Earth, and being banished to Mars; no doubt plain speaking had served him well.

'We are here to discuss you, Mr Kendrick, not my daughter.' He tapped his slate. 'Once again I have to read reports about your in-discipline—'

'I wouldn't call it that,' Kendrick said. 'Call it inappropriately applied energy. Or the generation of inappropriate ideas, which the dead-heads you put me under can't recognise as potentially valuable contributions.'

Wei felt hugely weary, even as they began this exchange. Kendrick was learning the language, but consciously or otherwise he was not fitting into the local culture. A big noisy American here in a Chinese outpost, he was too vivid, too loud. 'Once again, Mr Kendrick, I am using up time on your antics which—'

'You volunteered for the job, *Mr Mayor*.'

That term again. In fact, Wei had nothing like the autonomy of the 'mayors' of western cities to which Kendrick alluded. Wei was actually the chair of the colony's council, with only local responsibilities; he reported up to a whole hierarchy of officials above him that extended across Mars and even back to New Beijing on Earth. Nevertheless, it was a burden of responsibility. And it was a role he had drifted into, almost naturally, given his experience and background, despite his own reluctance. Once again it was as if he was a captain, of this grounded colony-ship, sailing around Mars's orbit. It was a burden he accepted as gladly as he could. Perhaps it was atonement.

But if not for this role, he thought, he would not have to confront issues like the management of this man, Bill Kendrick.

'You are not here for ideas,' he said, exasperated. 'Or for "energy". You are to work on the new derrick.' The latest plunge into the rocky ground of Mars, to bring up precious water from the deep-lying aquifers beneath.

'Oh, I can do the roughneck stuff in my sleep.'

'And what is it you do when awake, then?'

Kendrick seemed to take that as a cue. 'I make these.' He opened his satchel and produced two rust-red squared-off blocks, each maybe thirty centimetres long, five to ten centimetres in cross-section. He set these on the desk, the blocks shedding a little dust.

Wei picked one up; on Mars, like everything else, it was lighter than it looked. 'What's this? Cut stone?'

'No. Bricks. I made bricks, out of Martian dust.'

'Bricks?'

He half-listened as Kendrick briskly ran through the steps in his brick-making process: taking fine Martian dust, wetting it, adding a little straw from the domed gardens or shreds of waste cloth, then baking it in a solar-reflector furnace he had improvised from scrap parts. 'It's a process that's as old as civilisation.'

Wei smiled. 'Whose civilisation do you mean?'

'So simple a child could run it.'

'You say you need water—'

'Which is precious here, I know that. I'm breaking my back drilling for my own supply to avoid draining the communal reserve. But most of what I use can be recovered from the steam that comes off during baking.'

'Tell me why anybody would want to make bricks.'

Kendrick leaned forward. 'Because it's a quick and dirty way for this township to expand. Think about it. Most of your people are still living crammed into these domes, and most of *them* are still shipped from Earth. Your plastics industry here is in its infancy, along with everything else. In fact, I've got plans for two kinds of structure you can build from Martian brick. The first is dwelling spaces.'

Wei piled the two bricks one on top of the other. 'How could I build a useful dwelling of brick? Our buildings have to be pressurised. A brick structure would be blown apart by the internal pressure; remember that Martian air is at only a fraction of Earth's.'

'That's the whole damn point.' Kendrick rummaged in his satchel again. He showed Wei hand-drawn plans of domes and vaults, half-buried in the Martian ground. 'See? Pile it up with dirt, which you need for radiation shielding anyhow.' Which was true. On Mars there was no ozone layer, and the sun's ultraviolet reached all the way to the ground. 'And the weight of the dirt will maintain the compression you need. This is only a short-term solution but it could be an effective one. There's no shortage of dust on Mars, God knows; you could make as many bricks as you like, build as wide and deep as you can manage. It would give you room to grow your population fast, even before longer-term industries like plastics and steel kick in at production scales, and you can begin to achieve your strategic goals.'

Wei held up his hand. 'As always, you over-reach yourself, Mr Kendrick. Remember, you have no rank here, no formal role. You were sent here from the UN base at Eden because of the trouble you caused there; it is better that you are used as a labourer here at Fire City than to rot in some prison at Eden, breathing the expensive air—'

'I always think big,' Kendrick said, grinning unabashed. 'What got me in trouble in the first place. Even if I did achieve great things when I had a chance.'

'"Great things" which earned you banishment to Mars.'

Wei was overfamiliar with Kendrick's file. He was one of the youngest of a generation of entrepreneurs and engineers who had used the Jolts, a succession of climate-collapse shocks on Earth, as an opportunity; they had rushed through huge, usually flawed schemes to stabilise aspects of the climate, from sun-deflecting mirrors in space to gigantic carbon-sequestration plants in the deep oceans – schemes that, as had been revealed when the prosecutions started, had made their originators hugely wealthy, no matter how well they worked, or not. Even now, Wei thought, Kendrick probably carried around much of that wealth embedded in the very fabric of his body, in genetic therapies, cybernetic implants.

'Can you not see, Mr Kendrick, that if I allow you a role in influencing the "strategic goals" of this community, as you call them, suspicions will inevitably arise that you are simply reverting to type?'

Kendrick shrugged. 'I'm stuck on Mars, like you. I'm more interested in the common benefit than my own personal gain. Believe that or not, as you like. Sell this under your own authority if it makes you feel better.' Then he shut up.

In the lengthening silence Wei was aware of a seed of curiosity growing in his own mind, a seed planted by Kendrick. He suppressed a sigh. The man was a good salesman if nothing else. 'Tell me, then. You have described living shelters. What is the second kind of structure that could be built with your bricks?'

Kendrick glanced out of the window. 'The monument.'

'The cairn?'

'Look at it. It's kind of impressive, in its way. Everybody adds to it. I've seen the school kids climbing the ladders to add on another couple of rocks.'

Wei shrugged. It had been one of his initiatives to build up the cairn of Cao Xi as a cheap way to unite the community, and to remember a great hero.

'But how tall is it?' Kendrick asked now. 'A hundred metres? Listen – there were pyramids on Earth taller than that. And this is Mars, *Mr Mayor*. Low gravity, right? We ought to be able to build a pyramid three or four hundred metres tall, if we felt like it. Or . . .' Another expertly timed pause.

This must have been how the Heroic Generation made their plays, Wei thought. The sheer ambition of the visions, the scale – the chutzpah, to use one of Kendrick's own words – it was all dazzling. 'Or what?'

'Or we use my bricks. There were cathedral spires on Earth over a hundred and fifty metres tall. Here on Mars—'

'Spires?'

'Just imagine it, *Mr Mayor*.' Kendrick could clearly see he had hooked Wei's interest. 'If nothing else, you need something to keep me busy, and maybe a few other miscreants. You can't send me back to Earth, can you?'

Wei could not; that was no longer an option. A post-Jolt redistribution was shaping the home planet now; in China and around the rest of the world, whole populations were being displaced north and south from the desiccating mid-latitudes, and the central government had told the Martian colonists that they needed to find their own solutions to their problems. Yes, this would use up spare labour.

And anyway, Wei had long had an instinct that the first humans living on Mars should be doing more than merely surviving.

'A spire, you say?'

Kendrick grinned, and produced a slate with more diagrams. 'You'd start by digging foundations. Even on Mars a tree would need roots as deep as it is tall . . .'

Kendrick's rover was waiting for Wei outside the lock from the Summertime Vault. It was mid-morning and a break in the school timetable; at this time of day, as usual, most of the colony's hundred children were running around the big public space that dominated the

Vault, many of them low-gravity tall, oddly graceful. They were full of energy and life, and Wei, feeling old at fifty-two, regretted having to turn his back on them.

But Kendrick was waiting for him, his oddly youthful face full of calculation, eager as ever to draw Wei into his latest schemes.

To Wei's surprise, he and Kendrick were alone in the rover when it pulled away from the lock. 'I didn't know you were permitted to pilot one of these.'

Kendrick just grinned. 'There's a lot of stuff in this town that goes on under your personal radar, *Mr Mayor*. I've made a lot of friends here, a lot of contacts, and I call in favours every now and then.'

Wei glanced back at the heavy brick shoulders of the Summertime Vault, under its mound of rock and dust. 'You have accumulated these favours ever since we let you become so influential in the colony's destiny.'

'I'm doing no harm – you've got to admit that. Everybody benefits in the end. Xue Ling helped fix me up with this, actually.'

'She isn't your personal assistant. She merely volunteered to—'

'I know, I know.' Kendrick looked away hastily, as if seeking to close down the subject. 'It's the way the world works. Don't sweat it.'

Wei was sure Kendrick knew he disapproved of his relationship with Xue Ling, such as it was. The spurious glamour of the man seemed to draw in Xue Ling, as it drew in others. Wei didn't believe that Kendrick intended to push this too far. Nor did he suspect that Kendrick would succeed if he tried; Xue Ling, twenty-two years old now, was engaged to be married to a decent Chinese boy, a student. But still, something about Kendrick's interest in Xue Ling didn't feel right, given the paternal instincts Wei hoped he had developed as the girl's foster parent.

Heading out of town, they drove past the new Cao Xi monument. The old heap of rubble had long been demolished to make way for Kendrick's spire, a lofty cone nearly four hundred metres tall – almost three times the height of the tallest cathedral spires of medieval Europe, though constructed with much the same materials and techniques, of brick and mortar over a frame of tall Martian-grown oak trunks. The usual gaggle of protestors was gathered here, at the foot of the unfinished monument. Kendrick let the rover nose through their thin line, and Wei peered out, forcing an official smile for the benefit of any cameras present. Some were protesting because of the diversion of materials into what they called 'Wei's Folly', and it did Wei no good to point out that the building of the spire had kick-started the development of whole industries in the colony. Others protested because of the spire's echoes of the Christian west. And still others protested simply because they had liked the old cairn, the mound of stones they and their children had worked together to build up.

Kendrick, typically, ignored the people and peered up at the spire: slim, tall, already a monument impossible on Earth, at least with such basic raw materials. 'Magnificent, isn't it?'

'Magnificent for you,' Wei murmured. 'Is this how it was for the Heroic Generation? You build your monuments, overriding protests. You persuade the rest of us they are essential. And you grow fat on the profits, of one kind or another.'

'Binglin, my friend—'

'I am not your friend.'

'Sorry. Look, maybe I push my luck at times. But the reason I get away with it is, you're right, because you need what I do. Thanks to my brick-making you have the Vaults now, a huge expansion of space that would have been impossible without me. And that helps everybody, right? I've heard you talk of the Triangle. I read the news in the slates. I do pay attention, you know . . .'

The Triangle was the latest economic theory, of how Earth, Mars and the asteroids could be linked in a mutually supportive, positive-feedback trade loop. The asteroids were a vital source of raw materials that could be mined cleanly to support a starving Earth. So Earth, or rather the Chinese Greater Economic Framework down on Earth, exported expertise and high-tech goods into space, and got asteroid resources back in return. Mars, with its rapidly expanding colonies, served as a source of labour and living space for the asteroid development agencies, and in return received the raw materials *it* needed, particularly the volatiles of which the planet was starved.

But Mars's local administrators, Wei among them, were concerned that Mars should not be a mere construction shack on the edge of the asteroid belt. So a deliberate effort was being made to turn Mars's new communities, including Fire City, into hotbeds of communications, information technology, and top-class education. The dream was to start exporting high-quality software and other digital material both to the asteroids and to Earth – a dream that was already beginning to pay off.

And Kendrick had been right. To achieve those strategic goals Mars needed room, human space, to grow its population. Kendrick had managed to spot a kind of gap in the resource development cycle, and to fill it with his brick constructions. But that didn't make him necessary in any sense. Not as far as Wei was concerned.

Soon the centre of Fire City was far behind, and they passed the last colony buildings, the big translucent domes that sheltered the artificial marshland that was the hub of the city's recycling system. Then they drove through fields covered with clear plastic, where scientists were experimenting with gen-enged wheat and potatoes and rice, growing in Martian soil. Further out still the fields were open, and here banks of lichen stained the rocks, green and purple: the most advanced life forms on Mars, before humans arrived. Some of these lichen, which were some kind of relation to Earth life, were being gen-enged too, more experiments to find a way to farm Mars.

Beyond the lichen beds, at last they were out in open, undeveloped country. Even so they were still well within the walls of Mendel crater. And as the humming rover bounced over the roughly made track, Wei began to make out a slim form, dead ahead. It was a kind of tower, skeletal, with a splayed base. He peered forward, squinting through the dusty air. 'What is *that*?'

Kendrick grinned. 'What I brought you out here to see, *Mr Mayor*. You ever heard of the Eiffel Tower? In Paris, France. It was pulled down during a food riot in the 2060s, but—'

'Stop the rover.' As the vehicle rolled to a halt, Wei leaned forward, peering out of the blister window. Already they were so close that he had to tip back his head to see the peak. 'What is its purpose?'

Kendrick shrugged. 'It's a test. A demonstration, of what's possible to build with steel on Mars. Just as the spire—'

'Steel? Where did you get the steel from?' But of course Wei knew that; the city's new metallurgy plant, already up to industrially useful capacity, was pumping out iron and steel produced from hematite ore, the primary commercial source of iron on Earth, and an ore so ubiquitous on Mars it was what made the planet red. 'You diverted the plant's production for this?'

'Diverted – yeah, OK, that's the right word. Look, this is just a trial run. The steelworkers were keen too, to learn welding techniques in the Martian air, and so on . . . When it's proved its point we will tear this prototype down and put the materials to better use.'

'And that point is?'

'To see how high we can build, of course. We're still far from the tower, you don't get a sense of scale from here. Listen: that thing is almost eight hundred metres tall, twice the height of the Cao Xi monument. Nearly three times the height of Eiffel on Earth. That good old Martian gravity. This thing is already taller than any building on Earth before the late twentieth century. Think of that! Can you feel how it draws up the eye? That's the magical thing about Martian architecture. It baffles the Earthbound instinct.'

'You erected this without my knowledge.'

'Well, people live in holes in the ground here. You can get away with building almost anything you like, out in the big open Mars desert.'

'You are showing this to me now. Why?'

'I told you, this is a trial run. Just like the spire.'

'For what?'

'The monument of Cao Xi, Mark 3. You need to keep expanding, *Mr Mayor*. My brick has filled a gap, but in future Martian steel, Martian glass, and Martian concrete, are going to be the way to do it. But why keep burrowing into the ground? What way is that to bring up a new generation? Oh, I know we need to think about shielding, but...'

'What are you saying?'

'Tell me you can't guess. Tell me you aren't inspired. I know you by now, Wei Binglin.' Kendrick pointed to the brownish sky. 'No more cairns or spires, no more non-functional monuments. I'm telling you we should build a place for people to live. And I'm telling you that we should build, not down – but *up*.'

The chairman of the review committee, appointed directly by New Beijing on far-off Earth, was called Chang Kuo, and as the meeting came to order for its second day he regarded Wei and Kendrick solemnly. This conference room was deep underground, under the floor of the Hellas basin, which was itself eight kilometres beneath the Mars datum. Wei reflected that it would have been impossible for this place, the Chinese administrative capital, buried at the deepest point on Mars, to have been further away in spirit from what he and Kendrick were trying to build at Fire City.

Yet the room was dominated by a hologram, sitting in the centre of this circular room, a real-time relayed image of the Obelisk, as people were calling it, an image itself as tall as a human being. The real thing was already more than a kilometre tall, a great rectangular arm of steel and glass reaching to the Martian sky. And the damage done by the recent meteorite strike was clearly visible, a neat circular puncture somewhere above the three-hundredth level: the disaster that was the reason for this review.

The room shuddered, and Wei thought he heard a boom, deep and distant.

'What the hell was that?' Kendrick had lapsed into his native English. He looked alarmed, to Wei's unkind satisfaction.

Wei said, 'It was a nuclear weapon, detonated far beneath the fragmented floor of the Hellas crater. I would not have thought that a Heroic-Generation engineer like you would have been frightened by a mere firecracker.'

'Why are they setting off nukes? Oh. The terraforming experiments.'

'You heard about that. Well, of course you would.'

'Xue Ling showed me some of the documentation. Don't blame her. I pushed her to leak me the stuff. Blame her pregnancy; it's making her easier to handle.' But his smile was secretive, reluctant.

Wei thought he understood. Xue Ling, now twenty-eight years old, married and with child, had been campaigning to be allowed to leave Fire City – to come here, in fact, to Hellas, where she felt she could carve out a more meaningful career in administration than was possible back home. Her husband too, now a senior terraforming engineer, was having to commute to Hellas and back. It made sense in every way for Wei to allow her to go.

Every way but one: Kendrick.

There were other Chinese-Martian communities who were after Kendrick now, other opportunities, clandestine or otherwise, he might be tempted to pursue. Wei knew that part of Kendrick's long-term game plan had always been to make himself indispensable, to manoeuvre himself into a position where such opportunities would turn up. But it would be disastrous for Fire City if he were allowed to leave before the tower was finished – and disastrous too for Wei himself, of course, who had become so closely identified with the project, even in the eyes of these mandarins at Hellas. So Kendrick could not be allowed to leave. How, though, to keep him?

Xue Ling still seemed to be important to Kendrick, and therefore, for Wei, she served as a hold on him. She was also a conduit of information to Wei, information about his difficult, unpredictable, rogue of an ally. Regretfully, if Kendrick must be kept, *Wei could not allow Xue Ling to leave.* She was simply too useful. He assured himself that greater concerns, the good of the community as a whole, were paramount over her wishes. Besides, he told himself, it was better for

Xue Ling herself, whether she knew it or not, after the chaotic start to life she had endured, to stay close to what had become her nearest thing to home: close to her adoptive father, to himself . . .

The chairman, Chang Kuo, had spoken to him.

'I'm sorry, sir. Could you repeat that?'

'I said that this is the second day of our review of the project, of this "Obelisk" as the popular media are calling it. We must come to a verdict soon as to whether to allow the project to continue.'

Wei focused, and said carefully, 'Yesterday we reviewed the practical value of the tower. The living space it will afford. The stimulus it has given to local industries, to the development of skills and technologies specialised to Martian conditions. It is a great challenge, and as a people we are at our best when we rise to challenges.'

'Citizens have died. Its absurd vulnerability to meteorite strikes . . .'

Earth's thick atmosphere shielded the mother world from a variety of hazards. But just as Mars's thin air was no barrier to solar ultra-violet, so it did not screen the ground from medium-sized meteorite impacts.

Kendrick said confidently, 'That is a problem that can be solved, with warning systems, orbital deflection, laser batteries—'

'Ha! A typical Heroic-Generation answer. All at great expense, no doubt. Already the Obelisk project is distorting the whole of the regional economy. There are those who say it is a mere grandiose gesture.'

Kendrick stood up, eliciting gasps of shock at his ill manners. 'Grandiose? Is that what you think this is? Grandiose? Mr Chairman, the point of the Cao Xi Tower is to give this current generation a dream of their own to achieve – something more than a promise of a distant future they will never see . . .' He looked at Wei for support.

Wei stayed silent. They all looked at him now, even Kendrick, who sat down beside him. Wei felt old himself. He was only fifty-eight. He had already spent a decade of his life working with this man, this monster, Kendrick, and still he was not done.

One of the officials spoke into the silence. 'It was always a mistake to allow a pilot to assume a position of administrative power. The hero of the *Sunflower* was always liable to make some such gesture as this. Once a hero, always a hero – eh, Captain Wei? Is that your account of yourself?'

Chang Kuo nodded, stern. 'You have certainly bound yourself up personally to this monument, Wei Binglin. This monument, or folly.'

'Of course he has,' said Kendrick dryly. 'But he can't stop. *We* can't stop...'

Wei collected himself. He had to speak.

'None of us can stop,' he said now, firmly. 'The Obelisk is known across the planet, and at home, across the Framework – even in the UN-allied nations, thanks to satellites that image it from orbit. *We cannot stop*. The loss of face would be too great. That is the foundation of our argument for continuing, and it runs as deep and solid as the foundations we built for the tower itself.

'Now, shall we discuss how best to proceed from here?' And he glared at them, one by one, as if daring them to contradict him.

The word came to the two of them as they were having another long, wrangling meeting in Wei's office, in the old Summertime Vault.

The call came from her estranged husband, who was in Hellas, and who had in turn received a panicky call from a friend. She was heading for the top of the Obelisk. She had looked desperate as she left her apartment, on the prestigious fiftieth floor.

So they ran, the two of them, through the underground way to the base levels of the Obelisk, chambers carved into the tower's massive foundations. Both were in their sixties, neither as healthy as they once had been, Wei knew – he himself with an obscure cancer eating at his bones, and Kendrick limping along beside him, his oddly distorted face youthful yet slack. His expensive implants were, after decades without replacement, beginning to fail.

At the Obelisk, Wei had a priority card that enabled him to gain access to any of the fast-ascent external elevators. They were both breathless, and stayed silent as the elevator car climbed, smooth and effortless. Soon they rose above ground level, and the car began to make its way up one glass-coated side of the building. The car seemed to crawl, despite its speed, such was the scale of the building. A tremendous view of the city, and of Mars, opened up as they climbed.

Yet it was the Obelisk itself that captured the attention, as ever.

As he looked up through the elevator's clear roof, Wei saw the building's glass face shining in the low, buttery morning sunlight of Mars, climbing on and on, a dead flat plane that narrowed to a fine line and seemed to pierce the sky itself. And in a sense it did, for the Obelisk rose above the weather. The shell was complete now, a cage of Martian steel under tension, holding concrete piles in place, all of it glassed over. It was mostly pressurised, though the labour of fitting

out its interior would likely go on for years yet. To the external walls
were fixed a number of elevator channels, like the one they rode, and
inside, a steep staircase wound up within the pressurised hull. That
was the other way to ascend the building, to *climb* up, like ascending
a mountain.

The tower itself reached an astounding ten kilometres into the sky,
three times as tall as any conceivable building of the same materials
on Earth, and over five times as tall as any building ever actually
constructed there. Wei had seen simulations of the sight of it from
orbit – he himself had never left the planet since stepping off the
shuttle from the *Sunflower*. From space it was an astonishing image,
slim, perfect, rising out of the chaotic landscape to claw at the sky.
Even on the ground, you could see it from hundreds of kilometres
away, a needle rising up from beyond the horizon.

Ten kilometres! Why, if you laid it flat out it would take a reasonably healthy man two hours to walk its length. And the walk up the
stairs, if you took it, was itself fourteen kilometres long. Mars was a
small world but built on a big scale, with tremendous craters and deep
valleys; but only the great Tharsis volcanoes would have dwarfed the
Obelisk. All of mankind seemed to agree it was a magnificent human
achievement, especially to have been constructed so early in the era
of the colonisation of Mars.

And the Obelisk had transformed the community from which it
had sprung. Just as Kendrick had predicted, as a result of the forced
development that had been required for the building of the tower,
Fire City had become a global centre of manufacturing industry, of the
production of steel and glass, even Kendrick's venerable bricks. There
was even talk of moving the planet's administrative capital here, from
the gloomy dungeons of Hellas.

Yet there was still controversy.

'I received another petition,' Wei said, breaking the silence as they
rose.

'About what?'

'About the water you use up, making your concrete.'

He shrugged. 'We have plenty of water coming up from the aquifer
wells now. Besides, what of it? If civilisation falls on Mars, let future
generations mine the wreck of the Obelisk for the water locked up in
its fabric. Think of it as a long-term strategic reserve.'

'Are you serious?'

'Of course.'

'I should not be astounded by you any more, but I am. To think on such timescales! But have we really made much difference, despite all your arrogant bluster? Out there. What do you see?'

Kendrick turned to look out at the Martian landscape opening up beyond the confines of the city, the horizon steadily widening.

Beyond the walls of Mendel, they could see more crater walls, on a tremendous scale but eroded, graven with gullies, and dry valleys snaking between them. This was Terra Cimmeria, a very ancient landscape. It dated from the earliest days of the formation of the solar system, when the young worlds were battered with a late bombardment of huge rock fragments, some of them immature planets themselves. That was a beating whose scars had been eroded away on Earth, but they had survived on the moon, and on Mars. And here the cratering process had competed with huge flooding episodes, as giant underground aquifers were broken open to release waters that washed away the new crater walls, and pooled on the still-red-hot floors of the impact basins.

Terra Cimmeria, a museum of primordial violence, had itself endured for billions of years, a crazy geological scribble. And humanity had barely begun to touch this vast, primal disorder, Obelisk or no Obelisk. Yet there was beauty here. He spied one small crater where a dune field had gathered, Martian dust shaped by the thin winds, a fine sculpture, a variation of crescents. Maybe that was the proper role of humans here, he thought. Not to shape the world, but to pick out fragments of beauty amid the violence. Beauty like the spirit of Xue Ling, perhaps, who was fleeing from him into the sky.

But Kendrick said nothing. A mere planet, it seemed, did not impress him, save as raw material.

They climbed through a layer of cloud, of fine water-ice particles.

Once they were above the cloud, the ugly ground was hidden, and it was as if the Obelisk itself floated in the sky.

For the last few hundred floors, as the tower narrowed, they had to switch elevators to a central shaft. They hurried down a corridor inhabited only by patient robots, squat cylinders, which worked on an incomplete weld. There was no carpet here, and the walls were bare concrete panels; the very air was thin and cold. At the central elevator shaft they had to don pressure suits, provided in a store inside the car itself; pressurisation was not yet guaranteed at higher levels.

They rose now in darkness, excluded from the world.

Wei said carefully, 'We have not even spoken of why we are here.'

'Xue Ling, you mean. Neither of us is surprised to find ourselves in this position. Be honest about that, Wei Binglin. You know, I could never . . .'

'What? Have her?'

'Not that,' Kendrick said angrily. 'I knew I could never *tell* her how I felt. Mostly because I don't understand it myself. Do I love her? I suspect I don't know what love is.' He laughed. 'My parents didn't provide me with that implant. But she was something so beautiful, in this ugly place. I would never have harmed her, you know. Even by loving her.'

'I knew that.'

Kendrick looked at him bleakly. 'And yet you kept her close to me. That was to control me, was it?'

Wei shrugged. 'Once the Obelisk was begun, you could not be allowed to leave.'

'How could I leave anyhow? I'm a criminal, remember. This is a chain gang for me.'

'I've known you a long time, Bill Kendrick. If you had wished to leave you would have found a way.'

'So you nailed me in place with her, did you? But at what cost, Wei? At what cost?'

The elevator slid to a halt. The doors peeled back to reveal a glass wall, a viewing gallery as yet unfinished. They were near the very top of the tower now, Wei knew, nearly ten kilometres high, and the horizon of this small world was folded, a clear curve, with shells of atmosphere visible as if seen from space. A layer of cloud draped the lower storeys of the Obelisk, concealing the ground. To the east there was a brownish smudge: possibly a dust storm brewing.

And there, on a ledge, *outside* the wall of glass, was Xue Ling. She was aware of their arrival, and she turned. Wei could easily make out her small, frightened face behind her pressure suit visor. She was still only thirty-three, Wei realised, only thirty-three.

The two men ran to the wall, fumbling with gloved hands at the glass. Wei slapped an override unit on his chest to ensure they could all hear each other.

'*Now* you come,' Xue Ling said bitterly. 'Now you see me, as if for the first time in my life.'

Kendrick looked from left to right desperately. 'How do we get through this wall?'

'What was it you wanted? You, Bill Kendrick, creating a thing of stupendous ugliness to match the crimes you committed on Earth? You, Wei Binglin, building a tower to get back to the sky from which you fell? And what was I, a token in your relationship with each other? You call me your daughter. Would you have treated your blood daughter this way? You *kept* me here. Even when I lost my baby, even then, and my husband wanted to go back to Hellas, even then... You never saw me. You never heard me. You never listened to me.'

Wei pressed his open palm to the glass. 'Ling, please. Why are you doing this? Why now?'

Kendrick touched his arm. 'She asked again to leave, to go to Hellas.'

'She asked *you*?'

'She wanted me to persuade you this time. I said you would forbid it. It was one refusal too many, perhaps...'

'Your fault, then.'

Kendrick snorted. 'Do you really believe that?'

Ling cried, 'You never saw me! See me now!'

And she let herself fall backwards, away from the ledge. The men pressed forward, following her descent through the glass. The gentle Martian gravity, which had permitted the building of the Obelisk, drew her down gently at first, then gradually faster. Her breathing, in Wei's ears, was as if she stood next to him, staying calm even as she fell away, drifting down the face of the tower. He lost sight of her as she passed through the cloud, long before she reached the distant ground.

ESCAPE FROM EDEN

Yuri had to kick Lemmy awake. Lemmy stirred slowly, feeling around for his jumpsuit in the dark of the barrack.

Yuri always thought it was amazing the kid slept at all, what with his scurvy, as the Martians called it, the stuffy head and the nausea and the disorientation, the result of a profound non-adaptation to the low gravity, and that was despite him having spent half his nineteen years up here. Whereas Yuri sometimes wondered if *he'd* slept properly at all since being thawed out, eighty years out of his time. He lay there in his narrow bunk every night, listening to the snoring of the men around him in the barrack, and the shuffling of the bed-hoppers, like it was some border-control prison back in Manchester. And behind all *that* there were the uncomfortable sounds of Mars itself, the unending wheeze of the dome's pumps and fans, the popping of the dome shell as the temperature swung through its day and night extremes, and the occasional distant artillery-shell crump that might be a meteorite, or something worse. Sleep, for Yuri, was a luxury on Mars. But Lemmy slept like a baby.

Anyhow, as soon as Lemmy woke up he remembered what they'd planned for today, and he grinned as he pulled on his bright green jumpsuit, his wheezy breath rattling.

The two of them padded barefoot through the barrack. A few inmates were awake, Yuri could tell; eyes gleamed in the dark, predatory or fearful. But nobody bothered them. Yuri still had enough of his Earthborn strength to be able to swing a fist pretty effectively, and they mostly stayed away. Which was one reason why Lemmy, smart but small and sickly, hung around with him.

Once out of the barrack they hurried through corridors, heading for the dome wall. All was quiet, save for a couple of squat maintenance robots working their dull way across the scuffed plastic floor. Partitions sliced up the dome's inner space, and Yuri imagined sleepers racked up in their bunk beds behind those smooth walls. But over their heads the bland surface of the main dome stretched, shutting out the sky. They passed a row of VR booths, all occupied. Always somebody trying to escape from life on Mars, and prepared to spend their hard-earned scrip to do it, whatever the time of day or night.

'Told you it would be quiet,' Lemmy murmured. 'Supposed to be a twenty-four-hour shift pattern here, WorkTherapy all day and all night. But the handover from late night to early morning is always a slack time.'

'Good for us.'

They reached the outer wall of the dome, a sheet of plastic reinforced by ribs of Martian steel, which sloped sharply down to meet the flooring in a tight seal. Lemmy led the way with a shambling run around the curve of the wall, which was plastered with UN posters in Spanish, English, French, Russian, even some in Chinese, exhorting you to eat, sleep, exercise, to obey the Peacekeepers and accept whatever verdict the Community Council handed down to you, and to throw yourself into your WorkTherapy. All the posters had been systematically marred by graffiti.

'So where is this lock?'

'Not far now. Keep your voice down.' Lemmy looked up nervously at the black snubs of the Peacekeepers' surveillance cameras, everywhere. Of course they would be seen, their identities revealed, every movement recorded; it was just a question of whether they could get to where they wanted to be before they were stopped.

They came to a stretch of wall covered by a new poster, taller than Yuri was, plastered against the inward-sloping face. It showed an astronaut in a snazzy pressure suit with a helmet of pale UN blue, smiling out at you while pointing to a cluster of stars in the night sky: JOIN ME AT FAR CENTAURUS, said the slogan, in the blocky modern font Yuri had so much trouble reading. Somebody had scratched a UN-dollar sign into his forehead. Lemmy briskly ripped this off the wall, to reveal another poster reassuring you that gen-enged Martian wheat from the province of Cadiz was wholesome to eat despite the rumours, and under *that* ...

A hatchway. A metal door with rivets, rounded corners.

'Told you.' Lemmy punched a bypass code into a panel, then worked a heavy manual handle, a stiff bar that needed all his weight to turn. 'Used when they first built this place, but now it doesn't pass the safety-standard checks. But they never seal anything up. You never know.'

The door hissed open, pulling inward. Yuri had been born on Earth in the year 2067, nearly a hundred years ago, and, dozing in a cryo tank, had missed mankind's heroic expansion out into the solar system. But after a year in this place he understood a few details. Like this door, that it was designed to open inward so that the dome's inner air pressure would keep the hatch closed rather than push it open.

Beyond, the hatch fluorescents blinked reluctantly to life. The pair hurried down a short corridor towards another hatch. The air smelled musty.

The second hatch was stiffer, but Lemmy got them through.

Now they entered a small compartment, which had windows to the outside showing streaky Martian dawn light, and the domes and blocks of Eden, this UN township. Yuri went straight to the window and pressed his hands against it. He'd been taken through spacesuit and airlock drills for the sake of emergency training, but he'd never been outside. Mostly he never even got to look through a window.

He stepped back and looked around. There was nothing in this chamber but four holes in the wall, each about as wide as his waist and sealed with some kind of plastic diaphragm, and shelves with a clutter of elderly gear: jars of skin cream, an empty water bottle, a heap of dirty clothing.

'Is this an airlock? How do we get outside?'

Lemmy grinned. 'Shoes off.' He kicked off his own soft-soled slippers. Then he got hold of a handrail over one of those holes in the wall, lifted himself up with a grunt, and slid his legs feet-first through the hole. The diaphragm, flaps of flexible plastic, swallowed his lower body. He looked back at Yuri. 'Try it. One size fits all.' And he raised his arms above his head, and slipped bodily through the hole and out of sight.

Yuri had no choice but to trust him. He kicked away his own shoes, grabbed the bar, jumped up and swung. The plastic flaps slid around him easily, and he felt his legs being guided into tubes of fabric. With a faint misgiving he let go of the bar, wrapped his arms around his torso, and let himself fall through the hole – and found himself standing up, in some kind of pressure suit, *outside*, on the Martian surface. His head had ended up in a bubble visor. His legs had slid easily into the lower part of the suit, the leggings and boots, but his arms were still clasped around his chest. He heard the suit come alive now he was inside it, the high-pitched hum of fans, and the material squirmed around his legs and feet, evidently adjusting to fit.

The helmet, and the whole back of the suit, was fixed to the wall behind him, as if glued. But he was outside. Through the visor he saw a panorama of dusty buildings and equipment.

Beside him, Lemmy stood inside another suit, pinned at the back to the wall like his own. Lemmy was working his arms into dangling sleeves, and a neck light inside his helmet showed his face. 'Told you.' His voice came over a crackly radio link.

Yuri found the arms of his own suit, and pushed his hands down the sleeves and into gloves. The suit chafed in places, and he could see the outer layer was grubby and worn.

Lemmy sneezed spectacularly, spraying the inside of his dome helmet. 'Shit. Dusty.' A small white shape wriggled around inside the helmet, pink eyes peering out fearlessly.

'So you brought Krafft along.'

'What, you think I'd leave him in the barrack? Good boy, Krafft.' The rat wriggled and disappeared.

'What kind of suits are these, that you don't put on inside a lock?'

'Planetary protection gear. Designed to keep humans and their mucky bodies sealed off completely from Mars. And vice versa. From back in the day when they cared about such things.'

'They don't any more?'

'Look, you just have to pull away from the wall. One, two, three—' He braced, leaned, and Yuri saw his suit part from the wall, with a spray of ancient dust. Everything got dust-covered on Mars.

Yuri knew nothing about the air of Mars, except there wasn't much of it and he couldn't breathe it, and he'd freeze to death even before he got a lungful. He didn't let himself hesitate, didn't stop to think what would happen if the decades-old suit failed on him. He just pulled himself forward, there was a smacking sound like somebody noisily kissing the back of their hand, and there he was, free of the wall, standing independently on Mars. He tried a step or two. He felt just as light as he did inside the dome, and the suit wasn't much of an encumbrance; he could hear the whir of elderly exoskeletal artificial muscles helping him bend the joints.

There was dust heaped everywhere, the relic of many storm seasons; this area was evidently unused. When he kicked, the dust fell like crimson snow, in the gathering red-brown light of a Martian dawn.

Out!

Lemmy coughed again; his breath was a wheezy rattle.

Yuri said, 'So which way's the rover?'

'This way. Come on. Let's get to it before some Peacekeeper crawls out of bed and comes after us . . .'

*

Yuri followed Lemmy away from the dome. Just to be out was a relief, to be able to walk more than fifty metres or so and not be stopped by a wall. But he longed to rip off this enclosing suit, he longed to *run*, off into the lapping desert.

Eden was the UN's largest outpost on Mars, and one of the oldest. You could see its history in the jumble of buildings around the dirt-track streets. The cylindrical bulks like Nissen huts were the remains of the first ships to land, tipped over and heaped with dirt and turned into shelters. Then had come domes like the one Yuri had been assigned to, built of panels prefabricated on Earth and shipped out here, and covered over with dirt as a shield from meteorites and solar radiation. Then there were a few buildings of blocks of red Martian sandstone – the newest structures, and made of local materials, but oddly they looked the oldest to Yuri's Earthborn eye, like the archaeological remains that survived among the sprawl of the cities of his native North Britain. The whole place had the feel of a prison to Yuri, or a labour camp.

And this was pretty much all the UN held on Mars these days. The scuttlebutt was that a colony like this would be dwarfed by the giant cities the Chinese were building on the rest of the planet, like their capital, Obelisk, in Terra Cimmeria.

They came to a kind of parking lot where ground vehicles were gathered around big pressurised maintenance workshops. The vehicles ranged from little one-person dust buggies to huge drilling rigs with anchors to hold themselves down against the low gravity while they sought for water from deep aquifers. All these great engines were coated with the clinging dust of Mars, all reduced to the same washed-out reddish-brown, their paintwork obscured. The area was quiet, nobody around; Lemmy had been right about this window of small-hours stillness.

'Here.' Lemmy led him to a boxy vehicle with a big sealed compartment at the back, and a smaller two-seat cabin up front. With six big bubble wheels and a boat-like lower hull, the rover was dust-covered like the rest, but Yuri saw from scuffs and smears that a big heavy airlock door at the rear had been opened recently.

'Just a rover, for getting workers from A to B. It ain't pretty, but it is fast. And stupid enough to do what we tell it.'

Lemmy walked up to a smaller lock that led into the driver's cabin, punched a code and pushed open the lock door. Lemmy was good at this kind of stuff, knew his way around. Which was one reason why Yuri hung around with him – the other being, Yuri sometimes admitted to himself, a need to protect somebody even weaker than himself here on Mars. Like Lemmy with his rat Krafft, so it was with Yuri and Lemmy.

The cabin was a two-seater, with two sets of controls, two wheels. A hatch at the back evidently led to the rear pressurised bay. Lemmy deferred to Yuri and let him take the left-hand seat. As the cabin pressurised they opened up their suits. Settling in the right seat, Lemmy punched a few panels and murmured a few commands, while his pet rat crawled around his neck and inside his jacket. 'That's it. Safety overrides off. Of course alarms will be ringing in the domes.'

'So we'll get our butts kicked.' Yuri strapped himself in tightly with a wraparound belt. 'But not yet. Let's do this.' He started punching buttons, and grabbed the joystick before him. Soon they were rolling away from the vehicle lot. Panels lit up with red flags, and a ponderous automated voice in what sounded to Yuri like a Bostonian accent instructed them to turn back, but Lemmy shut it all down.

It was the first time Yuri had driven since his cryo-freezing, and the first time he'd driven any kind of vehicle on Mars. But he found the controls hadn't changed much in a century, even on a different world; you just pointed and steered with the joystick and squirted the gas with your foot, even if the 'gas' here was methane manufactured out of Martian air and water. There was even some kind of manual override on the transmission if you needed it. Since his waking, he'd found twenty-second-century technology easy to work. User interfaces seemed to have settled down to common standards some time before he'd been frozen. Even the language had stabilised, more or less, if not the accents; there was a huge mass of recorded culture, all of which tended to keep languages static. Vehicles and vocabularies of the year 2166 were easy. It was the people he couldn't figure out.

Lemmy performed another miracle. He produced a plastic flask full of a clear liquid from inside his pressure suit. Yuri grabbed it, unscrewed the cap using his teeth, and swigged. He knew what it had to be: illicit vodka made by a group of Russians in their illegal still in Y Dome, from stolen gen-enged potatoes. 'Suddenly the day got better yet.'

'You bet.'

'So, this Chaos we're heading for. Which way?'

'North.'

The sun was rising now, a small, pale, distorted disc whose light turned the sky a kind of diarrhoea-brown, washing out the last of the starlight. Yuri knew where he was on Mars, more or less, in an area called Atlantis in the southern hemisphere, so he took his alignment from the sun. They roared north, following a dusty trail, not much more than a braid of overlapping tyre tracks. He got up some speed, and a plume of dust rose up behind them, ancient Martian dust that, he was told, got endlessly sifted around this snow globe of a planet, never settling, never washing out, never consolidating. Lemmy whooped in exhilaration, though it quickly broke up into a cough.

They soon left the colony behind. Now, under the dung-coloured sky, there was nothing but the trail, and the vehicle, and the two of them, and barely a sign that humans had ever come this way before. Directly ahead Yuri made out what looked like a range of low, eroded hills, looming on the close horizon. That was the Chaos, whatever it was, where they were going to have some fun.

Lemmy pointed to a mound of stuff that they passed a little way off the track, a heap of boxes and canisters, some of them broken open already, and a fallen parachute draped over the dirt. All of it was stamped with UN roundels, evidently a supply drop gone wrong. Eden relied on supplies dropped from orbit, because the rest of Mars was owned by the Chinese. It was an operation like the Berlin airlift to keep them alive, somebody had once told Yuri, as if he would remember an event that had happened over a century before he was even born.

They went over a pothole in the track, and the rover bounced on its fat tyres, lifting off the ground with an eerie low-gravity slowness. As they hit the dirt once more Yuri thought he heard a noise in the rear compartment, like a grunt. But though he listened closely, he heard no more.

After that Lemmy went quiet, and when Yuri looked over he saw he had fallen asleep. Even the rat was dozing on his shoulder. Lemmy was only nineteen, a year younger than Yuri biologically, but he looked older, sallow, the dirt accentuating the lines in his face, even when he slept.

Well, his silence suited Yuri. He wanted nothing more in all this shrivelled-up cage of a world than to be left alone. And here in this hijacked rover, with his only companions sound asleep, Yuri was about as alone as he'd been since the medics had woken him up from his cryo tank. He grinned, and put his foot down harder.

*

He came upon the Chaos before he knew it. Distances were evidently tricky to judge here, with the near horizon, the dry but dusty air.

The Chaos was a bunch of irregular mounds sticking out of the ground, big slabs like some huge piece of Martian crust had been picked up and dropped and allowed to shatter. All of it was softened, eroded under the dusty yellow-brown sky, but he could see a few sharp edges and sheer cliffs.

He drove into shadow, between two huge hill-sized slabs, like the paws of some tremendous animal. He found himself in a kind of valley, a gully. He could tell no water had ever run here, or not enough to carve this feature; it was just a break in the slabs.

A screen on the dash pinged and lit up with some kind of map, along with more red warning lights. Lemmy, woken by the ping, tapped a pad until the flags went away. 'Safety off. But you might want to slow down—'

'Not just yet.' Yuri put his foot down harder.

They raced through a nest of mesas, buttes and hills, chopped through by valleys that looked as if they had been carved out by some huge laser beam. It was a hell of a country, like nothing he'd ever seen on Earth – not that landscapes had ever been his bag anyhow. It was kind of like a ride he'd once had on a high-speed two-man jetski through the concrete canyons of a drowned Canary Wharf, in Londres. He whooped, and ignored the pinging of the warning flags, and pushed the rover even harder, and the vehicle bounced on its tyres. Again he thought he heard some kind of grunt come from the rear cabin, but it must be a creaking of the hull.

Now the valley he was following narrowed suddenly, like a funnel. He couldn't slow down in time, he was charging down its throat. And a slope rose up out of the dust under his left wheels, like a purpose-built ramp.

The hurtling rover flipped neatly up and over. Suddenly he was sailing through the thin air, through the shifting shadows of this canyon, *upside down*. The flight seemed to take an age in the low gravity.

Lemmy closed his eyes. The rat squealed. Yuri laughed out loud.

The rover hit with a slam, and slid on its roof deeper into the canyon. Yuri, strapped upside down in his seat, was enough of a Martian by now to listen for the signs of a hull breach, the whistling of a leak, the ear-popping of decompression. But whoever had built this rover had done a good job, and the hull held.

The rover rammed itself between narrowing walls, and came to a sudden, juddering halt.

Yuri and Lemmy exchanged a look.

'They'll put us in the shit marsh for a year after this,' Lemmy said, slightly strangulated, his harness around his neck.

'It was worth it. Ten years would be worth it.' Yuri reached to his waist, hit the release, and tumbled out of his seat and down into the inverted cabin roof. He reached up to help Lemmy down. The rat clung to Lemmy's collar as if nothing had happened. 'So now what?'

'So now we wait for rescue, and to have our asses kicked by the Peacekeepers. I think there's a coffee maker—'

Yuri held up his hand. A distinctive scraping was coming from the hatch to the rear compartment. The sound of a handle turning, a wheel.

Both of them turned and watched the hatch. Even the rat sat still.

The hatch swung back, awkwardly pushed; whoever was back there was upside down too. Then a head and shoulders thrust through the hatch. The face was a tattooed mask, under a scalp shaven in elaborate whorls. A woman's face. She had some kind of white dust scattered over her shoulders and the black jacket she wore. She was mad as hell. 'Which of you two fuckers is the driver?'

'I am.'

The woman reached through the hatch with a clenched fist, every finger laden with a massive steel ring, and slammed a punch into Yuri's nose.

When he woke, his whole face felt like a bruise. He was lying on his back, over the steering wheel which dug into his spine, with his head resting on the windscreen. He touched his nose cautiously to find both nostrils bunged up by bits of ripped cloth.

They were both looking at him.

Lemmy was huddling in a corner of the cab, with a swelling over his right eye, either from the crash or from a second punch. 'Sorry about the first aid, man. Your nose wouldn't stop bleeding.'

The woman sat in the open hatchway. She was chewing what looked like shreds of tobacco. The tattoos on her face were solid black slabs that brought out the glare of her pale blue eyes. He could see more of that white dust on her black tunic and charcoal-coloured leggings.

Yuri struggled to sit up; his back ached like hell, and his face was a mass of throbbing pain. When he was settled on the inverted cabin roof, Lemmy handed him a plastic bulb of water that he sucked down gratefully. He said to Lemmy, 'So we've not been saved yet.'

Lemmy shrugged. 'You've only been out about five minutes.'

'Don't worry,' said the woman. 'Peacekeeper Tollemache is on his way.'

'Why him? How do you know?' But the woman just glared back at him, and he filled in the blanks: because Tollemache already knew about whatever she was up to, in the back of this anonymous rover. That was Peacekeepers for you, always in somebody's pocket.

She said, 'Give me more of that water, you little prick.' Lemmy scrambled to comply. 'My name is Delga. And you owe me money.' She glanced down at the powder spilled on her tunic.

Yuri had no intention of paying anything, come what may. 'How much?'

'I'll let you know. I'll want it in UN dollars, by the way, not the local scrip.'

'And how much for Peacekeeper Tollemache?'

That might have earned him another punch. Instead she just grinned. Her front teeth were filed to points. 'The Peacekeepers know I provide a necessary service.'

'Drugs.'

'I offer escape from this place. What were you doing in this rover but escaping?'

'You're a regular social worker.'

She frowned. 'A what? I know who you are. You're a curiosity. The ice boy, right? Your name is Yuri. What the hell kind of a name is that?'

'Not my name.'

'Then why are you called it?'

'Some joker called me that when they woke me up, here on Mars.'

'So what's your real name?'

He looked away.

There was movement outside. Somebody in a pressure suit, the helmet UN blue, shone a flashlight through the cabin window. Then there was more movement, vehicle lights, a big bundle being offloaded from a rover.

'They'll put a dome up around us,' Lemmy said. 'Get us out that way. It's a whole squad of Peacekeepers, out here because of us. Look at how they're moving. See, that jerky way? They've got military enhancements. Oh, boy, are we in trouble.'

While they waited, Delga was still staring at Yuri, faintly curious. He wondered how old she was – mid-thirties, maybe. Under the tattoos it was hard to tell. She said, 'This is Mars, ice boy. It's the dream of a thousand years to be here. I bet that's how they talked in your day, right?'

'Not me. It's not my dream. Who would raise a kid in a place like this? Like in a prison, or a cage.'

'They want us to have kids,' Lemmy said. 'Kids are the future, on Mars. You get breaks if you have 'em. But there are a lot of stillborn, and births that don't go right. Kids that don't grow right.' He whirled a finger by his ear. 'You know.'

'They have a Public School, they call it,' said Delga, 'in Phlegra Montes. That's in the northern hemisphere, a long way from here. That's where they dump all those kids. The UN runs the Phlegra camp in cooperation with the Chinese. Think of that, the great rivals cooperating to cover up what becomes of their kids.'

'Cover up? From who?'

'From the folks on Earth. The voters, whoever props up the UN. Mars is a dream of the frontier. You can't have some blank-eyed broken kid spoiling the image, can you? So it's all hidden away.'

'How do you know all this?'

She shrugged.

But Lemmy said now, 'Because she has a kid of her own there. Don't you, Delga?'

She didn't take her eyes off Yuri. 'We all have secrets. Except for you, boy cosmonaut. You don't have secrets; you're just a blank.'

At last the hatch opened, with a hiss of equalising air pressure. A man, hefty, thrust his head and shoulders into the inverted cabin. He wore a pressure suit, military specification, but he had his helmet off. He looked maybe forty years old. Behind him Yuri could see the translucent walls of a temporary bubble-dome, heard the clatter of a portable air supply system. The guy glared around the cabin at the three of them. 'Who's responsible for this?'

Delga smiled easily. 'Good morning, Peacekeeper Tollemache. Not me. I was asleep in the back, after my last shift. You can check the records. I only woke up when—'

'It was me,' Yuri said. 'My idea. My plan, my driving. I made Lemmy here show me how.'

'Sure you did.' Tollemache inspected the bits of cloth stuck in Yuri's nose. 'Disgusting.' He leaned into the cabin and loomed over Yuri. Smiling, spacesuited, he suddenly reminded Yuri of the astronaut in the 'Far Centaurus' poster. 'You're the ice boy, right? Nothing but a pain in the butt since they defrosted you. Well, you won't be my problem much longer.' With a gloved fist he jammed a needle into Yuri's neck.

Once again the red-brown Martian light folded away.

OTHER YESTERDAYS

THE JUBILEE PLOT

Murmurs ran through the crowd. 'She is coming! The Queen is coming!' 'Listen – you can hear the whistle of her Trevi!' Under the high sun of this June morning, top hats were raised and lacy parasols twirled.

Giles Romillie was as thrilled as the rest at the sound of the steam whistle. Above all he dreamed of the race across the Channel bridge at six that evening, after which he himself was to be presented to Her Majesty – if he won! And somewhere in the crowd around him was Edith Wilcox, and he imagined her warm gaze on him when he returned from the French side and raised the trophy in victory.

It was 20 June 1887, the day of Victoria's Golden Jubilee. Later Giles would remember these heady morning moments and marvel at how little he had anticipated of the hours to come, when, as the Jubilee Plot unfolded, at peril would not be racing glory or the love of a serving girl, but his very life – and the life of a Queen-Empress.

His immediate problem was that he couldn't see what was going on. Lost in a forest of tall men wearing shiny black morning suits and women in elaborate gowns and bonnets, he could see nothing but Kentish sky. Giles, twenty years old, already dressed in his bright scarlet racing leathers, was stocky and strong, but tall he was not. He had to witness the Queen's arrival. He cast about, looking for inspiration.

He was a hundred paces away from a raised bandstand that stood on the bridge slip road. That might do.

With muttered apologies he pushed his way through the crowd. He knew most of these people, by sight if not by name; his father's class, the land-owning aristocracy, was powerful and supremely wealthy but not numerous, and everybody knew everybody else. He was rewarded with irritated glances from the loftily pompous – and, in his tight-fitting leathers, frankly lustful looks from some of the ladies, and one or two men.

He reached the bandstand. Its delicate wrought-iron roof was supported by slim pillars. In its shade, players of a Grenadier Guards band were sorting out their music and brass instruments. They ignored Giles. He stepped onto the stage, but it was only eighteen inches off the ground and he could see little more than he had before.

A trombone player, a big man wearing campaign ribbons from the Ottoman War of a decade before, took pity on him. 'Looking for a view, sonny? Why don't you follow the other lad's example and go up top?' He indicated the iron roof.

'What other lad?' But the man had already turned away. So Giles, relishing a bit of adventure, set his peaked cap back on his head and scaled a pillar's ornate ironwork. His thin-soled boots slipped on glossy white paint.

A hand in a black leather glove reached down. 'Let me help you.'

Giles looked up at a handsome, grinning face, a shock of blond hair silhouetted against the sky. 'Ulrich,' he growled. 'It would be you.'

Ulrich Zuba laughed. 'You may as well get used to me finishing first today!'

Giles grudgingly took the offered glove, and let Ulrich haul him up to the roof. So they sat side by side, Giles in his red racing leathers, Ulrich Zuba, Giles's deadliest rival, in his black.

At least the view, over a sea of top hats and parasols, was as magnificent as Giles had hoped.

He was only a hundred yards from the mighty abutment of the Jubilee Bridge, whose iron roots had been planted firmly into this chalky coastal ground a few miles from Folkestone. The bridge was a cantilever design, with iron trunks striding away towards France, supporting dual-level trackways inside shaped boxes of girders. It was hard to grasp the scale of the structure until you remembered that the lower track bore a four-track rail line, a route for the continental railway companies to reach the British Isles, and the upper, a route for autocars, was as wide and true a road as anything the Romans had ever built. A vision of Sir Benjamin Baker, architect of the Forth Bridge, the whole was painted post-box red, vivid against the blue of the sea. Tall ships passed under its mighty spans.

And it was across that upper roadway that, later that day, Ulrich and Giles would be racing for the honour of being the first ever to cross the freshly opened bridge.

Away from the bridge, a broad new Telford road ran straight as an arrow off to the north to join the main south coast route, and this the national network. Meanwhile the rail link rather petered out, ending only in the rusty old military line to London. One short troop train stood idle on the tracks, its carriages black with soot. Closer by, a select crowd milled around the bandstand, looking from Giles' vantage like a flock of exotic birds. A pavilion sheltered the most notable, including several foreign heads of state, and there were distractions for the rest, including a fair and a display of country dancing.

But most eyes were turned north, where a short road train was approaching. As its mighty ten-feet-diameter wheels turned steadily, the Trevi's whistle blasted again, a puff of steam rising like a flag, and the onlookers cheered. Giles strained to glimpse the little woman who must be riding within one of those ornate carriages, in her black widow's weeds. She had been on the throne of Britain since the death of her father fifty years ago today. Beside her should be her son, Edward Prince of Wales, the heir to the throne to whom would fall the honour of starting the race, as well as hammering home the bridge's last rivet, of solid gold.

'It is good news for you, Giles,' Ulrich said in his slightly laboured English, and he pointed. 'Look, the Queen herself drives your autocar to the starting line!'

'Oh, very witty. I'll have you know that famous old omnibus drew her carriage to her coronation. One of Gurney's designs, I believe, deriving from Trevithick's prototypes. The Queen cleaves to tradition. That is her role.'

'She chose not to risk her royal neck in a put-put coal-gas autocar like your Boulton. Very wise! Perhaps she has merely been waiting to purchase a sound petrol-driven design like my Daimler.'

'If so, she might change her mind after she sees you lost in my dust this evening.'

'We will see.' Ulrich glanced around. 'Chancellor Bismarck is intending to be here in time to witness my triumph. He will be travelling, in fact, on the very first railway train to arrive from the continent over the bridge.'

'Trains. Pah! The rail carriageway spoils the line of the bridge, if you ask me. They should have left it as a dual-level roadway.'

Ulrich raised plucked eyebrows. 'But without the money from the continental iron-road companies, who are impatient to get at your ore and coal, the bridge would never have been built in the first place. Surely you know that. Do you read the newspapers, Herr Romillie?'

Actually Giles rarely did, save for the reports on motors and racing – and in particular on himself.

Ulrich laughed again. 'I will not tease you further. Look.' He pointed. 'A young lady is waving to you.'

Giles's heart beat faster.

She was a slight girl, her complexion olive, her jet black hair set off well against the cream-coloured gown she wore. She grinned up at Giles, and mouthed, 'I've been looking for you!'

'You have found me!' he mouthed back.

'You lucky dog,' Ulrich said.

'She is called Edith.'

Edith Wilcox worked in the royal household. Giles had met her when his father took him to Hampton Court to discuss protocol surrounding the race events. Today Edith's duties would start when the patient Trevi brought the Queen to the royal pavilion.

'Such a pretty girl,' Ulrich said. 'But such poor taste in men! And forward too, if I may say so. She has an exotic look about her – Mediterranean, is she?'

'Actually she's from London – Euston. Her father is Irish, her mother black, a freed slave.'

Again Ulrich raised his eyebrows. 'Well, she's a beauty for all that. But she's hardly a marriage prospect, is she? Not for a scion of such a family as yours.'

The very question surprised Giles. 'Of course not.' Yet his own quick answer rather shamed him.

'That's the attitude,' came a growling voice from the ground. Sir Joshua Romillie spoke around a fat cigar, his face as red as Giles's racing jacket.

'Good morning, Father.'

Ulrich tipped his peaked cap. 'Sir Joshua.'

Sir Joshua grunted. 'Should have known I'd find you up there, Giles. Can't resist making a spectacle of yourself, can you? Like a ruddy peacock in those leathers.'

Ulrich defended him. 'I rather think more eyes are drawn to Her Majesty this morning, Sir Joshua. Or else to the loveliness of Edith Wilcox.'

'Who? Oh, Giles's latest flibbertigibbet. Well, I was young once. Any engine must be run in. Just so long as you don't wear out your piston, eh, boy?'

Giles, blushing, glanced at Edith's sweet face. She was whispering to her friend, another palace servant, a flame-haired Irish beauty called Gemma whom he had met once or twice. Perhaps they were talking about him. Edith winked at him boldly. He felt his heart soften, just a little.

But he said, 'Of course not, sir.'

'Oh, for heaven's sake get down from there, you pair.'

They made their way to pillars and clambered down from the roof.

Ulrich asked, 'And what do you think of the bridge, Sir Joshua?'

He frowned, an intimidating expression exaggerated by his dense grey sideburns. 'I heard you taunting the boy over the rail deck. I'd have nothing to do with railways if it was my choice. Shunting the poor around the country might be good enough for you continentals, but it's not the English way, and never has been. The English yeoman lives on the ground his ancestors have tilled since before the Conquest, and he's best left there. My own father opposed George Stephenson himself...'

Ulrich responded with words about the efficiency and economic growth delivered by rail transportation.

And as they politely argued, Edith came pushing past Sir Joshua, towards the bandstand. Her face was drawn. 'Oh, Giles – Giles, it's awful!'

'Edith?' He was shocked. He had lost sight of her while he climbed down. From the smiling coquette of just a minute ago she was transformed, on the verge of tears. 'Whatever is the matter?'

'Gemma's been telling me things – oh, Giles! *You must not race,*' she said, her voice earnest, a half-whisper. 'You mustn't go on that bridge. Promise me!'

He was bewildered. 'Edith – the race, it's everything to me – how can I possibly promise such a thing?'

'But you must.' She glanced around, evidently scared. 'I'll get myself in the most frightful fix if I say more. Please, don't race – I must go –'

With that she was gone into the crowd. Ulrich had witnessed the little scene, and watched Giles curiously.

And there was a bang like a clap of thunder, so loud it was like a physical force, a blow in the chest.

Everybody flinched. There were screams. Sir Joshua took his cigar out of his mouth and turned around. 'What in blazes was that?'

Giles quickly shinned a couple of feet back up the bandstand pillar. And he saw, over the heads of the crowd, that the Queen's Trevi steam omnibus had exploded. Its big boiler was broken open like a burst paper bag, and it had careened off the roadway. The passenger carriages had become detached, but seemed unharmed. Soldiers were already running towards the shattered road train. People seemed stunned, but now the screaming started, shouts of fear and anger.

And Giles, clinging to the pillar, sensed that his life had changed forever.

Sir Joshua strode into the crowd, trying to exert control. He insisted Giles stayed close to him in the chaos that followed, for the sake of Giles' own safety.

Police and even military officers knew who Sir Joshua was, and deferred to him; he spoke to members of parliament, ministers, members of the royal household and other senior figures as an equal, giving advice and commands. Indeed, Sir Joshua held a parliamentary seat of his own, representing a 'rotten borough' on the outskirts of Luton whose few hundred electors were mostly his relatives or employees.

And through his father's conversations Giles, shocked, learned that although the royal party was unharmed by the explosion, an elaborate plot was unfolding this day of the Queen's Jubilee.

The detonation of the Queen's Trevi had been no accident. A bomb had broken the seam of its high-pressure steam boiler. The saboteurs had got their timing wrong, as the road train had been running too slowly to do any harm. But that wasn't all. There had also been an attempt to blow up Westminster Abbey, intended, presumably, to detonate at the time of the Queen's attendance at a thanksgiving service tomorrow. That had been uncovered because of a stray remark in a London pub by an Irish labourer. The Metropolitan Police had quickly broken the man, using techniques honed against strikers and other agitators over the decades, and had exposed a conspiracy by Irish Home Rule campaigners.

So two attacks had been thwarted, but the police and senior soldiers wondered aloud if there were more plots to be uncovered. Giles fretted over what Edith had said to him, which had seemed to imply that there must indeed be such a threat – something to do with the race perhaps. He needed to talk to her.

But Edith and the other girls had been sent home, whisked away in a fast road-train to London. He knew her address, in Euston, though he had never in his life been to such a district. But how was he to get there, on this day of confusion?

He mused on this with Ulrich, who had witnessed his fraught conversation with the girl. Ulrich disappeared for a while.

Then he returned, and tapped Giles on the shoulder. 'I have found a way. Come with me.'

'Found a way to do what?'

'To get you to Euston in a hurry. Isn't that what you want?'

Giles hesitated. 'And leave me stranded in north London and out of the race – is that the game?'

Ulrich sighed. 'Oh, do not be a fool. I know you say you care little for this girl, Edith. But I saw her agitation for myself. Might this not be more important than a mere race? Anyway, you will be back by six. I will accompany you, so you can be sure there is no deceit involved! Will that satisfy you?'

Giles felt mollified, and faintly ashamed; the man did seem to be trying to help him. 'All right. But how are we to get there and back in a few hours? In your smelly Daimler?'

Ulrich grinned. 'I have been speaking to a few of your troops. I know soldiers. I have relatives in the military.'

'*All* Germans have relatives in the military.'

'Well, with a little sweet talk, and a promise of a grandstand seat to see the race's finish, I have secured us places on the next troop train back to London.'

Giles wrinkled his nose in disgust. 'A train? The railway? I've never ridden the railway in my life!'

'Then it is a day of novelties. Come *on*.' He led the way.

Giles followed with a backward glance at his father, who had apparently not yet noticed his son slipping away. But then Sir Joshua paid him little attention at the best of times.

The troop train was a row of grimy wooden carriages behind a hissing locomotive of French design. With a smile and a promissory note Ulrich talked them past the corporal guarding the train.

There was no station here, no platform; they climbed into the carriage up a short wooden ladder directly from the rusty tracks. The carriage was like a barn on wheels, with a wooden floor and slats for walls, and rows of simple, backless benches. There were only a few troops aboard, tired-looking men cradling packs and rifles, with red coats unbuttoned. They glanced at Ulrich and Giles, uninterested, then turned back to their cigarettes and card games. Giles settled reluctantly on a bench, trying to keep his leathers clean.

Just minutes after they boarded, a whistle shrieked and the train jolted into motion. Giles had to grab the bench to avoid being thrown to the floor. As the train picked up speed, the breeze whistled through the slatted walls, and Giles was glad it was such a hot day, but was dismayed when smoke and soot and even sparks came blowing into the carriage.

Ulrich laughed at his discomfort. 'You are an iron-road virgin.'

'I told you, I've never ridden a rail train before in my life. And this is why.'

'But you should visit Germany some time.' He had to speak up over the chuffing of the locomotive, the rattle of the wheels on the track. 'There you travel in heated coaches, with dinner served to you by a pretty waitress. Why, German cattle are transported in better conditions than this!'

'But even so, who wants to ride a train? To be shunted from fixed point to fixed point – you have none of the freedom you have in an autocar. *And* you can't choose what sort you travel with. No offence.'

'But look at the economics. As I explained to your father, the rail can transport high volumes at low cost and high speeds. For industry's needs—'

'Canals will do for England, and turnpike roads, as they have always done. My father owns shares in the Silver Cross, the country's greatest canal system, connecting the Thames, Trent, Severn and Mersey. Once we had a cruising holiday, a summer in a houseboat. The canals were fair crowded with commercial vehicles and cargo.'

Ulrich grunted. 'Lumbering along at the pace of a broken-down horse! The British *invented* modern industrial society. You have an empire that spans the world. Yet you are the poor man of Europe! And now continental entrepreneurs will come over the Jubilee Bridge to take away your coal and iron ore and other raw materials as if you are a colony to be exploited. You should come to Germany, my friend,' he said again.

Giles was relieved when the train picked up more speed, and the noise drowned out Ulrich's voice.

The train cut briskly across the country, heading north-west. It stopped at Ashford, Maidstone and Sevenoaks, where troops and equipment were disembarked, and others loaded aboard. Then it turned north towards the capital, and joined the London Loop south of Greenwich. This grand circle of rail track, designed to ferry troops rapidly to trouble spots around the city, was the only major rail development to have taken place in Britain for forty years.

On the Loop, the train headed west and rattled through Deptford,

Peckham and Camberwell. Ulrich peered out curiously at the capital's sprawling, grimy acres, houses and factories jammed in together under a pall of smoke, cut through here and there by the tracks of the motor roads – shining paths kept empty of pedestrians by law, to make way for the coal-gas-powered autocars of the rich, and the occasional steam omnibus.

Giles felt proud of this vision of London's roads, for his own family had had a great deal to do with its creation. In the 1830s a man called Sir Goldsworthy Gurney had run a trial steam-driven road train service between Gloucester and Cheltenham. After the early railway experiments by Stephenson and the rest failed, the Romillies and other interested parties had argued for Gurney's system, and poured money into resolving the attendant technical problems: high pressure boilers to make engines powerful enough, road surfaces toughened by Thomas Telford's expensive processes, pneumatic tyres to make the ride itself bearable for passengers. Sir Joshua always said that it was a much more civilised solution to Britain's transport needs than the rail, a solution that did *not* involve laying waste to whole swathes of ancient English countryside with bridges and cuttings and embankments, and shrieking locomotives putting the cows off their milk.

But Ulrich did not seem impressed. 'London is not like Berlin.'

'Well, I should hope not.'

'The roads are so poor, save for the motor routes. And without rail how do people travel to work?'

Giles was puzzled by the question. 'In their autocars.'

'Not the rich,' Ulrich said. 'The workers, the ordinary people.'

'They don't. Well, they walk. If everybody travelled about it would ruin the character of the place, wouldn't it?'

'Why, look there – a cow!' Behind every grimy house or terraced row was a scrap of green, populated by cows, sheep, chickens. 'Cows, in your capital!'

'How else are you supposed to get fresh milk in the city?'

'You transport it in from the countryside. By rail!'

'Maybe you like your milk sour in Berlin,' Giles said defensively. 'Here we take it warm and udder-fresh.'

'How medieval!'

Giles cast about for a way to shut him up. 'Look – you're starting to sound like an agitator.'

'Oh, I would not dream of causing trouble.' But, glancing at the soldiers with whom they shared the carriage, Ulrich fell silent.

The line swept over the river at Vauxhall, and they peered out sullenly at the crowded, grimy Thames.

The train stopped at Marylebone, and here Giles and Ulrich alighted. It was a walk of only a mile or so east to Euston. But this was a slum area. The old Marylebone road was lined by shabby houses and tenements and jammed with traffic, most of it horse-drawn. In one doorway they saw a man fallen down drunk, though it was barely past lunchtime; in the next a sad-looking prostitute bared bony ankles. And over it all hung the foetid stink of the city.

Ulrich muttered, 'In Berlin such areas have been cleared. The penetration of the railways into the city saw to that alone. In Berlin we have a *hauptbahnhof*, a big central station from which tracks push out in all directions. This is the north of London, is it not? Perhaps a great rail terminus might have grown up in Euston, if the iron roads had come this way, connecting the city to the northern provinces. Instead' – he waved a hand at the crowded squalor – '*this*.'

'I think I've heard enough about Berlin, thanks very much.'

Edith's home, when they found it, was a common lodging house, where you could stay for threepence a night. They had to tip the woman on the door, the deputy, a shilling to be allowed in.

Edith and her family inhabited two basement rooms. Here a black woman of about fifty held court over children of all ages, both black and white – there might have been a dozen, but they squirmed around so much it was hard for Giles to keep count. The walls were flaking and unpainted, and a kind of green mould was breaking through the ceiling. The only partitions were grimy blankets hung from ropes, and there was a stale stink of drying clothes, cooking and unwashed bodies.

And Edith was here, still in her cream uniform, but her hair was undone. She looked shocked when Giles entered, and with a squeal she hurried out, primping her hair.

The black woman sighed. She was going through a child's hair, evidently searching for lice. 'Don't you mind her, gentlemen. She'll come round. Does like to look nice always, like a china doll, that's what's wrong with her...' Her accent was strong and hard for Giles to place, a mixture perhaps of the African of only a generation back, and of the Liverpool area from where the family had recently come. She offered them tea, which they politely refused.

And as they waited for Edith their hostess told them something of herself.

Her name was Patience Wilcox, and she was Edith's mother. Edith's father, a white man from Liverpool, was only recently dead – killed, in fact, during the Jubilee Bridge construction, along with a thousand others, drowned when working in a caisson that had failed. Not all of these children were Patience's. Some of them belonged to the *other* family that shared these two rooms, two families living here without partition or boundary like animals in a pen. Patience was trying to encourage some of the children to sleep, while preparing others for work; all these little ones worked in factories or shops, all save the very smallest.

Patience herself, born in Britain, was the daughter of an African who had been captured by slavers on the Gold Coast; she barely remembered him. After slavery was formally abolished in Britain in the 1820s, Liverpool, which had made its fortune from the slave trade, had looked to a future as an imperial port. But when the pioneering Liverpool & Manchester railway had failed following the notorious 1838 Olive Mount disaster, the industrial trade from Manchester was choked. In those desperate times for the port, slaving returned – illicitly at first, and later legally when parliamentary bills set out various 'exemptions' to the abolition act. The trade ceased at last in the 1860s after the American Civil War, and any slaves in Britain at the time were given their liberty. Freedom – but no work, not from the great land-owning aristocrats who dominated the region's economy. So Patience's family had come to London, which was big and hungry enough to offer them employment.

'Edith herself was born a slave.' Patience cackled, opening a mouth with only a couple of stubby teeth. 'Scrubs up well, doesn't she?'

As if on cue, Edith returned. Giles and Ulrich stood. She was freshly washed and with her hair properly done up, her royal household uniform spick and span. 'Giles. Thanks ever so for coming. I'm sorry to be so silly.'

'It's all right. Your mother has been most gracious. Look, I've come because I thought we should talk. What you said about the race – and then the Trevi bomb going off like that—'

'It was Gemma who told me! You know, my friend, you met her. I got it all from her. She just warned me to stay away from the Queen's Trevi, that was all. We are good pals, you know. She was only looking out for me. She made me promise not to tell, not even you! But I was shocked. I couldn't let you go ahead with the race, could I?' She looked at him with an intensity of affection that disturbed him. 'Not if—'

'Not if what?' Giles crossed to her, took her hands and tried to calm her. 'Start at the beginning, Edith. It's all right. I'm sure we can sort this out.'

'*Are* you sure? I'm not.'

And she told him what her friend Gemma had told her, of the Jubilee Plot.

It was to have been a threefold strike: the already-foiled Irish assault on Westminster Abbey, the sabotage of the Queen's Trevi – and finally, Edith told him, her voice trembling, the most devastating assault of all, a detonation that would sever one of the long spans of the new Jubilee Bridge, just as the inaugural autocar race reached that point.

She whispered, 'Oh, nobody expected all the bombs to work. But if just one did it might be enough. It's all about striking back, you see. That's what Gemma told me. About showing they are strong.'

'And how,' Ulrich asked sternly, 'does this Gemma know such things? And who are these saboteurs?'

The saboteurs, it turned out, were a mixed bunch with mixed motives, all of them unhappy under the regime. Gemma Brady had family connections to the Home Rule campaigners who had attacked Westminster. But the Irish had links to other groups, anarchists, agitators for universal suffrage, campaigners against poverty, who together had worked out this spectacular multiple plot timed for a most symbolic moment, the Queen's own Jubilee.

Giles shook his head. 'Do these fools imagine they will win their arguments by blowing up the Queen?'

'But what else are they to do, Giles? Call it an experiment in revolution! I've talked this through with Gemma and others. There are a lot of very clever people working below stairs, believe me! I've even been to a few meetings to hear for myself.' But she hesitated; almost certainly any such meeting would be regarded as an illegal combination. 'Look, for decades reform in this country has been thwarted at every step. The last attempt at parliamentary reform failed in 1832. The Chartists were prosecuted in 1838. Laws about factory inspections and the hours you can work a child were defeated or repealed in the 1840s. Efforts to repeal the Corn Laws were defeated in 1846, and the poor stayed hungry . . .'

This litany of history dismayed Giles, who knew little of these events; he found it slightly obsessive. And yet there was something admirable in this girl's self-taught understanding.

'It's amazing we haven't had revolts before, as they have in Europe. In 1848—'

'You should have gone to the police,' Ulrich said sternly.

'What, and get locked up as a conspirator myself? You know what the police are like – at least *you* do, Giles. And it's worse for a woman, believe me. And what if the agitators find out I've been talking to you, what if *they* come after me? Who will protect me then?'

Giles was moved, if astonished. 'So you risked your life to save mine?'

Ulrich murmured, 'Evidently she cares about you, Romillie. Can't imagine why.'

Giles looked uneasily into his own soul. He had never thought of Edith in such terms at all – not at all. She was from a different category of society from him, and always would be. How could he love such a girl? And how could he deal with the prospect that such a girl loved him?

Ulrich said, 'We must set off if we are to be back in time.'

Edith stared at Giles. 'You won't give me away—'

'Of course not,' Giles said, distressed she thought him capable of it.

'And, oh, say you won't race! You can find some way to cry off. Say you're ill. Or get the race cancelled, or at least postponed... There must be a way.'

But Giles recoiled from the very thought. He glanced at Ulrich, and saw in the German's eyes that he understood.

Giles wanted to race. At that moment he cared nothing for Chartists or resentful Irishmen. Even when he looked at the children crowding around Patience Wilcox, he felt that way. *Tomorrow I will find out all about the history of electoral reform*, he promised his Lord. *For today, let me race.*

But did he have the courage to see that resolution through?

Six o'clock approached, as measured by clocks set to Paris time – England had no universal standard time of its own, for it had no national rail system that required it.

Giles climbed into his Boulton coal-gas autocar alongside the other racers in their American Selden designs and German four-stroke petrol engines, and Ulrich in his Daimler. It was a magnificent setting, the gleaming autocars lined up across the clean new roadway, the bridge set straight before him in bold, intimidating perspective, and the bright blue sky of a June evening over it all. The morning scare had much reduced the crowd, but the few spectators remaining were being rewarded with a cold collation, and beer for the men and tea for the women and children. And, it was said, the Prince of Wales was still here, braving out the panic, determined to open the bridge and start the race.

It would all have seemed perfect, the culmination of Giles's young life so far, if not for the doubt that still churned in his stomach.

Even if Edith were correct about the bomb being placed on the bridge, there was no reason to suppose it would work as planned – the Jubilee Plot conspirators had failed twice today already – but still, if he raced he would be gambling with his life.

Or he could tell his father or the police all he had learned from Edith. If he did so, he would be safe, come what may. But he would show his father who he had been dabbling with. A floozy was one thing, but a girl with a brain and exposure to radical ideas was quite wrong for him. And the race would surely be stopped; he would lose his chance of glory.

And, worst of all, he would show himself to his father to be a coward: to be unwilling to take the ultimate risk in search of glory. It made it worse that Ulrich was sat patiently waiting for the start, as aware of the risk as Giles was.

Then, minutes before the off, his father walked up and clambered into the passenger seat beside him.

'Don't mind me stowing away, do you?'

Giles, astonished, could only reply, 'Not at all, Father.'

'I thought we should chat.' Sir Joshua ran a finger along the leather surround of the dashboard. 'Look, boy – do you understand what you're doing here? Do you understand *why* you're here?'

'What do you mean?'

Sir Joshua shifted in his seat to look at his son. 'Just this. We're an old lot, we Romillies. For centuries we got our money and power from land, the oldest asset of all. But that all started to change in my father's time – your grandpapa's, God rest his soul. Suddenly there was industry everywhere; suddenly there was trade; suddenly there were these absurdly wealthy fellows in grimy northern cities making demands for parliamentary representation. And then that wretched man Stephenson started throwing down his railway lines.

'Well, your grandpapa and others of like mind had soon had enough. Once they had rid of Grey and his Reform Bill, they decided to deal with Stephenson and his crew. We were all for transport, it was obvious the old canals and roads weren't sufficient, but railways were far too – ugh! – *common*. Grandpapa told me of one of his workers who spent his pennies on a train ride to the coast. Do you know what it does to a man, to see the sea for the first time? Fills his head full of longings that can't be fulfilled. No, the railways had to go. Of course the argument mightn't have been won if not for the Olive Mount disaster.'

In that notorious catastrophe, a cutting close to the Liverpool terminus of Stephenson's Liverpool & Manchester line had collapsed, crushing two packed passenger trains and killing hundreds – including Stephenson himself. The collapse was supposedly caused by poor excavation and vibration from the trains themselves.

Giles said, 'Nobody wanted to ride the railway after that. I remember Grandpapa saying so.'

Sir Joshua smiled. 'Fortuitous, wasn't it? And good riddance to ruddy Stephenson, of course.'

Fortuitous. Suddenly Giles saw what his father was telling him. The Jubilee Plot wasn't the only conspiracy he was learning about today.

'After that we Romillies didn't look back. We made a fortune during the Crimean War, when we poured buses and wagons into the conflict, and bought the lot back afterwards, along with an army of trained veteran drivers, the beginnings of a new industry of motor-driven hauliers. The recent war with the Ottomans was almost as profitable.'

'I never really understood why we had to fight the Ottomans ...'

'Oil,' Sir Joshua said firmly. 'That's all. The oil under the provinces we took: Baghdad, Basra, Mosul. Oh, don't look so shocked! All the experts assure me that the Germans' petrol technology is the way of the future. That doesn't mean to say the race can't be won by good old British coal gas, today ...'

Engines were throttled. Giles looked around. A box had been set up at one side of the road; a number of men surrounded a portly figure in a military uniform who must be the Prince of Wales. A white flag was raised: one minute to the start. Giles tested his throttle and choke, and squeezed the foot bulb that controlled the flow of gas. The engine hummed sweetly. He glanced across at Ulrich, who looked back at him sombrely.

Sir Joshua sat back in his seat, fixed a harness across his chest, and adjusted his goggles before his eyes. 'So you do understand what's happening here, do you, Giles? This new bridge, this race, this very autocar, they all represent the England *we* have built, we and others of our class. And now at this moment of national celebration the eyes of the empire and the world are on us – on *you*. That is why what you are about to do is so important . . .'

The flag remained poised. Only seconds remained for Giles to make his choice.

It all swirled around in his head.

Above all, he found, *he still wanted to race*, that was the iron frame of his thinking. Even if it cost him Edith – even if there were other costs, and for some reason he thought uneasily of the hollow faces of Edith's brothers and sisters – even if it cost him his life, he had to race. And even if he were weighed down by his father's baleful presence, and the autocar by his weight, he would win.

He made his decision.

The flag fell. He engaged the engine. The Boulton shot forward.

He had travelled perhaps half a mile before he realised that his was the only vehicle that had started. The rest remained lined up on the grid.

Sheepishly he turned the autocar around and drove it back to the start.

'You arranged this,' he said to his father.

'Surely that's obvious! Oh, don't worry, the bridge has been made safe. I set up this little trial with the race starter. Prince Edward himself thought it was all rather a lark!'

'So you know. About the Jubilee Plot, the bomb, Edith—'

'Of course I know. The police picked up that silly Brady girl even before you sneaked away from me in the crowd. Well, you were followed. The police should have collected Edith Wilcox too by now.'

'She wasn't involved,' Giles said hotly. 'She only knew what Gemma told her.'

'That's what she told *you*. But even if so, she didn't report it as she should have done, did she?

'As for you, I saw an ideal opportunity to test you, boy. I merely wanted to see if you had the courage, the sheer blind bloody-minded guts to hurl yourself into a race for glory, even if there was a good chance you would kill yourself in the process – and me, by God! And that was precisely what you did.' He patted Giles's shoulder. 'Good boy! You are a Romillie after all.'

Giles reversed the autocar back into its starting place. The other drivers applauded him ironically. He glanced across at Ulrich, who shrugged at him and grinned. 'I see you shared this plot with Zuba.'

'Oh, yes. I didn't want *him* babbling about potential bombs. He was happy to go along with it. He too wants to win. And he sees a better chance of doing so without you in the race.'

Giles frowned. 'What do you mean, without me? I could win this yet.'

'No.' Sir Joshua leaned past him and opened his door. 'Out you get.'

'What?'

Sir Joshua's face became thunderous. 'You kept the truth from me, boy! And, worse, you *hesitated*. You should have hauled the girl by her ear down to a police station, or brought her to me. *I* make family decisions, not you; you come to me, you do not act alone. You need to learn a lesson.'

'And this is the lesson?'

Sir Joshua grinned. 'Certainly. To watch me take the glory that should have been yours. Never mind! There might be another chance for you when Victoria reaches her Diamond Jubilee in ten years' time. Out you hop. Shoo, shoo!'

So Giles got out of the autocar, pulled off his goggles, gloves and cap, and walked away, off the bridge. The spectators smirked and giggled. Everybody else seemed to have been in on his father's joke, save him.

There was a roar of engines. The spectators cheered. So the race was under way. Giles didn't bother turning around.

His father had set him a test he believed Giles had passed. Giles wasn't so sure, not any more. Perhaps, in fact, he had failed.

He thought of Edith, who had winked at him boldly when he was on the roof of the bandstand; Edith, daughter of a freed slave, and her toiling siblings; Edith who had tried to save his life, and would pay for it with her own liberty. He didn't even know if he loved Edith. He had never posed the question to himself before. But now he wondered if he deserved such loyalty, such love from her. Perhaps that was the next test he would have to pass.

And as for her 'experiment in revolution' – well, now that she seemed to have provoked a revolution in his own heart, perhaps other tests lay ahead. A role in such a revolution for the heir of a family who had grown so rich while so many others had stayed so poor might be difficult to find...

But first he must find *her*. He looked around for a policeman to ask him where Edith might be held and how he could see her.

FATE AND THE FIRE-LANCE

'Imogen. Oh, Imogen, you must wake up. He's dead, Imogen. Gavrilo, the son of a Roman emperor, killed in London! It's such a frightful mess, and I don't know what I'm going to do...'

The thin, tremulous voice dragged Imogen Brodsworth out of a too-short sleep. Her eyelids heavy, she had trouble focusing on the face before her: young, oval-shaped, with big eyes but a small nose and mouth, not pretty despite all the efforts of the cosmeticians. And Imogen, just for a moment, couldn't remember where she was. The bed was big, too soft, and there was a scent of old wood, a whiff of incense – and, oddly, cigarette smoke.

Incense. This was Lambeth Palace, residence of archbishops.

The day was bright, the light streaming through the big sash window where a servant had pulled back dusty curtains. She glanced at the small clock on her bedside table. At least that was her own, an ingenious French-Louisianan contraption that told you the time and date on little dials. It was 29 June 1914, fifteen minutes past six on this summer morning.

The girl before her, her face swollen with crying, was Alice, daughter of the English king Charles VII. A princess babbling of killing. She had a maidservant with her, who flapped and fluttered as Alice's mood shifted.

Imogen struggled to sit up. 'Ma'am? What did you say of Gavrilo?'

'That he's been murdered, Miss Brodsworth.' That was a male voice, grave, and Imogen reflexively ducked back down under the covers.

A soldier stepped forward, crisply uniformed, immaculately shaved, walrus moustache trimmed despite the earliness of the hour. He was perhaps forty. He held a small cigarette in his right hand. He kept his eyes politely averted. 'My intrusion is unforgivable, but it is a bit urgent. We met yesterday at the reception at St James's Palace—'

'I remember. Major Armstrong.'

Imogen was a teacher of Latin and Greek, employed by a small private girls' school in Wales. She had been attached as an interpreter with special responsibilities to support the Princess Royal at the reception for her fiancé, the second son of Caesar Nedjelko XXVI Princip. She had encountered Major Archibald Armstrong who was charged with the security of the party, working with a splendidly dressed Roman prefect called Marcus Helvidius.

Imogen had little interest in politics, but she could imagine the implications of the murder of an imperial scion on British soil. 'My word,' was all she could think of to say.

Alice's tears were turning to temper. 'What about *me*? Gavrilo was my fiancé, if you've forgotten! I'm a widow before I was even married – I'm not even eighteen – everybody will look at me and laugh!'

Imogen glanced at Armstrong. 'Major, please...'

Armstrong coughed, and turned his back.

Imogen got out of bed. Her nightdress was thick and heavy, too hot but quite suitable for spending the night in the residence of the Archbishop of Canterbury. She faced Alice and took her hands; they were weak and clutched a soggy handkerchief. 'My lady. You must be strong. Dignified. Today is bound to be difficult, and your father will be relying on you.'

Admonished, Alice did calm a little. 'Yes. I know. It's just – is my whole life to be defined by this moment? I hardly knew the man, Imogen. I spent more time with him yesterday on his quireme than we've ever spent before. Even when I visited his palace in Moscow he was always off hunting. Marie Lloyd sang for us on the ship, you know. "Everything in the Garden's Lovely"...'

And you did not love him, Imogen thought. *Of course not, how could you?* 'I'm sure the future will take care of itself. For now, I know you will do your duty.'

'Yes...' Alice let her maid lead her away.

'You're good with her,' Armstrong said, back turned, puffing calmly on his cigarette.

'I have pupils older than her. I think you'd better let me perform my toilet, Major.'

'Thirty minutes,' Armstrong said briskly. He nodded and walked out.

On the bedside table, her little clock chimed the half-hour.

In the event she took only twenty minutes.

She checked her appearance in the mirror behind the door: her hair tied up in a neat, practical bun, high-necked blouse and long black skirt, her sensible schoolmistress's shoes for a day she expected to spend on her feet. She was twenty-five years old, and prettier than at least one princess, she told herself defiantly. But she knew she had a sensible air about her, and tended not to attract the eye of any but the most sensible of men. For sensible, she meant *dull*, she conceded wryly. Certainly none of the exotic grandees from across the globe present at the sessions yesterday had noticed her, not like that. None, perhaps, save Marcus Helvidius, who had, she thought back now, smiled at her once or twice...

She was wool-gathering, and blushing like a girl. She glared at her own pink cheeks, ordering herself to calm down; she would not have Major Armstrong think she was a ninny. She picked up her handbag and left the room.

Armstrong was waiting outside, puffing on another skinny American cigarette. Without a word he hurried her down a broad staircase and out of the palace.

An automobile was waiting for them on the embankment. They clambered aboard. An armed soldier sat up beside the driver, and two more climbed in behind them. The driver worked the ignition bulb, the engine started up with a smoky roar, and they pulled away into the road. More automobiles joined them, so it was quite a convoy that headed up along the embankment towards Lambeth Bridge. They all sported Union flags, but like most of the automobiles on London's roads they were Roman designs powered by Roman petrol; innovation in the automotive industry was driven by the demands of the empire's huge battlefields in central Asia.

The sun was still low but the sky was a bright cloudless blue, and the air was already warm. London's buildings and bridges were adorned with wreaths, flags and streamers, marks of celebration for the coming of a Roman prince to the city. But there was no air of celebration this morning. Soldiers lined the route, alternating with police, rifles at their shoulders. Aside from them there was nobody to be seen, and only Navy boats moved on the Thames.

Armstrong said, 'I do apologise for hoiking you out of your bed like that. Had to force my way in to make sure the summons got through to you. And I know you were up until the small hours with those ecclesiastical types.'

'Well, it's true,' she admitted. 'And coping with all that theological language does make the brain spin...'

The Romans were in London for the formal announcement of the engagement of Princess Alice to Gavrilo. The marriage was essentially political, a way to unite the British Bourbon dynasty to the house of Caesar Nedjelko XXVI Princip, a Serbian line of emperors who had ruled in Constantinople for more than a century. The British government, ever eager to maintain a balance of power on the continent, had used the occasion to host a summit conference of the great powers, notably the French and the Ottomans, territorial rivals of the Romans in central Europe and Mesopotamia, and the Americans, locked in their own perpetual rivalry with the French over their long border with the Louisiana Territory. The churches had been communing too, and while the temporal leaders had been gathered at St James's, the Archbishop of Canterbury had used Lambeth Palace to host delegations from the Vatican and the patriarchate of Constantinople to discuss theological issues and ecumenical ventures.

Imogen murmured, 'It was a long evening. Compared to the princes at St James's, the prelates might be long-winded, but they enjoy their wine just as much.' *And* a good few of them had roving eyes and wandering hands, she and the other girls had found.

Armstrong laughed. 'Well, I'm afraid you have another long day ahead of you today, Miss Brodsworth. Only a few of us are being summoned back to St James's. He asked for you specifically.'

'Who did?'

'The prefect, Marcus Helvidius. He was impressed by your language skills, and your sobriety. I think he believes you will be an asset today.'

Thinking of the prefect, she blushed again.

They were crossing Lambeth Bridge now, and they both turned to see the centrepiece of the Roman presence in London. Drawn up at a quay not far from the shimmering sandstone cliff that was the Palace of Westminster, the Roman ship that had brought Gavrilo here was a quireme. With her rows of oars she might not have looked out of place in the imperial fleets of two millennia before. But smokestacks thrust out of a forest of masts, and rows of gun ports were like little dark windows in the hull.

Having crossed the bridge the convoy turned right and sped up Millbank towards Westminster Abbey and Parliament Square.

'That ship's a remarkable sight, isn't she?' Imogen breathed.

'Oh, yes. But she's more than a floating hotel, you know. And this morning, after the fuss yesterday – well, look what she's disgorged.'

The convoy drove up Horse Guards Parade, past the government buildings, and turned into the Mall. And Imogen saw that a row of massive vehicles had been drawn up here, great blocks of steel that towered over the automobiles speeding past. Mounted on caterpillar tracks, with gun nozzles peering from every crevice, these were the vehicles of war the Romans called *testudos*, and the standards of the 314th Legion Siberian fluttered over their ugly flanks.

'A statement of strength,' Armstrong muttered. 'Given that we let their prince be assassinated we could hardly refuse, though nobody's happy about it. After all, it's hardly *our* fault; this unfortunate incident just happened to have occurred on our territory, that's all.'

Of course there was an implicit assumption in what he said that the assassin had not been British. She wondered what basis he had for believing that. But she did not question him, knowing nothing yet of the case.

More soldiers had set up a perimeter of sandbags and barbed wire around St James's Palace. Imogen and Armstrong were made to wait while a sergeant checked papers and telephoned his headquarters, and photographers wearing Roman insignia took their pictures. Armstrong accepted this delay laconically; he lit up another cigarette.

Inside the palace, Marcus Helvidius was waiting for them. He was conferring with a Roman senator, representatives of the French and Ottomans, British commanders – and a stout, bristling man dressed in a drab black morning suit who Imogen, feeling faintly bewildered, recognised as the British Foreign Secretary, David Lloyd George. They were speaking in broken Latin, their only common tongue.

When Imogen entered with Armstrong, Marcus turned to her. 'Miss Brodsworth. Thank you for coming.' He spoke Greek. He was a prefect of the 314th Legion, which, supplementing the Praetorian Guard, had been given responsibility for the security of Gavrilo during this expedition. Yesterday he had worn an archaic ceremonial costume of plumed helmet, cloak, breastplate, short tunic and laced-up boots; this morning he was dressed more functionally in an olive-green coverall, though the number and standard of his legion had been sewn into the breast. Aged perhaps thirty, he was a heavy-set, powerful man with thick dark hair; his look was more Slavic than Latin, she thought. But his blue eyes were clear, his jaw strong.

She glanced around, and replied in Greek, 'Am I the only interpreter you've called?'

'My decision,' Marcus said firmly. 'It's not seven hours since Gavrilo was murdered. I think it's best if we involve as few people as possible until we know what we're dealing with. Don't you agree?'

'It seems sensible. But why me?' The party yesterday had included senior academics from the great universities, experts in all the languages of the empire: Greek, Latin, Serbian, Georgian, Russian, German. 'I'm just a schoolteacher, you know. I was only attached because it was thought best that Princess Alice should be accompanied by somebody closer to her own age—'

'You are too modest,' said the Roman. 'I saw how you handled that most difficult of charges, a Princess Royal! You are evidently able, and sensible, Miss Brodsworth. I think you will be a great help today.'

He smiled at her, and she thought she would melt. But he wanted her only for her sobriety, she reminded herself. 'I'll do my best, I'm sure.'

Armstrong coughed. 'Now, the only Greek I have is what they managed to beat into me at Harrow, Miss Brodsworth, and I think I can follow, but you'd better start earning your corn.'

Imogen glanced at the party. The Foreign Secretary was waiting for her with a face like thunder. As she hastened over and slipped into her role, she seemed to become invisible to them – all save Marcus, who smiled at her again.

Marcus led the party through a part of the palace Imogen hadn't seen before. One particularly grand chamber had to be the Hall of the Ambassadors, with its famous ceiling depicting a vision of an austere Protestant heaven, painted by Michelangelo under the patronage of Henry VIII, who had built the palace in the first place. Imogen wondered how many other commoners had ever got to see it.

Marcus said, 'As it happens, Gavrilo received only a few visitors yesterday evening, in a small reception room at the back of the palace. Exchanging gifts and so forth. In fact, he spent much of the day aboard the ship. He did receive Princess Alice during the day, but in the evening was rather unwell.'

They all took this with straight faces. The rumours circulating among the interpreters was that Gavrilo, who had served on the Chinese front, had come back with an unhealthy liking for opium. He had spent the evening indulging with his companions and a few guests, including Jack Dempsey, the famous American-born gladiator, who had put on a show of mock combat against the empire's finest.

'Of course, that makes our task easier,' Marcus went on. 'Since only a small number of people had access to the prince, we have a small number of suspects to consider.' Imogen, attuned by now to diplomatic niceties, chose to translate 'suspects' as the more neutral word 'personages'. Armstrong caught her eye and gave her an approving nod.

They came at last to the reception room where Gavrilo had, from eleven in the evening onwards, grudgingly greeted his handful of visitors. More Romans took their pictures, the flashes dazzling, and British soldiers and police stood by uncomfortably among the legionaries.

Imogen was shocked by the state of the room. The portraits on the walls were scorched and blistered, the heavy wallpaper blackened; the moulded plaster of the ceiling was cracked, and at the very centre of the room a thick pile carpet was as scorched as if it had been used as a hearth. Many of the fittings had been soaked, by the water that must have been used to put out the fire that had blazed here. Over that scorched patch of carpet a chair had evidently been blown to bits; Imogen recognised scattered fragments, an arm, a seat cushion, a carved leg. The cushion was stained with a brown pigment – blood, perhaps.

The party poked around the mess. The Foreign Secretary pressed a handkerchief to his face. There was a prevailing smell of smoke and soot, and a heavy underlying iron smell that reminded Imogen of a butcher's shop.

Marcus was at her side. 'Are you all right?'

'I'm fine,' she said.

'Then you're stronger than me,' he murmured. 'I've seen war – I've fought in the east. One never gets used to the smell of dried blood.'

'This is where Gavrilo died?'

He pointed. 'He sat in that chair. He was blown apart in the explosion; he probably died instantly. The body has been taken away – returned to his ship.'

'Was he alone in here?'

'Alone save for his own companions, and one of our legionaries. Their injuries were minor. They reacted well, actually; they raised the alarm, got rid of the fires.'

'But what caused all this? Was it a bomb?'

'You can see it here, Miss Brodsworth,' Armstrong said in his Harrovian Greek. He pointed to a metal tube on the floor. 'Don't touch it – Scotland Yard, you know.'

It seemed to be a primitive weapon, an iron lance, perhaps. At its tip, bound with cord, were the remains of a rolled-up tube of paper, perhaps two feet long. The paper tube was blackened, blown apart, like a failed firework. And scattered around the lance were bits of joinery, the remnants of a smashed wooden box.

'Ironically,' Marcus said, 'the force of the explosion preserved the remnants of the fire-lance itself, even the paper tube; the fire was blown towards the walls. But poor Gavrilo was not spared, of course.'

Imogen inspected the weapon. 'A "fire-lance"?'

'A very early gunpowder weapon,' Armstrong said. 'Actually of Roman design. In battle you would carry a small iron box of glowing tinder to light the tube. Flames would shoot out, perhaps covering ten, twelve, fifteen feet.'

'It's a flamethrower, then.'

Marcus said, 'This particular specimen was captured during our war with the Seljuk Turks, over eight hundred years ago. It was a gift, presented in a display case – a Roman weapon captured by the Turks and returned centuries later. You can see the remnants of the case, reduced to matchwood. It appears Gavrilo was pleased with the gift, and was cradling it, box and all, when it detonated.'

'But how could it have exploded?'

'Well, it was rigged,' said Marcus. 'Aside from the gunpowder in the lance itself, there was a simple fuse, and a trigger mechanism like a flintlock attached to a clockwork timer, all concealed in the body of the presentation box.' He pointed, and she could just make out an intricate mechanism amid the wreckage.

She nodded. 'So that's how he died. But who's responsible? Who gave him this gift?'

'Ah,' Armstrong said. 'That's where it gets tricky... It was a gift from Vizier Osman Pasa.' Who was, Imogen knew, a senior official of the Ottoman government. 'So this appears to be the murder of a Roman prince, by an Ottoman assassin, carried out right here on British soil.' He shook his head. 'Shocking business.'

Imogen frowned. 'The Ottomans I've met haven't been fools, Major. Would Vizier Pasa really implicate himself so obviously? And do the Ottomans actually want conflict with the Romans right now? I've read that on the contrary—'

Armstrong snorted. 'I doubt very much that whatever racy stuff you read in the penny papers has much relation to a complicated diplomatic reality, Miss Brodsworth.'

Offended, she withdrew. 'Yes, Major.'

But Marcus would have none of it. 'No, no. You have a good point,

Miss Brodsworth. We must not jump to conclusions. Gavrilo was a scion of an imperial house two thousand years old, and here we are at the meeting point of empires. It's hardly likely that anything about his death would be simple, is it? What would *you* suggest we do, Miss Brodsworth?'

Armstrong was starting to get agitated. He stubbed out his latest cigarette and protested, 'Now look here, prefect, Miss Brodsworth is an able translator, but a mere slip of a girl who . . .'

Marcus wasn't listening. He kept his eyes on Imogen until the Major fell silent.

Imogen smiled at Marcus, flattered. 'Well, you need to find out who had access to the prince. One of them was the murderer – or more than one – that seems clear. When you know who the suspects are, you can begin to eliminate them, one by one.'

'Eminent common sense,' said Marcus. 'But I disagree on one point.'

'Yes?'

'You said "you". You meant "we". I want you to work with me on this, Miss Brodsworth.'

Armstrong seemed outraged. 'Oh, now look here, this is all—'

'Just for a period of grace. The police can continue their work in parallel. Miss Brodsworth is surely right, Major. We need to establish the truth of this incident before we start murdering each other's populations over it. Fresh eyes, untainted by diplomatic calculation, British eyes at that, might help a great deal. And we do need an interpreter, too, of course.' He turned back to Imogen. 'You spoke of who had access to Gavrilo. That at least is easy to establish.' He glanced at the photographers. 'A thorough lot, we Romans. We keep a record of everything . . .'

It wasn't yet nine o'clock. As the relevant photographs were assembled, hastily developed overnight, Imogen took the opportunity to have a breakfast of pastries and Brazilian coffee.

Aside from the prince's companions and guards, only four men had been admitted to the reception room last night while Gavrilo held his bleary court. 'The prince was in such a delicate temper,' Marcus said carefully, 'that it was decided to restrict the interview to representatives of the three great powers, other than the Romans: the British, the French and the Ottomans.'

So the Americans, the Spanish, and the German and Italian

princelings had all been left kicking their heels. 'That must have pleased the others.'

'But at least they are not under suspicion. Well, the photographs match the testimonies,' Marcus said.

Imogen stared at the grainy plates. There was a fresh chemical smell about them. She studied the Romans first: legionaries in traditional costumes, though armed with automatic weapons; a handful of the prince's companions in stylish American-fashion modern dress; senators and other ministers in togas. Gavrilo had himself worn a toga, and a wreath of laurels on his head.

'I know none of these people,' Imogen said.

'I think we can rule them out as suspects,' Marcus said rather grimly. 'They're all now in the hands of the Praetorian Guard.' This traditional bodyguard of the Caesars had evolved into a secret police. 'After several hours we can be sure they've nothing to reveal. Why, the very threat of being handed over to the Praetorians is enough to keep any Roman in line, believe me.' If he harboured any fear of what might be done to *him* as punishment for his failure to protect Gavrilo, he showed no sign of it.

Imogen studied the photographs of the visitors. Here was Vizier Osman Pasa carrying the fateful wooden case containing the firelance, and Prince Philippe, second son of the French king come to greet the second son of Caesar, and the Foreign Secretary representing the British government – and Lloyd George had Armstrong at his side. Even as he had been admitted to the Roman's presence, Imogen saw, Armstrong had been smoking his customary cigarette.

'I'm surprised you were there, Major,' Imogen said.

'I do have a responsibility for security,' Armstrong said. 'In this case it was actually the Foreign Secretary's welfare I was concerned with, for you'll notice we had no British soldiers in the chamber at that time.'

Marcus studied another photograph, which showed the visitors submitting to searches by helmet-clad legionaries. 'You're still smoking in this picture, Major. They left you your cigarette! Few Romans smoke, you know.'

'Well, I know that. In fact, I only lit up to annoy the Frenchies, if you must know.' His schoolboy Greek was studded with English: "Frenchies".

He was referring to a rivalry that dated back to Napoleonic times, when the French emperor, confronting the Romans in Europe and locked in war with the British, had refused to sell the Louisiana Territory to the new United States. A century later, as if in spite, the French refused any imports of tobacco products from the former English colonies, and very few Europeans smoked.

'Well.' Marcus lined up four photographs of the Foreign Secretary, the Major, the vizier and the French prince. 'Our suspects.'

'I do find it hard to suspect the Foreign Secretary,' Imogen admitted.

Marcus referred to a sheaf of documents. 'I have testimony from the prince's companions and the legionaries. It was after all these men left the prince's presence that the explosion went off. It was indeed the fire-lance that killed Gavrilo, and all the witnesses confirm that it was the vizier who brought it in personally. Though of course that is not proof that he knew of its lethal adjustments.'

The Major sat back, hands behind his head. 'It all seems clear enough to me.'

Marcus ignored him. 'What now, Miss Brodsworth?'

'We should interview our suspects. I would start with the man who brought in the fire-lance in the first place.'

Marcus summoned a runner. Then he set about finding an office suitable for interviews.

Armstrong raised his eyebrows, but did not object.

It took forty minutes for Osman Pasa to be brought to the palace from his suite at the Savoy.

Pasa's title was vizier, but Imogen understood this was something of a formality; power under the Ottoman sultan Mehmed V lay with parliament, and the vizier had little influence outside the court. Pasa was an elegant man, perhaps fifty, his dark complexion set off by the sharp, silver-grey suit he wore. He spoke fluent Latin, the nearest thing to a common international language, and Imogen translated for the Major.

'The fire-lance was of course a Roman artefact,' Pasa said languidly. 'Captured during the Seljuk war of 1071, as the Christian calendar has it. It has languished on palace walls or in museums ever since. This seemed an appropriate occasion to hand it back. After all, that conflict, so little known to western historians, was a turning point in the fortunes of the Romans...'

The East Roman empire, with its capital at Constantinople, had survived the collapse of its western counterpart. But the explosive advance of Islam in the seventh century had seen it lose Syria,

Palestine, Mesopotamia, even Egypt to the Arabs. And in the new millennium the Seljuk Turks assaulted Asia Minor, the very heart of the empire.

'As something of an amateur student of history myself, I've always been convinced that if not for the fire-lances, Asia Minor would have been lost,' the vizier said. 'And the final decline of the empire would have been assured. But the fire-lances, just like this one, and other gadgets like crude bombs, turned the tide. The Seljuk armies had nothing like them, and were driven back.

'It's said that gunpowder was brought to Constantinople by a single man, a Chinese dissident who fled the Sung emperors and came wandering down the Silk Road. And he carried a new idea out of China, as many ideas had travelled to the west before – silk, paper... In China, as you may know, gunpowder was an accidental discovery of Taoist chemists who sought an elixir of life.' Pasa grunted. 'What they discovered was a recipe for death. Of course, the East Romans had always used Greek fire against the Islamic armies; they knew how to develop super-weapons, and how to keep them secret. As a result, they had a monopoly on gunpowder weapons in Europe for two hundred years. Remarkable, isn't it, the difference one man can make?'

Imogen pressed the vizier, 'But as to the fire-lance itself – you did not intend to hand over a live weapon to the prince, did you?'

'Of course not.' He glanced at Marcus, quite relaxed. 'There should have been no gunpowder in it at all – only black pepper – certainly not such a potent modern mix. To place such a weapon in the hands of a young man so liable to, ahem, confusion? It would have been asking for trouble.'

Imogen said, 'And did the lance leave your possession at any time before you handed it over to the prince?'

'Yes. Both Roman and British soldiers, and British police, checked over the weapon and its box.' He glanced meaningfully at Armstrong.

'I oversaw some of this myself,' the Major said. 'We were looking for poison – doped needles, that sort of thing; we thought *that* was the most likely way one might get at the prince. We missed the gunpowder, I admit.'

'A bit of an oversight,' Marcus said in English, mocking the Major's tone.

Armstrong eyed him stonily. 'We're not as experienced with assassinations and palace coups as you are in your ancient empire, prefect.'

'Really?' Osman Pasa asked, glaring at Armstrong. 'I wonder if these questions of yours are directed at the right party, prefect.'

Armstrong just laughed at him.

They asked further questions of the Ottoman diplomat, but learned nothing new.

Prince Philippe was fat, fifty, his face red and puffy, his hair elaborately coiffed. He smelled of perfume, pomade and Roman vodka.

As he tried to squeeze his ample frame into a hard, upright English chair, Armstrong murmured to Imogen, 'Always the same, the Frenchies. Every diplomatic occasion they send over a prince of the blood – if not Fat Phil here, one if his equally unappealing brothers. They know these Orleanist princes get up the noses of our Bourbon royal family.'

Philippe's own gift to Gavrilo had been a remarkable jewelled cane, still in the possession of the Romans, beautiful and quite harmless. What Philippe chose to talk about, however, was the gift Gavrilo had handed to him. It was a bit of cloth mounted in a glass case, very old, coarsely woven. It bore a red cross, faded with time, and was stained with rust-brown splashes.

'It is a relic of my own ancestor,' Philippe said, speaking defiant French. 'Georges de Boulogne took the cross of Christ in 1203; this was stitched to his tunic when he died before the walls of Constantinople . . .'

The East Romans had always had a prickly relationship with the crusades. Those great military missions, aimed at recovering the Holy Land from the Muslims, were seen from Constantinople as grabs for power by the popes in Rome, who hoped to rule the squabbling statelets of Christendom. At last resentment had boiled over, and western Christians assaulted the capital of the east Christian power. But by now the East Romans had advanced weapons, bombs and mines, cannon, rockets, even handguns, at a time when gunpowder was still entirely unknown west of Constantinople. The crusaders were scattered; the city was saved.

'The cross was ripped from the chest of my fallen ancestor, and stored in some vault in Constantinople for eight hundred years. And now here it is,' Philippe said. 'Hurled back in my face!'

Imogen frowned. 'Perhaps the Romans meant to honour you, and the memory of Georges.'

Philippe said dismissively, 'Perhaps there is honour in defeat for you British; not for us. Remember, we have kept the Romans at bay for centuries, while you sit behind *la Manche* building ships . . .'

This was an old gripe. Even before the East Romans had acquired their fire-lances, Orthodox Christendom had spread far from Constantinople, with the conversion of Bulgaria, Georgia, Russia, Serbia. When in the thirteenth century the Mongols had erupted from central Asia to assault Georgia and Russia, the East Romans struck back, using their firearms to drive off the ferocious nomads: the Battle of Kiev in 1240 was remembered as the day the Mongols were repelled, and a dream reborn. After this victory a new geographically contiguous empire was born, absorbing the Orthodox countries, sweeping from the Balkans to the Baltic.

By then the secret of gunpowder was out; the Mongols acquired it from the Chinese, and through them the technology was adopted by Islam and western Christendom. But the East Romans were the first to reorganise their society as a gunpowder empire, with an expansion of mining and manufacture, government control of resources, the raising of vast armies, and a centralising of the state. To do this they reached back consciously to the forms of the old Roman Empire. By 1300 the Caesars once more wore the imperial purple, and legions armed with muskets and field artillery marched in Central Asia.

The empire cautiously expanded, east across Asia, south into Mesopotamia and Persia, and west into Europe. By 1500, Europe had been partitioned between the Roman and French spheres, with a hinterland of petty German and Italian statelets between the two – ironically, Rome itself was an independent city state, governed by the pope.

'We stood against them,' the French prince said bitterly. 'If not for France the eagle standard would fly in London as it does in Baghdad and Vladivostok—'

'I'm sure we're all jolly grateful to you Frenchies,' Armstrong said dryly. 'But getting back to the matter in hand...'

Marcus said, 'You regarded the gift of your ancestor's cross as an insult. Was it grievous enough to kill for?'

Philippe sneered. 'I would not trouble myself to spit upon a dissolute boy like Gavrilo. The Caesar will feel France's wrath at the next round of trade negotiations.'

'His motive is flimsy,' Marcus said after the prince had gone.

Armstrong said, 'Flimsy unless he, or the Ottoman, or both, wanted to start a war. You heard what he said about trade negotiations. There are always factions in such courts spoiling for a fight...'

As they argued about motives, Imogen, impatient, felt convinced they were on the wrong track. She begged leave to take some lunch, and left them to it.

She walked back to the Hall of Ambassadors. A butler on the palace staff brought her lunch: a sandwich and a glass of fresh milk.

Eating slowly, she peered up at Michelangelo's marvellous ceiling. She knew that historians thought it an irony that King Henry, who had enriched himself by plundering the wealth of the Church through the English Reformation, had used those funds to hire great artists like Michelangelo who could not find suitably wealthy sponsors in the impoverished city states of Catholic Italy, trapped as they were between the flaring ambitions of the French and Roman empires. She was grateful the work had not been harmed by the previous night's fire.

The others kept talking of motives. Certainly you could say that both Ottoman and French had a motive to murder Gavrilo, if you really believed that one of them wanted to start a war. Conceivably Philippe also had a personal motive, if he felt insulted by the crusader rag. But Philippe certainly did not have the means, as far as she could see, however strong his motive, for there was absolutely no evidence he had ever come into physical contact with the fire-lance.

Perhaps Osman Pasa could have done it. But he wasn't alone in handling the murder weapon; the British and Roman authorities had both had a hold of it, and could perhaps have tampered with it. She supposed some of the Romans might have a motive to do down Caesar's son, if they despised his reign sufficiently – even if it meant their own death. What she couldn't work out was what possible motive the British could have for killing Gavrilo. After all, he was here to be betrothed to a British princess. And yet the means existed.

Means, not motive, had to be the key to this murder: *everybody* involved had a motive, if you looked hard enough, and so it was only means that could lead to the truth. That was what she kept telling Marcus, and here she was forgetting it herself.

On impulse she made her way back to Gavrilo's reception room, alone. The police stationed there recognised her and allowed her in.

She looked again at the bloodstained carpet, the fire-damaged walls. Aware of the stern warnings not to disturb anything, she knelt down, peering at the weapon and the damage it had caused: the smashed chair, the remains of the lance itself, the trigger, the traces of the fuse. The timer was a mass of components, like the innards of a watch. The parts gleamed, finely worked. The trigger was simpler, but was just as well made. It looked remarkably *clean*, she thought. Too clean, perhaps. She leaned closer yet, holding her hair back from her forehead.

And she saw something. A trace she longed to take away. She left it in place.

She sat back on her heels, thinking hard. A British peeler, standing alongside a Roman centurion, watched her cautiously.

Then she walked slowly back to the office Marcus had requisitioned.

Marcus and Armstrong were still arguing about motives.

Marcus said, 'Perhaps we should suspect the Pope, then, Major! After all, Martin Luther nailed his Ninety-Five Theses to a church door in Wittenberg, a Roman city. Was it all a Roman plot to destabilise the Vatican? Or what of the natives of the Americas? If the Romans had not blocked off trade routes to the east, Columbus would never have sailed...'

'Now you're being absurd.'

'Of course I am. But my point is... Oh! Never mind.'

As Imogen sat down, Armstrong folded his arms. 'I think we've spent enough time on this. It seems perfectly obvious that the culprit is our Ottoman friend, for his was the gift that turned out to be the murder weapon. He had the motive, he had the means. I think the best thing we can do now is announce our conclusions to our superiors.'

'And risk a war?' Imogen asked softly. 'Without being *sure*, Major?'

They both looked at her. Marcus said, 'Miss Brodsworth? Do you have something?'

She considered the conclusion she had been forced to come to, hoping to find holes in it. Unfortunately it seemed to her as complete and perfect as the jewelled cane Philippe had given to Gavrilo.

'Means and motive,' she said to Armstrong and Marcus. 'We kept talking about motive. But the means was the key to this crime. *How* was it committed? That would tell us *who*. That was what I was thinking after my lunch. I went back to Gavrilo's reception room. I suppose I hoped I would find some bit of evidence, something clinching, which would establish the means beyond doubt, no matter what the motive. Perhaps I was being absurd...'

'Yes,' said Armstrong heavily. 'You were. What did you imagine you would spot that evaded the Criminal Investigation Department?'

Marcus hushed him. 'What have you found, Miss Brodsworth? Tell us plainly.'

She took a breath, avoiding Armstrong's eye. 'A shred of tobacco.'

'What?'

Armstrong said with a dangerous calm, 'This sounds like nonsense to me, Miss Brodsworth, and dangerous nonsense at that.' He made to stand up, pushing back his chair. 'I think it's time you were removed from this comical investigation—'

'Sit down,' said Marcus. And for the first time Imogen thought she could hear the authority of the Caesars in his voice.

Armstrong, glowering, complied.

Marcus asked, 'A shred of tobacco?'

'There was something odd about that trigger mechanism,' she said. 'I don't pretend to understand the clockwork of the timer. But the trigger itself was such a simple thing. And perhaps it's because it is so simple, there is something about it nobody seems to have noticed.'

'Yes?'

'*It was never fired.* Even though the bomb detonated, the trigger never fired. You can see it quite clearly from the cleanness of the hammer. And so, I wondered, what was it that could have lit the fuse?'

'Ah. And when you looked closer...'

'I found a shred of tobacco, stuck in the trigger mechanism of the bomb. I left it in place for the detectives to find – I'll show you later, prefect.'

'Well, well.' Marcus turned to the Major.

For long seconds Armstrong stared at them stonily. Then he relaxed, subtly. 'Miss Brodsworth, I now rather regret getting you out of your bed this morning.'

Marcus faced him. 'You were the only smoker, Major. The legionaries would have removed any weapon from you – even your matches, a lighter. But you walked into the presence of Gavrilo with a lit cigarette in your mouth.'

Armstrong shrugged. 'I suppose you may as well know the rest. It was simple enough to rig the fire-lance and the box; we worked on it through the night after purloining it from the Ottoman's room on his first arrival at the palace.

'I always had it in the back of my mind that I might need a backup, though. And I was quite right. Bloody cheap bit of American clockwork – I could *hear* the timer fail even while I stood beside the prince, smelling his wine-sodden breath. I knew the lance wasn't going to go off of its own accord. So, just as I was leaving ...' He mimed reaching down with a lit cigarette to light the fuse.

'As simple as that,' Marcus said, marvelling.

'It was always a cock-eyed sort of plot,' Armstrong admitted. 'But I thought we'd get away with it. I never had much faith that the earnest peelers of Scotland Yard would work out what had happened. Besides, I thought that the incident itself would soon be overwhelmed by a storm of diplomatic notes and ultimatums. The balance of power is, after all, precarious.' He mimed a series of topplings. 'And so, after the assassination of a crown prince, the empires would fall into war, one after the other.'

Imogen shook her head. 'But why would you want that?'

Marcus added more sternly, 'You and whoever is behind you.'

'National interest,' Armstrong said simply. 'The guiding light of all British policy, Miss Brodsworth. The Ottomans and French have a pact, you see, of mutual protection against the Romans. They both rightly fear the rather awesome arsenal of weapons the Romans have developed in their Chinese wars. If war came it would be the pair of them against the Romans, a war of two fronts, and a right mess it would be.'

Marcus listened, stone-faced. 'And the British?'

'We would come in on whichever side was winning. The Romans, even, if necessary, though I would expect that antique empire to implode. For what we want is not victory for one side or the other.'

'What, then?'

'Oil,' Armstrong said simply. 'Those oceans of oil, locked up under Baghdad, and in the Caucasus – all under the sway of the Romans. Oil that will drive our industries, and our own *testudos*, and especially our ships – we are a maritime nation, and you may know we recently converted most of our ships from coal. It's oil we need, prefect, oil to fight the wars of the twentieth century, and it's oil we mean to take.'

Imogen said, 'If war comes from this, the slaughter will be immense.'

'Miss Brodsworth, you will never grasp the solemn contemplation of empires.'

'No,' she said, 'and listening to you I'm jolly glad of it.'

Marcus said coldly, 'By cable, the Emperor will hear of this within the hour.'

Armstrong was relaxed. 'Fine. Everything I've told you is for your benefit only – I've come to feel rather fond of you two idiots. Tell Caesar what you like. No evidence will be found; my boys will make sure of that. The death of Gavrilo will no doubt be put down to an accident, muddy and unresolved. And even if some link were proven between the death and myself, the British government would deny all knowledge of it. I would be seen as a rogue, a maverick acting without instruction.'

Imogen stared at him. 'And is that the truth? That His Majesty's government knows nothing about this dreadful plot?'

He looked at her steadily. 'If that's what you want to believe, then it's the truth. I'll tell you this, Miss Brodsworth. You have done your country a disservice today. A great disservice.'

Marcus and Imogen walked to the embankment, breathing in air that was fresh with barely a hint of soot. The security cordon had not yet been relaxed, but it was a relief to Imogen not to be surrounded by the usual crush of Londoners.

They stared at the powerful lines of the quireme on the Thames. 'I feel giddy,' Imogen said. 'It's been such a long day.'

The Roman glanced at Big Ben. 'It isn't yet three o'clock. Yet so much has happened. A shred of tobacco has unravelled a plot that might have toppled empires!'

'I can't believe we allowed him simply to walk away.'

Marcus shrugged. 'What else could we have done? He's right; he and his conspirators will only refute everything, having destroyed the evidence. Let him go. With the British government's fervent denials, I have at least a fighting chance of convincing Caesar that the death of his son was the action of a rogue element, and not worth going to war over.'

'But there are surely other men like him in Britain, and the other powers. Men who long for war, for what they imagine is in their country's interests.'

'Yes. And he was right, you know, that the world is a precarious place. In Europe you have four empires, counting Britain, all jealous of their interests, all armed to the teeth. If this incident does not drive us to war, it seems more than likely that *something* will trigger it all.'

Imogen tried to imagine an all-out European war fought with modern weapons, with immense guns and steel-hulled ships, and *testudos* crawling over the broken bodies of men. 'That Chinaman who came wandering down the Silk Road has a lot to answer for.'

He laughed. 'But perhaps we would all have ended up in this situation even if he had stayed home. Fate is stronger than the will of any of us.'

On impulse she grabbed his hand. 'But if war is to come in the autumn, or in the winter, or the spring of next year, at least we have this summer's day. Spend it with me, Marcus Helvidius.'

'Are you serious?'

'Never more.'

'I have duties,' he said. 'I will be missed—'

'I know the city well enough. There are places they'll never find us. Come on. I've had enough of being sensible!'

Laughing, he let her pull him away. They hurried down the embankment, not quite running, until they had slipped through the cordon of British and Roman troops, and had lost themselves in the bustle of London.

THE UNBLINKING EYE

Under an empty night sky, the Inca ship stood proud before the old Roman bridge of Londres.

Jenny and Alphonse pressed their way through grimy mobs. Both sixteen years old, as night closed in they had slipped away from the dreary ceremonial rehearsals at St Paul's. They couldn't resist escaping to mingle with the excited Festival crowds.

And of course they had been drawn here, to the *Viracocha*, the most spectacular sight of all.

Beside the Inca ship's dazzling lines, even the domes, spires and pylons of the Festival, erected to mark the anniversary of the Frankish Conquest in this year of Our Lord Christus Ra 1966, looked shabby indeed. Her towering hull was made entirely of metal, clinkered in some seamless way that gave it flexibility, and the sails were llama wool, coloured as brilliantly as the Inca fashions that had been the talk of the Paris fashion houses this season.

Jenny Cook was from a family of ship owners, and the very sight excited her. 'Looking at her you can believe she has sailed from the other side of the world, even from the south—'

'That's blasphemy,' Alphonse snapped. But he remembered himself and shrugged. What had been blasphemy a year ago, before the first Inca ships had come sailing north around the west coast of Africa, was common knowledge now, and the old reflexes did not apply.

Jenny said, 'Surely on such a craft those sails are only for show, or for trim. There must be some mighty engine buried in her guts – but where are the smoke stacks?'

'Well, you and I are going to have months to find that out, Jenny. And where you see a pretty ship,' he said more darkly, 'I see a statement of power.'

Jenny, as a scion of a prominent merchant family, was to be among the party of friends and tutors who would accompany sixteen-year-old Prince Alphonse during his years-long stay in Cuzco, capital of the Inca. Alphonse had a sense of adventure, even of fun. But as the second son of the Emperor Charlemagne XXXII he saw the world differently from Jenny.

She protested, 'Oh, you're too suspicious, Alphonse. Why, they say there are whole continents out there we know nothing about! Why should the Inca care about the Frankish empire?'

'Perhaps they have conceived an ambition to own us as we own you Anglais.'

Jenny prickled. However, she had learned some diplomacy in her time at court. 'Well, I can't agree with you, and that's that,' she said.

Suddenly a flight of Inca air machines swept overhead like soaring silver birds, following the line of the river, their lights blazing against the darkling night. The crowds ducked and gasped, some of them crossing themselves in awe. After all, the *Viracocha* was only a ship, and the empires of Europe had ships. But none of them, not even the Ottomans, had machines that could fly.

'You see?' Alphonse muttered. 'What is that but a naked demonstration of Inca might? And I'll tell you something, those metal birds don't scare me half as much as other machines I've seen. Such as a box that can talk to other boxes a world away – they call it a farspeaker – I don't pretend to understand how it works; they gave one to my father's office so I can talk to him from Cuzco. What *else* have they got that they haven't shown us? Well, come on,' he said, plucking her arm. 'We're going to be late for Atahualpa's ceremony.'

Jenny followed reluctantly.

She watched the flying machines until they had passed out of sight, heading west up the river. When their lights had gone the night sky was revealed, cloudless and moonless, utterly dark, with no planets visible, an infinite emptiness. As if in response the gas lanterns of Londres burned brighter, defiant.

The Inca caravan was drawn up before the face of St Paul's. As grandees passed into the building, attendants fed the llamas that had borne the colourful litters. You never saw the Inca use a wheel; they relied for their transport on such means as these haughty, exotic beasts.

Inside the cathedral, Jenny and Alphonse hastily found their places in the procession, just as it began to pass grandly along the cramped candlelit aisles, led by servants who carried the Orb of the Unblinking Eye. These were followed by George Darwin, archbishop of Londres, who chattered nervously to Atahualpa, commander of the *Viracocha* and emissary of Huayna Capac XIII, Emperor of the Inca. In the long tail of the procession were representatives from all the great empires of Europe: the Danes, the Germans, the Muscovites, even the Ottomans, grandly bejewelled Muslims in this Christian church. They marched to the gentle playing of Galilean lutes, an ensemble supplied by the Germans. It was remarkable to think, Jenny reflected, that if the Inca had come sailing out of the south three hundred years ago, they would have been met by ambassadors from much the same combination of powers. Though there had always been border disputes and even wars, the political map of Europe had changed little since the Ottoman capture of Vienna had marked the westernmost point of the march of Islam.

But the Inca towered over the European nobility. They wore woollen suits dyed scarlet and electric blue, colours brighter than the cathedral's stained glass. Most of the Inca wore face masks as defence against the 'herd diseases' they insultingly claimed infested Europe. The effect was to make these imposing figures even more enigmatic, for the only expression you could see was in their black eyes.

Jenny, at Alphonse's side and mixed in with some of the Inca party, was only a few rows back from Atahualpa and Darwin, and she could clearly hear every word they said as they conversed.

'My own family has a long association with this church,' the bishop said. 'My ancestor Charles Darwin was a country parson who, dedicated to his theology, rose to become Dean here. But the site is much older. The Anglais built the first Christian chapel on this site in the year of Christus Ra 604. After the Conquest, the Frankish emperors were most generous in endowing this magnificent building in our humble, remote city...'

As the interpreter translated this, Atahualpa murmured some reply in Quechua, and the two of them laughed softly.

One of the Inca party, walking beside Jenny, was a boy about her age. He wore an Inca costume like the rest, but without a face mask. He whispered in passable Frankish, 'The emissary's being a bit rude about your church. He says it's a sandstone heap he wouldn't use to stable his llamas.'

'Charming,' Jenny whispered back.

'Well, you haven't seen his llamas.'

Jenny had to cover her face to keep from giggling. She got a glare from Alphonse, and recovered her composure.

'Sorry,' said the boy. He was dark-skinned, with a mop of short-cut, tightly curled black hair. The spiral tattoo on his left cheek made him look a little severe, until he smiled, showing bright teeth. 'My name's – well, it's complicated, and the Inca never get it right. You can call me Dreamer.'

'Hello, Dreamer,' she whispered. 'I'm Jenny Cook.'

'Pretty name.'

Jenny raised her eyebrows. 'Oh, is it really? You're not Inca, are you?'

'No, I just travel with them. They like to move us around, their subject peoples. I'm from the South Land...'

But she didn't know where that was, and the procession had paused again as the emissary and the archbishop stopped to inspect the great altar, and Jenny and Dreamer fell silent.

Atahualpa said to Darwin, 'I am intrigued by the god of this church. Christus Ra? He is a god who is two gods.'

'In a sense...' Darwin spoke rapidly of the career of Christ. Long before His birth the Romans had conquered Egypt, but had suffered a sort of reverse religious takeover; their pantheon had seemed flimsy before the power and sheer logic of the Egyptians' ancient and enduring faith in their sun-god. After all the sun was the only point of stability in a sky populated by chaotic planets, mankind's only defence against the infinite dark. Who could argue against its worship? This was the religious background into which Jesus had been born. Centuries after Christ's execution, when His cult was adopted as the empire's official religion, the bishops and imperial theologians had made a formal identification of Christ with Ra, a unity that had outlasted the empire itself.

Atahualpa expressed mild interest in this. He said the worship of the sun was a global phenomenon. The Inca's own sun god was called Inti. Perhaps Inti and Christ-Ra were mere manifestations of the same primal figure...

The leaders moved on, and the procession followed.

'"Cook",' Dreamer whispered. He was evidently more interested in Jenny than in theology. 'That's a funny sort of name. Not Frankish, is it?'

'I don't know. I think it has an Anglais root. My family are Anglais, from the north of Grande-Bretagne.'

'You must be rich. You've got to be either royal or rich to be in this procession, right?'

She smiled. 'Rich enough. I'm at court as part of my education. My grandfathers have been in the coal trade since our ancestor founded the business two hundred years ago. He was called James Cook. My father's called James too. It's a mucky business, but lucrative.'

'I'll bet. Those Watt engines I see everywhere eat enough coal, don't they?'

'So what do your family do?'

He said simply, 'We serve the Inca.'

The procession reached a chapel dedicated to Isaac Newton, the renowned alchemist and theologian who had developed a conclusive proof of the age of the Earth. Here they prayed to their respective gods, the Inca prostrating themselves before Inti, and the Christians kneeling to Christ.

And the Inca servants came forward with their Orb of the Unblinking Eye. It was a sphere of some translucent white material, half as tall as a man; the servants carried it in a rope netting, and set it down on a wooden cradle before the statue of Newton himself.

Atahualpa turned and faced the procession. He may have smiled; his face mask creased. He said through his interpreter: 'Once it was our practice to plant our temples in the chapels of those we sought to vanquish. Now I place this gift from my emperor, this symbol of our greatest god, in the finest church in this province.' And, Jenny knew, other Inca parties were handing over similar orbs in all the great capitals of Europe. 'Once we would move peoples about, whole populations, to cut them away from their roots, and so control them. Now we welcome the children of your princes and merchants, while leaving our own children in your cities, so that we may each learn the culture and the ways of the other.' He gestured to Alphonse.

The prince bowed, but he muttered through his teeth, '*And* get hold of a nice set of hostages.'

'Hush,' Jenny murmured.

Atahualpa said, 'Let this globe shine for all eternity as a symbol of our friendship, united under the Unblinking Eye of the One Sun.' He clapped his hands.

And the orb lit up, casting a steady pearl-like glow over the grimy statuary of the chapel. The Europeans applauded helplessly.

Jenny stared, amazed. She could see no power supply, no tank of gas; and the light didn't flicker like the flame of a candle or a lamp, but burned as steady as the sun itself.

With the ceremony over, the procession began to break up. Jenny turned to the boy, Dreamer. 'Are you sailing on the *Viracocha*?'

'Oh, yes. You'll be seeing a lot more of me. The emissary has one more appointment, a ride on a Watt-engine train to some place called Bataille—'

'That's where the Frankish army defeated the Anglais back in 1066.'

'Yes. And then we sail.'

'And then we sail,' Jenny said, fearful, excited, gazing into the dark, playful eyes of this boy from the other side of the world, a boy whose land didn't exist even in her imagination.

Alphonse glared at them, brooding.

The dignitaries were still talking, with stiff politeness. Atahualpa seemed intrigued by Newton's determination of the Earth's age. 'And how did this Newton achieve his result? A study of the rocks, of living things, of the sky? I did not know such sciences were so advanced here.'

But when Archbishop Darwin explained that Newton's calculations had been based on records of births and deaths in a holy book, and that his conclusion was that the Earth was only a few thousand years old, Atahualpa's laughter was gusty, echoing from the walls of the cramped chapel.

Alphonse's party, with Jenny and his other companions and with Archbishop Darwin attached as a moral guardian, boarded the Inca ship.

The *Viracocha*, Jenny learned, was named after a creator god and cultural hero of the Inca. It was as extraordinary inside as out, a floating palace of wide corridors and vast state rooms that glowed with a pale, steady light. The Frankish and Anglais were allowed to stay on deck as the great woollen sails were unfurled and the ship pulled away from Londres, which sprawled over the banks of its river in heaps of smoky industry. Jenny looked for her family's ships in the docks; she was going to be away from home for years, and the parting from her mother had been tearful.

But before the ship had left the estuary of the Tamise, the guests were ordered below deck, and the hatches were locked and sealed. There weren't even any windows in the ship's sleek hull. Their Inca hosts wanted to save a remarkable surprise for them, they said, a surprise revealed to every crew who crossed the equator, but not until then.

And they were all, even Alphonse, put through a programme of inoculation, injected with various potions and their bodies bathed with a prickly light. The Inca doctors said this was to weed out their 'herd diseases'. All the Europeans resented this, though Darwin marvelled at the medicinal technology on display.

At least the Inca's faces were visible, however, now that they had discarded their masks. They were a proud-looking people with jet black hair, dark skin, and noses that would have been called Roman in Europe. None of the crew were particularly friendly. They wouldn't speak Frankish or Anglais, and they looked on the Europeans with a kind of amused contempt. This infuriated Alphonse, for he was used to looking on others in precisely that way.

Still, the ship's sights were spectacular. Jenny was shown the great smelly hold where the llamas were kept during the journey. And she was shown around an engine room. Jenny's family ran steam scows, and she had expected Watt engines, heavy, clunky, soot-coated iron monsters. The *Viracocha*'s engine room was a pristine white-walled hall inhabited by sleek metal shapes. The air was filled with a soft humming, and there was a sharp smell in the air that reminded her of the seashore. The smooth sculptures didn't even look like engines to Jenny, and whatever principle they worked on had nothing to do with steam evidently. So much for her father's fond hopes of selling coal to the mighty Inca empire!

Despite such marvels, Jenny chafed at her confinement below decks. What made it worse was that she saw little of her friends. Alphonse was whisked off to a programme of study of Inca culture and science, mediated by Darwin. And in his free time he monopolised Dreamer for private language classes; he wanted to learn as much Quechua as he could manage, for he did not trust the Inca.

This irritated Jenny more than she was prepared to admit, for the times she relished most of all were the snatched moments she spent with Dreamer.

One free evening Dreamer took her to the navigation bay. The walls were covered with charts, curves that appeared to show the trajectory of the sun and moon across the sky, and other diagrams showing various aspects of a misty-gold spiral shape that meant nothing to Jenny. There was a globe that drew her eye; glowing, painted, it was covered with unfamiliar shapes, but one strip of blue looked just like a map of the Mediterranean.

The most wondrous object in the room was a kind of loom, rank upon rank of knotted string that stretched from floor to ceiling and wall to wall – but unlike a loom it was extended in depth as well. As she peered into this array she saw metal fingers pluck blindly at the strings, making the knots slide this way and that.

Dreamer watched her, as she watched the strings. He said, 'I'm starting to think Alphonse is using the language classes as an excuse to keep me away from you. Perhaps the prince wants you for himself. Who wouldn't desire such beauty?'

Jenny pulled a face at this gross flattery. 'Tell me what this loom is for.'

'The Inca have always represented their numbers and words on quipus, bits of knotted string. Even after they learned writing from their Aztec neighbours, whom they encountered at the start of the Sunrise.'

'The Sunrise?'

'That is their modest name for their programme of expansion across the world. Jenny, this is a machine for figuring numbers. The Inca use it to calculate their journeys across the world oceans. But it can perform any sum you like.'

'My father would like one of these to figure his tax return.'

Dreamer laughed.

She said, 'But everybody knows that you can't navigate at night, when the sun goes down, and the only beacons in the sky are the moon and planets, which career unpredictably all over the place. How, then, do the Inca find their way?' For the Europeans this was the greatest mystery about the Inca. Even the greatest seamen of the past, the Vikings, had barely had the courage to probe away from the shore.

Dreamer glanced at the strange charts on the wall. 'Look, they made us promise not to tell any of you about – well, certain matters, before the Inca deem you ready. But there's something here I do want to show you.' He led her across the room to the globe.

That blue shape was undoubtedly the Mediterranean. 'It's the world,' she breathed.

'Yes.' He smiled. 'The Inca have marked what they know of the European empires. Look, here is Grande-Bretagne. See how small it is!'

'Why, even Europe is only a peninsula dangling from the carcass of Asia.'

'You know, your sense of wonder is the most attractive thing about you.'

She snorted. 'Really? More than my eyes and teeth and neck, and the other bits of me you've been praising? I'll believe that when a second sun rises in the sky. Show me where you come from – and the Inca.'

Passing his hand over the globe, he made the world spin and dip.

He showed her what lay beyond the Ottoman empire, the solemn Islamic unity that had blocked Christendom from the east for centuries: the vast expanses of Asia, India, the sprawling empire of China, Nippon, the Spice Islands. And he showed how Africa extended far beyond the arid northern regions held by the Ottomans, a great pendulous continent in its own right that stretched, thrillingly, right across the equator.

'You can in fact reach India and the east by sailing south around the cape of southern Africa,' Dreamer said. 'Without losing sight of land, even. A man called Columbus was the first to attempt this in 1492. But he lacked the courage to cross the equator. Columbus went back to the family business of trouser-making, and Christian Europe stayed locked in . . .'

Now he spun the globe to show her even stranger sights: a double continent, far to the west of Europe across the ocean, lands wholly unknown to any European. The Inca had come from a high country that ran north to south along the spine of the southernmost of those twin continents. 'It is a place of mountains and coast, of long, long roads, and bridges centuries old, woven from vines, still in use . . .'

Around the year 1500, according to the Christian calendar, the Inca's greatest emperor Huayna Capac I had emerged from a savage succession dispute to take sole control of the mountain empire. And under him, as the Inca consolidated, the great expansion called the Sunrise had begun. At first the Inca had used their woollen-sailed ships for trade and military expeditions up and down their long coastlines. But gradually they crept away from the shore.

At last, on an island in the ocean far to the west of the homeland, they found people. 'These were a primitive sort, who sailed the sea in canoes dug out of logs. Nevertheless they had come out of the south-east of Asia and sailed right to the middle of the ocean, colonising island chains as they went. Thus humans from west and east met for the first time.' The Inca, emboldened by the geographical knowledge they took from their new island subjects, went further, following island chains until they reached Asia. All this sparked intellectual ferment, as exploration and conquest led to a revolution in sky-watching, mathematics, and the sciences of life and language.

But the Inca probed even further west. At last they reached Africa.

And when in the early twentieth century they acquired lodestone compasses from Chinese traders, they found the courage to venture north, towards Europe.

Jenny stared at the South Land. There was no real detail, just a few Inca towns dotted around the coast, an interior like a blank red canvas. 'Tell me about your home.'

He brushed the image of the island continent with his fingertips. 'It is a harsh country, I suppose. Rust-red, worn flat by time. But there is much beauty, and strangeness. Animals that jump rather than run, and carry their young in pouches on their bellies. Don't laugh, it's true! My people have lived there for sixty thousand years. That's what the Inca scholars say, though how they can tell that from bits of bone and shards of stone tools, I don't know. My people are called the Bininj-Mungguy, and we live in the north, up here, in a land we call Kakadu.'

Jenny's imagination raced, and his strange words fascinated her. She drew closer to him, almost unconsciously, watching his mouth.

'We have six seasons,' he said, 'for our weather is not like yours. There is Gunumeleng, which is the season before the great rains, and then Gudjewg, when the rain comes, and then Banggerreng—'

She stopped up his mouth with hers.

After a week's sailing, the *Viracocha* crossed the equator. Atahualpa ordered a feast to be laid for his senior officers and guests. They were brought to a stateroom which, Jenny suspected from the stairs she had to climb, lay just under the deck itself. Tonight, Atahualpa promised, his passengers would be allowed on deck for the first time since Londres, and the great secret which the Incas had been hiding would be revealed.

But by now Dreamer and Jenny shared so many secrets that she scarcely cared.

For the dinner, while the Inca crew wore their customary llama-wool and cotton uniforms, George Darwin wore his clerical finery, Alphonse the powdered wig and face powder of his father's court, and Jenny a simple shift, her Sunday best. Dreamer was just one of the many representatives of provinces of the Inca's ocean-spanning empire aboard the ship. They wore elaborate costumes of cloth and feather, so that they looked like a row of exotic birds, Jenny thought, sitting there at the commander's table.

In some ways Dreamer's own garb was the most extraordinary.

He was stripped naked save for a loincloth, his face-spiral tattoo was picked out in yellow dye, and he had finger-painted designs on his body in chalk-white, a sprawling lizard, an outstretched hand.

The Inca went through their own equator-crossing ritual. This involved taking a live chicken, slitting its belly and pulling out its entrails, right there on the dinner table, while muttering antique-sounding prayers.

Bishop Darwin tried to watch this with calm appreciation. 'Evidently an element of animism and the superstitious has survived in our hosts' theology,' he murmured.

Alphonse didn't bother to hide his disgust. 'I've had enough of these savages.'

'Hush,' Jenny murmured. 'If you assume none of them can speak Frankish you're a fool.'

He glared defiantly, but he switched to Anglais. 'Well, I've never heard any of them utter a single word. And they assume I know a lot less Quechua than I've learned, thanks to your bare-chested friend over there. They say things in front of me that they think I won't understand – but I do.'

He was only sixteen, as Jenny was; he sounded absurd, self-important. But he was a prince who had grown up in the most conspiratorial and back-stabbing court in all Christendom. He was attuned to detecting lies and power plays. So she asked, 'What sort of things?'

'About the "problem" we pose them. We Europeans. We aren't like Dreamer's folk of the South Land, who are hairy-arsed savages in the desert. We have great cities; we have armies. We may not have their silver ships and flying machines, but we could put up a fight. That's the "problem".'

She frowned. 'It's a problem only if the Inca come looking for war.'

He scoffed. 'Oh, come, Jenny, even an Anglais can't be so naïve. All this friendship-across-the-sea stuff is just a smoke screen. Everything they've done has been in the manner of an opening salvo: the donation of farspeakers to every palace in Europe, the planting of their Orbs of the Unblinking Eye in every city. What I can't figure out is what they intend by all this.'

'Maybe Inca warriors will jump out of the Orbs and run off with the altar silver.'

'You're a fool,' he murmured without malice. 'Like all Anglais. You and desert-boy over there deserve each other. Well, I've had enough of Atahualpa's droning voice. While they're all busy here I'm going to see what I can find out.' He stood.

She hissed. 'Be careful.'

He ignored her. He nodded to his host. Atahualpa waved him away, uncaring.

Atahualpa had begun a conversation with Darwin on the supposed backwardness of European science and philosophy. Evidently it was a dialogue that had been developing during the voyage, as the Inca tutors got to know the minds of their students. 'Here is the flaw in your history as I see it,' Atahualpa said. 'Unlike the Inca, you Europeans never mastered the science of the sky. To you all is chaos.'

Jenny admired old Darwin's stoicism. With resigned good humour he said, 'Isn't that obvious? All those planets swooping around the sky – only the sun is stable, the pivot of the universe.'

But Atahualpa only smiled. 'The point is that the motion of the planets is *not* chaotic, not if you look at it correctly.' A bowl of the chicken's blood had been set before him. He dipped his finger in this and sketched a solar system on the tabletop, sun at the centre, Earth's orbit, the neat circles of the inner planets and the wildly swooping flights of the outer.

Servants brought plates of food. There was the meat of roast rodent and duck, and heaps of maize, squash, tomatoes, peanuts, and plates of a white tuber, a root vegetable unknown to Europe but tasty and filling.

'There,' said Atahualpa, pointing at his diagram. 'Now, look, you see. Each planet follows an ellipse, with the sun at one focus. These patterns are repeated and quite predictable, though the extreme eccentricity of the outer worlds' orbits makes them hard to decipher. *We* managed it, though – although I grant you we always had one significant advantage over you, as you will learn tonight! Let me tell you how our science developed after that ...'

He listed Inca astronomers and mathematicians, names which meant nothing to Jenny. 'After we mapped the planets' elliptical trajectories, it was the genius of Huascar that he was able to show *why* the worlds followed such paths, because of a single, simple law: the planets are drawn to the sun with an attraction that falls off inversely with the square of distance.'

Darwin said bravely, 'I am sure our scholars in Paris and Damascus would welcome—'

Atahualpa ignored him, digging into his food with blood-stained fingers. 'But Huascar's greatest legacy was the insight that *the world is explicable*: that simple, general laws can explain a range of particular instances. It is that core philosophy that we have applied to other disciplines.' He gestured at the diffuse light that filled the room. 'You cower from the light of the sun, and fear the lightning, and are baffled by the wandering of a lodestone. But we know that these are all aspects of a single underlying force, which we can manipulate to build the engines that drive this ship, and the farspeakers that enable the emperor's voice to span continents. If *your* minds had been opened up, your science might be less of a hotchpotch. And your religion might not be so primitive.'

Darwin flinched at that. 'Well, it's true there has been no serious Christian heresy since Martin Luther was burned by the Inquisition—'

'If only you had not been so afraid of the sky! But then,' he said, smiling, 'our sky always did contain one treasure yours did not.'

Jenny was growing annoyed with the Inca's patronising treatment of Darwin, a decent man. She said now, 'Commander, even before we sailed you dropped hints about some wonder in the sky we knew nothing about.'

As his translator murmured in his ear, Atahualpa looked at her in surprise.

Darwin murmured, 'Mademoiselle Cook, please—'

'If you're so superior, maybe you should stop playing games, and *show* us this wonder – if it exists at all!'

The officers were glaring at her.

But Atahualpa held up an indulgent hand. 'I will not punish bravery, Mademoiselle Cook, and you are brave, if foolish with it. We like to keep our great surprise from our European passengers – call it an experiment – your first reaction is always worth relishing. We were going to wait until the end of the meal, but – Pachacuti, will you see to the roof?'

Wiping his lips on a cloth, one of the officers got up from the table and went to the wall, where a small panel of buttons had been fixed. With a whir of smooth motors the roof slid back. Fresh salt air, a little cold, billowed over the diners.

Jenny looked up. In an otherwise black sky, a slim crescent moon hung directly over her head. She had the sense that the moon was tilted on its side – a measure of how far she had travelled around the curve of the world, in just a few days aboard this ship.

Atahualpa smiled, curious, perhaps cruel. 'Never mind the moon, Mademoiselle Cook. Look that way.' He pointed south.

She stood. And there, clearly visible over the lip of the roof, something was suspended in the sky. Not the sun or moon, not a planet – something entirely different. It was a disc of light, a swirl, with a brilliant point at its centre, and a ragged spiral glow all around it. It was the emblem she had observed on the navigational displays, but far more delicate – a sculpture of light, hanging in the sky.

'Oh,' she gasped, awed, terrified. 'It's beautiful.'

Beside her, Archbishop Darwin muttered prayers and crossed himself.

She felt Dreamer's hand take hers. 'I wanted to tell you,' he murmured. 'They forbade me...'

Atahualpa watched them. 'What do you think you are seeing?'

Darwin said, 'It looks like a hole in the sky. Into which all light is draining.'

'No. In fact it's quite the opposite. It is the *source* of all light.'

'And that is how you navigate,' Jenny said. 'By the cloud – you could pick on the point of light at the centre, and measure your position on a curving Earth from that. This is your treasure – a beacon in the sky.'

'You're an insightful young woman. It is only recently, in fact, that with our far-seers – another technology you lack – we have been able to resolve those spiral streams to reveal their true nature.'

'Which is?'

'The cloud is a sea of suns, Mademoiselle. Suns upon suns, so far away they look like droplets in a mist.'

The Inca sky-scientists believed that the cloud was in fact a kind of factory of suns – and that *the* sun and its planets couldn't have formed in the black void across which they travelled, that the sun must have been born in that distant sea of light, long ago.

'As to how we ended up here – some believe that it was a chance encounter between our sun and another. If they come close, you see, suns must attract each other, as they attract their planets. Our sun was flung out of that sea of light *northwards*, generally speaking, off into the void. The encounter damaged the system itself; the inner planets and Earth were left in their neat circles, but the outer planets were flung onto their looping orbits. All this is entirely explicable by the laws of motion developed by Huascar and others.' Atahualpa lifted his finely chiselled face to the milky light of the spiral. 'This was long ago, when the world was young. Just as well; life was too primitive to have been extinguished by the tides and earthquakes. But what a sight it would have been then, the sea of suns huge in the sky, receding majestically – if there had been eyes to see it!'

There was a commotion outside the stateroom. 'Let me go!' somebody yelled in Frankish. 'Let me go!'

An officer went to the door. Alphonse was dragged in, with two burly Inca holding his arms. His nose was bloodied, his face powder smeared, his wig askew, but he was furious, defiant.

Archbishop Darwin bustled to the side of his charge. 'This is an outrage. He is a prince of the empire!'

To a nod from the commander, Alphonse was released. He stood there massaging bruised arms. And he stared up at the spiral in the sky, open-mouthed.

'Sir, we found him in the farspeaker room,' said one of the guards. 'He was tampering with the equipment.' For the guests, this was slowly translated from the Quechua.

But Alphonse interrupted the translation. He said in Frankish, 'Yes, I was in your farspeaker room, Atahualpa. Yes, I understand Quechua better than you thought, don't I? And I wasn't "tampering" with the equipment. I was sending a message to my father. Even now, I imagine, his guards will be closing in on the Orb you planted in St Paul's – and those elsewhere.'

Darwin stared at him. 'Your royal highness, I've no idea what is happening here – why would you be so discourteous to our hosts?'

'Discourteous?' He glared at Atahualpa. 'Ask him, then. Ask him what a sun-bomb is.'

Atahualpa stared back stonily.

Dreamer came forward. 'Tell him the truth, Inca. He knows most of it anyhow.' And one by one the other representatives of the Inca's subject races, in their beads and feathers, stepped forward to stand with Dreamer.

And so, smiling at this petty defiance, Atahualpa yielded.

A 'sun-bomb', it turned out, was a weapon small enough to fit into one of the Inca's Orbs of the Unblinking Eye, yet powerful enough to flatten a city – a weapon that harnessed the power of the sun itself.

Jenny was shocked. 'We welcomed you to Londres. Why would you plant such a thing in our city?'

'Isn't it obvious?' Alphonse answered. 'Because these all-conquering

Inca can't cow Franks and Germans and Ottomans with a pretty silver ship as they did these others, or you Anglais.'

Atahualpa said, 'A war of conquest in Europe and Asia would be long and bloody, though the outcome would be beyond doubt. We thought that if the sun-bombs were planted, so that your cities were held hostage – if one of them was detonated for a demonstration, if a backward provincial city was sacrificed—'

'Like Londres,' said Jenny, appalled.

'And then,' Alphonse said, 'you would use your farspeakers to speak to the emperors and state your demands. Well, it's not going to happen, Inca. Looks like it will be bloody after all, doesn't it?'

Darwin touched his shoulder. 'You have done your empire a great service today, Prince Alphonse. But war is not yet inevitable, between the people of the north and the south. Perhaps this will be a turning point in our relationship. Let us hope that wiser counsels prevail.'

'We'll see,' Alphonse said, staring at Atahualpa. 'We'll see.'

Servants bustled in to clear dishes and set another course. The normality after the confrontation was bewildering.

Slowly tensions eased.

Jenny impulsively grabbed Dreamer's arm. They walked away from the rest.

She stared up at the sea of suns. 'If we are all lost in this gulf, we really ought to learn to get along together.'

Dreamer grunted. 'You convince the emperors. I will speak to the Inca.'

She imagined Earth swimming in light. 'Dreamer – will we ever sail back to where we came from?'

'Well, you never know,' he said. 'But the sea of stars is further away than you imagine. I don't think you and I will live to see it.'

Jenny said impulsively, 'Our children might.'

'Yes. Our children might. Come on. Let's get this wretched dinner over with.'

The stateroom roof slid closed, hiding the sea of suns from their sight.

DARWIN ANATHEMA

Trailed by a porter with her luggage, Mary Mason climbed down the steamer's ramp to the dock at Folkestone, and waited in line with the rest of the passengers to clear security.

Folkestone, her first glimpse of England, was unprepossessing, a small harbour in the lee of cliffs fronting a dismal, smoke-stained townscape from which the slender spires of churches protruded. People crowded around the harbour, the passengers disembarking, stevedores labouring to unload the cargo. There was a line of horse-drawn vehicles waiting, and one smoky-looking steam carriage. The ocean-going steamship, its rusting flank a wall, looked too big and vigorous for the port.

Mary, forty-five years old, felt weary, stiff, faintly disoriented to be standing on a surface that wasn't rolling back and forth. She had come to England all the way from Terra Australis to participate in the Inquisition's trial of Charles Darwin, a man more than a century dead. Back home in Cooktown it had seemed a good idea. Now she was here it seemed utterly insane.

At last the port inspectors stared at her passepartout, cross-examined her about her reasons for coming to England – they didn't seem to know what a 'natural philosopher' was – and then opened every case. One of the officials finally handed back her passepartout. She checked it was stamped with the correct date: 9 February 2009. 'Welcome to England,' the inspector grunted.

She walked forward, trailed by the porter.

'Lector Mason? Not quite the harbour at Cooktown, is it? Nevertheless I hope you've had a satisfactory voyage.'

She turned. 'Father Brazel?'

Xavier Brazel was the Jesuit who had coordinated her invitation and passage. He was tall, slim, elegant; he wore a modest black suit with a white clerical collar. He was a good bit younger than she was, maybe thirty. He smiled, blessed her with two fingers making a cross sign in the air, and shook her hand. 'Call me Xavier. I'm delighted to meet you, truly. We're privileged you've agreed to participate in the trial, and I'm particularly looking forward to hearing you speak at St Paul's. Come, I have a carriage to the rail station . . .' Nodding at the porter, he led her away. 'The trial of Alicia Darwin and her many-times-great-uncle starts tomorrow.'

'Yes. The ship was delayed a couple of days.'

'I'm sorry there's so little time to prepare, or recover.'

'I'll be fine.'

The carriage was small but sturdy, pulled by a pair of patient horses. It clattered away through crowded, cobbled streets.

'And I apologise for the security measures,' Xavier said. 'A tiresome welcome to the country. It's been like this since the 29 May attacks.'

'That was six years ago. They caught the Vatican bombers, didn't they?' Pinprick attacks by Muslim zealots who had struck to commemorate the five hundred and fiftieth anniversary of the Islamic conquest of Constantinople – and more than a hundred and twenty years since a Christian coalition had taken the city back from the Ottomans, in the 1870s Crusade.

He just smiled. 'Once you have surrounded yourself with a ring of steel, it's hard to tear it down.'

They reached the station where the once-daily train to London was, fortuitously, waiting. Xavier already had tickets. He helped load Mary's luggage, and led her to an upper-class carriage. Aside from Mary everybody in there seemed to be a cleric of some kind, the men in black suits, the few women in nuns' wimples.

The train pulled away. Clouds of sooty steam billowed past the window.

A waiter brought coffees. Xavier sipped his with relish. 'Please, enjoy.'

Mary tasted her coffee. 'That's good.'

'French, from their American colonies. The French do know how to make good coffee. Speaking of the French – have you visited Britain before? As it happens, this rail line follows the track of the advance of Napoleon's Grande Armée in 1807, through Maidstone to London. You may see the monuments in the towns we pass through . . . Are you all right, Lector? You don't seem quite comfortable.'

'I'm not used to having so many clerics around me. Terra Australis is a Christian country, even if it followed the Marxist Reformation. But I feel like the only sinner on the train.'

He smiled and spoke confidentially. 'If you think this is a high density of dog-collars you should try visiting Rome.'

She found herself liking him for his humour and candour. But, she had learned from previous experience, Jesuits were always charming and manipulative. 'I don't need to go to Rome to see the Inquisition at work, however, do I?'

'We prefer not to use that word,' he said evenly. 'The Sacred Congregation for the Doctrine of Faith, newly empowered under Cardinal Ratzinger since the 29 May attacks, has done sterling work in the battle against Ottoman extremists.'

'"Extremists." All they want is the freedom of faith they enjoyed up until the 1870s Crusade.'

He smiled. 'You know your history. But of course that's why you're here. The presence of unbiased observers is important; the Congregation wants to be seen to give Darwin a fair hearing. I have to admit we had refusals to participate from philosophers with specialities in natural selection—'

'So you had to settle for a historian of natural philosophy?'

'We are grateful for your help. The purpose of the Congregation's hearings is to clarify the relationship between theology and natural philosophy, not to condemn. You'll see. And frankly,' he said, 'I hope you'll think better of us after you've seen us at work.'

She shrugged. 'I guess I'm here for my own purposes too.' As a historian she hoped she could gather some good material on the centuries-long tension between Church and natural philosophy, and maybe she could achieve more at the trial itself than merely contribute to some kind of Inquisition propaganda stunt. But now she was here, in the heart of the great European theocracy, she wasn't so sure.

She'd fallen silent. Xavier studied her with polite concern. 'Are you comfortable? Would you like more coffee?'

'I think I'm a little over-tired,' she said. 'Sorry if I snapped.' She dug her book out of her bag. 'Maybe I'll read a bit and leave you in peace.'

He glanced at the spine. 'HG Wells. *The War of the Celestial Spheres.*'

'I'm trying to immerse myself in all things English.'

'It's a fine read, and only marginally heretical.' He actually winked at her.

She had to laugh, but she felt a frisson of unease.

So she read, and dozed a little, as the train clattered through the towns of Kent, Ashford and Charing and others. The towns and villages were cramped, the buildings uniformly stained black with soot. The rolling country beyond the towns was cluttered with small farms where people in mud-coloured clothes laboured over winter crops, and the churches were squat buildings like stone studs pinning down the ancient green of the countryside. She'd heard there was a monument to Wellesley at Maidstone, where he'd fallen as he failed to stop Napoleon crossing the Medway river. But if it existed at all it wasn't visible from the train.

By the time the train approached London, the light of the short English day was already fading.

As a guest of the Church she was lodged in one of London's best hotels. But her room was lit by smoky oil lamps. There seemed to be electricity only in the lobby and dining room – why, even the front porch of her own home outside Cooktown had an electric bulb. And she noticed that the telegraph they used to send a message home to her husband and son was an Australian Maxwell design.

Still, in the morning she found she had a terrific view of the Place de Louis XVI, and of Whitehall and the Mall beyond. The day was bright, and pigeons fluttered around the statue of Bonaparte set atop the huge Christian cross that dominated the square. For a historian this was a reminder of the Church's slow but crushing reconquest of Protestant England. In the eighteenth century a Catholic league had cooperated with the French to defeat Britain's imperial ambitions in America and India, and then in 1807 the French King's Corsican attack-dog had been unleashed on the homeland. By the time Napoleon withdrew, England was once more a Catholic country under a new Bourbon king. Looking up at Napoleon's brooding face, she was suddenly glad her own home was twelve thousand miles away from all this history.

Father Xavier called for her at nine. They travelled by horse-drawn carriage to St Paul's Cathedral, where the trial of Charles Darwin was to be staged.

St Paul's was magnificent. Xavier had sweetened her trip around the world by promising her she would be allowed to give a guest sermon to senior figures in London's theological and philosophical community from the cathedral's pulpit. Now she was here she started to feel intimidated at the prospect.

But she had no time to look around. Xavier, accompanied by an armed Inquisition guard, led her straight through to the stairs down to the crypt, which had been extended to a warren of dark corridors with rows of hefty locked doors. In utter contrast to the glorious building above, this was like a prison, or a dungeon.

Xavier seemed to sense her wary mood. 'You're doing fine, Lector.'

'I'm just memorising the way out.'

They arrived at a room that was surprisingly small and bare, for such a high-profile event, with plain plastered walls illuminated by dangling electrical bulbs. The centrepiece was a wooden table behind which sat a row of Inquisition examiners, as Mary presumed they were, stern men all of late middle age wearing funereal black and clerical collars. Their chairman sat in an elaborate throne-like seat, elevated above the rest.

A woman stood before them – stood because she had no seat to sit on, Mary saw. The girl, presumably Alicia Rosemary Darwin, Charles' grand-niece several times removed, wore a sober charcoal-grey dress. She was very pale, with blue eyes and strawberry hair; she could have been no older than twenty.

On one side of her sat a young man, soberly dressed, good-looking, his features alive with interest. And on the other side, Mary was astounded to see, a coffin rested on trestles.

Xavier led Mary to a bench set along one wall. Here various other clerics sat, most of them men. On the far side were men and women in civilian clothes. Some were writing in notebooks, others sketching the faces of the principals.

'Just in time,' Xavier murmured as they sat. 'I do apologise. Did you see the look Father Boniface gave me?'

'Not *the* Boniface!'

'The Reverend Father Boniface Jones, Commissary General. Learned his trade at the feet of Commissary Hitler himself, in the old man's retirement years after all his good work during the Missionary Wars in Orthodox Russia...'

'Who's that lot on the far side?'

'From the chronicles. Interest in this case is worldwide.'

'Don't tell me who's in that box.'

'Respectfully disinterred from his tomb in Edinburgh and removed here. He could hardly not show up for his own trial, could he? Today we'll hear the deposition. The verdict is due to be given in a couple of days – on the twelfth, Darwin's two hundredth anniversary.'

Xavier said that the young man sitting beside Alicia was called Anselm Fairweather; a friend of Alicia, he was the theological lawyer she had chosen to assist her in presenting her case.

'But he's not a defence lawyer,' Xavier murmured. 'You must remember this isn't a civil courtroom. In this case the defendant happens to have a general idea of the charges she's to face, as a living representative of Darwin's family – the only one who would come forward, incidentally; I think her presence was an initiative of young Fairweather. But she's not entitled to know those charges or the evidence, nor to know who brought them.'

'That doesn't seem just.'

'But the goal is not justice in the sense you mean. This is the working-out of God's will, as focused through the infallibility of the Holy Father and the wisdom of his officers.'

The proceedings opened with a rap of Jones's gavel. Alongside Jones on the bench were other Commissaries, and a Prosecutor of the Holy Office. Jones instructed the principals present to identify themselves. As they spoke, the clerk on the examiners' bench began to scribble a verbatim record.

When it was her turn, Mary stood to introduce herself as a Lector of Cooktown University, here to observe and advise in her expert capacity. Boniface actually smiled at her. He had a face as long and grey as the Reverend Darwin's coffin, and the skin under his eyes was velvet black.

A Bible was brought to Alicia, and she read Latin phrases from a card.

'I have no Latin,' Mary whispered to Xavier. 'She's swearing an oath to tell the truth, right?'

'Yes. I'll translate as we go along...'

Boniface picked up a paper, and began to work his way through his questions, in Latin that sounded like gravel falling into a bucket. Xavier whispered his translation: *'By what means and how long ago she came to London.'*

Mercifully the girl answered in English, with a crisp Scottish accent, which was smoothly translated back into Latin. 'By train and carriage from my mother's home in Edinburgh. Which has been the family home since the Reverend Charles Darwin's time.'

'Whether she knows or can guess the reason she was ordered to present herself to the Holy Office.'

'Well, I think I know.' She glanced at the coffin. 'To stand behind the remains of my uncle, while a book he published a hundred and fifty years ago is considered for its heresy.'

'That she name this book.'

'It was called *A Dialogue on the Origin of Species by Natural Selection.*'

'*That she explain the character of this book.*'

'Well, I've never read it. I don't know anybody who has. It was put on the Index even before it was published. I've only read second-hand accounts of its contents... It concerns a hypothesis concerning the variety of animal and vegetable forms we see around us. Why are some so alike, such as varieties of cat or bird? My uncle drew analogies with the well-known modification of forms of dogs, pigeons, peas and beans and other domesticated creatures under the pressure of selection for various properties desirable for mankind. He proposed that – no, he proposed a *hypothesis* – that natural variations in living things could be caused by another kind of selection, unconsciously applied by nature as species competed for limited resources, for water and food. This selection, given time, would shape living things as surely as the conscious manipulation of human trainers.'

'*Whether she believes this hypothesis to hold truth.*'

'I'm no natural philosopher. I want to be an artist. A painter, actually–'

'*Whether she believes this hypothesis to hold truth.*'

The girl bowed her head. 'It is contrary to the teachings of Scripture.'

'*Whether the Reverend Charles Darwin believed the hypothesis to hold truth.*'

She seemed rattled. 'Maybe you should open the box and ask him yersel—' Her lawyer, Anselm Fairweather, touched her arm. 'I apologise, Father. He stated it as a hypothesis, an organising principle, much as Galileo Galilei set out the motion of the Earth around the sun as a hypothesis only. Natural selection would explain certain observed patterns in nature. No doubt the truth of God's holy design lies beneath these observed patterns, but is not yet apprehended by our poor minds. Charles set this out clearly in his book, which he presented as a dialogue between a proponent of the hypothesis and a sceptic.'

'*Whether she feels the heresy is properly denied in the course of this dialogue.*'

'That's for you to judge. As I said, I have not read it. I mean, his intention was balance, and if that was not achieved, it is only through the poor artistry of my uncle, who was a philosopher before he was a writer, and—'

'*Whether she is aware of the injunction placed on Charles Darwin on first publication of this book.*'

'That he destroy the published edition, and replace it with a revision more clearly emphasising the hypothetical nature of his argument.'

'Whether she is aware of his compliance with this injunction.'

'I'm not aware of any second edition. He fled to Edinburgh, whose Royal Society heard him state his hypothesis, and received his further work in the form of transactions in its journal.'

Xavier murmured to Mary, 'Those Scottish Presbyterians. Nothing but trouble.'

'Whether she approves of his departure from England, as assisted by the heretical criminals known as the Lyncean Academy.'

'I don't know anything about that.'

'Whether she approves of his refusal to appear before a properly appointed court of the Holy Office.'

'I don't know about that either.'

'Whether she approves of his non-compliance with the holy injunction.'

'As I understand it he felt his book was balanced, therefore it wasn't heretical as it stood, and therefore the injunction was not applicable...'

So the hearing went on. The questioning seemed to have nothing to do with Darwin's philosophical case, which after all was the reason for Mary's presence here, but was more a relentless badgering of Alicia Darwin over the intentions and beliefs of her remote great-uncle – questions she couldn't possibly answer save in terms of her own interpretation, a line Alicia bravely stuck to.

To Mary, the trial began to seem a shabby epilogue to Darwin's own story. He had been a bright young cleric with vague plans to become a Jesuit, who had signed on to a ship of discovery, the *Beagle*, in the year 1831: the English had never assembled an empire, but they had been explorers. On board he had come under the influence of the work of some of the bright, radical thinkers from Presbyterian Edinburgh – the 'Scottish Enlightenment', as the historians called it. And in the course of his travels Darwin saw for himself islands being created and destroyed, and island-bound species of cormorants and iguanas that seemed obviously in flux between one form and another... Far from the anchoring certainties of the Church, it was no wonder he had come home with a head full of a vision that had obsessed him for the rest of his life – but it was a vision fraught with danger.

All that was a long time ago, the voyage of the *Beagle* nearly two hundred years past. But the Church thought in centuries, and was now exacting its revenge.

Alicia had volunteered to participate in this trial as an honour to her uncle, just as Mary had. Mary had imagined it would all be something of a formality. Yet the girl seemed slim, frail, defenceless standing there before the threatening row of theocrats before her – men who, Mary reminded herself uneasily, literally had the power of life and death over Alicia. Once, during the course of the questioning, Alicia glanced over at Mary, one of the few women in the room. Mary deliberately smiled back. *No, I don't know what the hell we've got ourselves into here either, kid.*

At last it ended for the day. Alicia had to look over and sign the clerk's handwritten transcript of the session. She was ordered not to leave without special permission, and sworn to silence. She seemed shocked when she was led away to a cell, somewhere in the crypt warren.

Mary stood. 'She wasn't expecting that.'

Xavier murmured, 'Don't worry. It's just routine. She's not a prisoner.'

'It looked like it to me.'

'Darwin will be found guilty of defying that long-ago injunction, of course. But Alicia will be asked only to abjure her uncle's actions, and to condemn the book. A slap on the wrist—'

'I don't care right now. I just want to get out of this place. Can we go?'

'Once the Reverend Fathers have progressed . . .' He bowed as Boniface Jones and the others walked past, stately as sailing ships in their black robes.

Mary got a good turn-out for her sermon in the cathedral the next day.

She'd titled it 'Galileo and the Holy Mystery of Relativity' – a provocative choice that had seemed a good idea from the other side of the world. Now, standing at the pulpit of St Paul's itself, dwarfed by the stonework around her and facing rows of calm, black-robed, supremely powerful men, she wasn't so sure.

But there in the front row, however, was Anselm Fairweather, Alicia Darwin's lawyer. He looked at her brightly, with an engaging, youthful sort of curiosity that she felt she'd seen too little of in England. Xavier Brazel sat beside him, faintly sinister as usual, but relatively sane, and relatively reassuring.

For better or worse, she was stuck with her prepared text. 'I'm well aware that to most churchmen and perhaps the lay public the

philosophical career of Galileo, in astronomy, dynamics and other subjects, is of most interest for the period leading up to his summons to
Rome in 1633 to face charges of heresy concerning his work regarding
the hypothetical motion of the Earth – charges which, of course, were
never in the end brought. But to a historian of natural philosophy,
such as myself, it is the legacy of the man's work *after* Rome that is
the most compelling...'

Nobody was quite sure what had been said to Galileo, by Pope
Urban himself among others, in the theocratic snakepit that was
seventeenth-century Rome. Some said the Tuscan ambassador, who
was hosting Galileo in Rome, had somehow intervened to soothe
ruffled papal feathers. Galileo had not faced the humiliation of an
Inquisition trial over his Copernican views, or, worse, sanctions afterwards. Instead the increasingly frail, increasingly lonely old man had
returned home to Tuscany. In his final years he turned away from
the astronomical studies that had caused him so much trouble, and
concentrated instead on 'hypotheses' about dynamics, the physics
of moving objects. This had been an obsession for him since, as a
young man, he had noticed patterns in the pendulum-like swinging
of church chandeliers.

'And in doing so, even so late in life, Galileo came to some remarkable and far-reaching conclusions.'

Galileo's later work had run ahead of the mathematical techniques
of the time, and to be fully appreciated had had to be reinterpreted
by later generations of mathematicians, notably Leibniz. Essentially
Galileo had built on common-sense observations of everyday motion
to build a theory that was now known as 'relativity', in which objects
moved so that their combined velocities never exceeded a certain 'speed
of finality'. All this properly required framing in a four-dimensional
spacetime. And buried in Galileo's work was the remarkable implica-
tion – or, as Mary carefully said now, a 'hypothesis' – that the whole
of the universe was expanding into four-dimensional space.

These 'hypotheses' had received confirmation in later centuries.
James Clerk Maxwell, developing his ideas about electromagnetism
in the comparatively intellectually free environment of Presbyterian
Edinburgh, had proved that Galileo's 'speed of finality' was in fact
the speed of light.

'And later in the nineteenth century, astronomers in our Terra Australis observatories, measuring the spectral shift of light from distant
nebulae, were able to show that the universe does indeed appear to

be expanding all around us, just as predicted from Galileo's work.' She didn't add that the southern observatories, mostly manned by Aboriginal astronomers, had also long before proved from the parallax of the stars that the motion of the Earth around the sun was real, just as Galileo had clearly believed.

She had often wondered, she concluded, if Galileo's attention had *not* been diverted to his dynamics work by his brush with the authorities – or, worse, if he had been left exhausted or had his life curtailed by their trial and sentencing – perhaps the discovery of relativity might have been delayed by centuries. She was rewarded with nods and smiles from churchmen accepting as if it were their own achievement this marvellous revelation by a man they had come close to persecuting, four hundred years before.

At the end of the Mass, Xavier and Anselm Fairweather approached her. 'We could hardly clap,' Xavier said. 'Not in church. But your sermon was much appreciated, Lector Mason.'

'Well, thank you.'

Anselm said, 'Points in your talk sparked my interest, Lector. What do you know of the Lyncean Academy? Named for the lynx, the sharp-est-eyed big cat. It was a group of free-thinking scholars, founded in Galileo's time to combat the Church's authority in philosophy. It published Galileo's later books. After Galileo it went underground, but supported later thinkers. It defended Newton at his excommunication trial, and protected Fontenelle, and, as was mentioned in court, helped Darwin flee to Scotland...'

She glanced at the churchmen filing out ahead of her – and at Xavier, whose impassive face carried an unstated warning. She asked, 'Is there something you want to tell me, Mr Fairweather?'

'Look, could we speak privately?'

Once out of the cathedral, she let Anselm lead her away. Xavier clearly did not want to hear whatever conversation Anselm proposed to have.

They walked down Blackfriars to the river, and then west along the Embankment. Under grimy iron bridges the Thames was crowded with small steam-driven vessels. The London skyline, where she could see it, was low and flat, a lumpy blanket of poor housing spread over the city's low hills, pierced here and there by the slim spire of a Wren church. The city far dwarfed Cooktown, but it lay as if rotting under a shroud of smoky fog. In the streets there seemed to be children every-where, swarming in this Catholic country, bare-footed, soot-streaked and ragged. She wondered how many of them got any schooling – and how many of them had access to the medicines shipped over from the Pasteur clinics in Terra Australis to the disease-ridden cities of Europe.

As they walked along the Embankment she addressed the issue directly. 'So, Anselm, are you a member of this Lyncean Academy?'

He laughed. 'You saw through me.'

'You're not exactly subtle.'

'No. Well, I apologise. But there's no time left for subtlety.'

'What's so urgent?'

'*The Darwin trial must have the right outcome.* I want to make sure I have you on my side. For we intend to use the trial to reverse a mistake the Church never made.'

She shook her head. 'A mistake never made ... You've lost me. And I'm not on anybody's side. I'm an outsider, outside your faith wars.'

He didn't seem to listen to that. 'Look – the Lynceans don't question the Church about morality and ethics, the domain of God. It's the Church's meddling in free thinking that we object to. For two millennia human minds have been locked in systems of thought imposed by the Church. First, Christianity was imposed across the Roman empire. Then Aquinas imposed the philosophy of Aristotle, his four elements, his cosmologies of crystal spheres – which is still the official doctrine, no matter how much the observations of our own eyes, of the instruments you've developed in Terra Australis, disprove every word he wrote! We take our motto from a saying of Galileo himself. "I do not feel obliged to believe that the same God who has endowed us with sense, reason and intellect –"'

'"– has intended us to forgo their use." I don't see what this has to do with Darwin's trial.'

'But it is an echo of the trial of Galileo – which the Church abandoned! Galileo was taken to a prison, given a good fright about torture and the stake, he agreed to say whatever they wanted him to say – but he was *not* put on trial.'

She started to see. 'But what if he had been?'

He nodded eagerly. 'You get the point. A few decades earlier the Church persecuted Giordano Bruno, another philosopher, for his supposed heresies. They *burned* him. But nobody knew who Bruno was. Galileo was famous across Europe! If they had burned *him* – even if they had merely put him through the public humiliation of a trial – it would have caused outrage, especially in the Protestant countries as they were then – England, the Netherlands, the German states.

The Church's moral authority would have been rejected there, and weakened even in the Catholic countries.

'And the Church would not have been able to cow those thinkers who followed Galileo. You're a historian of natural philosophy; you must see the pattern. Before Galileo you had thinkers like Bacon, Leonardo, Copernicus, Kepler . . . It was a grand explosion of ideas. Galileo's work drew together and clarified all these threads – he wrote on atomism, you know. His work could have been the foundation of a revolution in thinking. But after him, comparatively speaking – nothing! Do you know that Isaac Newton the alchemist was, covertly, working on a new mechanics, building on Galileo? If the Church had not been able to impeach Newton, who knows what he might have achieved?'

'And all this because the Church *spared* Galileo.'

'Yes! I know it's a paradox. We suspect the Church made the wise choice by accident. It would have been better if Galileo *had* been martyred! Then all honest souls would have seen the Church for what it is.'

Saying this, he seemed very young to Mary. 'And now,' she said carefully, 'you want to use this Darwin trial to create a new martyr. Hmm. How old is Alicia Darwin?'

'Just twenty.'

'Does she *know* she's to become some kind of token sacrifice for your cause?' When he hesitated, she pressed, 'You produced her as the family representative for this trial, didn't you? What's your relationship with her?'

'We are lovers,' he said defiantly. 'Oh, it is chaste, Lector, don't worry about that. But she would do anything for me – and I for her.'

'Would she be your lover if she weren't Darwin's grand-niece? And I ask you again: does she *know* what she's letting herself in for?'

He held her gaze, defiant. 'The Lyncean Academy is ancient and determined. If the Church has a long memory, so do we. And I hope, I pray, that you, Lector, if the need arises, will use your considerable authority in that courtroom tomorrow to ensure that the *right* verdict is reached.' He glanced around. 'It's nearly noon. Care for some lunch?'

'No thanks,' she said, and walked sharply away.

On Thursday 12 February, Darwin's two-hundredth anniversary, the final session of the hearing was held in another subterranean room, burrowed out of the London clay beneath St Paul's.

At least this was a grander chamber, Mary thought, its walls panelled with wood, its floor carpeted, and a decent light cast by a bank of electric bulbs. But this comparative luxury was evidently for the benefit of the eight cardinals who had come here to witness the final act of the trial. Sitting in their bright vestments on a curved bench at the head of the room, they looked oddly like gaudy Australasian birds, Mary thought irreverently.

Before them sat the court officials, led by Boniface Jones and completed by the earnest clerk with the rapidly scratching pen. The scribes from the chronicles scribbled and sketched. Anselm Fairweather, sitting away from his client-lover, looked excited, like a spectator at some sports event. Mary could see no guards, but she was sure they were present, ready to act if Alicia dared defy the will of the court.

That ghastly coffin stood on its trestles.

And before them all, dressed in a penitent's white robe and with her wrists and ankles bound in chains, stood Alicia Darwin.

'I can't believe I volunteered for this farce,' Mary muttered to Xavier Brazel. 'I haven't contributed a damn word. And look at that wretched child.'

'It is merely a formality,' Xavier said. 'The robe is part of an ancient tradition, which—'

'Does the authority of a two-thousand-year-old Church really rely on humiliating a poor bewildered kid?'

He seemed faintly alarmed. 'You must not be seen to be disrespecting the court, Mary.' He leaned closer and whispered, 'And whatever Anselm said to you, I'd advise you to disregard it.'

She tried to read his handsome, impassive face. 'You choose what to hear, don't you? You have a striking ability to compartmentalise. Maybe that's what it takes to survive in your world.'

'I only want what is best for the Church – and for my friends, among whom I would hope to count you.'

'We'll see about that at the end of this charade, shall we?'

As before, Boniface Jones began proceedings with a rap of a gavel; the murmuring in the room died down. Jones faced Alicia. 'Alicia Rosemary Darwin, daughter of James Paul Darwin of Edinburgh. Kneel to hear the clerical condemnation, and the sentence of the Holy See.'

Alicia knelt submissively.

Jones picked up a sheet of paper and began to read in his sonorous Latin. Xavier murmured a translation for Mary.

'*Whereas he, the deceased Charles Robert, son of Robert Waring Darwin of London, was in the year 1859 denounced by the Holy Office for holding as true the false doctrine taught by some that the species of living things that populate the Earth are mutable one into the other, in accordance with a law of chance and selection, and in defiance of the teaching of the divine and Holy Scripture that all species were created by the Lord God for His purpose, and having published a book entitled* A Dialogue on the Origin of Species by Natural Selection. *Whereas he the said Darwin did fail to respect an injunction issued by the Holy Congregation held before his eminence the Lord Cardinal Joseph McInnery on 14 December 1859 to amend the said work to ensure an appropriate balance be given to argument and counter-argument concerning the false doctrine . . .*'

The Commissary's pronouncements went on and on, seeming to Mary to meld into a kind of repetition of the details of the previous session. It struck her how little thought had been applied to the material presented to this court, how little analysis had actually been done on the charges and the evidence, such as they were. The sheer anti-intellectual nature of the whole proceedings offended her.

And Alicia, kneeling, was rocking slightly, her face blanched, as if she might faint. The reality of the situation seemed to be dawning on her, Mary thought. But with a sinking heart she thought she saw a kind of stubborn determination on Alicia's face. Was the girl preparing to defy the court?

At last Boniface seemed to be reaching the end of his peroration. '*Therefore, involving the most Holy name of Our Lord Jesus Christ and His most glorious Mother, ever Virgin Mary, and sitting as a tribunal with the advice and counsel of the Reverend Masters of Sacred Theology, we say, pronounce, sentence and declare that he, Charles Darwin, had rendered himself according to this Holy Office vehemently suspect of heresy, having held and believed a doctrine that is false and contrary to the divine and Holy Scripture, namely the doctrine known as "natural selection". Consequently, he has incurred all the censures and penalties enjoined and promulgated by the sacred Canons and all particular and general laws against such delinquents.*

'*For adhering to the doctrine of the Origin of Species, let Darwin be anathema.*'

The chroniclers scribbled, excited; Mary imagined the telegraph wires buzzing the next day to bring the world the news that Charles Darwin had been formally, if posthumously, excommunicated.

But Alicia still knelt before the panel. The clerk came forward, and handed her a document. 'A prepared statement,' Xavier whispered to

Mary. 'She's not on trial herself, not under any suspicion. She's here to represent Darwin's legacy. All she has to do is read that out and she'll be free to go.'

Alicia, kneeling, her voice small in the room before the rows of churchmen, began to read: '"I, Alicia Rosemary Darwin, daughter of James Paul Darwin of Edinburgh, arraigned personally at this tribunal and kneeling before you, most Eminent and Reverend Lord Cardinals, Inquisitors General against heretical depravity throughout the whole Christian Republic..."' She fell silent and read on rapidly. 'You want me to say the *Origin of Species* was heretical. And to say that my uncle deliberately defied the order to modify it to remove the heresy. And that I and all my family abjure his memory and all his words for all time.'

Boniface Jones' gravel-like voice sounded almost kind. 'Just read it out, child.'

She put the papers down on the floor. 'I will not.'

And this was the moment, Mary saw. The moment of defiance Anselm had coached into her.

There was uproar.

The chroniclers leaned forward, trying to hear, to be sure what Alicia had said. Anselm Fairweather was standing, the triumph barely disguised on his face. Even the cardinals were agitated, muttering to one another.

Only Boniface Jones sat silent and still, a rock in the storm of noise. Alicia continued to kneel, facing him.

When the noise subsided Boniface gestured at the clerk. 'Don't record this. Child – Alicia. You must understand. *You* have not been on trial here. The heresy was your distant uncle's. But if you defy the will of the tribunal, if you refuse to read what has been given to you, then the crime becomes yours. By defending your uncle's work you would become heretical yourself.'

'I don't care.' She poked at the paper on the floor, pushing it away. 'I won't read this. My family doesn't "abjure" Charles Darwin. We honour him. We're not alone. Why, the Reverend Dawkins said only recently that natural selection is the best hypothesis anybody ever framed...'

Mary whispered to Xavier, 'And I wonder who put that in her mouth?'

'You mean Anselm Fairweather.'

'You know about him?'

'He's hardly delicate in his operations.'

'This is exactly what Anselm and his spooky friends want, isn't it? To have this beautiful kid throw herself to the flames. Smart move. I can just imagine how this will play back home in Cooktown, and around the world.'

Xavier frowned. 'I can hear how angry you are. But there's nothing you can do.'

'Isn't there?'

'Mary, *this is the Inquisition.* You can't defy it. We can only wait and see how this is going to play out.'

His words decided her. 'Like hell.' She stood up.

'What are you doing?'

'Injecting a little common sense from Terra Australis, that's what.'

Before Xavier could stop her she strode forward. She tried to look fearless, but she found it physically difficult to walk past the angry faces of the cardinals, as if she was the focus of God's wrath. She reached the bench. Boniface Jones towered over her, his face like thunder.

Alicia still knelt on the floor, the pages of the statement scattered before her. Mary reached out a hand. 'Stand up, child. Enough's enough.'

Bewildered, Alicia complied.

Mary glared up at Boniface. 'May I address the bench?'

'Do I have a choice?' Boniface asked dryly.

Mary felt a flicker of hope at that hint of humour. Maybe Boniface would prove to be a realist. 'I hope we all still have choices, Father. Look, I know I'm the outsider here. But maybe we can find a way to get out of this ridiculous situation with the minimum harm done to anybody – to this girl, to the Church.'

Alicia said, 'I don't want your help. I don't care what's done to me—'

Mary faced her. 'I know you've never spoken to me before in your life. But just listen, if you don't want to die in prison, serving the dreams of your so-called lover.'

Alicia frowned, and glanced at Anselm.

Mary turned to Boniface. 'This is a spectacle. A stunt, so the Church can show its muscle. Even death doesn't put an enemy out of your reach, right? So you dug up poor Darwin here and excommunicated him posthumously. But in your wisdom, and I use the word loosely, you decided even that wasn't enough. You wanted more. But it's all unravelling. Can't you see, Commissary, if you prosecute this innocent kid for being loyal to her family, how much harm you will do to the Church's image – even in your home territories, and certainly outside? If you punish this girl, you'll be doing precisely what your enemies want you to do.'

'What would *you* have me do, Lector?'

'Your problem is with Darwin, not his remote grand-niece. If excommunication's not enough, punish *him* further. There are precedents in history. In the year 1600 Giordano Bruno was burned at the stake for his various heresies. But the punishment didn't end there. His bones were ground to dust! That showed him. So take Darwin's mouldering corpse out of that box and hang it from Tower Bridge. Grind his bones and scatter them on the wind. Whatever – I'm sure your imagination can do better than mine in coming up with ways to debase a dead man. Then you'll have the public spectacle you want, without the cruelty.'

Boniface considered, his eyes hooded over those flaps of blackness. 'But the holy court heard the girl defy me.'

Xavier approached now. 'I for one heard nothing, Holy Father. A cough, perhaps, a muttered apology. I'm sure there is no reliable transcript.'

Boniface nodded. 'Hmm. Lector Mason, you should consider a career in politics. Or the Church.'

'I don't think so,' she said vehemently.

'I must consult my colleagues. You may withdraw.' He turned away, dismissing her.

Mary grabbed Alicia by the arm and walked her away from the bench. 'Let's get you out of here, kid.'

Anselm followed, agitated. 'What did you do? Alicia, you need to go back – Lector, let her go.' He reached for Alicia.

Xavier said, 'I wouldn't advise it, Mr Fairweather.'

Mary hissed, 'Back off, kid. You'll get your martyr. Darwin's as much an intellectual hero as Galileo ever was. How do you think it's going to reflect on the Church to have his very bones abused in this grotesque way? You'll get the reaction you want, the anger, the disgust – with any luck, the mockery. And, look – you heard me speak about what the Aboriginal astronomers have discovered back home. The expansion of the universe, building on Galileo's own work? *We have proof.* The truth has a way of working its way out into the open. The Church has clung on for centuries, but its hold is weakening. You don't *need* to sacrifice Alicia to the Inquisition.'

The blood had drained from Alicia's face. Perhaps she saw it all for the first time.

But Anselm still faced her. 'Come with me, please, Alicia.'

Alicia looked from Mary to Anselm. 'Lector Mason – if I could stay with you – just until I get my thoughts sorted out.'

'Of course.'

Xavier leaned forward. 'Go away, Lyncean. And I'd advise you, boy, never to come to the attention of the Inquisition again.'

Anselm stared at the three of them. Then he turned and ran.

Mary looked at Xavier. 'So how long have you known he was with this Academy?'

'A while.'

'You're lenient.'

'He's harmless. You know me by now, I prefer to avoid a fuss. The Church survived the fall of Rome, and Galileo and Darwin. It will survive a pipsqueak like Anselm Fairweather.'

'So will you help us get out of here?'

He glanced back at Boniface. 'I suspect the court will find a way to close this hearing gracefully. Nothing more will be asked of Miss Darwin. Umm, her clothes . . .'

'I don't care about my clothes,' Alicia said quickly. 'I just want to get out of this place.'

'You and me both,' Mary said. 'You can borrow my coat.' She started walking Alicia towards the door.

'Anselm set me up, didn't he?'

'I'm afraid so, dear.'

'He said no harm would come to me if I refused to say anything bad about Charles Darwin. I believed him. Of course I did. He was my lawyer, and my, my . . .'

'Don't think about it now. Come see my hotel room. It's got a great view of the Place de Louis XVI. You can see right up Napoleon's nose. You know, I'm planning a trip up to Edinburgh. You have family there? I hear the air is cleaner. Why don't you come? And then I'm thinking of booking an early berth back home. Maybe you can come visit.'

'Are you serious?'

'Why not? After all, your uncle Charles was a traveller, wasn't he? Maybe it's in the blood. I think you'd like Terra Australis...'

Talking quietly, following Xavier through the warren under St Paul's, Mary led Alicia steadily towards the light of day.

MARS ABIDES

Hell City, Mars. 4 July 2026.

Well, at least one of us lasted long enough to see the fiftieth anniversary of the first human hoofprints on this rustball. *My* hoofprints. That's something, isn't it?

And I decided it's a good enough time to finish my autobiography, such as it is, and read it down the comms link for the benefit of a silent universe, and then bury the text in this tin chest in the Martian dirt in the probably vain hope that somebody will find it some day. Who, though? Or what? Maybe some radioactive super-roach from the ruins of Earth, or some smart semi-motile Martian of a future volcano summer, will read about our mistakes, and not repeat them.

Mars abides. Yes, I know the Bible verse (and by the way, I stowed Verity's copy of the Good Book in this chest): 'One generation passeth away, and another generation cometh: but the Earth abideth forever.' Ecclesiastes one, four. I always found that line a comfort, in the darkest days, and I always told Verity that it was a by-product of her Bible reading groups, although I have to admit I picked it up in the first place from the title of a pretty good science fiction novel.

But I digress. If you want to learn the story of me and Mars, and Verity and Alexei, and all the rest, you'll have to begin at the beginning.

Mount Wilson Observatory, Los Angeles, California. 21 July 1964.

The city lights washed to the foot of the hill on which the old observatory stood, but that night the sky above was crisp and cool and peppered with stars. The opened dome curved over Verity's head, a shell of ribbing and panels. I suppose that old dome is crushed like an eggshell now. The telescope itself was an open frame, vaguely cylindrical, looming in the dark.

I'd always been an astronomy buff. But I only had eyes for Verity Whittaker.

I was fussing around the telescope, talking too fast and too much, as usual. 'This is the Hooker telescope. When it was built, in 1906, it was the largest telescope in the world. These days it's not hard to book time on it. Most observers want better seeing conditions than you get here now. The city lights, you know . . . I guess it doesn't much look like what most people think a telescope is supposed to be. I mean—'

'You mean it's a reflector,' Verity murmured. 'Come on, Puddephat; I studied basic optics.'

'Sure.' I laughed nervously; in my own ears it was a painful, grating sound.

She walked around the small, cluttered space, more glamorous in her USAF uniform than Marilyn Monroe, in my eyes. I was twenty-one, a year younger than Verity, with my hair already thinning at the temples. Why, she was already all but a combat veteran, having flown patrols over Germany and gone toe-to-toe with the Soviets. What could she see in me? She wasn't even interested in astronomy, which was a subject for old men.

But we were both attached to NASA's long-term Mars programme, though both of us were at bottom-feeder level. And to fly the space-ships of the future, pilots like Verity Whittaker were going to have to learn astronomy from dweeb science-specialists like me.

So here she was, having responded to my invitation to come share some study time, and my heart was pounding. Even the heavy crucifix she wore on a chain around her neck didn't put me off.

Restless – she was always easily bored by science stuff – she went over to a small bookshelf laden with a range of volumes of varying ages and degrees of decrepitude. *Mars as the Abode of Life* by Percival Lowell, 1909; *Mars and its Canals* by Lowell, 1906 . . .

'Not too scientific,' I ventured. 'Old Lowell. But oddly prophetic in his way.'

'If you say so.' She picked out a fiction title: Bradbury's *The Martian Chronicles*.

I asked, 'You like science fiction? Me too. That's one of my favourites.'

'Too realistic for my taste. I grew up with Barsoom.'

'Maybe we could discuss books some time.'

She didn't actually say no. She put the volume back.

I got out of the chair. 'Come on over; I have the instrument set up.'

She sat in the chair and craned her head back. It took her a few moments to figure out how to see. You had to keep one eye closed, of course, and even then you had to align your head correctly, or your view would be occluded by the rim of the eyepiece. But when her lips parted softly – man, I could have kissed her there and then – I knew what she was seeing. A disc, washed-out pink and green, with streaks of lacy cloud, and patches of steel-grey ocean that would glint if the sun caught them at the right angle. All this blurred, softened, as if depicted in watercolour.

'I'm looking at Mars?'

'Right. We're nowhere near opposition, but the seeing is pretty good.' Her lips closed in a frown, and I knew she didn't know what I was talking about. 'At opposition Mars is almost opposite the sun, seen from Earth. So the planets are at the closest they get in their orbits. Verity, to do their jobs astronomers have always had to be able to figure out where they are in relation to the rest of the universe. Just the skills you interplanetary pilot heroes are going to need. Anyhow, I thought it was appropriate for us to see Mars tonight. It kind of ties in with the main thing I want to show you.'

She pulled back from the eyepiece. She looked suspicious, as if I was about to whip out my dong. 'And what's that, Puddephat?'

I went to a desk at the back of the observatory, and came back with a fat folder. 'Up until just a few days ago, that view of Mars was pretty much the best we had. But now everything's different. Look at this stuff.'

She took the folder. It contained photographs in grainy black and white. 'What am I looking at?'

'The pictures radioed back by Mariner 4. The NASA space probe that flew by Mars last week. Mariner sent back twenty-one pictures in all. They cover maybe one per cent of Mars's surface. Classified, but I've got contacts at NASA Ames,' I boasted desperately.

The first photo showed the limb of the planet, seen from close to; there was a curved horizon. Verity stared. In contrast to an astronomer's view, the misty, unreal disc, this was how Mars would look to an orbiting astronaut. I could see her imagination was snagged.

The next few monochrome images looked like aerial pictures of a desert. 'It's hard to make out anything at all.'

'You have to remember the geometry, Verity; the sun was more or less directly overhead here, so there are no shadows.'

'High noon on Mars. It looks kind of like Arizona, maybe, seen from a high-flying plane.'

'Well, you'd know.'

'Could Mars be like Arizona?'

'Something like it, but a higher altitude. Mariner confirmed the atmospheric pressure. You could walk around on the surface with nothing more than a face mask and sun cream...'

The seventh picture showed craters.

She stared. 'This looks more like the moon.'

'Mars is a small, geologically static world with a thin atmosphere, Verity. So, craters.'

'We're screwed.'

'Why do you say that?'

'Because nobody's going to spend billions of dollars to send us to a cratered rockball.'

'Just keep going.'

She flicked on, and stopped at the thirteenth frame. 'My God.' Suddenly she sounded electrified.

And well she might have been. The thirteenth picture showed more craters, but with what could only be forests sheltering inside them, bordering neat lakes. Life on Mars, unequivocal proof, coming after centuries of old men staring through telescopes at shifting grey-green patches...

Verity whooped. 'They're just going to hose money at the programme now!'

Jet Propulsion Laboratory, California. 21 January 1972.

We got out of the car and I smuggled Alexei past JPL security, with me in my bright astronaut-corps jumpsuit and flashing my best grin at the star-struck guards and clerks. I murmured, 'This is treason, probably. I could get shot for this.'

Alexei Petrov grinned back at me. 'Don't worry about it. No American soldier yet born can shoot straight.'

I hurried him nervously along the central mall, which stretched from the gate into the main working area of the laboratory. JPL was a cramped place, crowded between the San Gabriel Mountains and the upper-middle class suburb of La Canada. Alexei was distracted by the von Karman auditorium, for years the scene of triumphant news conferences. Today there was a crowd at the doors, for the rumour was that the Martian rainstorms had cleared enough for the Voyager mission controllers to attempt a landing. But I hurried him past.

'We will not go in there? I heard Arthur C. Clarke and Walter Cronkite were coming today.'

'What, you're hunting autographs now? We're going somewhere much more exciting.'

I led him to the Image Processing Laboratory, rooms full of chattering technicians and junior scientists, and screens and computer printouts showing crude black and white images being put through various enhancement processes. Here, away from the sanitised stuff being presented to the celebrities, the raw data sent back by the Voyager orbiters at Mars were being received.

In common with every other semi-public NASA facility, there were also TV feeds on the walls reporting on the agency's growing celestial dominion, such as live in-colour Earth-orbit images from the astronauts in the Skylabs, and grainier pictures of the second EVA by the Apollo 18 crew on the moon – even an image from the Cape of preparations for the latest unmanned test launch of the mighty Nova booster, big brother of the Saturn Vs. But Alexei, dedicated planetary scientist that he was, had eyes only for the Mars data: images transmitted across the gulf one dot at a time like newsprint wire photos and painstakingly reconstructed. The very latest pictures, live from Mars!

And, as I'd hoped and half-planned, Verity Whittaker came pushing out of the crowd. At twenty-nine she was more beautiful than ever, her hair cropped sensibly short, her body toned by years of astronaut training. She was still as remote from me as the moon, of course. But she smiled at an old colleague. 'Hi, Puddephat. Should have known you'd show up. Who's your friend?'

'Lieutenant Verity Whittaker, meet Doctor Alexei Petrov, from the Soviet Academy of—'

'Puddephat, are you insane? You smuggled in a Soviet?'

Alexei, a little older than us at thirty-two, wasn't the way you'd imagine a Soviet citizen. Coming from a relatively privileged stratum of Russian society – his father had been an Academician too – he was tall, slim, with slicked-back dark hair and movie-star looks. And, even as he and Verity faced each other down in those first seconds, I could see something sparking between them.

'I take it you never met a Soviet citizen before.' His rich Slavic accent was like warm butter.

'Maybe not, but I met a few Chinese Commie flyers during my tour in 'Nam in '68, and I don't care what the official histories say.'

I sighed; in the astronaut corps we'd had these arguments too many times. 'Verity, science can only proceed through openness. I've known Alexei for years. He's in the Soviet Mars cosmonaut cadre – he's flown in space, which is more than I've managed so far. And when I heard he was in the country—'

'I hunger for data,' Alexei said, his gaze roaming. 'My subject, astrobiology, is information-poor.'

Verity moved to block his view. 'In that case, go spend a billion roubles and retrieve your own data. Ah, but your landers failed, didn't they?'

Alexei said mildly, 'Some commentators say a massive investment in space technology is itself destabilising.'

'Maybe the way you Soviets do it.'

'But what of your militarised Skylabs? And is it true that the Apollo 16 crew tested weapons on the moon during their "dark" EVA?'

It's probably just as well that before she could answer a stir of excitement distracted us, as the technicians and scientists gathered around the TV monitors.

In this particular launch window, it had been unlucky for the twin Voyager-Mars spacecraft (and even more unlucky for their sturdy Soviet counterparts) to arrive in the middle of the worst Martian storm season the astronomers had ever seen. The JPL controllers didn't want to risk dropping their landers down into that planetary maelstrom, and for weeks the orbiters' cameras sent back nothing but images of rain clouds punctuated by lightning flashes.

But now the storms had settled out, and it seemed the mission planners had agreed to go for a descent attempt. The lander attached to Voyager-Mars 2 had already separated, and was shown in grainy images from cameras mounted on the orbiter. It was a squat glider, a trial of the manned landers to be built in a few years' time, and you could clearly see the Stars and Stripes and UNITED STATES boldly painted on its flanks. The scientists, Poindexter patriots all, whooped and cheered.

But at that pivotal moment I found myself alone.

When I looked around I saw Verity was shadowing Alexei as he went through an image archive. He was peering at striking images of liquid water running through the deep canyons, and the tough vegetation of Mars clumping in the crater basins. I saw how their slim bodies brushed close, and he turned his head, just subtly, as if distracted by the scent of her hair.

And, reader, my heart ripped apart.

Hesperia Base, Mars. 4 July 1976 (Mars dates given as at Houston meridian).

I took a step forward, moving away from the MEM, into pale sunlight.

This was me, Jonas Puddephat, aged thirty-three, walking on Mars

– the *first* on Mars! Who'd have thought it? Not Verity and the rest of our six-strong crew, that's for sure. We'd argued halfway to Mars about priority, and in the end it was pure diplomatic hypocrisy that had delivered me out the hatch first. President Nixon's office had decided that this mission, as much militaristic land-grab as science expedition, should be led down the ladder by the only authentic civilian aboard. Verity had always been a strange mix of Cold Warrior and religious zealot, and she retreated into her onboard Bible study group and tried to find some consolation for the snub in the pages of the Good Book.

But just then I didn't care about any of that. Let me tell you, it was a moment that made up for all the years of training, and the horrors of the flight itself, from the shattering launch of the Nova booster climbing into the sky on its fourteen F-1 engines, to the months of the cruise in our souped-up Skylab hab module with the growling NERVA nuclear rockets at our back, and finally the hair-raising descent to the ground in the Mars Excursion Module, an untried glider descending into a virtually unknown atmosphere. Not only that, we were rising out of the debris of too many accidents and disasters – too many lives lost, for our accelerated programme had put huge pressure on the resources and management structures of NASA, USAF and our main contractors.

And then add on the fact that, such had been our eagerness to sprint here and beat the Soviets, we had no way of getting home again before a relief mission arrived some twenty-five months later.

None of that mattered, for I'd lived through it all, and I was *here*. I whooped in my dweebish way and pumped the air.

Verity's voice murmured in his ear. 'Checklist, asshole.'

I sighed. 'I know, Verity, I know.'

So I got to work. I turned to face *Nixon*. The MEM was a biconic glider, its tile-clad belly and leading edges scorched, sitting on frail-looking skids. I made sure the camera mounted on my chest got a good view of the craft's exterior, so Mission Control could check for damage.

Then I set off again, across the Martian ground. Soon I had gone far enough that I could see no signs of raying from *Nixon*'s descent engines. The soil under my feet was unmarked, without footprints. Ahead of me I saw a dip in the ground, it might have been a crater, where what looked like a forest copse grew, crowding grey-green.

By God, I thought, we're here. We came for insane reasons, and probably by all the wrong methods, but *we're here*.

'Puddephat,' Verity said gently. 'Are you all right?'

I tried to focus. 'Fine, Verity.' She didn't need to tell me I was well behind schedule. I hadn't even got the flag set up yet. But I walked forward, further from the MEM.

And Verity murmured, 'Look up.'

Again I tilted back, and peered up at the zenith. I saw a single, brilliant star passing overhead. Not one of Mars's moons – it had to be the *Stalingrad*. The Soviet vessel was an unlikely jam-up of Proton booster stages, a Salyut-derived space habitat, and some kind of lander, launched by three firings of their huge N-1 boosters – or four, if you count the one that blew up – but they had made it too, and here they were. Somewhere up there was Alexei Petrov, peering down at me through a telescope, with envy no doubt eating into his soul. I lifted an arm and waved.

Again Verity pressed me. 'We only beat them here by days, Puddephat. And if they manage to land before you get around to making the claim—'

'All right, damn it.'

It took me only a moment to set up the flagpole, and take the Stars and Stripes from its bag and fix it to the pole. 'Can you see me, *Nixon*?'

'Clear as crystal, Jonah.'

I straightened up and saluted. 'On this, the bicentenary day of my nation's declaration of independence from foreign tyranny, I, Jonas James Puddephat, by the authority vested in me by the government of the United States of America, do hereby claim all these lands of Mars . . .'

While I spoke, I heard Verity and the others discussing contingencies in case the Soviets landed close by. We had rifles and revolvers, engineered to work in Martian conditions and trialled on the moon, and the *Nixon* even packed a couple of artillery pieces. For years, even before we humans got there, Mars had been an arena projected from our Earthbound Cold War.

When I was done, despite squawks from the MEM, I started unbuckling my mask. Somebody had to be first to try it. I ripped off my mask and took a deep lungful of that thin, cold, Martian air . . .

United States Hellas Base, Mars. 9 November 1983.

From the beginning we got visits from the Russians. Occasionally, some of us would go over there.

We'd share tips on operational matters, and under the radar Alexei and I and the other scientists would pool data. It was never more than semi-official. But in the end it was our sheer humanity that united us; in the two bases combined there were just forty-some human souls stuck up here on Mars, and we needed company, no matter what was going on back on Earth.

So, that November morning – that terrible morning, as it would turn out – I watched Alexei and the others come rolling over the horizon in the rovers we called Marsokhods, having driven from their own base, which we called Marsograd, tucked deep in the rift we called Voyager Valley, a quarter-way around the planet's circumference. Few of us knew (or could pronounce) the names the Russians themselves gave to these things. But we admired the hardy 'khods, more robust than anything we had, although our vehicles ran on methane fuel from our wet-chemistry factory, which was better than anything *they* had.

And on this particular visit, Verity was riding back with Alexei and the rest. Despite the fact that she was a veteran Cold Warrior she was one of the most frequent American visitors to the Soviet base, and if you saw her with Alexei you'd have known exactly why. My last hope that she would reject him as a godless Commie was dissipated when it turned out his family was Catholic.

So there you are. I was forty years old, and still mooning over the woman. Even Mars was no cure for that.

The arrival of a 'khod at the dismal, half-buried collection of shacks we called Hell City was usually a cause for a party. Well, most anything was. This time, though, the mood was sour and stiff, and it wasn't hard to understand why. Up on that blue dot in the sky – thanks to Soviet atrocities in Afghanistan, thanks to the US deploying Pershing intermediate-range missiles throughout Europe thereby increasing our capability to launch a first strike, thanks to the increasing weaponisation of space, a process even we on Mars were a part of – the armed forces of our respective nations had come to a pitch of tension that hadn't been matched since Cuba twenty years earlier. As soon as Verity got through the lock she hurried to her cabin to tune into her encrypted comms channel back to NORAD, to get the straight skinny on what was going on at home.

Meanwhile I hosted Alexei and the rest in our galley area, the only place large enough to accommodate us all. On the wall-mounted TV set an ice hockey game was playing, another sublimated US-USSR confrontation, beamed directly from the Earth for the benefit of both sides of our ideological divide.

Alexei glanced over his coffee at me. 'You are preparing for home, yes?'

The cycler habitat, a half-dozen ganged Skylabs looping endlessly between the orbits of Earth and Mars, was due in a few days, ready to collect us and take us home.

I said, 'I've been preparing a geology package to help train up my replacements. I ought to walk your people through it. I think we've established the basic parameters pretty well now. Aside from the lava fields around the Tharsis giants, you basically have a surface of impact ejecta mixed with debris from mudflows and floods. In many ways Mars is a mix of conditions on Earth and the moon, and I've recommended to Houston they should have crews trained up in the field on both those bodies before being sent over here.'

He smiled. 'That sounds a wise geological synthesis, for an astronomer.'

He was needling me, affectionately enough. 'Well, we all cross-trained, Alexei...'

Verity came bustling in. Her face was pale and drawn, with Martian dust ingrained in her pores. She poured herself a cup of coffee from a perc on the bar, the liquid slopping in the low gravity. Her earpiece whispered continually. 'The stupid fuckers,' she muttered.

Alexei asked, 'Which particular stupid fuckers do you have in mind?'

'My bosses, and yours.' She sat with us and leaned closer so the ice hockey fans couldn't hear. 'I got a feed from NORAD. Allied forces across the world have been put on Defcon Two. It's an exercise. But a big one, spanning all of western Europe. They call it Able Archer 83. It will be over in a couple of days. But it's giving the Soviets nightmares. Seems nobody told *them* it's just a drill. We're trying out new comms systems and protocols, so they can't follow what we're doing. And the clincher is that the USAF has decided it's a good opportunity to launch their OWP.'

That was a new acronym for me. 'Say what?'

'An orbital weapons platform,' Alexei said grimly.

'A Skylab with nukes,' Verity said. 'Hell, you Russians have your Salyuts—'

'Peaceful scientific and reconnaissance platforms.'

'Sure they are. And what about the Polyus programme? What's that but a space battle station? Anyhow, no wonder the old men in the Kremlin are freaking out. We're spending billions of dollars on this excrcise and the build-up to it, but not one grain of thought is being given to how it looks to the other side – or how the Soviets might react.' She stared at her coffee cup. Then, without looking up, she reached across the table and took Alexei's hand.

'Let's talk about something else,' I said sharply. 'How's your own work going, Alexei?'

So we turned away from those dangerous topics to the strange life forms of Mars.

The best biological results had been retrieved by the Soviets, in the diverse environments they had explored in the Voyager Valley – judging by the results they'd leaked to us, anyhow. And they seemed to have established the basic parameters of life on Mars. You had a substrate of microbial communities, some of them stretching for hundreds of miles in the shallow, moist soil, together with the very photogenic multicellular stars on the surface, mostly the forms we colloquially called 'cacti' and 'trees'. The cacti had tough, leathery skin, which almost perfectly sealed in their water stores. The trees had trunks as hard as concrete, and leaves like needles to keep in the moisture. Both forms photosynthesised busily.

But Alexei had always thought there was more to it.

Now he leaned towards us, confidential. 'As it happens, I do have new observations. We have believed there is no animal form here on Mars. Nothing but the microbes and the plants. We have no fossil traces—'

'No spikes on the cacti.' That had been my own first observation, on my second Marswalk, when I had explored that crater I saw after my first footfall, full of cacti and dwarf trees. There were no Martian teeth against which those cacti might have needed to evolve protection.

'And not enough oxygen in the air to enable motility anyhow,' Verity put in.

'Yet there are sites in the valley where I believe I have seen *tracks*. Channels dug deep into the strata. Even,' Alexei said dramatically, 'a kind of footprint. Very small, bird-like or lizard-like, and embedded in mud and mudstone. Not new – but not more than a few thousand years old, I would guess. Why do we *not* see these forms being created now?'

In terms of observations of Mars he had come a long way since first staring at those grainy Voyager orbiter pictures in JPL, I thought.

Nevertheless I shook my head. 'We don't yet know enough about Mars to eliminate non-biological causes, Alexei.'

'Of course not. But there could be something we are not expecting – for example, some equivalent of slime moulds, which alternate between static and mobile forms. I have a feeling that there is more to this biosphere than we have yet discovered, aspects we do not comprehend . . .'

There was a hiss of static.

We turned. The TV image had fritzed out, the hockey game lost. Some of our colleagues dug comms links out of their coverall pockets.

And Verity, touching her earpiece, got up and went straight to the galley's small window, looking east.

Alexei and I glanced at each other, and followed. Through the window we looked out over our base, a collection of domes and shacks, and the greenhouse bubbles where we grew our potatoes and beans. A child ran by, with her mask off, just five years old and breathing the air of Mars.

'They went to Defcon One,' Verity said, listening to her earpiece. 'The USAF Skylab didn't make its correct orbit after launch. Looked like it was descending over Soviet territory. Like a bombing run. It was just a malfunction – but the Russians responded—' I could hear the squeal of static. She pulled the little gadget out of her ear.

And an evening star flared, low in the Martian sky. It was as sudden, as brutal, as that. Verity had known where to look, to see Earth in the sky.

I didn't know what to feel. I retreated to my default mode, the science dweeb. 'Quite a stunt, to make bangs bright enough to be visible across interplanetary space.'

Verity glanced at me. 'I guess you have a choice to make about going home when the cycler comes, Puddephat.'

The star had seemed to be dimming. But then, only moments after the peak, there was another surge of light.

'The second strikes,' murmured Alexei. He put his arm around Verity's shoulders. 'This is home. Earth is gone. Mars is our mother now. And the future is our responsibility, those of us here.'

Standing alone, I comforted myself with the thought that the conflict was already minutes in the past, even as its light seared into my eyes.

Hell City, Mars. 28 October 2010.
Alexei Petrov died. He was seventy years old.

The skin cancer took him, as it's taken too many of us, that remote sun spitefully pouring its ultra-violet through the thin air here on this mountaintop we call Mars.

When he knew the game was up, he wrote out a kind of will. Naturally he left all his meagre material possessions to Verity and their kids and grandchildren. But he also willed a gift to me, a box of notes, a lifetime's research on the Mars ground, beginning with records from the fancy instruments our mission designers gave us and finishing with eyewitness observations written out in his own cramped handwriting, like a Victorian naturalist's journal.

The point was, Alexei had come to certain conclusions about Mars, mankind's second home, which he hadn't shared with anybody – not even Verity. But when I'd gone through it all, and checked his results, and reworked his findings – and found they tallied with some tentative conclusions of my own – I called on Verity Whittaker Petrova, and asked her to take a walk with me around our little township.

We lived in a huddle of yellowing plastic domes. Some of the youngsters – we already had second-generation Martians sixteen or seventeen years old – were building houses of the native 'wood', hacked out with stone axes and draped over with alpaca skin, houses that looked like tepees, or Iron Age roundhouses from Europe. But the houses had to be sealed up with ageing polythene sheets, and connected by piping to our elderly air circulation and scrubbing plants, driven by the big Soviet solar cell arrays now that our small NASA nuke plant had failed. Verity had led the effort to build a pretty little chapel, using materials scavenged from the MEM.

All this was set down on the floor of Hellas basin, a feature so vast that from anywhere near its centre you can't see the walls. After the One-Day War we had all come here to live together, Soviets and Americans together, including the crew of the abandoned interplanetary cycler. The logic was that we needed as large a gene pool as possible. Besides, once the last signals from the moon bases went silent, we huddled for companionship and warmth.

Well, we got along in reasonable harmony, save for the occasional fist fight, despite the fact that our two nations had wiped each other out. We avoided political talk, or any discussion of constitutions or voting rights or common ownership of means of production. We were too few to need grand political theories; we would let future generations figure it out. We thought we would have time, you see.

We walked on towards the farm domes, with their laboriously tilled fields of potatoes and yams and green beans. The work we'd put in was heartbreakingly clear from the quality of the soil we'd managed to create from Martian dirt. We'd even imported earthworms. But a spindly, yellowed crop was our only reward.

The native Mars life seemed to be struggling too. Between the domes was a small botanical garden I'd established myself, open to the Martian elements. The native stock looked *different* from my first impression, on that wonderful Independence Day of discovery. The cacti were shrivelled and tougher-looking, and the trees I'd planted had hardly grown. Adult specimens, which had littered the north-facing slopes of Hellas in tremendous forests, were dying back too.

A gaggle of kids ran by, coming from the alpaca pens, yelling to each other. They were bundled up in shabby coats and alpaca-wool hats, and they all wore face masks. The kids had always loved the alpacas. Verity and I, two fragile old folk, had to pause to let them by.

'Do you know,' she said, 'I didn't understand a single word any of them said.' After her decades with Alexei she had a faint Slavic accent. 'The kids seem to be making up their own language, a kind of pidgin. Maybe we should call it Russ-lish. Rung-lish.'

'How about Wronglish?'

That made her laugh, just for a second, this dust-ridden, careworn, sanctimonious matriarch at my side.

We paused by the alpaca domes ourselves, where those spindly beasts, imported as embryos from the mountains of South America, peered out at us, or scraped apathetically at the scrubby grass that grew at their feet.

'I think it was the alpacas I noticed first,' Verity said slowly. 'How reluctant they became to leave their domes.'

I took a deep breath, sucking in the stale odours of my own mask. 'Did Alexei ever talk to you about his conclusions?'

'No, he didn't. But I was married to the man for twenty-five years, Puddephat, and I was never completely dumb, even though I was no double-dome like you two. I learned to read his moods. And I knew that *the air pressure is dropping.* That's obvious. A high-school barometer would show it. The partial pressure of oxygen is falling even faster. There's something's wrong with Mars.'

I shook my head. 'Actually, I think Mars is just fine. It just isn't fine for us, that's all.'

She stood, silent, grave.

I sighed. 'I'll tell you what Alexei concluded, and I agree with him. Look.' I scratched axes for a graph in the crimson dirt with my toe. 'Here's a conventional view of Mars – what we believed must be true before we landed here. When it was young, Mars was warm and wet, with a thick blanket of air, and deep oceans. Like Earth, in many ways. That phase might have lasted a couple of billion years. But Mars is smaller than the Earth, and further from the sun. As the geology seized up and the volcanoes died back, and the sunlight got to work breaking up the upper atmosphere, Mars lost a lot of its air. Here's the air pressure declining over time . . .' I sketched a graph falling sharply at first, but then bottoming out before hitting zero. 'Much of the water seeped away into deep underground aquifers and froze down there, or at the poles. But still you finished up with conditions that were only a little more extreme than in places on Earth. Mars was like high country, we thought. Scattered lakes, vegetation. Verity, this decline took billions of years – plenty of time for life to adapt.'

She nodded. 'Hence the cacti and the trees. Now you're telling me this is all wrong.'

'We, and Alexei especially, have had decades now to take a good close look at Mars. And what we find doesn't tally with this simple picture of a one-off decline.

'We found extensive lava fields much younger than we'd expected – a whole series of them, one on top of the other. Sandwiched in between the lava strata we found traces of savage glaciation, and periods of water flows – river valleys, traces of outflow events, even shorelines. And we found thin bands of fossils, evidence of life growing actively for brief periods, overlaid by featureless sandstone – the relics of dead ages of windblown dust storms. You can date all this with crater counts. Cycles, over and over.

'Here's what Alexei came to believe.' I scuffed out the graph with my toe, and sketched another. 'Mars did start out warm and wet. It had to be so; we see the trace of huge oceans. The biosphere itself is the legacy of that age. But that warm phase was short-lived. Mars lost almost all its air, catastrophically.' I drew a new line that cut right down to the zero line.

'How low?'

'Hard to say. To no more than one per cent of Earth's sea-level pressure. You can tell that from the evidence of the dust transport, the rock-shattering extremes of temperature, the solar weathering...'

I sketched it for her, speaking, drawing. Mars's natural condition is dry and all but airless. All the water is either locked up in polar ice caps or is sunk deep in a network of subterranean aquifers. The air is so thin there's virtually no shielding from the sun, and no heat capacity to keep in the warmth at night; you swing daily from heat to a withering cold. The only thing that moves is the dust, swirling around in a trace of air.

'And life, Verity, life huddles underground, living off the planet's inner warmth, and seeps of liquid water in the cracks in the rocks. Spores and seeds and microbes, hiding from the raw sunlight.'

She pulled off her mask and breathed in, a deep gulping, rasping breath. 'It ain't that way now, Puddephat.'

'No. But the way it is *now*, as it happens, is unusual for Mars. We're coming to the end of a volcano summer.'

'A what?'

'Which is when things change.' I drew a series of spikes reaching up from the flatlined graph. 'Mars is still warm inside. Every so often the big Tharsis volcanoes blow their tops. They pump out a whole atmosphere, of carbon dioxide and methane and other stuff, and a blanket of dust and ash that warms the world up enough for the permafrost to melt...'

'And life takes its brief chance.'

'You've got it. Mars turns green in a flash, maybe just a few thousand years. The native life spreads seeds and spores far and wide. At the peak of each summer there probably is some motility – Martian moulds squirming in the dirt, Alexei was right about that – but we came too late to see them directly.

'But, just as quickly, the heat leaks away, and the air starts to thin. The end, when it comes, is probably rapid – a catastrophic decline – lots of feedback loops working together to destroy the life-bearing conditions.'

Her face was hard. 'And then it's back to the dustbowl.'

'Yes. Alexei thought he mapped six such episodes, six summers. The first was about a billion years after the planet formed. The second a one-and-a-half billion years ago, and then eight hundred million years ago, two hundred million, one hundred million—'

162

'And now.'

'Yeah. We were lucky, Verity, we humans, to come along just now, to see Mars bloom, for it's a rare event.'

'Or unlucky,' she said acidly.

'I suppose so. In normal times, we couldn't even have landed the way we did, in a big glider of a MEM. Air too thin. You'd need heat shields, parachutes, rockets...'

'We maybe wouldn't have come here. And maybe we wouldn't have had all this extra tension over Mars, over the future in space. Maybe we wouldn't have gone to war at all. And now...' She looked around at the shabby huddle of our settlement, the yellowing plastic, the broken-down machines, the dying crops, the bundled-up, wheezing children. 'We thought we were safe, here on Mars. Or at least that we had a chance. A new world, a new roll of the dice for humanity. But if the atmosphere collapses we won't be able to live here.'

'No. In, say, a century, tepees and bonfires won't cut it. You might as well be living on the moon. If we'd had more time, more resupply from home—'

'We were lured here by a lie. A transient phenomenon.'

I reached out and took her hand. 'Verity – all these years. When I close my eyes I can still see you sitting in the chair in Mount Wilson, smiling as I showed you Mars... It seems like yesterday. I don't begrudge you Alexei. You had a good life, I can see that. But now he's gone, and maybe—'

She snatched her hand away. 'What are you talking about, Puddephat? My children are going to die here, and their children, without meaning, without hope. What do you think we're going to do, in your head – sit together on a porch, holding hands and smiling as we give out the suicide pills?'

'Verity...'

She stalked off.

And I was left alone with the alpacas, and my graph in the dirt.

Hell City, Mars. 4 July 2026.

Even now I'm not alone, probably. Some other group may be huddled up against another air machine, bleeding power off peeling Soviet solar cells. We could never reach each other. Doubt if my old pressure suit would fit me any more – but it's a moon suit you need on Mars now.

Anyhow, that's it for me. At eighty-three, I'm probably the oldest man left alive on any of the worlds. I'll raise Old Glory one more time over the sands of Mars, and toast her with the very last drop of my Soviet potato vodka, and bury this tin chest, and wait for the dust storms to bury *me* . . .

I guess I should finish the story.

We didn't need suicide pills in the end. When the youngsters figured out that my generation had blown up one world and dumped them into lethal conditions on another, they went crazy. A war of the age cadres, you could call it. Verity died in the chapel, praying to God for succour, telling the young ones they would be damned for their sins; her own grandchildren blew the chapel up. I daresay we could have lasted longer, if we'd eked everything out as carefully as we could. But to what end? So we could live to see the last molecule of oxygen rust out of the air?

Mars abides. Yes, it's a consolation that in the far future, in fifty or a hundred million years, when my bones are dust, and Earth has healed over and is a mindless green point in the sky, the great volcanoes will shout again and bring Mars to life once more, though we will be gone. There's always that, and – whoever you are, whoever reads this – I hope you won't think too badly of us.

It was one heck of a ride, though, wasn't it?

JONAS JAMES PUDDEPHAT.

EAGLE SONG

7510 BC

Wolf Cry led Spring Snow out of the camp and up the track to the ridge and the Giant's Stone. It was deep in the night, but this was midsummer, and the huge sky was a deep blue speckled with stars. The way was easy to find.

They were both breathing hard by the time they reached the Stone. But Wolf was just fifteen years old, Spring sixteen, both lean and fit, and they recovered quickly. 'There.' Wolf pointed high in the sky. 'See that? The new star.'

Spring looked up. Her eyes were wide, her small mouth open, and a pretty pin of carved antler held her skin cloak fixed at her throat. Wolf felt something churn deep inside him, churn with longing. She said, 'Well, I can hardly miss it.' She looked away uneasily, and glanced back the way they had come, to the camp by the lake.

From here they could see the sweep of the landscape, the lake flat and still, the huts hunched by the shore, cages of bent-over poles draped with skin and reed thatch. Thin threads of smoke rose up from the ruddy glow of the hearths. Wolf could hear a dog growl in its sleep, and somebody snoring – old Speaker, probably – small sounds that rose up into the still air. Around the camp the wildwood was black in this light and foreboding, but it was broken by the smouldering scars of fire. The people burnt the reeds; the new growth that followed attracted the deer to the water.

Spring said, 'I could have seen your star from down there, at my mother's side. Why did you need to bring me up here?'

But there was something about this particular star that Wolf Cry longed to share with her. 'Spring – it changes. The star.'

She frowned. 'What do you mean? Does it wander? Will it fall? Do you think it will sprout hair? I've seen *that* before.'

'No. I never heard anybody talking about any other star like this. Sometimes it's there. And sometimes it's not.' He opened and closed his fist, trying to make her understand. 'I saw it. A few nights ago it was fast, like this,' and he flapped his fingers quickly. 'But it slowed down. I counted it with my breath. One breath. Another. Then two, then three, then five.' Fingers flapped, flapped.

'You're talking nonsense,' she said. She was shivering despite the warmth of the night. 'Stars don't blink like, like an *eye*. It's not blinking now, is it?'

'No,' he admitted. 'It kept getting longer between blinks. I tried to count it, five and five until there were four fives, and it blinked again, and then—'

She shook her head, denying this strangeness. The people knew the sky as intimately as they knew the land, for it informed them of the times when the deer and horses and aurochs ran, when the forest's fruit ripened, and when the snow would return. Any change was something to be wary of. 'I don't like this, Wolf.' She moved away from him into the shadow of the Stone, and stepped on something that crunched under her feet. 'What's *this*? Oh, it's Speaker's old mask . . .' She reached down and picked up a skull adorned with antlers, one broken in two. She dropped it in disgust. 'I think I cut my foot. *And* I dropped my antler pin. What a mess this is.' She clutched her skin cloak, which had come loose. 'I'm going back to my mother. Wolf, you should come too. Stars that blink –'

'I saw it,' he insisted.

'Nobody has told of such things, so they can't be real, and that's that.' She stomped back down the track, her irritation and nervousness obvious in her stride.

Alone, Wolf sat miserably with his back to the Giant's Stone. If he'd hoped to impress Spring Snow by bringing her up here, he had done the opposite. He picked up the skull mask. Speaker had worn it during his dream dances, the times when he spoke to the animals and the birds and the fish. He had discarded it for a more handsome stag's skull. And Wolf saw something else that gleamed white, like the skull. It was Spring's deer-antler needle. Idly he used the needle to scrape at the skull, scratching spirals and starburst patterns into the worn, much-handled surface.

He looked up at the new star. It was so bright it looked like a fleck of the sun, he thought, and the same sort of colour. If only it had blinked for Spring, even just once, she would have believed him and everything would have been different. But no star was going to perform for his benefit.

Or would it? Why would a star blink at all? What *was* a star? A stone, an animal, a bird, a person, a god? What could a star see of the tiny movements of the people, their little camp? But he glanced over at the smoke that rose from the reeds they had set burning, and further across the hillside at the great gash of the clearing they had burned two years ago and later abandoned, a scar not yet healed. Could a star see such vast burnings, such changes in the land? If it was trying to speak to him, what was it saying? But even as he formulated the questions he knew he would never find an answer.

And just then the star blinked again, turning dark for a heartbeat, two, three, before shining down on him once more.

949 BC

It was chance that revealed the strange star to Gouen, that cold summer night. Chance that her eyes were drawn up to its unnatural flickering, from the decomposing corpse of her child by the lake.

It was midsummer, but it was cold, cloudy, wet – a dismal season, nothing like the brilliant summers Gouen remembered from her own childhood. And it was lonely too. The family's great cone-shaped house was abandoned save for herself, and the fields marked out across the hillside by reeves and low walls were populated only by weeds and young trees, come to take back their ancient domain.

Her sisters and their children had already fled the hunger, to throw themselves on the mercy of Podraig in his brooding fort further down the valley. Nobody could farm here on the uplands any more, only in the valleys and the lowlands, all of which were owned by men like Podraig with his swords of iron.

Gouen, twenty-five years old, knew she would have to follow her sisters. For Gouen's own husband was gone, dead of overwork. And she would have to trade the last pitiful remnants of her father's legacy, the pottery, the bits of fine fabrics, the bronze daggers nobody wanted any more, for a place in Podraig's petty domain.

But she would not leave, not yet. Not while her only daughter Magda, just eight years old when she died, still lay on the sky burial platform by the water; not until the birds and the worms and the flies had done their work, and Gouen could take her cleansed bones to inter them in the barrow of her grandmothers.

When the weather permitted, she sat through the night on her blanket by the lake shore, by Magda's platform. Tonight was mild, relatively, and the stars shone through breaks in the cloud cover. The midsummer sky was pale, and she could easily see the ridge and the brooding mass of the Giant's Stone and its ring of pillars, on a spot where, it was said, the skull of the Giant who had carried the great Stone was buried, with horns sprouting out of his broken face, and the bone marked with spirals and stars. Gouen had been very small the last time anybody had worshipped up there. When the weather failed them the farmers had abandoned the old stone gods and had taken to sacrificing and propitiating at the edge between land and water, the border between this world and the next.

And tonight, praying for repose for her daughter, Gouen would make another sacrifice to the water gods: one of her last daggers, a thin blade of bronze that had been handled by her grandfathers since time out of mind.

It was just as she was about to jam the dagger between two boulders, meaning to break the blade before casting it in the water, that she noticed the flickering in the sky.

Entranced, she watched the new star come and go, shining longer and more steadily with each return, as if it were trying to say something to her. She counted the shining by her own breaths: two breaths, three, five, eight, thirteen... The glow of the star was bright, surely brighter than any other star in the sky, and it had a yellowness to it that reminded her of the sun.

Magda's white face was turned up to the star: poor Magda who had never known a single summer of warmth and play.

Gouen lurched to her feet, stiff from sitting on the damp ground, pulled her woollen blanket around her shoulders, and stumbled over to the platform of the dead. Worms curled in Magda's vacant eye sockets, and flies rose up from her open mouth. It was unbearable to Gouen that Magda could not see the sunny star. How it would have delighted her!

Her father's dagger was in her hand.

She leaned over Magda and scraped hard at the bone forehead, her movements jerky and anxious. She drew a star shape, there on the pale bone under the remnants of flesh. It would be a mother's last gift to a lost daughter, to show her this shining jewel of light that rode over the petty concerns of the human world, the rain and the mud, the grasping of men like Podraig. She scraped and scraped.

But the skull rolled loose on its neck. And before she was done, the bronze tip blunted. She threw away the dagger and fell weeping on her daughter.

1238 AD

At the close of the sixth day of the new star's apparition, Brother Wilfred summoned Ibn Mazur to his side. Wilfred had the Moor set out chairs and a table on the green beside the abbey's cloister, with parchment and quills and ink, and books and hourglasses.

From here Ibn Mazur had an uninterrupted view of the countryside, of the lake and the village on the upland beside it, and the crag with its brooding rock and silent attendant monoliths. It was midsummer. The sun had set but the sky was still a powder blue, and only a few stars yet shone – one of them the enigmatic newcomer.

For just a moment this dismal corner of Wales evoked some of the beauty of far-off al-Andalus. Ibn Mazur could never return to the land of his birth. But he was alive, thanks to the charity of the brothers of this Christian house.

Wilfred saw nothing of the evening. For days he had been staring at the sun through his bits of parchment with their pinprick holes, determined to discover if the star's light was indeed the same as sunlight. Now his eyes were tired, he said; as he waited impatiently for the day to fade he sat back in his chair with a damp towel over his eyes, white hair sticking up around his shaved scalp. Unseeing he might be, but his mind bubbled with speculation. 'You say you have the date I asked of you, Ibn Mazur?'

'I do.'

Wilfred breathed, a frail old man's excitement apparent in the way his bony fingers flexed. 'Then tell me – but not yet...'

When the winking star had first appeared in the sky, Wilfred had been excited to learn of local legends that seemed to be connected to it. Seven centuries after Augustine's mission of conversion, the people of this remote place still clung to remnants of pagan belief. And they said this had been a holy land long before the Norman abbey had been built here to replace a Saxon church, which in turn had been built over a sylvan temple of the pre-Roman British. All of this was a link to the deep past, Wilfred believed, to legends of a dead child with a third eye that had gazed up at a winking star, and to even older legends of the primordial giant who built the landscape and was now buried under the great Stone. Wilfred had seized on Ibn Mazur's scholarship, and had urged the Moor to check through the almagests he had carried since his enslavement in Granada to determine if the

Moors had any record of those earlier apparitions. After all, a winking star must have been visible all across the world, if it existed.

Somewhat to his own surprise, Ibn Mazur had been successful. More than two thousand years before, long before the Prophet's revelation, such a sighting had been made by a Chinese court astronomer, and written down in a book of astronomical oddities that had eventually been brought to al-Andalus by traders along the Mongols' Silk Road.

It was this Chinese date that Wilfred now deferred hearing, like a child putting aside a strawberry the better to enjoy its flavour later. 'Let us review what we know. The star itself—'

'Is known to the Arabs as Altair.'

'And to Ptolemy as Alpha Aquilae, the first star of the constellation of the Eagle.'

Ibn Mazur bowed his head. 'But the light we see, so like sunlight as you have observed, is not that of the star itself. In the intervals when the new star is dark, we still see Altair shining as we remember it.'

'We know that it has shone in its intermittent way for six days now, in which time it has undergone two cycles of pulsing – starting with the rapid flickering, the shining intervals gradually lengthening.'

'So we believe. But we cannot see the star easily in the day, and our observations of the beginning of the first cycle are uncertain, being based on the ramblings of a wide-eyed boy and an old woman of the village.'

Wilfred waved that away. 'Well, we have one more chance to observe a full cycle with scholarly precision.'

Ibn Mazur frowned. 'Why just one? Why not many?'

'The star is ruled by numbers – or so I believe, Ibn Mazur. We have had two cycles of three days; a third cycle would round off the set neatly.' The talk of numbers made Wilfred agitated; despite his great age he had a boyish enthusiasm for his studies. 'I cannot wait any more. The date, Ibn Mazur! Tell me what the Chinese said!'

Ibn Mazur had managed to convert the date from an archaic Chinese form to the Arabs' elegant calendar and then work it through the Christians' own error-ridden calculations. 'The Chinese saw the star nine hundred and forty-nine years before Christ.'

Wilfred's mouth worked. 'Nine hundred and forty-nine! How long ago is that? Added to our date, which is one thousand, two hundred and thirty-eight years – oh! Numbers enchant but baffle me.'

Wilfred was a computistor; his primary job was to figure the movable date of Easter each year. But Ibn Mazur had never yet met a

Christian who could do computations much beyond nine hundred, not even a computistor. 'I worked it out on my abacus,' he said dryly. 'The apparition was two thousand, one hundred and eighty-seven years ago.'

'Two thousand, one hundred...' Wilfred muttered, adding up figures in his head. 'Why, I believe that number is divisible by three!'

Ibn Mazur took a bit of parchment and a pen, and wrote down the figure in his own Arabic numbers. Because of his affliction all but two of his fingers were bandaged stumps, and his writing was clumsy and slow. 'You are correct,' he said at length. 'The product of the division is also divisible by three...'

It took them a few minutes to establish that two thousand, one hundred and eighty-seven was in fact three multiplied by itself seven times.

Wilfred was so excited by this result that he sat upright and his towel fell from his face. Ibn Mazur was shocked at how red and watery his eyes were. 'Numbers, Moor! I told you, New Altair is a star made up of numbers, woven by God and hurled into the sky!'

Ibn Mazur looked up with some unease. 'Perhaps you are right. But why should God speak to us in this way?'

'To reassure us, perhaps, that there is an order in all things? To remind us that He is *here*, in an age of chaos that crowds around us...'

Like all thoughtful Christians Ibn Mazur had met, Wilfred fretted over the trajectory of history. Across Europe, save only for Iberia, Islam was triumphant against the forces of Christianity. Further afield, the pagan Mongols were ripping in turn into the bellies of the great Islamic empires of the east. It was a world where Christ's triumph seemed very distant indeed.

And yet there were gentler consolations, Ibn Mazur thought. He looked down at the village. Tithed to the abbey, it was a rude collection of longhouses where, Ibn Mazur had been horrified to learn, the people lived *with* their animals. Tonight those few villagers not yet in their houses kept their eyes averted from the sky, for these Welsh were a superstitious lot who feared the new flickering star.

But Ibn Mazur had experienced great kindness here. There were no slaves in Wales or England, or none that Ibn Mazur had encountered; he himself had been set free after his purchase in Bristol by a lord who valued his skills in arithmetic. There was law: the manorial courts ensured that a rough balance was maintained between the interests of the peasants and the lords and bishops. And the Christian Church, for all its infantile theology, cared for its flock from cradle to grave in return for devotion and moral rectitude. Wilfred spoke earnestly of the Fourth Lateran Council, when the Church had resolved that salvation was available to all, not just the most righteous. This was not Islam, but there were worse systems.

Ibn Mazur himself had cause to be grateful for Christian charity. He had caught his ailment when the Viking raiders who had captured him had traded him through African ports. When it became impossible to hide his condition, his lord had not thrown him out or put him to death, but consigned him to the care of this remote abbey with its hospital of St Lazarus, patron saint of lepers.

Would a star, or a being riding on a star, be able to see such petty sufferings and kindnesses? Perhaps such a being would make out only the greater works of man: the walls of Hadrian and Offa, or the way humans had turned so much of their world into a patchwork of farms. Perhaps, then, the flickering star transcended human divisions among men. Perhaps the star presaged a better future in which Christian and Muslim would be able to put aside centuries of warfare, and work together on loftier purposes.

Wilfred was agitated. 'Tell me, Moor, I cannot see well, my eyes are tired . . . Has the star gone dark? Has the new cycle of flickering begun?'

Ibn Mazur glanced up. The sunlight sliver had indeed gone out, and only the pale, familiar light of Altair shone. 'It has,' he said softly; and even as he said it the brighter light returned.

'Quickly, man,' Wilfred said. 'The hourglasses . . .'

As the star resumed its flashing, each glare longer than the one preceding, the two of them went into the routine they had rehearsed, of hourglasses and counting and scratched numbers on parchment. It soon became apparent to Ibn Mazur that each successive glow lasted a little more than half as long again as its predecessor.

But Wilfred was after more precision. 'Yes, yes – look at these numbers! It is as I suspected. If you take the first pair, each as a unit of duration, then the next beaming was two units long, and then three, then five, then eight, then thirteen, then—'

'I see the sequence,' Ibn Mazur said. 'I do not understand it.'

'It is additive, man! Look – one plus one is two; I don't need your abacus for *that*. One plus two is three. Two plus three is five . . .'

'Ah.' Each number in the sequence was the sum of the two preceding. Something in Ibn Mazur warmed with satisfaction at the realisation, and yet another part of him cringed. Abstract philosophy was all very well, but could Wilfred be right, that something divinely numerate really was at work above his head, visibly, in the mid-summer sky of Wales?

The two of them continued to work long into the night, measuring the lengthening intervals until they could count no more.

Wilfred turned out to be right that the final sequence of flashes lasted three days, as had the first two, and then the star turned dark, leaving only patient Altair. Wilfred babbled speculation, wondering what strange eyes might see the star when it returned in another three-to-the-seventh years, or three to the sixth or three to the eighth... But Wilfred was not able to see even the end of the new star's nine days, for his eyes were ruined from staring into the mid-summer sun.

After that Ibn Mazur stayed with him, a leprous Moor with a blind Christian. They let the days slide by, neither of them with anywhere else to go, and waited for more messages from a silent sky.

1967 AD

'Neolithic SETI, man,' Neville had promised on the phone. 'That's what I'm talking about. That *and* the Beatles. You've got to be there...'

On that June Sunday, it was early evening by the time Barry Morgan drove up to the ruins of the abbey. The place hadn't changed in the eight or ten years since he and Neville had come up here when they were both still geeky kids at school in Cardiff, fascinated by maths and scared of girls. The abbey still stood gaunt beside its lake, a shell since the dissolution of the monasteries four centuries before. And, older yet, there was the Giant's Stone, a great glacial erratic with its ring of standing stones. But the pale light of the four-day-old new star – the sunlight beacon, as astronomers like Neville were calling it – was already visible in the evening sky. And Barry could see the TV aerial Neville had fixed to the stone wall of the abbey.

Barry took the box of bottled beer from the boot of his car and strolled up to the abbey. Neville Wilson was on his hands and knees tinkering with the TV's tuning and its battery pack. He had brought blankets, a hamper of sandwiches, flasks – a regular picnic. Barry had brought nothing but beer. He dumped his bottles on the floor. 'I can't believe you actually brought that bloody set up here, you mad bugger.'

Neville got to his feet, awkward and shy-looking as ever, and wiped his hands on his corduroy trousers. 'Wotcher, Barry. Or should I say – peace and love?'

'Shut up and have a beer.' Barry sat on a blanket, threw Neville a bottle, and used the flat of his hand and the edge of a tumbled stone to open a bottle for himself. He took a long pull; the beer was warm after the drive up from his mum's home in Cardiff.

The 'Our World' show had already started, Barry saw. This was, he had been surprised to learn, a broadcasting stunt dreamed up by the staid old BBC. For the first time twenty-four countries, something like two hundred million people, were to share a single live show with contributions from each of the individual countries. Right now, rather bafflingly, jolly Swedes were showing off their canoeing skills. 'Is that what they spent all those millions of quid on comsats for? Canoeing?'

Neville grinned. 'Wait until the Beatles come on. You're looking tanned, as far as I can tell under all that facial hair.'

'Ah, that Californian sun. You can't beat it . . .'

But while Barry dressed like a West Coast American, Neville wore pale-brown cords and a crumpled white shirt, and his eyes were hidden behind big Roy Orbison glasses, as if he had been deep-frozen since the fifties. Barry was struck by how much the two of them had grown apart. After their first degrees, while Barry had gone into the private sector, Neville had stayed on at Cambridge to do an astronomy PhD. Not surprising they looked so different, then.

Barry felt like winding him up. 'What a season. The Summer of Star Love, they're calling it now. Out in 'Frisco those hippy chicks just fall over with a bit of banter about peace and love. And a British accent.'

'That's all it means to you, is it? Getting inside the knickers of some spaced-out teenage bird? I wonder what they'd think if they knew you work at a weapons lab like Livermore.'

'Make no difference probably. It's all bollocks, man, all of it. While one end of America is handing out flowers, the other is using helicopter gunships to strafe straw huts in Vietnam. You take what you can grab, just like always.'

'Well, not everybody thinks that way.' Neville pointed at the beacon. 'And besides, that's not bollocks, is it?'

'Ah.' Barry stood, beer in hand, and looked hard at the sunlight beacon. He felt a prickle of scientific curiosity, and envy, for Neville had managed to get involved with the global effort to study the new star. 'Repeating the flickering pattern, is it?'

'Yes. The beam lengths are running through the Fibonacci sequence, as far as we can tell. The SETI boys in America – the search for extraterrestrial intelligence, searching for radio signals from the stars – always thought the aliens would send us a sequence of prime numbers. But if you're going to communicate in mathematics, the Fibonacci series is even more obvious. I mean, it's there in nature, embedded in the spiral shape of the galaxies for instance...'

'And it's definitely coming from Altair.'

'Oh, yes. Seventeen light years away. If we had more time we might be able to get a parallax and prove it for sure, but that depends on the signal lasting longer than nine days – time for the Earth to move significantly in its orbit.' Neville held to a controversial view that there had been previous sightings of the beacon, perhaps in the thirteenth century – there was supposedly a note left by a monk of this very abbey to that effect. That sighting had lasted no longer than nine days; maybe this apparition would cut short too.

'But the light we see,' Barry said, 'has nothing to do with Altair.'

'No way. It's pretty much monochromatic.'

'A laser, then.'

'We think so. Very narrow beam. Pointed right at us. *And* tuned to the peak wavelength of our own sunlight. Not only that, it's got an almost identical apparent magnitude as Sirius, the brightest star in our sky.'

Barry thought that over. 'They intended it for us, then. The Altaireans. They could see us, see the Earth. They designed it, knowing what our sunlight is like, how bright our brightest star must be. Jesus.'

Neville was grinning. 'It's scary, or thrilling, depending how you look at it. We've actually been able to dig out a lot more information. There are slight Doppler shifts on two periodic cycles, one of a few days, the other of years. We think their transmitting station is on a planet. We're seeing the station move towards and away from us, as the planet turns, and travels around its sun.'

'You've worked out their day and year.'

'Yeah. Altair is maybe eleven times as bright as the sun. We think their planet is a big one, turning slowly, about three times as far from Altair as Earth is from the sun.'

'Cool enough for liquid water?'

'We think so.'

'All that from Doppler shifts.' Barry sat again, finished his beer and cracked another bottle. 'I think I'm more interested in the reaction down here on Earth.'

He had seen some of it for himself. For the few days of its patient signalling the sunlight beacon had been a wonder in the press, even crowding Vietnam and the aftermath of Israel's Six Day War off the front pages. The scientists were crowing. The Pope had made an earnest statement about sending the Altaireans evidence of Christ's incarnation. Wernher von Braun had declared, 'With the right funding we'll be at Altair in fifty years.' The UFOlogists said it was a government hoax designed to distract attention from the truth about aliens.

And all over the western world a generation of young people, already blissed out on drugs and music and sunshine, had kicked off a kind of global party. Barry had bluffed his way into one of them, a 'star happening', just a few days ago, at the feet of the Golden Gate Bridge. The drugs and sex had been on tap.

'I suppose the hysteria will wear off,' he said. 'I mean, as far as alien life is concerned the beacon is only a proof of existence, as old Prof Morton would have said at Cambridge. I figure most people believed in aliens anyhow, and half of *them* think they've met them.'

'I don't know,' Neville said thoughtfully, pushing his heavy glasses up his thin nose. 'Yes, it will pass out of the headlines. But even a proof of existence represents a philosophical upheaval – like Copernicus, like Darwin. From now on, we can still theologise if we like, but we're going to have to separate religion from the knowledge that we really do share the universe with a higher power. They might even be here soon; seventeen light years isn't all that far.'

'Um.' Barry swigged his beer and watched the TV. 'Speaking of God . . .' The screen had filled up with an image of John Lennon in a flowery shirt, strumming a guitar and chewing gum.

Neville turned the volume up. He had always been a Beatles fan.

The Beatles were singing in a flower-strewn studio with a string orchestra and acolytes sitting at their feet. Barry recognised Mick Jagger, Donovan, Keith Moon. The song was slow, dreamlike, littered with what sounded like sitars, and very beautiful.

Barry said flatly, 'I see they've all dressed up again. What are they singing?'

'A new song by George. "Eagle Song" – for Aquila, see. Apparently they were going to do something by Lennon, but scrapped it when the sunlight beacon lit up.'

'I hope the Altaireans enjoy this when they get to hear it in seventeen years.' He eyed Neville. 'And this is why they are speaking to us, right? They detected our first radio broadcasts, and now they're flashing their beacon to show they know we're here.'

Neville shook his head. 'That's the consensus. You know I don't agree. I'm convinced they've been signalling since long before the radio age.' Hastily, he ran over the evidence for previous sightings of the beacon. 'Those Chinese were good astronomers; we *know* they made accurate sightings of novas whose relics we can see. And there's a pattern to the dates . . .' He picked up a pad and scribbled: 1967 AD, 1238 AD, 949 BC. 'Look at the intervals. Going back in time, seven hundred and twenty-nine years, then two thousand, one hundred and eighty-seven years – which is precisely three times the previous interval. I'm willing to bet there was a previous event another threefold years before then.'

Barry could never resist a puzzle. 'Three times twenty-one eighty-seven is six thousand, five hundred and sixty-one. Add that to your oldest date . . .' He wrote the result on Neville's list: 7510 BC. 'That's back in the Mesolithic.'

'They can see us. They know how long our year is, and used it as a unit of time.'

'Why all the threes?'

Neville waggled his hand. 'Maybe they have three fingers.'

'Or three cocks. How could they have known we were here in the Mesolithic? We weren't using radios then.'

'No, but we were changing the world already. The big forest clearances came with the farming revolution in the Neolithic, but even in the Mesolithic we were slashing and burning, starting to domesticate plants and animals. You can imagine viewing the composition of a remote planet's atmosphere with some kind of spectroscope. Maybe you can *see* that kind of global change. It would be distinguishable from natural events like volcanoes or asteroid strikes, for instance by the characteristic timescale.'

'And when they saw us starting to farm—'

'They hit us with a beacon. They didn't expect we had radio telescopes, but it was a good guess we had eyes that could see our own sun. God knows what they intended our ancestors to make of the signal, mind. Could have kick-started a Neolithic astronomical revolution, I guess. Pity we weren't a bit smarter. I hope whoever saw it back then found some consolation. Which begs the question, what use will we make of this latest signal?'

'Time will tell,' Barry said.

'I guess so. Anyhow, it's a falsifiable hypothesis. If the pattern persists we can predict the next sighting, after a third of seven hundred and twenty-nine years.' He added another date to the list: 2210 AD.

'Well, you and I won't be around to see it.' Barry had drained another beer, and cracked a third. The Beatles were finishing their song with a long, repetitive coda. Neville stared at them wistfully, a true fan. On impulse Barry dug into his pocket and produced a couple of sugar lumps wrapped in tin foil. 'Here. You ever tried this?'

Neville took one dubiously. 'LSD, right?'

'Makes the world sparkle.' He nibbled his own lump.

'I can't afford to pay you—'

'In Cardiff it costs about a quid a tab. Forget about it. Listen, Neville. What you said about the Altaireans being a higher culture. How much power would you need to send a signal like the sunlight beacon?'

Neville put down the lump and rubbed his nose. 'Well, we're not sure. The laser will cast a spot of some size across the solar system, like a searchlight. We don't actually know how big the spot is, how far it extends beyond the Earth. NASA are trying to measure it using their Mariner deep-space probes. It depends how good their aim is, and how tight the beam is. I mean, you'd have to fire the laser to where Earth was going to be in seventeen years' time... Across that target spot you need to maintain a flux equivalent to the light reaching us from Sirius.'

'So how much power?'

'In the terawatts. That's surely beyond us for the near future, but a Kardashev Type II culture could manage it easily.'

'A what?'

The Kardashev types were a theoretical grading of alien civilisations based on the power they could muster: Type II controlled the entire output of a star, and Type III a galaxy. Humanity was somewhat less than a Type I, controlling a planet's energy supply.

Barry nibbled his sugar, thinking that over. 'A terawatt laser would be a hell of a weapon.'

Neville frowned. 'Typical of you to think that way. Anything's a weapon, potentially. I could choke you with flowers.'

'I guess so.' But Barry thought of himself as a realist. Tanks burned in the desert around Israel: *that* was the truth of the world, and maybe the universe. His thinking loosened by the booze and the drugs, he let ideas run around in his head. The Altaireans had offered evidence of the *possibility* of a pretty powerful technology ... Hell, more than that. The demonstration of a working model, evidence of its performance parameters. And knowing that, you could back-fit a design. He began to run over proposals he could make back at Livermore.

Neville handed back the sugar cube. 'Sorry, man. Not for me.'

'Forget it.'

The Beatles had gone now, to be replaced by a feature on trams in Australia. Neville turned the set off and they sat in the dark, gazing up at the beacon. Barry was content with the silence, as he waited for the drug to kick in.

2210 AD

By the time he had finished his walk to the weapons installation in the shade of the Giant's Stone crag, Owen Wilson was out of breath. At sixty-eight he was too old for this, too old to be sneaking around in the dark.

He knew he didn't have much time before he was detected. But he gave himself one minute to rest. Leaning against a bit of surviving wall of the old abbey, he took a swig of his water, and a deep breath of the hot, smoky air. There actually wasn't much left of the ruined abbey, whose stones had been ground up to make the concrete base of the weapon.

He got on with it.

He stepped forward towards the installation, his way illuminated by a torch strapped to his forehead; the sky was a lid of smog. The Morgan laser was surrounded by an electrified fence and monitored by a surveillance system, but Owen had used a microgrenade to knock out the fence's juice, and smart viruses were already at work in the Unitary Authority's data processing systems to make him invisible to these electronic eyes. He just snipped through the wire and walked in.

He soon reached the weapon.

It looked like a cannon, its metres-wide snout poking stubbornly at the obscured sky. He had studied its design carefully, and knew just which maintenance hatch to open, just where to plug in the software patch he had prepared. In only minutes, with a grind of massive servomotors, the laser prepared to move, obeying his commands. Owen allowed himself to punch the air.

And yet his triumph was muted. He looked up into the sky. It was midsummer day – not that you'd know it any more, every day was as murky and warm as the rest, right through the year. And today, somewhere above the obscured sky, he was sure, the sunlight beacon from Altair was once again pinging Earth with its hopeful Fibonacci sequence. The story of many-times-great-grandfather Neville, who had witnessed the last apparition back in the twentieth century, had been passed down as a family legend. As Owen had grown up, in between his work in the big offshore food factory in Cardiff Bay, he had been able to verify the old story with a bit of data mining. And he had been thrilled to discover that his long-dead ancestor had predicted that the next apparition from Altair would come in Owen's lifetime.

But he would see nothing of it. The sky was entirely shrouded, and deliberately so, to protect Britain, Russia, North America and the rest of the Unitary Authority commonwealth from the Chinese laser mounts on the moon. Make the air opaque with aerosols and endless fires and you could scatter the light of the most intense laser weapon, even the big Chinese petawatt monsters; the laser war continued between the space platforms, but at least the planet itself had some degree of protection.

And then there was political control. With the sky covered you could make the sunlight beacon invisible for the first time in its ten-thousand-year history of interaction with mankind. The citizens of the Authority need never be troubled by the existence of another world, another civilisation – or by the idea that other possibilities might exist, a destiny other than a war that had now ground on for a century.

But tonight, Owen believed, the air might clear enough, if not for him to see the sunlight beacon for himself, at least enough to give this big old beast a shot at *replying*, on behalf of mankind. The Morgan was antiquated by comparison with the latest Chinese weapons, capable of no more than a few megawatts, and much of its brightness would be lost even before the signal got out of the murky atmosphere of Earth, let alone began its seventeen-year journey to Altair. But Owen was confident the Altaireans would be able to pick up the signal, and to read the message he intended to encode into it: 'SOS' in Morse code, easy to decipher for a culture that had surely been monitoring human radio broadcasts since Marconi. A weapon used to send a cry for help.

Help us – that was all he wanted to say. Help us, for we have misused your gift and your example; we used the idea of your beacon and turned it into a weapon. Neville Wilson had long ago calculated that if the beacon continued to recur at intervals reducing by a factor of three every time – after another eighty-one years, twenty-seven, nine, three, one – the ten-thousand-year sequence would come to an end in 2331, not much more than a century away. What would happen then? Would the Altaireans' mighty ships slide into the solar system?

But Owen was by no means sure mankind would still be around on that date. So he needed to send his reply today. *Help us now—*

The shot's noise was soft, from a silenced gun, but the round ricocheted noisily off the barrel of the repositioning laser.

Owen turned off his torch and stood stock-still. In the murky light he couldn't even see who was shooting at him or how many there were. There were no voices, no sounds of footsteps, only that single shot. With a grind of seized-up bearings the laser began to tilt up. He crept round towards its muzzle. His programme might yet be completed, his signal sent—

Another shot. This one slammed into the weapon's concrete base; he felt chips fly up and dig into his heel, through his sock. The petty pain seemed absurd. Surely they could see him, even if he couldn't see them. It occurred to him that they were playing with him.

Another shot screamed past his head.

He cried out, and found himself stumbling forward against the laser's open barrel. He held onto its rim, and as the cannon tilted back he was lifted up bodily. He heard a hum, felt in his gut the huge energies gathering. His fingers strained to hold his weight. Another shot cracked past his head.

The laser grumbled, as if waking.

His eyes registered the light for the briefest of instants before his retinas were seared.

And he cast a shadow kilometres long as the beam punched through the air, seeking Altair.

OTHER TODAYS

THE PEVATRON RATS

'Mr Hathaway, it's Amanda Breslin. Ms Breslin from the high school?'

A call from Penny's teacher wasn't particularly welcome in the middle of the working day. I kicked closed the office door. 'Yes, Ms Breslin. Is something wrong?'

'Not exactly...'

That hesitation triggered memories of meeting her at the last parent–teacher night: a slim woman, intense, shy, eyes that drew you in. Penny, twelve years old, was on a school field trip to Harwell today, the nuclear lab. I had lurid imaginings of what might have gone wrong. 'Go on.'

'Penny found some rats.'

'What?'

'Two rats, to be precise. Babies. The problem is, the rats shouldn't have been where they were. Couldn't have been, in fact. The lab authorities suspect this is some kind of hoax played by the kids. And since it was Penny who found them...'

Ever since the cancer that had taken her mother three years before, I had fretted continually about Penny's welfare. Now Ms Breslin's prevaricating about what seemed a trivial matter irritated me. 'What's this all about? Where exactly did she find these damn rats?'

I heard Ms Breslin take a breath. 'In a particle accelerator.'

'I'll be there.' And I hung up, rudely. I made some excuses to old Harrison, the senior partner, and went to get my car.

That was the start of it for me. Soon, of course, the whole county was going to be getting calls and mails about rats turning up where they shouldn't be. I suppose it's my peculiar distinction to have been the very first.

Harwell is only a couple of miles west of Didcot, where we lived. It didn't take me long to drive over.

Penny was doing fine at school, as far as I could tell. That was the trouble – I was increasingly unsure that I *could* tell. The school itself

185

was very alien to a twentieth-century relic like me, with more tablets than teachers, who all had job titles like 'motivational counsellor'. Penny and I had muddled through the first couple of years after we lost her mother, when she was still essentially a child. Now, at twelve, I knew she was moving into a more complex phase of her life – still fascinated by horses, but increasingly distracted by bad-boy soccer players with sculpted hair.

I was an office manager for a firm of solicitors. I can handle people reasonably well, I think – crusty old lawyers and their clients, anyhow. How well I could handle the moods and dilemmas of a teenage daughter I was much less sure. Maybe today was going to be a test.

On the way in I looked up Harwell on my phone. The place had been founded after the Second World War as a nuclear laboratory, on an old RAF airfield close to Oxford University. Some good work was done there, in fission reactor designs and fusion experiments. But as the decades wore away the slowdown of government science and the reduced threat of nuclear war saw the place go through complicated sell-offs. RAL, the Rutherford Appleton Laboratory, still operates within what is now known, almost inevitably, as the Harwell Science and Innovation Campus. A few months back RAL had briefly made the headlines when the public were first allowed to see the revolutionary new Pevatron, a new breed of particle accelerator, which was due to come online in a couple more years. And that was why Penny's school party had gone there that day.

As I approached the gate I had to drive through a sullen picket line of protestors. They were calm and sane-looking, and their placards, leaning against the outer fence, were wordy warnings about the dangers of doing high-energy physics in the middle of the English countryside: black holes might be created, or wormholes, or 'vacuum collapses' might be triggered, none of which meant very much to me.

Ms Breslin met me at the security gate, as I signed bits of paper and submitted to retinal and DNA scans. I even had to pass through a Geiger-counter trap, as if I might try to smuggle radioactive materials *into* a nuclear laboratory. Then we walked across the laboratory campus, side by side, her pace rapid, edgy. 'Harwell's a major local employer, of course,' she said, talking too fast, 'and for the kids to be able to see a world-class science facility in development right on their doorstep is a great opportunity – it helps that I know a couple of the scientists on staff here personally . . .'

It was a bright spring day, late April, with a bit of wind that blew

Ms Breslin's hair around her face. She was a slim woman, tall, in her late thirties, a bit younger than me, with hints of grey in her tied-back brown hair. She struck me as wistful, a woman at the end of her youth and, I guessed, alone; she wore no rings.

The lab buildings were blocky and old-fashioned, laid out in a rough grid pattern, like a military base. But every so often I glimpsed a dome, silent and sinister, rising beyond the tiled rooftops, and much of the site was sealed off by fences plastered with warning signs and radiation symbols.

The facility we were approaching was a kilometre across, but unprepossessing, like a ring of garden sheds set out across the scarred runway of the old airfield.

'That's the Pevatron,' I prompted her.

'It is a fantastic development,' she said. 'Called the Pevatron because it can reach energies of peta-electron volts – that's ten to power fifteen, a million billion. Orders of magnitude more even than the big new International Linear Collider in Japan, and at a fraction of the cost and scale thanks to the new methods they've developed here. It's all to do with room-temperature superconductors controlled at the femtosecond scale by a new quantum computer – I have a physics PhD myself and I barely understand it . . .'

Given that qualification I wondered how she had ended up teaching high school kids. 'And it's infested by rats,' I said.

'Apparently.' Ms Breslin's nervousness was overwhelming her now. 'I'm sorry to have caused you so much trouble.'

I smiled at her. 'Don't be. You should try running elderly solicitors. Stuff happens. And thanks for getting me out here so quickly.'

She seemed surprised to be thanked. Her eyes widened, those eyes I remembered, seawater green.

Schoolkids, teachers, white-coated lab workers and a couple of management suits gathered by an entrance. I saw Penny, slim and small in her school uniform. Penny was actually cradling the two baby rats that were the cause of all the trouble, pink slivers of flesh. She smiled at me in the wry, almost adult way she had. 'Hello, Dad. Look what I found.'

It was where she had found the animals that was the problem.

An apologetic site manager showed me a ball of glass and steel a couple of metres across, sealed save for vents to either side. 'When the Pevatron is operational the particle beams will run through this sphere.' The manager was about fifty, greying, a scientist turned administrator. He used his fists to mime particles colliding. 'Electrons and positrons will slam into each other at a whisker below the speed of light. Because they're elementary particles, you see, unlike the protons they use in the LHC in Switzerland, which are bags of quarks, we can control the energies of collision very precisely... Well. The point is this chamber will be evacuated when the facility is in use.'

'A vacuum.'

'And so it's entirely sealed off, save for the valves to either side.'

'There must be air in it today, or these baby rats wouldn't have survived.'

'There's nothing wrong with the rats, Dad,' Penny said brightly. 'In fact they were nice and warm when I picked them up, warm little bellies.'

'But,' said the manager, 'there's no way the rats could have got in there in the first place...'

I inspected the cage for myself. A hermetically sealed sphere, two baby rats, no sign of a mother or nest. It was a locked-room mystery, with rats.

When Penny found the rats, the junior technician who had been hosting the school party immediately got suspicious.

'Which is why we called you,' said the site manager. 'Ben's guess that Penny had planted the rats did make sense. Occam's razor, you know. The simplest hypothesis is likely to be correct. We have to take such allegations seriously – terrorism and all that. But in this case Occam let us down. We looked over the sphere; there's simply no way the brightest child, and I'm sure Penny is bright as a button, could have set this up. Well, we got into the sphere and saved the baby rats. Didn't want a gaggle of traumatised schoolchildren on our hands.' He sighed. 'Of all the issues I've had to wrestle with over this project – academic rivalries, funding cuts, anti-science protestors – I never expected to have to deal with vermin! Well. I do apologise for your trouble. Of course we'll take care of those two beasts for you.' He reached out for the baby rats.

Penny clutched them to her chest. 'What will you do, destroy them?'

'Well...'

'Oh, Dad, can't we keep them? They've already been locked up in a particle accelerator. And they're only babies.'

'Penny, be serious.'

'Lots of people have rats for pets,' Penny said, more in hope than belief.

Ms Breslin said, 'Actually that's true. We keep a few at the school. I could help you get set up if you like. They're so young they might need their mother's milk for a while . . . Oh.' She glanced at me. 'I'm not helping, am I?'

What she had said had made no difference; I had already seen there was only one positive outcome from what might have ended up being a very difficult day. I said to Penny, 'OK, you can keep them. But you're responsible for cleaning them out. Clear?'

Ms Breslin asked, 'What will you call them?'

Penny, beaming, held up the rats. 'Rutherford and Appleton – Ow! Rutherford just *bit* me.'

'Let me hold them for you – I've gloves.'

So Ms Breslin held them carefully in her gloved hands as the party walked out of RAL, all the way back to the gate. And as we passed back out through security, that Geiger gate bleeped. Ms Breslin held up the little animals and inspected them curiously.

We saw a lot of Ms Breslin in the weeks after that, although we became 'Amanda' and 'Joe' when she started to visit us at home. The house I had bought with Mary, Penny's mother, was too big for the two of us, but neither of us had wanted to move away from the memories. I could see Amanda working some of this out as she glanced around the place.

She found a big old parrot's cage in a charity shop for our rats, and she and Penny worked on making runs and providing toys and litter. Amanda helped us 'rat-proof' our home, as she put it. I had to lift my piles of books off the floor and up onto shelves, and we put covers over the soft furnishings as a guard against territory-marking urine spurts, and I slit lengths of old hosepipe to cover electric flex. We kept the rats in a corner of our dining room, close by a window. I didn't mind the little beasts save for a lingering stink of urine. And I enjoyed Amanda's visits.

After a few weeks the rats were very active, with jet black hair and bright, glittering little eyes. Amanda said they were growing unusually fast. She was also curious about the way they'd triggered the RAL Geigers. She asked if she could bring some instruments home from the school's physics lab to test them.

She showed up on a rainy May day, about four weeks after we had acquired the rats, with instruments that turned out to be advanced forms of radiation detectors.

My own physics GCSE was in the dim past. 'In my day we didn't have this kind of stuff – just crackling Geiger counters.'

'Fantastic, isn't it? Instrumentation has gotten so cheap. Now schoolkids can detect cosmic rays...' Penny and Amanda manipulated the rats, holding them up before the detectors, while Amanda inspected them. 'They *are* growing fast,' she said. 'I mean, they can't have been more than a few days old when Penny found them, but their eyes were already open.' And though they should have been dependent on their mother's milk until they were four weeks old, from the beginning they'd been able to take solid food – high-protein puppy food, recommended by Amanda.

Appleton, it turned out, was a female – a doe, as Amanda put it. 'And she's pregnant,' Amanda said now, feeling the rat's tiny belly.

Penny stared. 'By her brother? *Eughh.*'

'She's young to be fertile but it's not impossible... You generally try to separate siblings, always assuming Rutherford *is* her sibling.' One of her sensor boxes bleeped.

I asked, 'And she's giving off cosmic rays?'

'Dad,' Penny said, 'cosmic rays come from supernovas and stuff. Rats do *not* give off cosmic rays.'

'OK, so why is Amanda's box bleeping?'

Amanda was downloading a record onto a tablet. 'There is some kind of high-energy radiation. Just a trace.' She passed a plastic wand over Appleton's stomach. 'A source, around here.'

'Inside her?' Penny asked.

'Is it dangerous?' I asked immediately. 'For us, I mean.'

'Oh, no, it's the merest trace – you have more energetic particles lacing through your body all the time, from all sorts of natural sources. This would make no difference. Odd, though.'

Penny said, 'Maybe the rats ate some plutonium in that atomic lab. They were just babies. They must have been hungry. They'd have eaten anything.'

But there is no plutonium in a particle accelerator. 'Another mystery,' I said.

'Ow!' Penny pulled her hands back and dropped Rutherford, who scampered off behind a radiator. 'That little bugger nipped me again!'

'Language,' I said. This time the rat had made her hand bleed. 'That one's getting vicious.'

'Some do,' Amanda said. 'He's probably just being macho. Like a teenage boy.' She put Appleton back in her cage. 'Joe, I'll fetch some TCP if you round up Rutherford.'

'OK. You sit still, Penny, and try not to bleed on anything.'

So I picked up a hearth brush and fish net and went after Rutherford.

After a month we were working out a protocol for such incidents. I was confident the beast couldn't get out of the room; the trick was to shepherd him with the brush, and then swipe him gently with the net. I soon backed him into a corner of the room. He stood on his haunches looking back at me, and I thought I saw traces of Penny's blood around his mouth. I dropped the brush to block his exit to my left, and when he made a run for it I dropped the net to my right, in his path.

And missed him. He ended up running between my legs as if I was a nutmegged goalkeeper, following a course a good thirty degrees away from the one I'd thought he'd chosen. I couldn't believe I'd managed to miss him so badly.

I tried again. This time I chased him down to a corner of the room's blocked-off fireplace, and tried the same routine: brush in one hand, net in the other. But again he ran off on a course very different from the one I *saw* him choose.

'Curiouser and curiouser,' Amanda said. She'd returned and was dabbing at Penny's bitten hand. 'Joe – do you mind if I film you?'

'What for? To give your buddies in the staffroom a laugh?'

'I wouldn't do that.' She swivelled her tablet so it faced me. 'There's something funny going on, I think. Try catching him again.'

It took me three more goes to trap him. Each time he fooled me, as if sending me chasing a ghost. I got him in the end by using a rucked-up bit of carpet to create a channel he couldn't escape from.

With both rats safely back in the cage Amanda ran over her footage. 'Well, that's very odd. Look. Your second attempt is the clearest...'

Rutherford looked as if he had been heading towards my right. That was the way I dropped the net, and as Penny's shoulder happened to be in the frame, I could see from her reaction that she thought he was heading that way too. But he headed left, and darted off the screen.

'I'm sure I reacted *after* he made his move.'

'You did, every time I watched you.' Amanda said carefully, 'Each time it's as if he got another chance. As if, knowing what you would do, he went back and made a second choice.'

'"Went back"? What's that supposed to mean?'

Amanda might have been careful in her choice of words, but Penny wasn't. 'We did fish them out of an atomic lab, Dad. What did you expect? Time-travelling mutant radioactive rats! Brilliant,' she said gleefully.

We continued to see a good deal of Ms Amanda Breslin as the rats grew into two big, heavy, hungry, snappy animals. Amanda devised tests to try to establish the truth of their mysterious 'time-hopping'. She and Penny built elaborate mazes of cardboard and plastic, baited with cheese and timed locks, but their results were inconclusive. Penny, designing experiments and keeping notes, loved all this. Amanda must have been a hell of a teacher, I thought.

And every so often I was reminded of that doctorate in physics.

'I mean, think what an evolutionary advantage it would be,' she said. 'When you're chasing your lunch, or trying to keep from being somebody else's lunch – if you make a mistake you can *go back*, even just a few seconds, and choose the option that keeps you safe, or fed. Once such a facility rose in a population you'd expect it to propagate fast.'

'If they're changing the past,' Penny said, 'why would we remember? Our memories should be changed too.'

'Good question,' Amanda said respectfully. 'Maybe any changes to the time stream are localised – the effects travelling no wider than the rats need them to be. After all, time travel must be energy-consuming. In general it ought to be a last resort. Maybe the time-travel reflex cuts in only as an emergency option when the rat is cornered. We might be able to use that to test them...'

But Penny absolutely vetoed doing any kind of experiment that would put her rats under stress.

I couldn't really have cared less about rats, even time-travelling rats. But it was a pleasure to come home after another dull day with dusty solicitors to help Penny with the rats' feed or with cleaning them out, and to talk over their latest exploits. 'Who would have thought,' said Penny, who could be disturbingly wise beyond her years, 'that a pair of glow-in-the-dark rodents would bring us together?'

And then there was Amanda. At first it was odd to have a woman of my own age around the house again. Even after weeks with us she was awkward, oddly shy, but with that sharp brain and a healthy dose of empathy she was always good company.

I did try to find out more about her. 'You said you did a PhD. Wouldn't you rather be working in a place like RAL, than with rats and schoolkids?'

'Not me.' She pushed back her hair. 'Academia is a pretty brutal world, you know. Petty bullying when you're junior, and lifelong rivalries when you're older.'

'Like a rat pack,' Penny said.

'Oh, academics make rats look civilised.'

She seemed to enjoy our company in turn, as long as we had the rats as neutral ground between us. She evidently had nobody at home, no partner or kids. Penny clearly hoped that some kind of relationship was going to bloom between us, that her mother would be replaced in her life's hierarchy of security by a favourite teacher. It wasn't impossible. I was drawn into those seawater eyes. But I could see nothing but complications, and held back, taking it slowly.

Too slowly, in the event. In the brief time we had left, I learned little more about Amanda's past and her private life, and nothing about her few sad, failed love affairs. For in the end, of course, the rats got in the way.

On the day Appleton gave birth, Amanda stayed with us late into the evening, as the rat suckled her babies, a dozen of them.

It had been about seven weeks since we'd brought the rats home from RAL. It was early June now, and the evening was long, the air through the open window fresh and full of the scent of cut grass. Didcot's not an exciting place, but on a warm summer evening, with the birds singing and the lawns green, middle England is as pretty a place as you'll find anywhere. And the baby rats had made Penny happy. It was a good day, and by about eleven p.m., hours after the rat had given birth, I felt pretty mellow, and was vaguely wondering how I could arrange for some time alone with Amanda.

Then Penny broke the mood with a sudden scream. Amanda and I rushed to see what was wrong. Of the dozen babies, only two remained in the cage with Appleton, who seemed to be sleeping soundly.

Penny was distressed. She thought the babies must have been eaten by their mother, a gruesome thought, and I hugged her.

But Amanda calmly pointed out there was no evidence of such cannibalism. 'If Appleton had eaten all those babies,' she said reasonably, 'we'd have heard, and we'd see the by-products. The mess.'

'Then where are the little beggars?' I snapped. 'We've been sitting by this damn cage all day. Baby rats don't just disappear—'

'Baby rats just *appeared*,' Penny pointed out. 'Inside the accelerator, remember? Maybe they time-travelled out.'

Now, given what had gone before, that was a reasonable suggestion. But with my mood shattered I'd had enough of mutant rats. I snorted, and as Amanda and Penny exchanged glances, I turned up the lights and started a more conventional search around the room. I soon found a hole, gnawed through the skirting board. When I dug into the hole with a probing finger, I found bits of paper, stinking of urine. A rat nest.

I sat back on my heels, looking at the hole, and Penny and Amanda joined me.

'Baby rats can't gnaw holes that size,' Penny said.

'Adults can,' said Amanda. She ran a finger around the rim of the hole. 'The nest looks weeks old to me. Three or four?'

'The thing is,' I said reluctantly, 'I checked this board this morning. I checked the whole room. I usually do. There was no hole here. I'm sure of it. And certainly not a three-week-old nest.'

Penny grasped the situation immediately. 'The babies travelled back in time, three or four weeks. They went back in time, and built a nest here and grew up.'

Amanda nodded. 'They changed the past. So a nest exists here now where it didn't before.'

'Oh, come on,' I said. 'What happened to Occam's razor? Isn't it simpler to suppose that we've just got another bunch of rats, that just happened to show up now – or were drawn by the scent of Rutherford and Appleton?'

Penny shook her head. 'Won't wash, Dad. That doesn't explain the way the hole just magically appeared.'

Amanda, kneeling down, was still inspecting the hole. 'I wish I had a torch . . . I can't see evidence of more than a couple of animals here. Three at the most? But we lost maybe ten of our dozen babies. So where are the rest?'

Penny ran to her tablet and immediately began scanning news sites, blogs, police and health resources, for unusual sightings of rats. That night there were four sightings in the Didcot area – four encounters with rats where no rats had been seen before, big, aggressive animals that were hard to catch. One report claimed a rat had attacked an infant in her cot. Penny looked at us, her eyes shining in the screen's silver light. 'Oops,' she said.

Amanda stood up. 'I think it's time we took this a bit more seriously. Penny, do you mind if I take one of these babies into RAL for some tests? I have contacts there...'

That was week seven, as we started to count it later: the seventh week since Penny first spotted those baby rats in their sealed-up sphere at RAL.

The sightings of the rats continued through spring and summer, spreading out through Oxfordshire and Berkshire, the range increasing by roughly a couple of kilometres every three weeks. Penny and I set up an Ordnance Survey map on the wall of the dining room, and tracked the sightings with sticky coloured dots. By the beginning of September – week twenty – our dots had got as far as Abingdon, about eight kilometres away. The attacks on food stores, pets, livestock and, unfortunately, people, were getting more serious, and there were reports of the creatures causing other problems by gnawing through power lines, telephone optic-fibre cables and plastic water pipes. The rats were ferociously difficult to kill or contain, baffling the vermin controllers. The health authorities and the police were considering quarantining off an infected zone to try to stop the spread of the tabloids' 'super-rats'.

Amanda came to visit us on the first Saturday in September, the last weekend before school started again – although it wasn't yet clear if the schools would open because of the continuing rat problem – and brought back the baby she had borrowed for testing in a cat box; it was now fully grown. Rutherford, Appleton and their unnamed babies, now separated by sex, watched impassively.

Amanda professed admiration for our map.

'Look,' Penny said. 'We used a different colour code for each week since I found the first two at RAL. See how it spreads out? And there's more of them all the time. I counted it up with Dad. There were four nests sighted that first night when the babies were born. Three weeks later there were twenty-six. Three weeks after that a hundred and twenty-eight...'

'Show her your graph,' I said.

Penny brought up a graph of the number of reports of independent nests versus time, plotted on logarithmic scales. There was a scatter of points around a neat straight-line trend. 'Dad showed me how to do this. See that? It's a power-law line. That's what Dad says. Every three weeks the nests seem to multiply by about five. So it grows quickly. This is week twenty and we're up to over three thousand, spread across a circle about sixteen kilometres wide.'

Amanda nodded. 'You should show this to Mr Beauregard. He keeps saying you're underachieving at maths.'

She pulled a face. 'This isn't maths. This is *real*.'

Amanda raised her eyebrows at me. 'Which tells you all you need to know about Bob Beauregard's teaching methods. That fivefold increase maybe makes sense. You get typically ten or a dozen babies per litter. Maybe five breeding pairs each generation? But the generations are coming too close together, though, even for these rats . . . I'll have to think about that. Do some mathematical modelling.'

I went to put the kettle on. 'So how's the youngster? Survived its tests at RAL?'

'Oh, yes.' She leaned down to look at the rat in its cat box. 'Although my friends in there couldn't agree on an interpretation of their scan results.'

Penny said, 'Tell us what you think.'

Amanda said slowly, 'Well, I think this rat has got a wormhole in its stomach. A flaw in spacetime. And I think it was born that way, born with the wormhole.' She smiled at us. 'Isn't that a wonderful idea?'

Penny clapped her hands.

I poured out mugs of tea for me and Amanda, handed Penny a soda, and we sat at the table. ' "A flaw in spacetime." I'm not sure what that means.'

'The classical description of a wormhole is the Einstein-Rosen bridge, which—'

'Einstein didn't keep rats, as far as I know. This, this *flaw* in its stomach, is how the rat can travel back in time. Is that what you mean?'

She nodded. 'But not voluntarily, I don't think. It must be connected to the rat's nervous system somehow – like a muscular reflex. When it's cornered, it flexes this spacetime spring, and flips back.'

'Just a few seconds,' Penny said.

'Yes. That would be enough to escape most entrapment situations. But I'm speculating that a deeper reflex can work when the rats are very young. What if some babies in a litter can hop back *weeks*? It would be a random jump into the unknown, but at least they would be safe from any predators who might be attracted to the nest.'

'Or the vermin controllers.'

'Well, yes. And we know this strain of rat is able to survive preco-ciously young – especially if it finds some kind human like Penny to look after it.'

Penny frowned. 'They'd be separated from their mother. For *ever*.'

'But rats don't have the same kind of parental bond as we do, Penny. We, with our ape lineage, only have a few children, whom we cherish. The rats have lots of babies, expecting to lose most of them to predators. Being able to throw at least some of your babies back to the safety of the past is a valid survival option.'

I said, 'And this is what the RAL people wouldn't believe.'

'Well, would you? Although you'd think by now others would have noticed something odd. The police and the rest keep saying they're just an extreme strain of ordinary rat.'

'So how did spacetime wormholes get into the bellies of rats?'

'It started – or will start – in the place we found the first pair.'

'The Pevatron?'

'You recall those anti-science protesters outside the facility? They may have a point. The Pevatron will work at unprecedented high energies, and even some of the RAL people are expecting it to create extremely exotic objects . . .'

Objects such as wormholes and black holes, she told us. The ener-gies released by the Pevatron's colliding electrons and positrons could be enough to rip the fabric of spacetime and leave it stitched back together again *wrong*, with points that should be separated in space or in time unnaturally connected together.

'Miniature time machines,' Penny said.

'Yes. The RAL people are actually figuring out ways to detect such things. If a particle got trapped in such a wormhole it might bounce back and forth so you'd see multiple copies of it. Or, you might see a flash as all the light that fell in the wormhole in the future, as long as it existed, was sent back to the instant of its creation and emerged all at once.'

I nodded, half understanding, not quite believing. 'And if such a wormhole did form, at high energy . . .'

Amanda spread her hands on the table. 'I'm speculating. You'd get not one but a whole population of the things. The wormholes would interact and self-select – I think we might see a kind of evolution, a physical evolution, as the wormholes spiralled into stable, low-energy modes that could persist even outside the Pevatron, in our low-energy environment.'

'Until one got swallowed by a rat,' I said sceptically.

'Well, something like that. After that we're talking about biological evolution. It's obvious what a competitive advantage an ability to time-travel would confer. And, remember, if these creatures are some-how looping back in time, a lot of generations could be compressed into a short interval. Evolution could work very quickly, the time-travel gene spreading fast.'

'OK. But even if I buy all that, the Pevatron doesn't work yet. It isn't due to come online for two whole years! So how did those first time-travelling rats end up back in April?'

'That's obvious, Dad,' Penny said, admonishing. 'They come from the future. They are infesting the past.' She smiled at the idea. 'Cool.'

Amanda and I shared a glance.

That didn't seem so cool to me. Mankind has waged war against rats since we became farmers. Even before the Pevatron rats came along, there were thought to be more rats than all the other mammals put together; and rats and the diseases they brought were thought to have killed more humans in the second millennium than all our wars. If this new strain really did have the ability to time-travel – even to plant their young in the deep past – how could humanity stop them?

We weren't about to alarm Penny, who clearly hadn't thought it through that far. I raised the pot. 'More tea?'

A population increasing fivefold expands fast. By the end of Septem-ber there were over fifteen thousand nests, being spied as far out as Wantage. That was when we were evacuated out of the expanding infestation zone. It broke Penny's heart when Rutherford and Apple-ton were taken away.

Amanda sent us a video clip. It had been caught by chance, by a webcam in a bird's nesting box: it was the arrival of a baby rat, apparently sent from the future into its past, our present. At first you saw a sort of outline, flattened like roadkill, that gradually filled up to become a living, breathing, three-dimensional rat. Amanda said it was as if the rats were using their wormhole muscles to *fold* up into a higher spacetime dimension, and then back down into ours. She had hacked this footage out of data being gathered by government science units at the heart of the infected zone. The scientists didn't know what to make of it – or if they did, they weren't admitting it.

By week twenty-nine, mid-November, the rats were being seen in Wallingford, around thirteen kilometres from Harwell. In our government-issue caravan we kept up our map, and the centre of it was covered with dots; the rats weren't just spreading outward but were filling in the spaces they had already colonised. The authorities estimated there were over three hundred and fifty thousand nests in the area. Penny extrapolated her graph and made lurid predictions of how quickly the rats would reach Birmingham, London, the Channel Tunnel. 'It's the end of the world, Dad, for humans anyhow,' she said, thrilling herself by half-believing it.

By the end of November, the authorities were making provisional plans to evacuate Oxford.

That was when Amanda called me and asked me for help. 'We need to sort this out before it's too late.'

I met her at the edge of the control zone, near Wallingford. She had requisitioned an NHS ambulance, rat-hardened with cages over its tyres and netting over its doors. She was already wearing her spacesuit, as she called it, a coverall of tough Kevlar fabric with thick gloves and a hood like a nuclear engineer's. She had one for me; I had to put it on as she drove us briskly into the zone. I was impressed by the resources she'd assembled, through leaning on her contacts within Harwell itself. She was always far smarter, more resourceful than she appeared, and was rising to this challenge. She was having a good war. That's one reason why I'll miss her.

Inside the infected zone the towns and villages were deserted of people. The rats were everywhere, swarming out of doorways and windows and over the streets in a black tide. Even out in the country I could hear their heavy bodies thumping against the chassis of the ambulance as we drove.

'They've eaten everything there is to eat,' Amanda said. 'The super-markets, larders, granaries, fields, all stripped. The population must be near its peak. Soon they'll turn on each other, if they haven't already...'

As we neared Harwell we passed the hub of the emergency control, a heavily fenced-off group of trailers, vehicles and comms masts – Gold Command, as it was called, under the control of the local chief constable, and patrolled by squaddies armed with rifles and flame-throwers. Rats scurried across the ground even inside the soldiers' perimeter. That was the nature of them.

At Harwell itself we left the ambulance at RAL's security gate, were passed through the unmanned security barriers by Amanda's retinal scans, and walked across a campus deserted save for the shadowy black forms of rats. Amanda wore a canvas pack on her back that looked suspicious even to me, but none of the campus's security measures impeded us.

We passed through the rough ring of the Pevatron accelerator, and came to a group of more finished buildings at its centre. The area was heavily fenced off and the ground dosed with poison; this billion-pound facility had not yet been abandoned to the rats.

'In fact,' Amanda said, 'you could say the Pevatron's development is continuing, even now, as *that* works its way through its own, slow, superhuman calculations.'

That was the quantum computer. Contained within one of the largest of the central buildings and held behind a glass wall, it was a translucent ball maybe three metres across that hovered in the air, suspended by magnetic fields and contained in a perfect vacuum. Walking back and forth in its hall I thought I saw hints of deeper structure, glimmering. Even aside from its engineering quality, that computer was one of the most beautiful pieces of sculpture I have ever seen.

'Nobody knows how it works,' Amanda said. 'Not in detail, anyhow. It bootstrapped itself. It finished its own physical design, and now is working out its own programming for the task of running the Pevatron.'

'That is one smart machine, then.'

'But vulnerable.' And she took off her pack, and pulled out pretty much what I expected: a lump of pale plastic, an explosive. I didn't ask her where she had got it from. She slapped the plastic against the glass window, where it stuck easily, and attached a detonator charge that would be controlled by a radio switch. She showed me what to do, just in case: it was a gadget like a TV remote, with a big red button to push.

'We need some distance,' she said, and led me out of the building to the open air. 'The quantum computer is the heart of the Pevatron – and where most of the money has been spent. If we destroy it there's a good chance the project will be derailed enough to be cancelled altogether, especially given it's in the middle of a disaster zone. Of course others might build equivalent facilities somewhere else, but at least we'd buy time to prove the reality of the time loops, and to protect against the danger.'

We stood near the edge of the ring, looking back at the unprepossessing control buildings. 'Do we really have to do this? To smash such a beautiful machine—'

'I know,' she said, smiling at me. 'I feel it too. Yes, we have to do this. Because this is just the start. Look . . .' She pulled a tablet out of her pack, and showed me how she had modelled the spread of the super-vermin. 'These rats are fertile at four weeks old, and have a gestation time of about three weeks. When a litter is born, a percentage of it is thrown back in time *four* weeks. So they are mature just at the point they were born – if you see what I mean. That's why we see this jump in the spread with each three-week generation.

'But I'm speculating that under conditions of extreme stress – such as the overcrowding we're already seeing here – some individuals, or their offspring, can be thrown back further still. Just as Penny suggested.'

'To escape the population crash.'

'That's it. Because if you dive deep enough into the past, you *always* find virgin territory: you are the first of your kind, and your offspring can fill their boots. So, think about it. The first boom will start when the Pevatron comes online. Forty weeks later, crash . . .' The authorities were predicting a crash for us around week forty, when the rats would have overrun Oxford, and there would be tens of millions of nests – hundreds of millions of rats, swarming over an area forty or fifty kilometres across. Amanda went on, 'But suppose that a few extreme individuals escape back, say, a hundred weeks into the past, into the virgin time *before* the Pevatron was even turned on. Forty weeks later, their ancestors are still ahead of the first origin. But then there's another crash—'

'And another leap into the past, even deeper.'

'Yes. And back they go, crash and leap, crash and leap, working their way ever deeper into history. Every time it will start as it did for us, with just a handful of cute-looking babies in a virgin world. Every time it will end with a crash.' Behind her scuffed faceplate those seawater eyes were grave. 'There's *nothing* ahead of us, Joe. Nothing but rats swarming and fighting and dying; whatever human future once existed has been *eaten*.' She waved a hand. 'And soon none of this will exist either. We won't just be dead; we will never even have existed. Our history, our very existence, consumed by the rats.'

I touched the hand that held the bomb control. 'And you think this will put it right?'

'This must be where it started. I can't think of anything else to do.'

I would never have believed that the timid teacher I had got to know only months before would ever have been capable of setting up an operation like this, which shows how much I know about people. But she was trembling inside her suit.

'I'm scared, Joe.'

I squeezed her gloved hand. 'Don't be. To have figured this out, to have got this far – I could kiss you.'

She looked away, shy even in that extreme moment. There were rats running around our feet. 'We shouldn't risk it.'

'I guess not,' I said. I will regret that choice for ever.

She held up her control, the button under her gloved thumb. 'I hope this works. Three, two, one—'

It took me a long time to recover from the injuries I suffered in the next few seconds, and even longer to figure it all out.

Amanda and I had talked about what the rise of the rats would mean for humanity – that is, our extinction. What we didn't talk about was what it would mean for the rats themselves.

Rats breed fast, and compete hard. In a future world empty of mankind there would be a quick radiation of forms; I imagined slavering wolf-like rats preying on big grazing antelope-like rats. And I imagined intelligence advancing. Why not? Rats are already smart and highly social, and the stuff we left behind would give a start to any tool-users. Whatever society they built would surely be quite unlike ours, however. Rats, with their different breeding strategy, show little loyalty to their many offspring; there would be no rodent Genghis Khan. And natural time travellers would wage wars of a qualitatively different kind from ours. All this in a rat future.

But that future was always contingent. Suppose Amanda was right – suppose her one action in aborting the Pevatron was enough to stop the rise of the rats. Maybe a smart enough super-rat of the future would know that. And maybe he or she would come back in time to try to avert the extinction of its kind before it existed – or to confirm the defeat of mankind.

This is all speculation. But it would explain what I saw.

'Three, two, one—'

I saw Amanda's thumb press down on that red button.

And in the same instant I saw a vertical line appear in space before us, and fold out, like a cardboard cut-out rotating.

I've tried to describe it, even to draw it, for the doctors and physicists and policemen who have questioned me since. It was a rat, but a *big* rat, maybe a metre tall, upright, with some kind of metal mesh vest over its upper body, and holding a silvery tube, unmistakably a weapon, that it pointed at Amanda. Even as it appeared it opened its mouth wide – I saw typical rat incisors, just like Rutherford's – and it screamed.

And it started to glow.

Amanda had told me how the scientists had hoped to detect the Pevatron's miniature time machines by flashes of light: all the radiation that would ever fall on those wormholes, as long as they lasted, all pouring out at the moment of their formation. And right at the beginning of the affair Penny said the babies she found in the vacuum sphere were warm too, warm in their little bellies where the wormholes lay like tumours. Maybe there's a limit to how much of that gathered radiation an organic time machine can stand – a limit to how far a much-evolved rat thing can throw itself back in time.

I think the post-rat that tried to attack Amanda knew this. It was sacrificing itself in a hopeless attempt to save its timeline. If so, it was a hero of its kind.

I saw it die. Light shone out of its mouth, its boiling, popping eyes, and then out through its flesh and singed fur, as if it exploded from within. I closed my eyes, thus probably saving my sight. When its body detonated I was knocked to the ground, burned.

Amanda, closer, did not survive.

But she had pressed that button, and I felt a second concussion as her plastic explosive went up, and the quantum computer died.

When the Harwell security officers found us there was not a trace of that damn rat to be seen – and none of its swarming ancestors who had been under my feet moments before – nothing but the body of Amanda, and me with a head full of memories of the Pevatron rats that nobody else shares, not even Penny.

THE INVASION OF VENUS

For me, the saga of the Incoming was above all Elspeth Black's story. For she, more than anyone else I knew, was the one who had a problem with it.

When the news was made public I drove out of London to visit Elspeth at her country church. I had to cancel a dozen appointments to do it, including one with the Prime Minister's office, but I knew, as soon as I got out of the car and stood in the soft September rain, that it had been the right thing to do.

Elspeth was pottering around outside the church, wearing overalls and rubber boots and wielding an alarming-looking industrial-strength jackhammer. But she had a radio blaring out a phone-in discussion, and indoors, out of the rain, I glimpsed a widescreen TV and laptop, both scrolling news – mostly fresh projections of where the Incoming's decelerating trajectory might deliver them, and new deep-space images of their 'craft', if such it was, a massive block of ice like a comet nucleus, leaking very complex patterns of infrared radiation. Elspeth was plugged into the world, even out here in the wilds of Essex.

She approached me with a grin, pushing back goggles under a hard hat. 'Toby.' I got a kiss on the cheek and a brief hug; she smelled of machine oil. We were easy with each other physically. Fifteen years earlier, in our last year at college, we'd been lovers, briefly; it had finished with a kind of regretful embarrassment – very English, said our American friends – but it had proven only a kind of speed bump in our relationship. 'Glad to see you, if surprised. I thought all you civil service types would be locked down in emergency meetings.'

For a decade I'd been a civil servant in the environment ministry. 'No, but old Thorp –' my minister '– has been in a continuous COBRA session for twenty-four hours. Much good it's doing anybody.'

'I must say it's not obvious to the layman what use an environment minister is when the aliens are coming.'

'Well, they're trying to anticipate, worst case, some kind of attack from space. And a lot of what we can dream up is similar to natural disasters – a kinetic-energy weapon strike could be like a meteor fall, a sunlight occlusion like a massive volcanic event. And so Thorp is in the mix, along with health, energy, transport. Of course we're in contact with other governments – and NATO, the UN. The most urgent issue right now is whether to signal or not.'

She frowned. 'Why wouldn't we?'

'Security. Elspeth, remember, we know absolutely nothing about these guys. What if our signal was interpreted as a threat? And there are tactical considerations. Any signal would give information to a potential enemy about our technical capabilities. It would also give away the very fact that we know they are here.'

She scoffed. '"Tactical considerations." Paranoid cobblers! And besides, I bet every kid with a CB radio is beaming out her heart to ET right now. The whole planet's alight with radio messages, probably.'

'Well, that's true. You can't stop it. But still, sending some kind of signal authorised by the government or an inter-government agency is another step entirely.'

'Oh, come on. You can't really believe anybody is going to cross the stars to harm us. What could they possibly want that would justify the cost of an interstellar mission?'

So we argued. I'd only been out of the car for five minutes.

We'd had this kind of discussion all the way back to late nights in college, some of them in her bed, or mine. She'd always been drawn to the bigger issues – 'to the context,' as she used to say. Though we'd both started out as maths students, her head had soon expanded in the exotic intellectual air, and she'd moved on to study older ways of thinking than the scientific – older questions, still unanswered. Was there a God? If so, or if not, what was the point of our existence? Why did we, or indeed anything, exist at all? In her later student years she took theology options, but quickly burned through that discipline and was left unsatisfied. She was repelled, too, by the modern atheists, with their aggressive denials. So, after college, she had started her own journey through life – a journey in search of answers.

Now, of course, maybe some of those answers had come swimming in from the stars in search of her.

That was why I'd felt drawn here, at this particular moment in my life. I needed Elspeth's perspective. In the wan daylight I could see the fine patina of lines around the mouth I used to kiss, and the strands of grey in her red hair. I was sure she suspected, rightly, that

I knew more than I was telling her – more than had been released to the public. But she didn't follow that up for now.

'Come see what I'm doing,' she said, sharply breaking up the debate. 'Watch your shoes.' We walked across muddy grass towards the main door. The core of that old church, dedicated to St Cuthbert, was a Saxon-era tower; the rest of the fabric was mostly Norman, but there had been an extensive restoration in Victorian times. Within was a lovely space, if cold, the stone walls resonating. It was still consecrated, Church of England, but in this empty agricultural countryside it was one of a widespread string of churches united in a single parish, and rarely used.

Elspeth had never joined any of the established religions, but she had appropriated some of their infrastructure, she liked to say. And here she had gathered a group of volunteers, wandering souls more or less like-minded. They worked to maintain the fabric of the church. And within, she led her group through what you might think of as a mix of discussions, or prayers, or meditation, or yoga practices – whatever she could find that seemed to work. It was the way religions used to be before the big monotheistic creeds took over, she argued. 'The only way to reach God, or anyhow the space beyond us where God ought to be, is by working hard, by helping other people, and by pushing your mind to the limit of its capability, and then going a little beyond, and just *listening*. Beyond *logos* to *mythos*.'

She was always restless, always trying something new. Yet in some ways she was the most contented person I ever met – at least before the Incoming showed up.

Now, though, she wasn't content about the state of the church's foundations. She showed me where she had dug up flagstones to reveal sodden ground. 'We're digging out new drainage channels, but it's a hell of a job. We may end up rebuilding the founds altogether. The very deepest level seems to be wood, huge piles of Saxon oak...' She eyed me. 'This church has stood here for a thousand years, without, apparently, facing a threat such as this before. Some measure of the true impact of climate change, right?'

I shrugged. 'I suppose you'd say we arseholes in the environment ministry should be concentrating on stuff like this rather than preparing to fight interstellar wars.'

'Well, so you should. But maybe a more mature species would be preparing for positive outcomes. Think of it, Tobe! There are now creatures in this solar system who are *smarter than us*. They have to be, or they wouldn't be here – right? Somewhere between us and the angels. Who knows what they can tell us? What is their science, their art – their theology?'

I frowned. 'But what do they want? For that's what may count from now on – their agenda, not ours.'

'There you are being paranoid again.' But she hesitated. 'What about Meryl and the kids?'

'Meryl's at home. Mark and Sophie are at school.' I shrugged. 'Life as normal.'

'Some people are freaking out. Raiding the supermarkets.'

'Some people always do. We want things to continue as normally as possible, as long as possible. Modern society is efficient, you know, Elspeth, but not very resilient. A fuel strike could cripple us in a week, let alone alien invaders.'

She pushed a loose grey hair back under her hard hat, and looked at me suspiciously. 'But you seem calm, considering. You know something. Don't you, you bastard?'

I grinned. 'And you know me.'

'Spill it.'

'Two things. We picked up signals. Or, more likely, leakage. You know about the infrared stuff we've seen for a while, coming from the nucleus. Now we've detected radio noise, faint, clearly structured, very complex. It may be some kind of internal channel rather than anything meant for us. But if we can figure anything out from it—'

'Well, that's exciting. And the second thing? Come on, Miller.'

'We have more refined trajectory data. All this will be released soon – it's probably leaked already.'

'Yes?'

'The Incoming *are* heading for the inner solar system. But they aren't coming here – not to Earth.'

She frowned. 'Then where?'

I dropped my bombshell. 'Venus. Not Earth. They're heading for Venus, Elspeth.'

She looked into the clouded sky, the bright patch that, I knew, marked the position of the sun and the orbits of the inner planets, Venus and Mercury. 'Venus? That's a cloudy hellhole. What would they want there?'

'I've no idea.'

'Well, I'm used to living with questions I'll never be able to answer. Let's hope this isn't one of them. In the meantime, let's make ourselves useful.' She eyed my crumpled Whitehall suit, my patent leather shoes already splashed with mud. 'Have you got time to stay? You want to help out with my drain? I've a spare overall that might fit.'

Talking, speculating, we walked through the church.

We used the excuse of Elspeth's Goonhilly event to make a family trip to Cornwall.

We took the A-road snaking west down the spine of the Cornish peninsula, and stopped at a small hotel in Helston. The pretty little town was decked out that day for the annual Furry Dance, an ancient, eccentric carnival when the local children would weave, skipping, in and out of the houses on the hilly streets. The next morning Meryl was to take the kids to the beach, further up the coast.

And, just about at dawn, I set off alone in a hired car for the A-road to the south-east, towards Goonhilly Down. It was a clear May morning, and, I reflected, about eight months since I'd seen Elspeth at her church. As I drove I was aware of Venus, rising in the eastern sky and clearly visible in my rear-view mirror, a lamp shining steadily even as the day brightened.

Goonhilly is a stretch of high open land, a windy place. Its claim to fame is that at one time it hosted the largest telecoms satellite earth station in the world – it picked up the first live transatlantic TV broadcast, via Telstar. It was decommissioned years ago, but its oldest dish, a thousand-tonne parabolic bowl called 'Arthur' after the king, became a listed building, and so was preserved. And that was how it was available for Elspeth and her committee of messagers to get hold of, when they, or rather she, grew impatient with the government's continuing reticence over sending signals to the Incoming. Because of the official policy I'd had to help with smoothing through the permissions, all behind the scenes.

Just after my first glimpse of the surviving dishes on the skyline I came up against a police cordon, a hastily erected plastic fence that excluded a few groups of chanting Shouters, and a fundamentalist-religious cabal protesting that the messagers were communicating with the Devil. My ministry card helped me get through.

Elspeth was waiting for me at the old site's visitors' centre, opened up that morning for breakfast, coffee and cereals and toast. Her volunteers cleared up dirty dishes under a big wall screen showing Venus: a live feed from a space telescope – the best images available right now, though every major space agency had a probe to the planet in preparation, and NASA had already fired one off. The Incoming nucleus (it seemed inappropriate to call that lump of dirty ice a 'craft', though such it clearly was) was a brilliant star, too small to show a disc, swinging in its wide orbit above a half-moon Venus. And on the planet's night side you could clearly make out the Patch, that strange, complicated glow in the cloud banks tracking the Incoming's orbit precisely – evidence, it seemed, of Venusians, evidence of intelligence on the planet responding to the visitor from the skies. It was strange to gaze upon that choreography in space, and then to turn to the east and see Venus with the naked eye.

And Elspeth's volunteers, a few dozen earnest men, women and children who looked like they had gathered for a village show, had the audacity to believe they could speak to these godlike forms in the sky.

There was a terrific metallic groan. We turned, and saw that Arthur was turning on his concrete pivot. The volunteers cheered, and a general drift towards the monument began.

Elspeth walked with me, cradling a polystyrene teacup in the palms of fingerless gloves. 'I'm glad you could make it down. Should have brought the kids. Some of the locals from Helston are here; they've made the whole stunt part of their Furry Dance celebration. Did you see the preparations in town? Supposed to celebrate St Michael beating up the Devil – I wonder how appropriate *that* symbolism is. Anyhow, this ought to be a fun day. Later there'll be a barn dance.'

'Meryl thought it was safer to take the kids to the beach. Just in case anything gets upsetting here – you know.' That was most of the truth. There was a subtext that Meryl had never much enjoyed being in the same room as my ex.

'Probably wise. Our British Shouters are a mild bunch, but in rowdier parts of the world there has been trouble.'

The loose international coalition of groups called the Shouters was paradoxically named, because they campaigned for silence; they argued that 'shouting in the jungle' by sending signals to the Incoming or the Venusians (if they existed) was taking an irresponsible risk. Of course they could do nothing about the low-level chatter that had been targeted at the Incoming since it had first been sighted, nearly a year ago already.

Elspeth waved a hand at Arthur. 'Well, if I were a Shouter, I'd be here today. This will be by far the most powerful message sent from the British Isles.'

I'd seen and heard roughs of Elspeth's message. As well as a Carl

Sagan-style prime number lexicon, there was digitised music from Bach to Zulu chants, and art from cave paintings to Warhol, and images of mankind featuring a lot of happy children and astronauts on the moon. There was even a copy of the old Pioneer space probe plaque from the seventies, the one with the smiling naked couple. At least, I thought cynically, all that fluffy stuff would provide a counterpoint to the images of war, murder, famine, plague and other sufferings that the Incoming had no doubt sampled by now, if they'd chosen to.

I said, 'But I get the feeling they're just not interested. Neither the Incoming nor the Venusians. Sorry to rain on your parade.'

'I take it the cryptolinguists aren't getting anywhere decoding the signals?'

'We still think they're not so much "signals" as leakage from internal processes. In both cases, the nucleus and the Patch.' I rubbed my face; I was tired after the previous day's long drive. 'In the case of the nucleus, some kind of organic chemistry seems to be mediating powerful magnetic fields – and the Incoming seem to swarm within. I don't think we've really any idea what's going on in there. We're actually making more progress with the science of the Venusian biosphere . . .'

If the arrival of the Incoming had been astonishing, the evidence of intelligence on Venus, entirely unexpected, was stunning. Nobody had expected the clouds to part right under the orbiting Incoming nucleus – like a deep storm system, kilometres deep in that thick ocean of an atmosphere – and nobody had expected to see the Patch revealed, swirling mist banks where lights flickered tantalisingly, like organised lightning.

'With retrospect, given the results from the old space probes, we might have guessed there was something on Venus – life, if not intelligent life. There were always unexplained deficiencies and surpluses of various compounds. We think the Venusians live in the clouds, far enough above the red-hot ground that the temperature is low enough for liquid water to exist. They ingest carbon monoxide and excrete sulphur compounds, living off the sun's ultraviolet.'

'And they're smart.'

'Oh, yes.' The astronomers, already recording the complex signals coming out of the Incoming nucleus, had started to discern rich patterns in the Venusian Patch too. 'You can tell how complicated a message is even if you don't know anything about the content. You measure entropy orders, which are like correlation measures, mapping structures on various scales embedded in the transmission—'

'You don't understand any of what you just said, do you?'

I smiled. 'Not a word. But I do know this. Going by their data structures, the Venusians are smarter than us as much as we are smarter than the chimps. And the Incoming are smarter again.'

Elspeth turned to face the sky, the brilliant spark of Venus. 'But you say the scientists still believe all this chatter is just – what was your word?'

'Leakage. Elspeth, the Incoming and the Venusians aren't speaking to us. They aren't even speaking to each other. What we're observing is a kind of internal dialogue, in each case. The two are talking to themselves, not each other. One theorist briefed the PM that perhaps both these entities are more like hives than human communities.'

'Hives?' She looked troubled. 'Hives are *different*. They can be purposeful, but they don't have consciousness as we have it. They aren't finite as we are; their edges are much more blurred. They aren't even mortal; individuals can die, but the hives live on.'

'I wonder what their gods will be like, then.'

'It's all so strange. These aliens just don't fit any category we expected, or even that we share. Not mortal, not communicative – and not interested in us. What do they *want*? What *can* they want?' This tone wasn't like her; she sounded bewildered to be facing open questions, rather than exhilarated by mystery as she normally was.

I tried to reassure her. 'Maybe your signal will provoke some answers.'

She checked her watch, and looked up again towards Venus. 'Well, we've only got five minutes to wait before...' Her eyes widened, and she fell silent.

I turned to look the way she was, to the east.

Venus was flaring. Sputtering like a dying candle.

People started to react. They shouted, pointed, or they just stood there, staring, as I did. I couldn't move. I felt a deep, awed fear. Then people called, pointing at the big screen in the visitors' centre, where, it seemed, the space telescopes were returning a very strange set of images indeed.

Elspeth's hand crept into mine. Suddenly I was very glad I hadn't brought my kids that day.

Then I heard angrier shouting, and a police siren, and I smelled burning.

211

*

Once I'd finished making my police statement I went back to the hotel in Helston, where Meryl was angry and relieved to see me, and the kids bewildered and vaguely frightened. I couldn't believe that after all that had happened – the strange events at Venus, the assaults by Shouters on Messagers and vice versa, the arson, Elspeth's injury, the police crackdown – it was not yet eleven in the morning.

That same day I took the family back to London, and called in at work. Then, three days after the incident, I got away again and commandeered a ministry car and driver to take me back to Cornwall.

Elspeth was out of intensive care, but she'd been kept in the hospital at Truro. She had a TV stand before her face, the screen dark. I carefully kissed her on the unburnt side of her face, and sat down, handing over books, newspapers and flowers. 'Thought you might be bored.'

'You never were any good with the sick, were you, Tobe?'

'Sorry.' I opened up one of the newspapers. 'But there's some good news. They caught the Goonhilly arsonists.'

She grunted, her distorted mouth barely opening. 'So what? It doesn't matter who they were. Messagers and Shouters have been at each others' throats all over the world. People like that are inter-changeable... But did we all have to behave so badly? I mean, they even wrecked Arthur.'

'And he was Grade II listed!'

She laughed, then regretted it, for she winced with the pain. 'But why shouldn't we smash it all down here? After all, that's all they seem to be interested in up *there*. The Incoming assaulted Venus, and the Venusians struck back. We all saw it, live on TV – it was nothing more sophisticated than *The War of the Worlds*.' She sounded disappointed. 'These creatures are our superiors, Toby. All your signal analysis stuff proved it. And yet they haven't transcended war and destruction.'

'But we learned so much.' I had a small briefcase that I opened now, and pulled out printouts that I spread over her bed. 'The screen images are better, but you know how it is; they won't let me use my laptop or my phone in here... *Look*, Elspeth. It was incredible. The Incoming assault on Venus lasted hours. Their weapon, whatever it was, burned its way through the Patch, and right down through an atmosphere a hundred times thicker than Earth's. We even glimpsed the surface—'

'Now melted to slag.'

'Much of it ... But then the acid-munchers in the clouds struck back. We think we know what they did.'

That caught her interest. 'How can we know that?'

'Sheer luck. That NASA probe, heading for Venus, happened to be in the way ...'

The probe had detected a wash of electromagnetic radiation coming from the planet.

'A signal,' breathed Elspeth. 'Heading which way?'

'Out from the sun. And then, eight hours later, the probe sensed another signal, coming the other way. I say "sensed". It bobbed about like a cork on a pond. We think it was a gravity wave – very sharply focused, very intense.'

'And when the wave hit the Incoming nucleus—'

'Well, you saw the pictures. The last fragments have burned up in Venus's atmosphere.'

She lay back on her reef of pillows. 'Eight hours,' she mused. 'Gravity waves travel at lightspeed. Four hours out, four hours back ... Earth's about eight light-minutes from the sun. What's four light-hours out from Venus? Jupiter, Saturn—'

'Neptune. Neptune was four light-hours out.'

'Was?'

'It's gone, Elspeth. Almost all of it – the moons are still there, a few chunks of core ice and rock, slowly dispersing. The Venusians used the planet to create their gravity-wave pulse—'

'They *used* it. Are you telling me this to cheer me up? A gas giant, a significant chunk of the solar system's budget of mass–energy, sacrificed for a single warlike gesture.' She laughed, bitter. 'Oh, God!'

'Of course we've no idea *how* they did it.' I put away my images. 'If we were scared of the Incoming, now we're terrified of the Venusians. That NASA probe has been shut down. We don't want anything to look like a threat ... You know, I heard the PM herself ask why it was that this space war should break out now, just when we humans show up on Earth. Even politicians know we haven't been here that long.'

Elspeth shook her head, wincing again. 'The final vanity. This whole episode has never been about us. Can't you see? If this is happening now, it must have happened over and over. Maybe all we see, the planets and stars and galaxies, is just the debris of huge wars – on and on, up to scales we can barely imagine. And we're just weeds growing in the rubble. Tell that to the Prime Minister. And I thought we might ask them about their gods! What a fool I've been – the questions on which I've wasted my life, and *here* are my answers – what a fool.' She was growing agitated.

'Take it easy, Elspeth—'

'Oh, just go. I'll be fine. It's the universe that's broken, not me.' She turned away on her pillow, as if to sleep.

The next time I saw Elspeth she was out of hospital and back at her church.

It was another September day, like the first time I visited her after the Incoming appeared in our telescopes, and at least it wasn't raining. There was a bite in the breeze, but I imagined it soothed her damaged skin. And here she was, digging in the mud before her church.

'Equinox season,' she said. 'Rain coming. Best to get this fixed before we have another flash flood. And before you ask, the doctors cleared me. It's my face that's buggered, not the rest of me.'

'I wasn't going to ask.'

'OK, then. How's Meryl, the kids?'

'Fine. Meryl's at work, the kids back at school. Life goes on.'

'It must, I suppose. What else is there? No, by the way.'

'No what?'

'No, I won't come serve on your minister's think tank.'

'At least consider it. You'd be ideal. Look, we're all trying to figure out where we go from here. The arrival of the Incoming, the war on Venus – it was like a religious revelation. That's how it's being described. A revelation witnessed by all mankind, on TV. Suddenly we've got an entirely different view of the universe out there. And we have to figure out how we go forward, in a whole number of dimensions – political, scientific, economic, social, religious.'

'I'll tell you how we go forward. In despair. Religions are imploding.'

'No, they're not.'

'OK. Theology is imploding. Philosophy. The rest of the world has changed channels and forgotten already, but anybody with any ima-gination knows the truth ... In a way, this has been the final demo-tion, the end of the process that started with Copernicus and Darwin. Now we *know* there are creatures in the universe much smarter than we'll ever be, and we *know* they don't care a damn about us. It's the indifference that's the killer – don't you think? All our futile agitation about if they'd attack us and whether we should signal ... And they did nothing but smash each other up. With *that* above us, what can we do but turn away?'

'You're not turning away.'

She leaned on her shovel. 'I'm not religious; I don't count. My congregation turned away. Here I am, alone.' She glanced at the clear sky. 'Maybe solitude is the key to it all. A galactic isolation imposed by the vast gulfs between the stars, the lightspeed limit. As a species develops you might have a brief phase of individuality, of innovation and technological achievement. But then, when the universe gives you nothing back, you turn in on yourself, and slide into the milky embrace of eusociality – the hive.

'But what then? How would it be for a mass mind to emerge, alone? Maybe that's why the Incoming went to war. Because they were outraged to discover, by some chance, they *weren't* alone in the universe.'

'Most commentators think it was about resources. Most of our wars are about that, in the end.'

'Yes. Depressingly true. All life is based on the destruction of other life, it seems, even on tremendous scales of space and time... But our ancestors understood that right back to the Ice Age, and venerated the animals they had to kill. They are so far above us, the Incoming and the Venusians alike, yet maybe *we*, at our best, are morally superior to them.'

I touched her arm. 'This is why we need you. For your insights. There's a storm coming, Elspeth. We're going to have to work together if we're to weather it, I think.'

She frowned. 'What kind of storm? Oh. Neptune.'

'Yeah. You can't just delete a world without consequences. The planets' orbits are singing like plucked strings. The asteroids and comets too, and those orphan moons wandering around. Some of the stirred-up debris is falling into the inner system.'

'And if we're struck—'

I shrugged. 'We'll have to help each other. There's nobody else to help us, that's for sure. Look, Elspeth – maybe the Incoming and the Venusians are typical of what's out there. But that doesn't mean we have to be like them, does it? Maybe we'll find others more like us. And if not, well, we can be the first. A spark to light a fire that will engulf the universe.'

She ruminated. 'You have to start somewhere, I suppose. As with this drain.'

'Well, there you go.'

'All right, damn it, I'll join your think tank. But first you're going to help me finish this job, aren't you, city boy?'

So I changed into overalls and work boots, and we dug away at that ditch in the damp, clingy earth until our backs ached, and the light of the equinoctial day slowly faded.

OTHER TOMORROWS

TURING'S APPLES

Near the centre of the moon's far side there is a neat, round, well-defined crater called Daedalus. No human knew it existed before the middle of the twentieth century. It's a bit of lunar territory almost as far as you can get from Earth, and about the quietest.

That's why the teams of astronauts from Europe, America, Russia and China went there. They smoothed over the floor of a crater ninety kilometres wide, laid sheets of metal mesh over the natural dish, and suspended feed horns and receiver systems on spidery scaffolding. And there you had it, an instant radio telescope, by far the most powerful ever built: a super-Arecibo, dwarfing its mother in Puerto Rico. Before the astronauts left they christened their telescope Clarke.

Now the telescope is a ruin, and much of the floor of Daedalus is covered by glass, moon dust melted by multiple nuclear strikes. But, I'm told, if you were to look down from some slow lunar orbit you would see a single point of light glowing there, a star fallen to the moon. One day the moon will be gone, but that point will remain, silently orbiting Earth, a lunar memory. And in the further future, when the Earth has gone too, when the stars have burned out and the galaxies fled from the sky, still that point of light will shine.

My brother Wilson never left the Earth. In fact he rarely left England. He was buried, what was left of him, in a grave next to our father's, just outside Milton Keynes. But he *made* that point of light on the moon, which will be the last legacy of all mankind.

Talk about sibling rivalry.

2027 AD

It was at my father's funeral, actually, before Wilson had even begun his SETI searches, that the Clarke first came between us.

There was a good turnout at the funeral, at an old church on the outskirts of Milton Keynes proper. Wilson and I were my father's only children, but as well as his old friends there were a couple of surviving aunts and a gaggle of cousins mostly around our age, mid-twenties to mid-thirties, so there was a good crop of children, like little flowers.

I don't know if I'd say Milton Keynes is a good place to live. It certainly isn't a good place to die. The city is a monument to planning, a concrete grid of avenues with very English names like Midsummer, now overlaid by the new monorail. It's so *clean* it makes death seem a social embarrassment, like a fart in a shopping mall. Maybe we need to be buried in ground dirty with bones.

Our grandfather had remembered how the area was all villages and farmland before the Second World War. He had stayed on even after our grandmother died twenty years before he did, him and his memories made invalid by all the architecture.

At the service I spoke of those memories, or rather of my father's anecdotes about *his* father – for instance how during the war a tough Home Guard had caught Granddad sneaking into the grounds of Bletchley Park, not far away, scrumping apples while Alan Turing and the other geniuses were labouring over Nazi codes inside the house. 'When my brother and I turned out academic, Granddad always said he wondered if he picked up a mathematical bug from Turing's apples,' I concluded, 'because, he would say, for sure Wilson's brain didn't come from him.'

'Your brain too,' Wilson said when he collared me later outside the church. He hadn't spoken at the service; that wasn't his style. 'You should have mentioned that. I'm not the only mathematical nerd in the family.'

It was a difficult moment. My wife and I had just been introduced to Hannah, the two-year-old daughter of a cousin. Hannah had been born profoundly deaf, and we adults in our black suits and dresses were awkwardly copying her parents' bits of sign language. Wilson just walked right through this lot to get to me, barely glancing at the little girl with the wide smile who was the centre of attention. I led him away to avoid any offence.

He was thirty then, a year older than me, taller, thinner, edgier. Others have said we were more similar than I wanted to believe. He had brought nobody with him to the funeral, and that was a relief. His partners could be male or female, his relationships usually destructive; he brought them into the family like unexploded bombs.

'Sorry if I got the story wrong,' I said, a bit caustically.

'Dad and his memories, all those stories he told over and over. Well, at least it's the last time I'll hear about Granddad and Turing's apples.'

That thought hurt me. 'We'll remember. I suppose I'll tell it to Eddie and Sam someday.' My own little boys.

'They won't listen. Why should they? Dad will fade away. Everybody fades away. The dead get deader.' He was talking about his own father, remember, whom we had just buried. 'Listen, have you heard they're putting the Clarke through its acceptance test run?' And, there in the churchyard, he actually pulled a tablet out of his inside jacket pocket and brought up a specification. 'Of course you understand the importance of it being on Farside.' For the millionth time in my life he had set his little brother a pop quiz, and he looked at me as if I was catastrophically dumb.

'Radio shadow,' I said. To be shielded from Earth's noisy chatter was particularly important for SETI, the search for extraterrestrial intelligence to which my brother was devoting his career. SETI searches for faint signals from remote civilisations, a task made orders of magnitude harder if you're drowned out by very loud signals from a nearby civilisation.

He actually applauded my guess, sarcastically. He often reminded me of what had always repelled me about academia – the barely repressed bullying, the intense rivalry. A university is a chimp pack. That was why I was never tempted to go down that route. That, and maybe the fact that Wilson had gone that way ahead of me.

I was faintly relieved when people started to move out of the churchyard. There was going to be a reception at my father's home.

'So are you coming for the cakes and sherry?'

He glanced at the time on his tablet. 'Actually I've somebody to meet.'

'He or she?'

He didn't reply. For one brief moment he looked at me with honesty. 'You're better at this stuff than me.'

'What stuff? Being human?'

'Listen, the Clarke should be open for business in a month. Come on down to London; we can watch the first results.'

'I'd like that.'

I was lying, and his invitation probably wasn't sincere either. In the end it was over two years before I saw him again.

By then he'd found the Eagle signal, and everything had changed.

2029 AD

Wilson and his team quickly established that their brief signal, first detected just months after Clarke went operational, was coming from a source six thousand five hundred light years from Earth, somewhere beyond a starbirth cloud called the Eagle Nebula. That's a long way away, on the other side of the Galaxy's next spiral arm in, the Sagittarius.

And to call the signal 'brief' understates it. It was a second-long pulse, faint and hissy, and it repeated just once a *year*, roughly. It was a monument to robotic patience that the big lunar ear had picked up the damn thing at all.

Still, it was a genuine signal from ET, the scientists were jumping up and down, and for a while it was a public sensation. But the signal was just a squirt of noise from a long way off. When there was no follow-up, when no mother ship materialised in the sky, interest moved on. The whole business of the signal turned out to be your classic nine-day wonder.

Wilson invited me in on the tenth day. That was why I was resentful, I guess, as I drove into town that morning to visit him.

The Clarke Institute's ground station was in one of the huge glass follies thrown up along the banks of the Thames in the profligate boom-capitalism days of the early noughties. Now office space was cheap enough even for academics to rent, but central London was a fortress, with mandatory crawl lanes so your face could be captured by the surveillance cameras. I was in the counter-terror business myself, and I could see the necessity as I edged past St Paul's, whose dome had been smashed like an egg by the Carbon Cowboys' bomb of 2025. But the slow ride left me plenty of time to brood on how many more *important* people Wilson had shown off to before he got around to his brother. Wilson never was loyal that way.

Wilson sat me down and offered me a can of warm Coke. His office could have been any modern data-processing installation, save for the all-sky projection of the cosmic background radiation painted on the ceiling. An audio transposition of the signal was playing on an open laptop, over and over. It sounded like waves lapping at a beach. Wilson looked like he hadn't shaved for three days, slept for five, or changed his shirt in ten. He listened, rapt.

Even Wilson and his team hadn't known about the detection of the signal for a year. The Clarke ran autonomously; the astronauts who had built it had long since packed up and come home. A year earlier the telescope's signal processors had spotted the pulse, a whisper of microwaves. There was structure in there, and evidence that the beam was collimated – it looked artificial. But the signal faded after just a second.

Most previous SETI searchers had listened for strong, continuous signals, and would have given up at that point. But what about a lighthouse, sweeping a microwave beam around the Galaxy like a searchlight? That, so Wilson had explained to me, would be a much cheaper way for a transmitting civilisation to send to a lot more stars. So, based on that economic argument, the Clarke was designed for patience. It had waited a whole year. It had even sent requests to other installations, asking them to keep an electronic eye out in case the Clarke, stuck in its crater, happened to be looking the other way when or if the signal recurred. In the end it struck lucky and found the repeat pulse itself, and at last alerted its human masters.

'We're hot favourites for the Nobel,' Wilson said, matter of fact.

I felt like having a go at him. 'Probably everybody out there has forgotten about your signal already.' I waved a hand at the huge glass windows; the office, meant for fat-cat hedge fund managers, had terrific views of the river, the Houses of Parliament, the tangled wreck of the London Eye. 'OK, it's proof of existence, but that's all.'

He frowned at that. 'Well, that's not true. Actually we're looking for more data in the signal. It is very faint, and there's a lot of scintillation from the interstellar medium. We're probably going to have to wait for a few more passes to get a better resolution.'

'A few more passes? A few more years!'

'But even without that there's a lot we can tell just from the signal itself.' He pulled up charts on his laptop. 'For a start we can deduce the Eaglets' technical capabilities and power availability, given that we believe they'd do it as cheaply as possible. This analysis is related to an old model called Benford beacons.' He pointed to a curve minimum. 'Look – we figure they are pumping a few hundred megawatts through an array kilometres across, probably comparable to the one we've got listening on the moon. Sending out pulses around the plane of the Galaxy, where most of the stars lie. We can make other guesses.' He leaned back and took a slug of his Coke, dribbling a few drops to add to the collection of stains on his shirt. 'The search for ET was always guided by philosophical principles and logic. Now we have this one data point, the Eaglets six thousand light years away, we can test those principles.'

'Such as?'

'The principle of plenitude. We believed that because life and intelligence arose on this Earth, they ought to arise everywhere they could. Here's one validation of that principle. Then there's the principle of mediocrity.'

I remembered enough of my own studies to recall that. 'We aren't at any special place in space and time.'

'Right. Turns out, given this one data point, it's not likely to hold too well.'

'Why do you say that?'

'Because we found these guys in the direction of the centre of the Galaxy . . .'

When the Galaxy was young, star formation was most intense at its core. Later a wave of starbirth swept out through the disc, with the heavy elements necessary for life baked in the hearts of dead stars and driven on a wind of supernovas. So the stars inward of us are older than the sun, and are therefore likely to have been harbours for life much longer.

'We would expect to see a concentration of old civilisations towards the centre of the Galaxy. This one example validates that.' He eyed me, challenging. 'We can even guess how many technological, transmitting civilisations there are in the Galaxy.'

'From this one instance?' I was practised at this kind of contest between us. 'Well, let's see. The Galaxy is a disc a hundred thousand light years across, roughly. If all the civilisations are an average of six thousand light years apart – divide the area of the Galaxy by the area of a disc with a diameter of six thousand light years – around three hundred?'

He smiled. 'Very *good*.'

'So we're not typical,' I said. 'We're young, and out in the suburbs. All that from a single microwave pulse.'

'Of course most ordinary people are too dumb to be able to appreciate logic like that. That's why they aren't rioting in the streets.' He said this casually. Language like that always made me wince, even when we were undergraduates.

But he had a point. Besides, I had the feeling that most people had already believed in their gut that ET existed; this was a confirmation, not a shock. You might blame Hollywood for that. But Wilson sometimes speculated that we were looking for our lost prehistoric cousins. All those other hominid species, those other kinds of mind, that we killed off one by one, just as in my lifetime we had destroyed the chimps in the wild – sentient tool-using beings, hunted down for bushmeat. We evolved on a crowded planet, and we know something is missing, even if we forgot what we did and don't know what's wrong.

'A lot of people are speculating about whether the Eaglets have souls,' I said. 'According to St Thomas Aquinas...'

He waved away St Thomas Aquinas. 'You know, in a way our feelings behind SETI were always theological, explicitly or not. We were looking for God in the sky, or some technological equivalent. Somebody who would care about *us*. But we were never going to find Him. We were going to find either emptiness, or a new category of being, between us and the angels. The Eaglets have got nothing to do with us, or our dreams of God. That's what people don't see. And that's what people will have to deal with, ultimately.'

He glanced at the ceiling, and I guessed he was looking towards the Eagle Nebula. 'And they won't be much like us. Hell of a place they live in. Not like here. The Sagittarius arm wraps a whole turn around the Galaxy's core, full of dust and clouds and young stars. Why, the Eagle Nebula itself is a stellar nursery, lit up by stars only a few million years old. Must be a tremendous sky, like a slow explosion – not like our sky of orderly wheeling pinpoints, which is like the inside of a computer. No wonder the development of our own science began with astrology and astronomy. How do you imagine *their* thinking will be different?'

I grunted. 'We'll never know. Not for twelve thousand years at least, if we have to send a question and wait for the answer.'

'Maybe. Depends what data we find in the signal. You want another Coke?'

But I hadn't opened the first.

That was how that day went. We talked of nothing but the signal, not how he was, who he was dating, not about my family, my wife and the boys – all of us learning sign, incidentally, to talk to little Hannah. The Eagle signal was inhuman, abstract. Nothing you could see or touch; you couldn't even hear it without fancy signal processing. But it was all that filled his head. That was Wilson all over.

This was, in retrospect, the happiest time of his life. God help him.

2033 AD

'You want my help, don't you?'

Wilson stood on my doorstep, wearing a jacket and shambolic tie, every inch the academic. He looked shifty. 'How do you know?'

'Why else would you come here? You never visit.' Well, it was true. He hardly ever even mailed or called. I didn't think my wife and kids had seen him since our father's funeral six years earlier.

He thought that over, then grinned. 'A reasonable deduction, given past observation. Can I come in?'

I took him through the living room on the way to my home study. The boys, then twelve and thirteen, were playing a hologram boxing game, with two wavering foot-tall prize fighters mimicking the kids' actions in the middle of the carpet. I introduced Wilson. They barely remembered him and I wasn't sure if he remembered *them*. The boys signed to each other: *What a dork*, roughly translated.

I hurried him on, but Wilson noticed the signing. 'What are they doing? Some kind of private game?'

I wasn't surprised he wouldn't know. 'That's British Sign Language. We've all been learning it for years – actually since Dad's funeral, when we hooked up with Barry and his wife, and we found out they had a little deaf girl. Hannah, do you remember? She's eight now. We've all been learning to talk to her. The kids find it fun, I think. You know, it's an irony that you're involved in a billion-pound project to talk to aliens six thousand light years away, yet it doesn't trouble you that you can't speak to a little girl in your own family.'

He looked at me blankly. I was mouthing words that obviously meant nothing to him, intellectually or emotionally. That was Wilson.

He just started talking about work. 'We've got six years' worth of data now – six pulses, each a second long. There's a *lot* of information in there. They use a technique like our own wavelength-division multiplexing, with the signal divided into sections each a kilohertz or so wide. We've extracted gigabytes . . .'

I gave up. I went and made a pot of coffee, and brought it back to the study. When I returned he was still standing where I'd left him, like a switched-off robot. He took a coffee and sat down.

I prompted, 'Gigabytes?'

'Gigabytes. By comparison the whole *Encyclopaedia Britannica* is just one gigabyte. The problem is we can't make sense of it.'

'How do you know it's not just noise?'

'We have techniques to test for that. Information theory. Based on experiments to do with talking to dolphins, actually.' He dug a tablet out of his pocket and showed me some of the results.

The first was simple enough, called a 'Zipf graph'. You break your message up into what look like components – maybe words, letters, phonemes in English. Then you do a frequency count: how many letter As, how many Es, how many Rs. If you have random noise you'd expect roughly equal numbers of the letters, so you'd get a flat distribution. If you have a clean signal without information content, a string of identical letters, A, A, A, you'd get a graph with a spike. Meaningful information gives you a slope, somewhere in between those horizontal and vertical extremes.

'And we get a beautiful log-scale minus one power law,' he said, showing me. 'There's information in there all right. But there is a lot of controversy over identifying the elements themselves. The Eaglets did *not* send down neat binary code. The data is frequency modulated, their language full of growths and decays. More like a movie of a garden growing on fast-forward than any human narrative. I wonder if it has something to do with that young sky of theirs. Anyhow, after the Zipf, we tried a Shannon entropy analysis.'

This is about looking for relationships between the signal elements. You work out conditional probabilities: given pairs of elements, how likely is it that you'll see U following Q? Then you go on to higher-order 'entropy levels', in the jargon, starting with triples: how likely is it to find G following I and N?

'As a comparison, dolphin languages get to third- or fourth-order entropy. We humans get to eighth or ninth.'

'And the Eaglets?'

'The entropy level breaks our assessment routines. We think it's around order thirty.' He regarded me, seeing if I understood. 'It is information, but much more complex than any human language. It might be like English sentences with a fantastically convoluted structure – triple or quadruple negatives, overlapping clauses, tense changes.' He grinned. 'Or triple entendres.'

'They're smarter than us.'

'Oh, yes. And this is proof, if we needed it, that the message isn't meant specifically for us.'

I got it. 'Because if it were, they'd have dumbed it down. How smart do you think they are? Smarter than us, certainly, but—'

'Are there limits? Well, maybe. You might imagine that an older culture would plateau, once they've figured out the essential truths of the universe, and a technology optimal for their needs... There's no reason to think progress need be onward and upward forever. Then again, perhaps there are fundamental limits to information processing. Perhaps a brain that gets too complex is prone to crashes and overloads. There may be a trade-off between complexity and stability.'

I poured him more coffee. 'Am I supposed to feel demoralised? I went to Cambridge, remember. I'm used to being surrounded by entities smarter than I am.'

He grinned. 'That's up to you. But the Eaglets are a new category of being for us. This isn't like the Incas meeting the Spaniards, a mere technological gap. *They* had a basic humanity in common. We may find the gulf between us and the Eaglets is *forever* unbridgeable. Remember how Dad used to read *Gulliver's Travels* to us?'

The memory made me smile. 'Those talking horses used to scare the wits out of me.'

'Yeah. They were genuinely smarter than us. And how did Gulliver react to them? He was totally overawed. He tried to imitate them, and even after they kicked him out he always despised his own kind, because they weren't as good as the horses.'

'The revenge of Mister Ed,' I said.

He just looked at me blankly. 'Maybe that will be the way for us – we'll ape the Eaglets or defy them. Maybe the mere knowledge of the existence of a race smarter than your own is death.'

'Is all this being released to the public?'

'Oh, yes. We're affiliated to NASA, and they have an explicit open-book policy. Besides, the Institute is as leaky as hell. There's no point even trying to keep it quiet. But we're releasing the news gradually and soberly. Nobody's noticing much. You hadn't, had you?'

'So what do you think the signal is? Some kind of super-encyclopaedia?'

He snorted. 'Maybe. That's the fond hope among the contact optimists. But when the European colonists turned up on foreign shores, *their* first impulse wasn't to hand over encyclopaedias or histories, but—'

'Bibles.'

'Yes. It could be something less disruptive than that. A vast work of art, for instance. But why would they send such a thing? Maybe it's a funeral pyre. Or a pharaoh's funerary monument. Look what I built.'

'So what do you want of me?'

He faced me. I thought it was clear he was trying to figure out, in his clumsy way, how to get me to do whatever it was he wanted. 'Well, what do you think? This makes translating the most obscure human language a cakewalk, and we've got nothing like a Rosetta stone. Look, Jack, our information processing suites at the Institute are pretty smart theoretically, but they are limited. Running off processors and memory store not much beefier than this.' He waved his tablet. 'Whereas the software brutes that do your data mining are an order of magnitude more powerful.'

The software I developed and maintained mined the endless torrents of data culled on every individual in the country, from your minute-to-minute movements on private or public transport to the porn you accessed and how you hid it from your partner. We tracked your patterns of behaviour, and deviations from those patterns. The terrorists and other trouble-makers were needles in a haystack, of which the rest of us were the millions of straws.

This continual live data mining took up monstrous memory storage and processing power. A few times I'd visited the big Home Office computers in their hardened bunkers under New Scotland Yard: giant superconducting neural nets suspended in rooms so cold your breath crackled. There was nothing like it in the private sector, or in academia.

Which, I realised, was why Wilson had come to me today.

'You want me to run your ET signal through my data mining suites.' He immediately had me hooked, but I wasn't about to admit it. I might have rejected the academic life, but curiosity burned in me as strongly as it ever did in Wilson. I had to put up a token fight, though. 'How do you imagine I'd get permission for that?'

He waved that away as a technicality of no interest. 'What we're looking for is patterns embedded deep in the data, layers down, any kind of recognisable starter for us in decoding the whole thing ... Obviously software designed to look for patterns in the way I use my travel cards is going to have to be adapted to seek useful correlations in the Eaglet data. It will be an unprecedented technical challenge.

'In a way that's a good thing. It will likely take generations to decode this stuff, if we ever do, the way it took the Renaissance Europeans generations to make sense of the legacy of antiquity. The sheer time factor is a culture-shock prophylactic.

'So are you going to bend the rules for me, Jack? Come on, man.

Remember what Dad said. We both ate Turing's apples... Solving puzzles like this is what we do.'

He wasn't entirely without guile. He knew how to entice me. He turned out to be wrong about the culture shock, however.

2036 AD

Two armed coppers escorted me through the Institute building. The big glass box was entirely empty save for me and the coppers and a sniffer dog. The morning outside was bright, a cold spring day, the sky a serene blue, elevated from Wilson's latest madness.

Wilson was sitting in the Clarke project office, beside a screen across which data displays flickered. He had big slabs of Semtex strapped around his waist, and some kind of dead man's trigger in his hand. My brother, reduced at last to a cliché suicide bomber. The coppers stayed safely outside.

'We're secure.' Wilson glanced around. 'They can see us but they can't hear us. I'm confident of that. My firewalls—' When I walked towards him he held up his hands. 'No closer. I'll blow it, I swear.'

'Christ, Wilson.' But I stood still, shut up, and deliberately calmed down.

I knew that my boys, now in their teens, would be watching every move on the spy-hack news channels. Maybe nobody could hear us, but Hannah, now a beautiful eleven-year-old, had plenty of friends who could read lips. That would never occur to Wilson. But it determined how I was going to play this. If I was to die today, here with my lunatic of a brother, I wasn't going to let my boys remember their father broken by fear.

I sat down. There was a six-pack of warm soda on the bench. I think I'll always associate warm soda with Wilson. I took one, popped the tab and sipped; I could taste nothing. 'You want one?'

'No,' he said bitterly. 'Make yourself at home, though.'

'What a fucking idiot you are, Wilson. How did it ever come to this?'

'You should know. You helped me.'

'And by God I've regretted it ever since,' I snarled back at him. 'You got me sacked, you moron. And since France, every nut job on the planet has me targeted, and my kids. We have police protection.'

'Don't blame me. You chose to help me.'

I stared at him. 'That's called loyalty. A quality which you, entirely lacking it yourself, see only as a weakness to exploit.'

'Well, whatever. What does it matter now? Look, Jack, I need your help.'

'This is turning into a pattern.'

He glanced at his screen. 'I need you to buy me time, to give me a chance to complete this project.'

'Why should I care about your project?'

'It's not *my* project. It never has been. Surely you understand that much. It's the Eaglets'...'

Everything had changed in the three years since I had begun to run Wilson's message through the big Home Office computers beneath New Scotland Yard – all under the radar of my bosses; they'd never have dared risk exposing their precious supercooled brains to such unknowns. Well, Wilson had been right. My data mining had quickly turned up recurring segments, chunks of organised data differing only in detail.

And it had been Wilson's intuition that these things were bits of executable code: programs you could run. Even as expressed in the Eaglets' odd flowing language, he thought he recognised logical loops, start and stop statements. Mathematics may or may not be universal, but computing seems to be – and my brother had found Turing machines, buried deep in an alien database.

Wilson translated the segments into a human mathematical programming language, and set them to run on a dedicated processor. They turned out to be like viruses. Once downloaded on almost any computer substrate they organised themselves, investigated their environment, started to multiply, and quickly grew, accessing the data banks that had been downloaded from the stars with them. Then they started asking questions of the operators: simple yes-no, true-false exchanges that soon built up a common language.

'The Eaglets didn't send us a message,' Wilson had whispered to me on the phone in the small hours; at the height of it he had worked twenty-four seven. 'They downloaded an AI. And now the AI is learning to speak to us.'

It was a way to resolve a ferocious communications challenge. The Eaglets were sending their message to the whole Galaxy; they knew nothing about the intelligence, cultural development, or even the physical form of their audiences. So they sent an all-purpose artificial mind embedded in the information stream itself, able to learn and start a local dialogue with the receivers. *Any* receivers.

This above all else proved to me how smart the Eaglets must be.

It didn't comfort me at all that some commentators pointed out that this 'Hoyle strategy' had been anticipated by some human thinkers; it's one thing to anticipate, another to build. I wondered in fact if those viruses found it a challenge to dumb down their message for creatures capable of only ninth-order Shannon entropy, as we were.

And of course the news that there was information in the Eaglets' beeps leaked almost immediately. For running the Eaglet data through the Home Office mining suites I was sacked, arrested – but, such was the evident priority of the project, I was bailed on condition I went back to work on the Eaglet stuff under police and Home Office supervision.

Because only the Clarke telescope could pick up the signal, the scientists at the Clarke Institute and the consortium of governments they answered to were able to keep control of the information itself. And that information soon looked as if it would become extremely valuable. Even the Eaglets' programming and data compression techniques, what we could make of them, had immediate commercial value. When patented by the UK government and licensed, an information revolution began that added a hundred billion euros to Britain's balance of payments in the first year. Governments and corporations outside the loop jumped up and down with fury.

Then Wilson and his team, through a variety of channels, started to publish what they were learning of the Eaglets themselves.

We still don't know anything about what they look like, how they live – or even if they're corporeal or not. But they are old, vastly old compared to us. Their cultural records go back a million years, maybe ten times as long as we've been human, and even then they built their civilisation on the ruins of others. But they regard themselves as a young species. They live in awe of even older ones, whose presence they have glimpsed deep in the turbulent core of the Galaxy.

Not surprisingly, the Eaglets are fascinated by time and its processes. One of Wilson's team foolishly speculated that the Eaglets actually made a religion of time, deifying the one universal that will erode us all in the end. That caused a lot of trouble. Some people took up the time creed with enthusiasm, and they looked for parallels in human philosophies, the Hindu and the Mayan. If the Eaglets really were smarter than us, they said, they must be closer to the true god, and we should follow them. Others, led by the conventional religions, moved sharply in the opposite direction. Minor wars broke out over a creed that had been entirely unknown to humanity five years before, and which nobody on Earth remotely understood.

Then the economic dislocations began, as those new techniques for data handling made whole industries obsolescent. That was predictable; it was as if the aliens had invaded cyberspace. Luddite types began sabotaging the software houses turning out the new-generation systems, and battles broke out in the corporate universe, themselves on the economic scale of small wars.

Amid all the economic, political, religious and philosophical turbulence, it was evident that if anybody had dreamed that encountering the alien would unite us around our common humanity, they were dead wrong.

'This is the danger of speed,' Wilson had said to me, just weeks before he wired himself up with Semtex. 'If we'd been able to take it slow, unwrapping the message would have been more like an exercise in normal science, and we could have absorbed it. Grown with it. Instead, thanks to the viruses, it's been like a revelation, a pouring of holy knowledge into our heads. Revelations tend to be destabilising. Look at Jesus. Just three centuries after the Crucifixion, Christianity had taken over the whole Roman empire...'

Then it got worse. A bunch of Algerian patriots used pirated copies of the Eaglet viruses to hammer the electronic infrastructure of France's major cities. As everything from sewage to air traffic control crashed, the country was simultaneously assaulted with train bombs, bugs in the water supply, a dirty nuke in Orleans. It was a force-multiplier attack, in the jargon; the toll of death and injury was a shock, even by the standards of the fourth decade of the bloody twenty-first century. And our counter-measures were useless in the face of the ETI viruses.

That was when the governments decided the Eaglet project had to be shut down, or at the very least put under tight control. But my brother wasn't having any of that.

'None of this is the fault of the Eaglets,' he said now, an alien apologist with Semtex strapped to his waist. 'They didn't mean to harm us in any way.'

'Then what do they want?'

'Our help...'

And he was going to provide it. With, in turn, my help.

'Why me? I was sacked, remember.'

'They'll listen to you. The police. Because you're my brother. You're useful.'

'Useful?' At times Wilson seemed unable to see people as anything other than assets, even his own family. I sighed. 'Tell me what you want.'

'Time,' he said, glancing at his screen, the data and status summaries scrolling across it. 'The great god of the Eaglets, remember? *Time*. Just a little more.'

'How much time?'

He checked. 'Twenty-four hours would let me complete this download. That's an outside estimate. Just stall them. Keep the coppers talking, stay here with me. Make them think you're making progress in talking me out of it.'

'While the actual progress is being made by *that*.' I nodded at the screen. 'What are you doing here, Wilson? What's it about?'

'I don't know all of it. There are hints in the data. Subtexts sometimes...' He was whispering.

'Subtexts about what?'

'About what really concerns the Eaglets. Jack, what do you imagine a long-lived civilisation *wants*? If you could think on very long timescales you would be concerned about threats that seem remote to us.'

'An asteroid impact due in a thousand years, maybe? If I expected to live that long, or my kids—'

'That kind of thing. But that's not long enough, Jack, not nearly. In the data there are passages – poetry, maybe – that speak of the deep past and furthest future, the Big Bang that is echoed in the microwave background, the future that will be dominated by the dark energy expansion that will ultimately throw all the other galaxies over the cosmological horizon... The Eaglets think about these things, and not just as scientific hypotheses. They *care* about them. The dominance of their great god time. "The universe has no memory".'

'What does that mean?'

'I'm not sure. A phrase in the message.'

'So what are you downloading? And to where?'

'The moon,' he said frankly. 'The Clarke telescope, on Farside. They want us to build something, Jack. Something physical, I mean. And with the fabricators and other maintenance gear at Clarke there's a chance we could do it. I mean, it's not the most advanced offworld robot facility; it's only designed for maintenance and upgrade of the radio telescope—'

'But it's the facility you can get your hands on. So you're letting these Eaglet agents out of their virtual world and giving them a way to build something real, in our world. Don't you think that's dangerous?'

'Dangerous how?' And he laughed at me and looked away.

'Don't you turn away from me, you fucker. You've been doing that all our lives. You know what I mean. Why, the Eaglets' software alone is making a mess of the world. What if this is some kind of Trojan horse – a Doomsday weapon they're getting us saps to build ourselves?'

'It's hardly likely that an advanced culture—'

'Don't give me that contact-optimist bullshit. You don't believe it yourself. And even if you did, you don't *know* for sure. You can't.'

'No. All right.' He pulled away from me. 'I can't know. Which is one reason why I set the thing going up on the moon, not Earth. Call it a quarantine. If we don't like whatever it is, there's at least a *chance* we could contain it up there. Yes, there's a risk. But the rewards are unknowable, and huge.' He looked at me, almost pleading for me to understand. 'We have to go on. This is the Eaglets' project, not ours. Ever since we unpacked the message, this story has been about them, not us. That's what dealing with a superior intelligence means. It's like those religious nuts say. We *know* the Eaglets are orders of magnitude smarter than us. Shouldn't we trust them? Shouldn't we help them achieve their goal, even if we don't understand precisely what it is?'

'This ends now.' I reached for the keyboard beside me. 'Tell me how to stop the download.'

'No.' He sat firm, that trigger clutched in his right hand.

'You won't use that. You wouldn't kill us both. Not for something so abstract, inhuman—'

'*Superhuman*,' he breathed. 'Not inhuman. Superhuman. Oh, I would. You've known me all your life, Jack. Look into my eyes. *I'm not like you*. Do you really doubt me?'

And, looking at him, I didn't.

So we sat there, the two of us, a face-off. I stayed close enough to overpower him if he gave me the slightest chance. And he kept his trigger before my face.

Hour after hour.

In the end it was time that defeated him, I think, the Eaglets' invisible god. That and fatigue. I'm convinced he didn't mean to release the trigger. Only seventeen hours had elapsed, of the twenty-four he had asked for, when his thumb slipped.

I tried to turn away. That small, instinctive gesture was why I lost a leg, a hand, an eye, all on my right side.

And I lost a brother.

But when the forensics guys had done combing through the wreckage, they were able to prove that the seventeen hours had been enough for Wilson's download.

2040 AD

After the explosion it took a month for NASA, ESA and the Chinese to send up an orbiter to the moon to see what was going on.

The probe found that Wilson's download had caused the Clarke fabricators to start making stuff. At first they made other machines, more specialised, from what was lying around in the workshops and sheds. These in turn made increasingly tiny versions of themselves, heading steadily down to the nano scale. In the end the work was so fine only an astronaut on the ground might have had a chance of even seeing it. Nobody dared send a human in, however.

Meanwhile the machines banked up moon dust and scrap to make a high-energy facility – something like a particle accelerator or a fusion torus, but not.

Then the real work started.

The Eaglet machines took a chunk of moon rock and crushed it, turning its mass-energy into a spacetime artefact – something like a black hole, but not. They dropped it into the body of the moon, where it started accreting, sucking in material, just like a black hole – and budding off copies of itself, unlike a black hole.

The governments panicked. A nuclear warhead was dug out of cold store and dropped plumb into Daedalus Crater. The explosion was spectacular. But when the dust subsided that pale, unearthly spark was still there, unperturbed.

Gradually these objects, these tiny black holes, are converting the substance of the moon into copies of themselves. The glowing point of light we see at the centre of Clarke is leaked radiation from this process. As the cluster of nano artefacts grows, the moon's substance will be consumed at an exponential rate. Centuries, a millennium tops, will be enough to consume it all. And Earth will be orbited, not by its ancient companion, but by a spacetime artefact, like a black hole, but not. That much seems well established by the physicists.

There is less consensus as to the purpose of all this. Here's my guess:

The moon artefact will be a recorder.

Wilson said the Eaglets feared that the universe has no memory. I think he meant that right now, in our cosmic epoch, we can still see relics of the universe's birth, echoes of the Big Bang, in the microwave background glow. And we also see evidence of the expansion to come, in the recession of the distant galaxies. We discovered both these basic features of the universe, its past and its future, in the twentieth century.

There will come a time – the cosmologists quote hundreds of billions of years – when the accelerating recession will have taken *all* those distant galaxies over our horizon. So we will be left with just the local group, the Milky Way and Andromeda and bits and pieces, bound together by gravity. The wider cosmic expansion will be invisible. And meanwhile the background glow will have become so attenuated you won't be able to pick it out of the faint glow of the interstellar medium.

So in that remote epoch you wouldn't be able to repeat the twentieth-century discoveries; you couldn't glimpse past or future. That's what the Eaglets mean when they say the universe has no memory.

And I believe they are countering it. They, and those like Wilson that they co-opt into helping them, are carving time capsules out of folded spacetime. At some future epoch these will evaporate, maybe through something like Hawking radiation, and will reveal the truth of the universe to whatever eyes are there to see it. The Eaglets are conscious entities trying to give the universe a memory. Perhaps there is even a deeper purpose: it may be intelligence's role to shape the ultimate evolution of the universe, but you can't do that if you've forgotten what went before.

Of course it occurs to me – this is Wilson's principle of mediocrity – that ours might not be the only epoch with a privileged view of the cosmos. Just after the Big Bang there was a pulse of 'inflation', superfast expansion that homogenised the universe and erased details of whatever came before. Maybe we should be looking for other time boxes, left for our benefit by the inhabitants of those early realms.

Not every commentator agrees with my analysis, of course. The interpretation of the Eaglet data has always been uncertain. Maybe even Wilson wouldn't agree. Well, since it's my suggestion he would probably argue with me from sheer reflex.

I suppose it's *possible* to care deeply about the plight of hypothetical beings a hundred billion years hence. In one sense we ought to; their epoch is our descendants' inevitable destiny. Wilson certainly did care, enough to kill himself for it. But this is a project so vast and cold that it can engage only a semi-immortal supermind like an Eaglet's – or a modern human who is functionally insane.

What matters most to me is the now. Little Hannah. The sons who haven't yet aged and crumbled to dust, playing football under a sun that hasn't yet burned to a cinder. The fact that all this is transient makes it more precious, not less. Maybe our remote descendants in a hundred billion years will find similar brief happiness under their black and unchanging sky.

If I could wish one thing for my lost brother it would be that I could be sure he had felt this way, this alive, just for one day. Just for one minute. Because, in the end, that's all we've got.

ARTEFACTS

You swim.

Why must you swim?

If you swim, where are you coming from, and where are you going to?

Why is there a 'you' separated from the 'not-you' through which you swim?

Why is there something rather than nothing?

Who are you?

You cannot rest. You are alone. You are frightened by the swimming. And you are frightened that the swimming must end. For – what then?

Morag's mother lay dead, behind the flimsy curtain that veiled her hospital bed, only feet away.

The little waiting area wasn't all that bad. It was carpeted, and had decent chairs and tables piled with newspapers and elderly magazines, *Hello* and *Country Life* and *Reader's Digest*, and a pot plant that Morag had watered a couple of times. A little window gave her a glimpse of Edinburgh rooftops. She had been awake all night, and now it was a sunny June morning, which felt a bit unreal. There was even a little TV up high on the wall, stuck on a news channel that looped headlines about water riots in Australia. In the year 2026 the news was always dismal, and Morag, fifteen years old, generally did her best to ignore it. No, it wasn't bad here, not as bad as you might have thought an NHS ward would be.

But it was all so mundane. It seemed impossible that the same reality, the same room, could contain curling copies of glossy celeb mags and the huge event that had taken place on the other side of that curtain, the final ghastly process as the bone marrow cancer overwhelmed her mother.

Her father, who always encouraged her to call him Joe, was helping himself to another cup of coffee. 'Fucking thing,' he said, as, not for the first time, he had trouble slotting the plastic coffee pot back into its little groove. He glanced at Morag. 'Sorry.'

'Like I never heard you swear before.'

'Fair enough.' He sat beside her.

They were silent a moment, both beyond tears, or between them. She hadn't seen him for a couple of years. His break-up with her mother had seemed to get more antagonistic as time passed, and his visits had become more sporadic and more fraught, at least until these final weeks and days. He was only forty-five. Tall, thin, always gaunt, Morag thought he looked hollowed out.

On impulse she smoothed out his sleeve. 'This shirt needs an iron.'

'Yes.' A flicker of a grin. 'Actually I need a new shirt. Can't afford it.'

They hadn't talked, not to each other, while Mum was still there. 'You quit your job, didn't you?' Joe had been working on computer systems in the City of London – something like that. 'Was it so you could be with Mum?'

'Partly.' He sipped his coffee, and grimaced at its strength. 'That and the fact of the illness itself. When I understood your mother was dying, the reality of it sunk home, I suppose.'

'The reality of what?'

'Life. Death. The finiteness of it all. When you're young you think you're immortal. Forty was a big shock to me, I can tell you, and now this. Hacking predictive algorithms so some City barrow boy could get even richer suddenly seemed an absurd way to spend my time.'

She thought she understood. 'It doesn't make any sense. There's a copy of the *Daily Mirror* sitting on that table. But behind that curtain—'

'I know. You go through life never facing up to the big questions. What is life? What is death? Why is there something rather than nothing? Anyhow, I'm going back to what I used to do.'

She frowned. 'Back to university?'

'I was a researcher,' he said. 'A whiz at maths. I went into theoretical cosmology. Let me tell you something.' He put his arm around her, the way he used to hold her when she was little. 'All of this, everything we see and feel, our whole three-dimensional universe with its unfolding arrow of time, is only a fraction of reality. Of course that was the message my father beat into me when I was your age, or tried to. He was a Presbyterian minister. When I started questioning his picture of the universe we fell out good and proper...'

Morag had only fragmentary memories of her grandfather, whom she'd met a mere handful of times.

Joe said, 'Our universe is like a snowflake in a storm, one among a myriad others, all floating around in a nine-dimensional continuum called the Bulk. The universes are called branes – after membranes – or D-branes, Dirichlet branes . . . Those other universes might be like ours, or they might not. Some of them might have one space dimension, or three or five or seven. They might have a time dimension, like ours, or none at all, so they're just static and eternal. We know all this is out there, you see, because of the effects of the higher reality on our universe. Primordial inflation, patterns in the cosmic microwave background radiation: all of these are influences from other universes approaching our own . . .' He glanced at her. 'I'm getting too technical.'

'No. But it's like when I was small and you'd distract me from the dark with fairy tales.'

He ruffled her hair. 'Well, all this stuff is real, as far as we can tell. Anyhow, it's out there, out in the Bulk, that the answers to the fundamental questions will be found some day. That's why I'm going back. I got sick of the academic life, the bitchiness and the infighting, the treadmill of always having to find a bit more money to keep going for a few more years. Nobody wanted to put money into fundamental research anyhow. But at least doing that I was closer to the big questions than slaving in the damn City.'

It all sounded foolish to Morag, a dream. But Joe had always been a dreamer. She wondered if he ever thought about how she was supposed to be supported through the rest of her schooling, her own college years. Well, she had Auntie Sheena, Mum's sister, cold, disapproving, but solid and generous enough. She wished she were a bit older, though, not so dependent on all these flaky, short-lived adults.

And she said, 'Joe – none of this stuff about D-branes and the Bulk will bring Mum back.'

'No. No, love, it won't.'

For some reason the tears came after that.

A nurse came to refill the coffee, and she dabbed with a tissue at the pot plant that Morag had overfilled with water.

It was a universe not unlike humanity's universe. But it was dark.

It lacked stars, for the intricate coincidence of fundamental constants that enabled stellar fusion processes had not occurred here; the dice had fallen differently. Yet complex elements had spewed out of this cosmos's equivalent of the Big Bang, atoms that combined, nuclei that fissioned. Rock formed, and ice. Grains gathered in the dark, drawn by gravity.

There were no stars here. But soon there were worlds.

On one of these worlds, creatures not entirely unlike those on Earth rose from the usual chemical churning. They were fuelled not by sunlight but by the slow seep of minerals and heat from the interior of their rocky planet. Crawling, swimming, flying, consuming each other and the world's raw materials, they built an ecology of a complexity that itself increased with time. There were extinctions as rocks fell from the sky, or when the cooling world spasmed as it shed its primordial heat, but each time life recovered, complexity was regained.

To those with minds this was a beautiful world, that empty sky a velvet heaven. They knew no different. Some of them dreamed of gods.

Few ever imagined, however, that a greater mind than any of theirs arose from the intricate workings of their ecology itself.

And that mind was troubled.

For she felt the grand cooling of her planetary body, and ached with the slow decay of the radioactive substances that replenished that heat. She remembered a time of hot youth, and she foresaw shrivelling cold, when the creatures that swarmed over her continents and oceans would die back, and her own thoughts would simplify and die back with them.

She remembered the birth of her universe. She anticipated surviving, in some reduced form, to see its end. To a being built on such a grand scale that future time of cold paralysis was not so terribly remote.

Questions plagued her. Why did it have to be so? Why must she die? Why should she have been born at all?

Why was there something in this universe, rather than nothing?

She longed for another to discuss these profound questions. There was no other like her, not in all this universe.

Not yet.

One was born, inchoate, utterly lacking symmetry. A mind formed immediately, like a snowflake crystallising from moist air, with questions: Where am I? What is this place? What must I do?

Others gathered around him. Answers slotted into the empty spaces of his mind.

Eight dimensions of space and one of time characterised this particular universe. That and symmetry.

Yet the symmetry was incomplete. There was an array of two hundred and forty-eight places to be filled, by ones like himself, as if you ascended to take a place in a constellation. That was the purpose of life, to ascend, to take your place, to contribute to the greater symmetry.

And when that vast symmetry was completed, the universe would end.

Even as he realised this, as he grasped the essential structure of his universe only moments after he was born, he was troubled by a faint doubt.

But in the meantime there was work to be done. Many of those two hundred and forty-eight places were already filled, and there were far more candidates than there were remaining places. All around him other young were gathering in simple clusters of four, eight, sixteen; others, more ambitious, sought to impress with explorations of twenty-three and thirty-one.

To shine in such gatherings was the only way to progress. A process of selection had to be gone through if you were to attain the heaven of perfected symmetry.

Grimly he got to work.

Morag's flight from Edinburgh was diverted to Luton because of flooding at Heathrow, but she was able to catch a short-haul connection to City Airport.

The plane took Morag over London along the line of the Thames and past the City, where her father had worked five years before. The ageing office blocks rose like thistles from the flood, and choppers flitted before impassive glass cliffs. Each of these huge developments contained as many people as a small town, stacked up into the sky; in the context of the latest London-wide flood emergency, each would require a major rescue operation of its own.

At the airport, passport control was perfunctory despite Scotland's independence. She caught a cab to the hotel at Hampstead, safely above the waterline, where her father was staying.

Joe was pacing around his tiny room, shirt rumpled as ever, tie loosened, shoes off, socks with holes in them. He looked as if he was longing for a cigarette. He was evidently wired on in-room coffee.

The remnants of his presentation to the government's Science and

Technologies Facilities Council were scattered on the small table and on the bed. Slides played over a slim laptop, mostly bullet-point argument summaries. There was one extraordinary image like a mutated sea anemone that Morag had come to recognise as a representation of a Calabi-Yau space, a possible configuration of the Bulk, the greater nine-dimensional continuum within which the universe swam.

'I'm sorry I missed your show,' Morag said. 'The plane, the flooding—'

'That's OK,' Joe said. Making an obvious effort to calm down, he came and kissed her cheek, took her coat and hung it on the back of the door. 'Not that you missed anything but another ritual humiliation. There's something else I want to talk about anyhow. You want a coffee?' He rummaged in the litter on the table, the little packets of granules and the plastic milk cartons. 'I've burned through most of it but there might be a packet of that fucking decaff stuff. Sorry.'

'I'm fine. Your need is greater than mine.' She pulled out the room's one chair from under the table and sat. 'I take it you didn't go down well, then.'

'Oh, hell, it's not just me. They announced another across-the-board cut in research spending last month. I was hoping to get hold of some American money, they're always more flush over there, but it's the same story, cuts to the National Science Foundation, the National Institute of Standards and Technology, the Office of Science at the Department of Energy. They're even making lay-offs at Fermilab.'

She pulled at her fingers. 'It's tough all over, Joe. There's money in ecosystem research but even that's getting tighter.' That was the direction she wanted to go herself, when she finished her first degree in biological sciences; she was twenty years old now and a couple of years into her course. 'And that's obviously applicable.'

'"Applicable!" How I hate that word. If your research doesn't have obvious "applicability" in flood defences or desalination or food production or, better yet, defence systems, you're screwed.'

'Well, you can understand it, Joe. The world can't afford as much as it used to. These are tough times.'

'The times are always tough,' he snapped back. 'There are always excuses not to spend on fundamental research.'

She reached over for the laptop and tapped a key to page through his slides. 'The trouble is, everything you ask for is just so expensive. This is big stuff...'

Over the years she'd learned something about the technologies

Joe needed to give him the data that would confirm or refute his theoretical meta-cosmic models. Evidence for other universes came in exotic and subtle forms, such as patterns in the cosmic background microwave radiation, a relic of the Big Bang which, Joe believed, had itself been caused by the close approach of one brane-universe to another, or even their collision. Other distortions in the radiation pattern could show the effect of more recent approaches to other branes – holes in the sky, such as a vast gap eight billion light years from Earth and all of a billion light years wide, where few galaxies swam. You needed satellite observatories to pick that up.

Or you could look for gamma rays, which might be relics of other exotic events. A supernova could produce gravitons, gravity-force-carrying particles, some of which, called Kaluza-Klein gravitons, were able to travel out of the 'surface' of a brane and into the greater Bulk. Falling back to a brane, such gravitons could produce a shower of high-energy gamma rays – which again, mostly, could only be detected from space. But NASA was mothballing its elderly gamma-ray satellite, called GLAST, the Gamma-Ray Large Area Space Telescope. You could even look for gravity waves, ripples in spacetime, more evidences of influences from beyond the universe's three-dimensional plane. But again those effects were subtle, minute, fiendishly difficult to track down.

You needed a big budget for any of this. And, in a world fraying under the multiple assault of climate change, resource depletion, disease and war, big budgets for cutting-edge physics experiments were hard to come by. Joe knew this as well as Morag did. It didn't make the results of his pitch any less disappointing.

She came to one striking image. It was geometrical, like a sphere picked out by a regular array of golden points, each apparently connected to the rest by a silver thread. It turned and pivoted in the computer's animation, its symmetries obviously profound. 'This is beautiful. What is it?'

'E8,' Joe said. 'A somewhat complicated mathematical pattern in eight dimensions. Two hundred and forty-eight points. It's a way of encapsulating the unification of physics. It's all to do with string theory, as is the whole idea of brane-universes... You place a fundamental particle or force at each of the points, say an electron or a quark, and if you get it right, the symmetries express the particles' relationships to each other.' He made the figure swivel this way and that, and projected various subsets of the particles down to two dimensions. 'See? This projection shows how the colour charge of a quark changes under the influence of the strong force carried by a gluon...'

'I'll take your word for it.'

'It's a bit of research from the noughties I've been following up, called the Lisi synthesis. The thing is, the same mathematical structure can be used in some models to describe the Bulk, the Calabi-Yau manifold. Remarkably rich, tens of thousands of interaction types expressed in the internal symmetries. Look, this is my theoretical underpinning. The core of my expression of physics, which in turn I'm using to construct my models of the Bulk.' He stared at the turning images in the laptop screen. 'I feel I'm close, at least to expressing the right questions, if not to getting the answers. All the other branes out there, all with their own time axes, or multiple times, or none at all... Time can pivot, you know. The time signature of a universe can change. You can have a static universe with several dimensions of space – a scrap of eternity – but then a space dimension evolves into time, and wham, you have the whole package, Big Bang and Big Rip, birth and death. Our universe could have been eternal once. Something could have happened to pivot the axes, to change the signature, to make it temporal, finite. Something bad.'

That word surprised her. *'Bad?'*

'Of course, bad. God wouldn't have made a finite, short-lived universe. Finitude isn't perfection. Even a trillion years isn't enough, if eternity is available.'

'That sounds like something Granddad might have said.' She had always wondered if Joe's obsessive quest for cosmological truth was really all about unresolved issues from his Presbyterian childhood.

'Well, that old monster asked some of the right questions, even if he didn't have the right answers.'

'Joe, you said there's something else you wanted to talk about.'

'Yes. Plan B.' He sat on the edge of the bed and faced her.

'Plan B?'

'Even if the research councils and governments won't fund me, I'm not giving up. Well, I can't.'

She looked around at the untidy room, the litter on the bed, the dirty clothes roughly shoved away on a wardrobe shelf. 'Joe, you can't fund high-energy physics research by yourself.'

He grinned. 'Can't I? We'll see. I do need a bit of money. Which is where you come in.'

She laughed. 'Joe, I'm a student. I don't have any money!'

'I know. But it's not you I'm tapping up,' he said bluntly.

'Then who? Oh. Not Sheena.'

'Your Auntie Sheena might look on the purchase of a bit of land as an investment,' he said. 'If it's put to her the right way. Such as by you . . .'

There were other worlds in this dark sky. She felt their gravitational tug, a pull deep in her belly. Sometimes she even felt a rain of meteorites, fragments blasted from the surfaces of those sister worlds and scattered through the void. But few of those worlds carried life of any kind, and none an ecology as complex as hers, none a mind as rich as her own.

There was a way to put that right.

It took an aeon of concentration, of a subtle shepherding of tensions.

Then an immense supervolcano ripped open one side of the planet. A wave of ash and dirt and toxic gases inflicted mortality on a global scale. No matter. The ecosystem would recover from this event, as it had from others.

And, briefly, as this one world shone like a star in the dark sky, from it spread a spray of rock and ash, blasted to escape velocity. Most of these fragments were inert, baked and smashed to sterility. But in a few of them life clung, hardy spores. And a few of those precious seed-carriers would fall on sister worlds.

It would take an aeon for new ecosystems to arise on barren worlds, for consciousness to arise on its multiple levels. To a world mind, that wasn't long to wait.

She rehearsed what she would say to the newborn.

Symmetries! Symmetries of squares and cubes! Symmetries of primes and perfect numbers! All these and more he fought to join and mould, while others, weaker or less determined, fell back into shapelessness – and new generations of novices, younger and still more hungry, fought to take away what he had achieved.

Joe Denham might have recognised the form to which he aspired. The structure of this cosmos was not unlike the E8 mathematical construct Joe used to model the fundamental forces and particles of his own universe. And indeed in this universe there were some advanced minds who posited a construct not unlike Joe's cosmos to serve as an analogical model of their own world. There was a duality in all things, a symmetry even across the branes.

But to one inhabitant at least, this universe had come to seem like a beautiful prison.

Very rapidly the remaining places among the two hundred and forty-eight elect were being filled. Yet even as he worked frantically to secure his own place, he was distracted by doubt.

The universe would end when the array of two hundred and forty-eight was filled, the symmetry completely expressed. And he, indeed, would die with it. Why? Why should this be so? Why should he be born, only to die? Why should the universe begin and end at all? And why so *soon*? If the universe were more complex it would last longer before its perfection were complete. Why should it not have been so?

More mysteries. There were other universes than this. Symmetry demanded it, the greater symmetry of the Bulk in which all cosmoses floated like fresh-born novices. He could *see* the other cosmoses, or at least he saw the necessity of their existence, in the way that a human theoretical physicist could gain insights into wider realities from the symmetries of his models and equations. Other universes were arrayed around his own, in pretty patterns. They too lived and died, those nearby.

Yet there was a cluster of other branes, further away, characterised by a different sort of symmetry. And they did not die.

Even as he fought for his place in the sky, he strained to understand how this could be so. And why.

Morag took the monorail from Edinburgh to Dunbar. From there she hired a pod car, fed in the coordinates her father had given her, and sat back.

In the car's electric silence she was driven south from Dunbar through arable country. This was a gently rolling landscape of dry stone walls. To the east the land fell away, affording a long view towards the Tweed valley, while to the west the land rose towards the Lammermuir Hills. But the road was empty of traffic, and it was heavily fenced off from the fields, even though there wasn't a sheep or a cow in sight, and the fields themselves were visibly unkempt.

It was the year 2046. Morag, in her mid-thirties now, was occupied full-time by her own ecosalvage projects in Africa, and rarely came home. It was difficult to absorb the changes this Scottish countryside had seen since Joe had first used Sheena's money to buy his few acres up here (and Sheena, long dead, had never seen a penny of it back). First had come the pathogen panics as bluetongue and other nasties, driven by shifting climate zones, had overwhelmed the farms. The countryside had walled itself off, hundreds of miles of barbed wire isolating the fields from spores carried on tyres and feet. But soon after that had come the pricing-out of private transport, the end of traffic, and then the great revolution in artificial food production that had led to the collapse of traditional agriculture everywhere. Now, even in Scotland and England, swathes of countryside were reverting to a state not seen since the Mesolithic, and ecologists like Morag mapped the changes as a depleted ecosystem tried to reassemble itself.

And in the middle of all this Joe Denham continued his patient, obsessive data-gathering, year after year.

Morag saw his installation from a rise a half-mile before the pod car reached it. Joe's cosmic-ray telescope was an array of several hundred tanks of water, each as tall as Joe was himself, gathered in a rough polygon nearly a mile across. Each tank was attached to a sensor pack and a communications antenna, and four big optical telescopes were set up around the perimeter of the array, including one that stuck out of the top of Joe's control centre, which was a garden shed with the roof cut open.

Morag knew the principle. The array was based on a properly funded design called the Pierre Auger Observatory in Argentina. It was designed to detect cosmic rays, high-energy particles coming in from space. When they hit the atmosphere such particles would create a shower of secondary particles, and as these passed through the tanks they would create tiny flashes of light in the water. From these bits of information, Joe's computers could reconstruct the nature and trajectory of the original cosmic rays – and he was able to use a subset of that data as evidence of the nature of the greater multiverse of the Bulk, and its interaction with the human universe.

It was a bold project, and it seemed to work, as far as Morag could tell. But it had taken Joe around fifteen years to get this far. His water tanks, scavenged one by one from oil refineries and other abandoned industrial facilities, were all shapes, sizes and colours, and his array looked less like a science project than an art installation. Or even just a folly, the obsession of a madman.

He met her outside his shed. He was in his mid-sixties now, but if anything he looked older than that. In his quilted coat and elderly boots and with his self-cut hair, he was like an eccentric hermit-like farmer.

He showed her into his shed and made her a coffee. There was a little bunk bed, and basic kitchen stuff, a fridge fed by a generator somewhere, a heap of clothes. But most of the space was taken up by science gear. A ferocious draught came in through the open roof, where the telescope peered out like some long-legged animal.

The 'coffee' was revolting. She wondered where he had got it. But she drank it for the warmth.

'It's good of you to come,' he said. 'Adam, the kids—'

'They're all fine. With me in Africa.'

'It's been too long.'

'Yes, it has,' she said fervently. 'Look at the state of you.'

'Oh, don't fuss,' he said, with a throaty old man's cackle. 'You're as safe out in the countryside as in the gated cities, they say. It's the shanty towns you have to avoid.'

'But you never were any use at looking after yourself, were you? When I was a kid I remember fretting over the way you never had your shirts ironed . . .'

He wasn't listening. He looked haunted. 'They're trying to take away my computers, you know, or most of them.'

'I know.' This was why she had come; he had emailed her, and she had checked up herself.

'The government say the hoard I have here, elderly and unreliable as it is,' and he gave one of his laptops a slap, 'is more than is "justifiable" for my needs. Justifiable! So much for the fucking singularity by the way, whatever happened to that? Sorry. They have no idea what I'm doing here.'

'That's the trouble, Joe. They don't have any idea. Why should they? I mean, you don't work for any reputable organisation. You don't even write up your results any more, do you?'

'What's the point? Nobody was paying any attention to partial results. I was getting no citations to speak of . . .'

'All the government cares about is the raw materials locked up in your computers. The germanium, the silver, even the copper – there are shortages of all these things now.'

'I'm biding my time, about writing up,' he said, as if he hadn't heard her. He stroked the computer he'd slapped, as if soothing it. 'I'll wait until I have conclusive results – the full Monty. Then I'll hit them with it all at once, fully backed up with data and references. None of this partial releasing. It will be unarguable.'

'What will?'

He looked at her, briefly puzzled, as if she hadn't been paying attention. 'My analysis of Calabi-Yau space. My map of the Bulk, and our place in it. There are branes all around ours, love, other universes, three, five, seven-dimensional constructs adrift in nine-dimensional space, influencing us with subtle whispers of gravity.

'There is a cluster of them close to us, self-attracting, orbiting like a swarm of asteroids. All of them time-ridden, and if anybody lives there they are as mortal as us. But I've detected *another* cluster of branes, further off, tighter, more orderly. And they are static – time-free, constructs of pure space. Fragments of eternity. Why mortality here, why eternity there? I can't answer that yet. But I feel I'm close to an understanding of *why* things are as they are . . .'

She reached out and took his hands. They were dry, the skin of his palms cracked. 'Joe – you've been obsessing about death and mortality since Mum died. I don't blame you. But don't you think all this work is maybe some kind of rationalisation? You're projecting your own life onto the whole of the rest of the universe. Isn't it better to let it go?'

He pulled back. 'The last time I went back to Edinburgh, I was after a grant, they assigned me to a counsellor who came out with the same kind of stuff as that. As if I'm a kid who can't cope with his hamster dying. Morag, the whole damn universe is dying. I know it's hard to grasp, but it's true. But, you see, I think . . .'

'What, Joe?'

'I think it didn't have to be that way. Now. Are you going to help me keep hold of my computers or not?'

The world minds were scattered in the dark, around the mother who had so explosively borne them.

Morag Denham might have understood their nature, if dimly. There was a great deal of information stored in the network of flows of mass and energy that characterised a world's ecosystem, flows which were in turn locked into the physical cycles of the planet. For example, Earth's interdependent geological and biological systems, all unconsciously, worked together in a giant feedback loop to keep the world's temperature at a level equable for life in the face of a steadily heating sun.

But in a complex ecosystem there was room for a great deal more information than what was needed to characterise a simple thermo-stat, as on Earth. Patterns of ecocycles, in their robustness and resilience, made for highly efficient memory and processing systems. Even in Morag's universe there were worlds where intelligence had arisen naturally from the data flows that cycled around complex entangled ecologies. On such worlds, thoughts were expressed in the swelling and dying of populations of plants and animals. Extinction events haunted million-year dreams.

So it was in that other dark sky.

The mother world waited for her children to develop complexity, to come to awareness, to formulate thoughts that crackled with the rise and fall of species, and to begin to ask questions: Where am I? What is this place? What must I do?

Then, when the offspring planets were ready, she began a slow process of dialogue.

The community of worlds shared tremendous deep thoughts via gravity waves generated by the churning of their cores, or even via the firing-off of life forms in fresh volleys of meteorites. An alien invasion was a sentence rudely despatched.

And gradually the mother and her children came to understand.

In the booming of gravity waves deeper and longer than any of them could generate, they sensed the structure of their own universe, and the architecture of the Bulk, the greater nine-dimensional cosmos in which it was embedded. They saw branes like their own, bound together by gravity just as the living worlds clustered, all living and dying. And they saw others, more distant, a handsome array of time-less universes, whose skies swam with heat, and where no world ever grew cold.

And they saw, beyond doubt, that such an arrangement was arti-ficial.

Whoever had done this, whoever had doomed whole universes to brevity and extinction, was surely much like themselves, surely as afraid of the gathering cold as they were. This the mother understood. But it was hard not to feel resentment when, as a consequence, her own universe so quickly aged, and the great chill gathered, and one by one her children shed their hard-won complexity and succumbed to the cold and the dark.

He had won. He had won! He had battled through a forest of sym-metries, and now those others already ascended prepared to welcome him to his place in the constellation of two hundred and forty-eight. It was all he had striven for, all his life, since the instant of his birth.

Yet now it was in his grasp he hesitated. Others watched him, doubtful and uneasy.

He understood that it would not be long after his ascension that the last of the places was filled, when the universe, complete, would die, and he would die with it. And he knew now that it did not have to be that way. He had glimpsed other universes, that far-off cluster of the undying, locked in their own changeless symmetries.

And he had glimpsed other types of symmetries, as far beyond his own as his was beyond a newborn novice's.

A simple regular polygon could have four points, a square; five or six points, a pentagon or a hexagon; it could have two-hundred and forty-eight points, any finite number. But as the number of points approached infinity, the angular form aspired to another sort of symmetry, that perfect regularity of the circle.

So it could have been in his universe, he saw now. Not the stifling closure of a mere two hundred and forty-eight vertices, but the unending symmetry of the sphere. A symmetry with room for all who aspired to join it – for ever. It could have been that way here, just as in those other realms.

And, once, that was how it had been.

Something, or somebody, had *changed* this universe, shattered its infinite order and blighted it with this crude spikiness. Replaced eternity with finitude. Replaced immortality with death.

Why should this have been done? He pondered this. Surely that greater agent was one not unlike himself. Surely that other had been born in asymmetry and struggled only for a symmetry of its own. That, at least, was a comforting thought, that in his own finitude and death he at least served the purposes of a greater symmetry, even if he could never understand how.

Enough. He was as content as he could ever be. He took his place, settling into the constellation of the elect. He shone, one among two hundred and forty-eight identical points of light.

Time ended.

Joe lay there inert. Morag sat beside him, outside his isolation tent, and waited for the ghastly process of his dying to run its course. He looked wasted by his illness, yet he was still as tall and ungainly as ever; he looked too big for the bed.

The hospital room reminded Morag of her mother's death, thirty-odd years before. Of course there were differences. There were few nurses around, only machines that tended to the needs of the ill and the dying. This wasn't the NHS; long before this year of 2056 an impoverished Scotland had seen its welfare state crumble, and the health care had exhausted Joe's own pitiful savings, and eaten up a good chunk of Morag's own.

But for all the changes, here was Joe spending his final hours lying on a curtained-off bed just as his wife had all those years ago. Although she hadn't had the indignity of a clear-plastic isolation bubble separating her from the touch of her family. And she at least had died of a cancer that had a name, instead of the exotic, species-crossing, nameless disease Joe had picked up when he had stayed out one winter too many in the Lammermuirs.

There were times during the night when Morag, sitting by his bed, thought he might not wake again. But then, as another bright Edinburgh summer morning dawned, his eyelids raised with a faint crumpling sound, like paper. 'Morag?'

She was startled. Perhaps she had been dozing, sitting in the hard chair. Impulsively she reached for him, but her fingertips only pushed against the clear isolation membrane. 'Dad. Joe. You're awake.'

He shifted his head slightly, and she saw some brownish fluid being pumped through a pipe and under the sheets into his body. And he saw her looking. 'Feeding time at the zoo. I could murder a burger. Even a fucking NHS coffee. Sorry. Are the kids here?'

The 'kids' were now both young adults. But they were here. 'They're exploring Edinburgh with Adam.'

'Good. Keep them away. Kids are more open to disease. Don't want them catching my mumbo jumbo syndrome. So it got me in the end, eh?'

'What did?'

'Death. The Bulk. All those branes and anti-branes swimming around. They're killing me in the end, just like every other fucker back to Adam—' He was interrupted by a cough that came out of nowhere. His whole body jerked, as if convulsed, and she saw blood spray over the inside of his bubble. The machines around him adopted a new constellation of displays. 'Sorry,' he said.

'Are you all right?'

He forced a smile. 'Jumping like a flea.' His voice was papery, audibly weaker. 'I'm seventy-five, you know. Not bad.'

'No,' she said. 'Not bad.'

'You haven't looked at my computers, have you?'

'Joe, there wasn't time. We just cleared out the shed. The council were already taking away your water tanks. The computers are safe, but—'

'Read my paper. It's backed up. The figures... I worked it out in the end.'

'Your map of the Bulk.'

'My analysis of the Calabi-Yau space, yes. I did it in the end. Like shining a torch up into all the dark, nine-dimensional halls we drift around in. Listen. This is what I found—'

'Joe—'

'Listen.' He tried to reach her, but his claw-like fingers just scraped feebly against plastic. 'Listen,' he whispered. 'I saw two clusters of branes, mutually orbiting, like a pair of solar systems. One, far from us, has two hundred and forty-eight members. All of them timeless, space dimensions only. All of them eternities. The other, the swarm we're part of, has one thousand, nine hundred and eighty-four. And they're all unstable, like our universe. All of them have at least one time dimension. All of them doomed to birth and death, the whole damn cycle, and every living thing in them.

'Here's the thing, Morag, here's what I saw. Our cluster is in a particular part of the Bulk. You saw my projections of it, the thing's covered in spines like a hedgehog. We are in one of those spines. We've been *shepherded* here. And all the brane universes are on trajectories that force them to intersect...' He fell back, wheezing. 'It needs more analysis. But I believe I saw the actual intersection, the close approach of another brane to our own, that destabilised our universe. I was able to track it back, like figuring out the flight of a bullet back to the assassin's gun.'

'Destabilised?'

'Before that we were an eternity. The close encounter pivoted one of our space dimensions into a time. Pow, Big Bang, inflation, Big Rip, death – it all came about in that moment. A moment of Bulk time, I mean.'

'The words you use,' she said uneasily. '"Shepherded". You said our cluster of branes was shepherded into the spine. What shepherded us there?'

'Or who.' He grinned; his teeth were discoloured, and she wondered when he had last been to a dentist. 'I believe it was intentional, Morag. And I can tell you what the intention was.'

'What, then?'

'To collect energy.' He raised one hand and feebly closed a fist, over and over. 'Universes exploding like gas in a piston chamber. The gravitational energy released by all those dying universes is just pumped down that spine – but what's it used for? Maybe that damn cluster of smug eternals is the payload.'

None of this made any sense. 'What are you saying, Joe?'

'That we're in an engine. Like a rocket ship. Each exploding cosmos is like a grain of gunpowder in a firework, driving the whole damn thing forward across the nine-dimensional Bulk. That's all we amount to, that's all we're *for*, our whole universe from beginning to end, Bang to Rip, all the galaxies and stars and planets, all the warriors and lovers and poets, all the births and deaths... And that's why they destabilised our universe, and thousands of others. Artefacts, all of them, embedded in a greater artefact. Whole universes used as propellant.'

'Who, Joe? Who's they?'

He tried to sit up. His mouth opened as he strained to speak, and she thought she saw the shape of his skull through his thin flesh, the dirty white hair in his scalp. 'Who? That's what I'd like to know. Where are we going? What is the purpose of this damn thing we're all trapped inside? Oh, maybe they're not unlike us. Aggressive expansionists, ripping up the environment. They must be, to build such a thing. We wouldn't care about a community of bugs swimming in a litre of petrol we poured into the tank, would we? But we aren't bugs. We *should* challenge them. Maybe we should team up with the other brane universes. Maybe we should demand what gave them the *right* to condemn billions of sapient beings to the agony of mortality...'

Another explosive cough sent a shower of thick blood over the bubble. Morag flinched. Red lights flashed across the face of the monitors. Morag heard human footsteps, running closer.

Joe fell back, shuddering, still trying to talk.

You swim.

Suspended in the nine-dimensional Bulk, you are a construct of Dirichlet branes.

Your mind emerges from the dances of a cluster of universes. These realms are internally timeless, eternal and perfect. The inhabitants of each tiny cosmos might believe they are gods. But you are entirely unaware of their existence, any more than a human watches the sparking of an individual neurone. It is the mutual orbit of the cosmoses themselves that is the foundation of your mind.

And you are driven forward in your swimming by the birth and collapse of a myriad more universes, each filled with minds, even with civilisations, blossoming and dying in hope and fear and longing, sent into the dark for your benefit. Again you are unaware of these miniature agonies.

You, arising from it all, are alone. And you swim.

Why must you swim? If you swim, where are you coming from, and where are you going to?

Why is there a 'you' separated from a 'not-you' through which you swim?

Why is there something rather than nothing?

Who are you?

You cannot rest. You are alone. You are frightened by the swimming. And you are frightened that the swimming must end. For... what then?

VACUUM LAD

It was the moment I first glimpsed my own secret origins, and, perhaps, my true destiny.

I was sitting in a shuttle, en route to a swank L5 orbital hotel where I was due to start another three-month residency for another seven-figure-euro fee. Of course I was in uniform, my suit and mask black and threaded with silver, a design suggestive of space, the vacuum. The uniform is what people expect. At the moment it happened, I was signing autographs, modestly fending off questions about my heroics during the Hub blow-out, and sipping champagne through a straw.

'It' was a scratch on the window. A scratch coming from *outside* a shuttle whizzing through the vacuum of space.

And a face. A human face beyond the window, no pressure suit, nothing. A mumsy middle-aged woman. When I looked, she beckoned and smiled, and mouthed words.

Welcome home, Vacuum Lad.

The world knows me as Vacuum Lad, the name Professor Stix gave me.

The only other thing the world knows about me, aside from my singular power, is that I'm from Saudi Arabia. That was another suggestion of Professor Stix. She said I should keep my own identity secret, for the sake of my family. But I should reveal my nationality, since wretched Saudi, in these shambolic post-oil days, could use a hero of its own.

Professor Stix designed my costume and had it made up, and did a pretty good job even though it's always chafed at the crotch. She even handles my business affairs. You could say Professor Stix created Vacuum Lad, the image, the commercial enterprise. She didn't create me, the boy inside the costume, born Tusun ibn Thunayan in Dhahran nineteen years earlier. But she did hold the copyright, as registered in the year 2157, as the Christians record the date.

And she didn't give me my power.

It was only an accident that my power was revealed to me, in fact, and an unlikely one. I mean, how many people do you know who've been exposed to space, to the hard vacuum and the invisible sleet of radiation?

When it happened I was just a kid, nineteen years old, on my way to study ecological salvaging in Ottawa, Canada, thanks to a European Union post-dieback Reconstruction scholarship. I think I would have been a poor student, and would pretty soon have been back home in Dhahran, working for my father's struggling business. We turned abandoned oil wells into carbon sequestration sinks by filling them with algae-rich slurry. It could have been a living for me, but my older brother Muhammad would have got the lion's share of the family fortune, such as it was. So I was exploring other options.

But all this is a story never to be told. I never got to Ottawa.

The shuttle was a Canadaspace suborbit hop from Riyadh to Ottawa. I wasn't sipping champagne or signing autographs then, I can tell you. Crammed in a cattle-class tube with forty-nine other marginally poor, I was squeezed against the wall by the passenger next to me, a jolly lady from Burundi who spoke pleasantly. 'You will study? Studying is beautiful. I myself am visiting a great-niece who is studying environmental ethics in Montreal. Do you know Montreal? Montreal is beautiful . . .'

I was polite, but I tuned her out, for I was enjoying my first taste of spaceflight.

From launch the ship sailed over the Gulf where, through the window to my left, I saw vapour feathers gleaming white, artificial cloud created by spray turbines to deflect a little more sunlight from an overheated Earth. The arid plains of the east were chrome-plated with solar-cell farms, and studded with silvered bubbles, lodes of frozen-out carbon dioxide. The Caspian Sea was green-blue, thick with plankton stimulated to grow and draw down carbon from the air. Asia was plunged in night, with little waste light seeping out of the brave new cities of southern Russia and China and India.

The Pacific was vast and dark. It was a relief to reach morning, and to pass over North America.

But all too soon we were starting our descent, banking over the desiccated Midwest. Far below us, tracing a line through the air, I saw the white glint of a sprayer plane, topping up faint yellow clouds of sun-shielding sulphur dioxide. And, given the position of the sun, if I had been able to see out to the right, towards space, I might have glimpsed the Stack, a cloud of smart mirrors a hundred thousand kilometres deep, forever poised between Earth and sun to scatter even more of the sunlight. But the right-hand window was eclipsed by the lady from Burundi.

That was when it happened.

The hull failure was caused by a combination of metal fatigue and, it is thought, a ding in the shuttle wall from some particle of orbital debris, probably a fleck of two-century-old frozen astronaut urine. Spacecraft are pretty safe. It took a compound failure to break through that shuttle's multiply-redundant safety features. And if not for that complicated accident I'd have quietly landed at Ottawa with the rest, and subsided back into anonymity, and that would have been that.

But the astronaut piss hit.

A blow-out is a bang, an explosive event. At first I thought some terrorist had struck. There are many on Earth who oppose spaceflight. But then I felt the gale, heard the howling wind, and saw the space in front of me filled with bits of paper and plastic cups, all whirling towards my right. I started to feel cold immediately, and a pearly fog formed in the air, misting cabin lights that flashed red with alarm.

Decompression. I had paid attention to the safety briefings. I opened my mouth wide, and allowed the air to rush out of my lungs, and from the other end let it go with the mother of all trumps.

I knew I had only seconds of consciousness. Almost calmly, I wondered what I should do.

But I was trapped in my seat by the lady from Burundi. Dying, she gripped my hand, and I squeezed back. She was trying to hold her breath. I imagined the air trapped in her lungs over-expanding and ripping open lung tissues and capillaries. The pain must have been agonising. And she was looking at her hands in horror, her bare arms. They were swelling. Soon the hand that held mine was huge, twice its size, comical, monstrous. Yet my hand was normal, almost. I thought I could see a kind of mist venting from my pores, and my skin seemed to be hardening, shrinking back. Not swelling at all.

As her grip relaxed I pulled away.

In the vacuum silence, the passengers around me were convulsing, or going limp. And then the stewardess, the solitary flight attendant in the cabin, came drifting over our heads, a broken air mask half-fitted over the swollen ruin of her pretty face, a drinks tray floating beside her. There would be no salvation from the crew.

Still I sat in my seat. I was cold. Frost on my lips. Glaze of ice on eyes. Acute pain in my ears, a dry tearing in my throat. All this in mere seconds since the blow-out.

Nobody else was moving. Was I the last one conscious?

I broke out of my shock. I punched my seat clasp and wriggled out from behind the bulk of the lady from Burundi. Now, as I floated over the heads of the bloated, inert passengers, I saw the hole in the opposite wall for the first time. It was a neat rectangle, less than a half-mctre wide, a slab of darkness. It was small.

Smaller, in fact, I saw, than the attendant's drinks tray.

I moved fast. I pushed off from the wall and fielded the tray from mid-air. The tray had handles underneath, and a Velcro top to hold the drinks. Dragging it behind me, I squirted my way out of the hole and out into space. Then I turned around and held the tray in the hole, bracing my feet against the soft insulation blanket of the shuttle's outer hull, pulling at the tray's handles with my hands to seal the hole. And through a window I saw mist, the reserve air supply at last having a chance to fill up the cabin.

It was only then that it occurred to me that I'd stranded myself outside the ship.

Well, there was nothing for it but to hang on as long as I could. I didn't feel scared, oddly, of death. I just imagined Muhammad's face when he learned how foolishly I'd met my end. It would have been fitting, given what followed, if at that moment I'd glanced up to see the Stack of Earth-protecting mirrors with my freezing eyes, but I did not. I just laughed, inside, thinking of Muhammad.

In a few minutes the cockpit crew, who wore their pressure suits all the time, were able to get through to the cabin and start delivering emergency medical aid. About half the passengers survived. Well, half is better than none. It took them fifteen more minutes to mount an operation to retrieve me from my impulsive spacewalk. I was unconscious by then. My flesh wasn't swollen, but my skin was desiccated – the co-pilot said it was like handling a mummy. I was smiling. My eyes were closed.

And my heart was beating, after fifteen minutes in space.

My new life went through a series of phases.

First I was a patient.

Once on the ground, along with the other survivors I was whisked into an Ottawan hospital. I'd suffered much less than some of the other passengers. Their tissue swelling went down quickly, but many had ruptured lungs from trying to hold their breath, and air bubbles in the bloodstream, and brain damage from hypoxia, and so forth. With me it was mainly dehydration. After a couple of days of sleep and a drip in my arm, I was walking around. I appeared to suffer no lasting harm save for a mild blotchiness about my rehydrated skin.

Then I was a media star, the boy who'd saved the spaceship. Even my shutting myself out of the ship was interpreted as bravery rather than crass stupidity. That was terrific, but it lasted mere hours. The world's gaze moves on quickly. My brother Muhammad said that it would have lasted longer if I'd been better looking. (Later, Professor Stix sent out software agents to minimise search-engine links between my Vacuum Lad incarnation and this first amateur outing. It wasn't hard, she said, which rather disappointed me.)

Then I was a hero at home in Dhahran. Even Muhammad was briefly impressed. But as I anticipated he was soon tormenting me for my brilliant plan to seal myself outside the spaceship hull. My mother made a fuss of me, however.

Then I became a medical curiosity. The doctors in Ottawa were unable to figure out how come I was still alive. So they called me back for tests, to which my family agreed after negotiation of a fee and some discussion of medical copyright.

And then I was referred to Professor Stix.

I was flown to Munich, Germany, at the heart of the European Union.

A driver met me at the airport and drove me into the city. I had never been to Europe before. I had never seen such wealth, even in Canada, never seen so much greenness, so much water.

We arrived at an imposing campus-like institute. There I met Professor Stix for the first time. 'Welcome,' she said, and shook my hand. 'I am Professor Maria Stix.'

'Hello, Maria.'

'You may call me Professor Stix.' She led me to her office.

She was perhaps forty. Her figure was sturdy yet voluptuous, her face beautiful but severe, her cheekbones set off by the way she wore her brown hair neatly swept back, her blue eyes if anything enhanced by the spectacles she wore. I lusted after her. I was, after all, nineteen years old.

In her office, which was equipped like a doctor's surgery, she immediately began a preliminary medical exam. 'This is the Max-Planck-Gesellschaft Zur Forderung der Wissenschaften e. V.,' she said briskly, as she measured my (rising) blood pressure. We spoke in English; her accent was light, not German. 'The institute, or its precursor, was founded in 1911 as the official scientific research organisation of Germany, and funded by the national government and later by the European Union to perform research in areas of particular scientific importance and in highly specialised or interdisciplinary fields.'

I stumbled over the words. 'Am I an interdisciplinary field?'

She smiled. 'Your survival is a puzzle.'

'And who's paying to solve that puzzle?' I asked bluntly.

'The European Space Agency. You can see the practicality.' She sniffed, elegantly. 'I myself am French. The Germans have something of a history in the field of extreme medicine, dating back to experiments performed on prisoners during the Second World War. You may debate the ethics of using such data.' She grabbed my testicles. 'Cough.'

That was the beginning of an extensive survey of my peculiar condition. I was pulled and prodded, scanned and sampled, at every level of my being from my genetic composition upwards. It was not long before Professor Stix, with my consent, subjected me to further vacuum exposures, in a facility designed to test robotic spacecraft in conditions approaching space, a chamber like a vast steel coffin. My exposure was gradually increased from seconds to minutes, though Professor Stix did not dare take me anywhere close to the fifteen minutes to which I was exposed after the accident on the Canadaspace flight.

After some weeks of this she gave me an informal précis of her results.

'Your recovery times are actually improving,' she said.

'Thanks.'

'Yet "recovery" is probably the wrong word. Your body accepts vacuum as an alien yet survivable medium, rather as my own body can survive underwater without ill effects.'

I said nothing, imagining the Professor's elegant figure underwater.

'Your body has a number of mechanisms that enable it to survive. Your lungs and indeed your bowels are unusually efficient at venting air.'

I grinned. 'I fart like a hero.'

'Hmm. And with internal gases removed, other conditions such as a rupture of lung tissues will not follow. In vacuum, most of us suffer ebullism, which is a swelling caused by the evaporation of water in the soft tissues. Your tissues, on the other hand, eject water rapidly through the pores, at least as deep as a few millimetres, and the outer skin collapses down to a tough, leathery integument. Like a natural spacesuit, protecting what lies beneath. There is also a unique film over your eyes, an extra layer which similarly toughens to retain your eyes' moisture, though they are always prone to frosting. Meanwhile the pumping of your heart adjusts, and the balance of venous versus arterial pressure reaches unique levels in your vacuum-exposed body. Oxygen-rich blood actually seems to be trapped in your brain, thus nourishing it beyond normal limits and reducing the risk of hypoxia—'

'How long could I survive in space?'

She shrugged. 'We could only discover that by testing you to destruction. I would suspect many hours – even days.'

The next briefing she gave me, some weeks later, was rather less encouraging.

In her office once more, she opened a drawer in her desk and produced a jar that she set on the table. It contained a kind of grub, dark brown, only a millimetre or two long.

'What is this?'

'A tardigrade. Known in some countries as a water bear. Very common.'

'Ugly little thing.'

'Tardigrades can survive desiccation. Some have been known to last a decade without moisture. There are other creatures that can survive extreme dryness – rotifers, nematodes, brine shrimp. And this makes them capable of surviving in space, for as long as several days in some flight experiments.'

'Like me.'

'Yes. You also, it appears, have the capability to recover from moderate doses of radiation better than the average human. You have a mechanism that I suspect is rather like that of the bacterium *Deinococcus radiodurans*, with a capability of repairing cellular damage, even recovery of damaged DNA strands. It has always been an open question why such creatures should have facilities to enable them to survive in deep space for extended periods. Perhaps this is a relic of our true origins, if we came here from another planet, wafted as spores across space. These traits may be ancestral.'

This sounded fanciful to me. I asked, indicating the tardigrade, 'What has this fellow to do with me?'

She said she believed she had discovered the cause of my peculiar abilities. There were traces of viral activity in my DNA, which had modified the genetic information there, leaving sequences that had some correlation with the genes of *Deinococcus* and the tardigrades and so forth. 'This appears to be the result of an infection when you were very small. There is no trace of similar modifications in your parents.'

'Something in the air.'

'Possibly something artificial,' she said. 'I am speculating. Why would anybody create such an infection? And how did it get into your bloodstream? Just chance, perhaps.'

I shrugged. 'What next for me?'

This was the bad news. The European Space Agency had hoped to use lessons from my anatomy as part of a conditioning regime for their own astronauts. But because my condition was genetic, and the result of agents Professor Stix had yet to identify, I was of no use.

I was disappointed. 'Perhaps I could become an astronaut.'

She smiled, not unkindly.

'Then is it over?' I was already forgotten as a space hero. Was I now to be discarded even as a medical specimen? And, worse, was the flow of money from the Planck Institute to my family about to be cut off? Was it back to the slurry wells for me?

Professor Stix seemed on the point of saying 'yes'. But then she pouted, quite prettily. 'Not necessarily. Let me give it some thought. In the meantime I will book you more time in the vacuum chamber.'

Once more I submitted to my ordeal in that metal coffin.

But I noticed a change in the testing regime. The intervals I was exposed to the vacuum were gradually increased. And, rather than lie inert on some bed with wires protruding from my body, now I was asked to perform various physical tasks – to walk around, to move weights, to complete small jobs of more or less complexity.

It was obvious to me, even before Professor Stix admitted it, that this was no longer a medical study. I was being trained.

After a couple more weeks, having thought it through, Professor Stix put her proposal to me.

'It seems a shame to waste your unique abilities. You have already demonstrated your value in an emergency situation. You have no place in ESA's exploration programme, but there are many commercial enterprises operating in near-Earth space – suborbital and orbital flights, hotels, factories, research establishments. At any given moment many hundreds of people are in orbit – and therefore subject to a risk of blow-out.'

'What are you suggesting, Professor?'

'That we hire you out, to the commercial organisations working in Earth orbit. You would serve as a fail-safe in case of the final catastrophe. Of course you could only be in one place at a time, on one flight at a time. But having you on hand, visibly present and ready for disaster, would be a profound psychological comfort for a lay passenger – much more so than theoretical assurances about fault-analysis trees and failure modes. You would be a luxury item, you see, in demand by high-paying customers. People fear decompression, however irrationally; people will pay for such comfort. It is very unlikely that you will ever have to face a real emergency again. I've already discussed this in principle with various insurance companies.'

I smiled. 'I like the idea. Tusun ibn Thunayan, life saver!'

'Oh, that's rather bland.' She glanced over my body, evidently sizing me up. 'We should think about branding. A costume of some kind. You would be your own walking advertisement.'

'A mask! I could wear a mask.'

She nodded slowly. 'Anonymity. Yes, why not? It might protect your family from ruthless competitors who might seek, in vain, to find another like you among them. You would need a name.'

'A name?'

'Such as "Rescue Man".'

'That sounds rather unspecific,' I said.

'Perhaps.'

'"Blow-Out Boy!"'

'Ugh! That sounds pornographic . . . "Vacuum Lad",' she said thoughtfully.

I think we both knew immediately that was the one. 'I like it! You know, my older brother Muhammad has many advantages over me, but not a secret identity.'

'Hmm. We will have to consider how to launch you as a commercial proposition. Once the costume is ready, other promotional material, a sound financial base in place, we should mount a demonstration to show your capabilities.'

'"We"?'

She smiled, as sweetly as she ever had at me. 'Do you have an agent?'

*

The public launch of Vacuum Lad went spectacularly well.

Professor Stix and I ran up a certain amount of debt, for the costume and various marketing materials, and most significantly for the hire of an orbital shuttle from a Britain-based spaceline. Our flight lasted four full orbits, for two of which, in the world's electronic gaze, I cavorted in space for up to ten minutes at a time. I performed simple tasks, demonstrated my lack of any supporting equipment, and, glamorous in my costume of silver and black, I shot through space powered by a small jetpack (with, at Professor Stix's insistence, the backup of an invisible monomolecular thread that tethered me to the shuttle).

The orders for my services came pouring in, through our chosen partners in the insurance industry. So did demands for media interviews, carefully filtered by Professor Stix. My family and countrymen rejoiced in my exploits. And then came the usual fringe contacts, from people who wanted to marry me or compete with me or assassinate me. (And that was the first I heard of the Earth First League, who opposed all human presence in space, and, therefore, me.)

Our debts were soon cleared, and we were in business.

Then followed months of a strangely idle, yet strangely exciting life. I was assigned to flights with various spacelines and stays at various orbital hotels, each of whom devised simple but effective failure-mode procedures for me to carry out in the event that my peculiar services should be required. In the uneventful hours I spent in flight, or the weeks I spent in the hotels, I was a celebrity, unmistakable in my dramatic costume. In return for my enigmatic company I was bought fine meals and wines, laden with gifts I shipped back to Professor Stix – and received offers of companionship, not all of which I turned down. Well, would you? I liked to boast about it to Muhammad. I did however often dream of the lovely Professor Stix rather than focus on whatever vacuously pretty rich girl was in my arms at the time. And I always kept my mask on.

The Professor had assured me that I would very likely never have to deal with a genuine disaster again. Yet she was wrong.

During my stay, the United Nations Hub was still little more than a torus, a tube of corridors and rooms, restaurants and fitness rooms, set slowly spinning about its midpoint to provide a small measure of apparent gravity. Its most spectacular features were big picture windows that looked down on the Earth far below, and on the ongoing construction all around the Hub, and a wheeling panorama of stars.

This was just the start. The Hub was set high above the world in a stationary orbit, turning with the Earth itself. One day it would be linked to the planet by a thread, a space elevator, the fulfilment of an old dream, at which time it would blossom into the most spectacular resort in cislunar space, and a key node for transportation beyond Earth orbit.

And that was why it was attacked by the Earth First League.

This North American terrorist cell publicly expressed fears about the elevator's economic impact on more traditional space industries. That was mere political cover. In fact it opposed all human presence in space for ideological reasons, as an expression of the technocratic thinking that, they say, led to the dieback and other horrors of recent centuries. So they tried to destroy the Hub – and they timed their attack for my presence aboard, so they could destroy *me*, an ultimate symbol of the human future in space. It was in this incident, you see, that I learned I had a sworn enemy.

They targeted the windows, the beautiful picture windows. They were of a toughened, thick but very clear plastic, set in robust frames. The designers had believed that the Hub itself would have to fall apart before the windows failed. But the saboteurs had infiltrated the construction operation and had embedded strips of explosive in the very frames of several windows.

In a blow-out you have to act fast. In vacuum, most people lose consciousness in ten seconds or so, and will be dead in a minute and a half, two minutes. I wore my jetpack as a matter of course, so it was strapped to my back when the explosion came. I hurled myself through a gaping, ripped-open window frame and for those two minutes retrieved the wriggling, convulsing bodies that had been hurled out into space, one after the other, and zipped them up in emergency pressurisation bags. I saved a dozen.

Then I spent the next several minutes retrieving the inert bodies of those who had been thrown too far for me to catch in time, a dozen or so more.

The incident cemented my fame. Demands for my services exploded, and my fees sky-rocketed. My life, already good, became better. I admit I felt as if I deserved this good fortune, this attention. Perhaps all nineteen-year-olds feel they are special.

Yet guilt nagged at me, for the dozen I had not saved. What's the point of a hero who can't rescue everybody?

And, in the sometimes lonely hours I spent in my luxury zero-gravity suites, waiting for emergencies that never came, I sometimes wondered if my abilities had been meant for more than this. Even Professor Stix, my one full confidante, could not answer such questions.

Oddly, it never occurred to me to wonder if I was unique. Not until I discovered that I wasn't.

The contact came at Mumbai spaceport, as I waited to be shipped to an upper-crust L5 orbital hotel for a three-month residency.

And there, in the first-class lounge, I was approached.

'Excuse me. Is this seat free?' He sat down beside me before I had a chance to reply.

The man was older than me, or Professor Stix, perhaps fifty. He was soberly dressed, if a little plainly for the exotic setting of that lounge; he did not look like a first-class passenger. Yet he carried a ticket folder. For my part I didn't recognise him. At first I thought he was a fan, and fretted vaguely that he might be some threat.

But from the moment I looked closely at him I knew why he had approached me. For, under a dark Indian complexion, I could see how his skin was mottled. Vacuum damage, you see.

He smiled. 'You've been enjoying yourself,' he said, in clear but accented English. 'But most of us prefer to keep a low profile.'

My heart beat faster. 'You are like me.'

'Yes. Once I thought I was unique, too. Then another approached me, as I approach you now. It is not yet time for my ascension, of course. Or yours.'

'Ascension? I don't know what you mean.'

'All your questions will be answered. Even those,' he said a bit sharply, 'you have apparently not had the wit to ask. Don't take your Sky Nigeria flight up to the Hilton.' He handed me the ticket he was holding. 'Take this one.'

I glanced at it. 'Peru Space.' I wasn't happy at the idea of switching. We were getting a kick-back from the shuttle company, Sky Nigeria.

'The flight is just as comfortable, and takes off not much later.'

'Why this one?'

'Because of the route. *This* shuttle's track takes you over the sub-solar point. That is, you will cross the line between Earth and sun. And on that line, of course, lies the Stack.'

'The Stack? The mirrors? What's the Stack got to do with it?'

He stood. 'The Damocletian will tell you that.'

'What Damocletian?'

'It's best you find out for yourself.' He bent down, prised up a corner of my mask, and laughed. '"Vacuum Lad". I don't want you to think I'm po-faced, that we all disapprove. Your life does seem rather fun. And useful. You're saving lives; you're not any sort of criminal. But there are other choices, more satisfaction to be had. Have a good flight.'

Of course curiosity burned. I could hardly refuse to go on the Peruvian flight. Could you?

I cleared it with Professor Stix. I could give her only evasive reasons as to why I wanted to switch. I was uncomfortable lying to her, for in my way, you see, I was hopelessly in love with her. And yet, even before I boarded the shuttle, I had the feeling that from then on Professor Stix would play an increasingly diminished role in my life.

And I was right. For it was on that flight, even as I sipped champagne and signed autographs, that there came that extraordinary scratch on the window.

The woman in space gestured, indicating that I should move down the spaceplane to the airlock at the rear. Of course the flight crew were by now aware of the woman's presence. It took me only a moment to persuade them to let me out through the lock; their human longing to be present at an historic moment in the career of Vacuum Lad overrode the safety rules.

When the last of the air sighed away, I felt the usual hardening of my skin, the prickly cold around my eyes, the gush of air from my mouth and belly, the peculiar arrhythmic thumping of my heart. It was no longer painful to me, more a welcome thrill, like a bracing cold shower. I had gone through this experience many times, including Professor Stix's experimental sessions in the vacuum tank in Munich.

But never before had I swum into vacuum to see another waiting, like me dressed only in everyday clothes – in her case, a tough-looking coverall with soft boots, gloves and tools tucked into her belt. Behind her, at the other end of a trailing tether, was a kind of craft, drifting alongside the shuttle: like a yacht, with a patchy, gossamer sail suspended from a mast. The sail was huge. A man, as naked to vacuum as the woman, clung to the yacht's slim body – and there was a child, I saw, astonished, no more than seven or eight years old, a boy playing restlessly with the rigging attached to the single mast.

The woman smiled at me. I mouthed, as clearly as I could, *How are we to speak?*

She reached for me. Her hands in mine were warm. She pulled me close, opened her mouth, and kissed me. It was an oddly polite, asexual gesture, but as our lips sealed I could feel her tongue, taste the faint spice of her trapped residual breath. And with that trace of trapped air she whispered to me. 'If we touch – see, let your teeth touch mine – speech carries through the bone, the skin.' Her accent was light American. 'My name is Mary Webb. I was born in Iowa. And you, Vacuum Lad?'

Suspended in orbit, my lips locked to this strange woman's, it was not a time for anonymity. I told her my full name.

'I suppose you're wondering why we sent for you.'

'You could say that.'

'Ask your questions.'

'Your yacht,' I said impulsively. 'Is that a solar sail?'

'Yes. We ride on the pressure of sunlight. Slow but reliable, and free. Ben loves it. My son, you see him playing there . . .'

'He was born in space?'

'Yes, he was born in space. But still, most of us are born on Earth and incubate there, as you have, before emerging.'

'"Incubate"?'

'You wonder where we live. The yacht is actually part of our home. We inhabit the Stack.'

'The Stack. The mirrors?' My lips locked to hers, I rolled my eyes to look up. The Stack was a swarm of mirrors, individually invisible, yet their cumulative effect was a subtle darkening and blurring of the sun.

'Each mirror is about a metre across. They are sheets of a silicon nitride ceramic. There are millions of them, of course. You can see our sail is stitched together from several mirrors. My husband made the sail. He's good with his hands.'

The man was grinning at me, across the gulf of space, grinning as I kissed his wife. Beneath me the Earth turned, and passengers and crew goggled at us from the shuttle's windows.

'You live on the Stack?'

'That's right. On it, in it, around it. It is why we exist. Why *you* exist. And why, some day, you will join us.'

I didn't like the sound of that. 'I don't understand any of this.'

'What,' she asked, 'do you know of AxysCorp?'

*

It was all a relic of the very bad days of a hundred years past, when the collapse of the planet's climate was acute. Some feared that the gathering extinction event might soon overwhelm mankind: the dieback. The governments and intergovernmental agencies at last reached for drastic measures.

'Geoengineering,' Mary Webb said. 'Massive human intervention in the processes of nature, everything from seeding the sea with iron to make it flourish, to building giant engines to draw down carbon dioxide from the air. A company called AxysCorp was responsible for the Stack, a system of mirrors at the Lagrange point designed to reduce the sunlight falling on the Earth.'

'It worked,' I murmured into her mouth. 'Didn't it? The climate was stabilised. Billions of lives were saved. The recovery began. That's what I learned at school.'

'Yes, that's so. But AxysCorp's projects were always controversial. What if the Stack, for example, were to fail? If so, the warming it had kept away would hit the planet in one fell swoop – worse than without the Stack in the first place. Can you see?'

'So it cannot be allowed to fail.'

'But every engineering system fails in the end. And so the Stack is not so much a shield as a sword of Damocles suspended over the world.'

'Ah. And you "Damocletians"—'

'Are AxysCorp's backup solution.'

AxysCorp, I learned now, had seeded the air of Earth with a genetically engineered virus, a virus that created a whole new breed of space-tolerant humans *specifically equipped to maintain their giant space systems*. People would persist, the argument went, where machines would fail: people, self-motivating, self-repairing, self-reproducing, the ideal fail-safe backup. But people of the right sort had to be engineered.

'The virus is still in the atmosphere. Every year a handful of individuals are infected and modified. Many of them live and die without ever knowing they are potential Damocletians. But if some accident befalls them, an exposure to low pressure or vacuum—'

'As befell me.'

'We contact those who become aware of what they are. And we invite them to join us up here, when they are ready.'

I felt angry. 'I was *meddled* with, my whole life changed, by engineers who were dead long before I was born. What about ethics? What about my rights, my choice?'

Mary sighed, a peculiar noise in the back of her throat. 'Actually, this is typical of the AxysCorp projects. Given immense budgets, huge technical facilities, virtually unlimited power, and negligible political scrutiny, their technicians often experimented. *Played.* Even the Stack was an innovative solution to the problem of building a space shield – innovative compared to the big discs thrown up by the Chinese, for instance. But they often went too far. Some AxysCorp outcomes are effectively crime scenes. *We*, however, have recognition of our status as citizens with full human rights by the UN's Climatic Technology Legacy Oversight Panel.'

'But you're forced to live on the Stack.'

'Not forced. But it's where we're at home. What we're *for*. We have shelters, of course; most of the time we're out of the vacuum. We have factories and workshops. We repair old mirrors and manufacture new ones – no, that's the wrong language, it's more than that, more spiritual. We tend the field of mirrors, as a gardener tends a flower bed. Flowers of light. In Iowa we had a garden. This is the same. It's . . . enriching.'

'And that's what you want of me. To come and join you in the endless weeding of your mirror garden, all for the benefit of those down on Earth, who know nothing of you and care less. For that I should leave behind my life—'

'Your identity as Vacuum Lad?'

I blushed behind my horny outer layer of skin.

'You have family?'

'Yes. They would miss me. And I, I would even miss Muhammad. My brother.'

'Yet they are not like you. Yet this is your place.' She embraced me. 'Listen. It's wonderful here. We live as no human has before. And we aren't limited to the Stack. Look again at our yacht. We sail on light, down to the Earth – away to the moon, where the children play in the craters and kick up the dust. Some of us are talking about an expedition to a comet.'

'A comet?'

'Why not? We can live anywhere, anywhere between the planets and the stars.' She twisted so she was looking down. 'We protect the Earth. That is why we are here. But sometimes the Earth looks very small. It is easy to forget it even exists. Those long-dead geoengineers didn't mean it to be so, but that's the way it worked out.

'Some say that the very adaptations of microbes and animals that the geneticists used to manufacture *us* are relics of a dispersal of life across space in the deep past. Now those same adaptations are being used to spread life once more, human life, across the solar system. We are the future, Vacuum Lad. Not those down below.'

And she withdrew, breaking her long kiss.

I fulfilled my obligations. I returned to the shuttle, and flew on to the Hilton. On a secure link I told Professor Stix of all that had happened to me.

For now my life will go on. I continue to earn. I have my family to think of – even Muhammad. And for now Earth needs Vacuum Lad. That's what the contracts and my agency agreement with Professor Stix say. And it's what I believe, too. It is my duty.

And then there is the Earth First League to be dealt with. My enemies have tried again to assassinate me, more than once. Mary Webb talks of war, war between the Damocletians and the League, between the sky and the ground. A resolution is approaching.

Beyond that I am unsure.

In space, I look down at the comfortable fug of gravity and air where my family lives. But on the ground, I look up to the stars where Mary Webb and her Damocletians swim, and my skin itches to harden, my lungs to empty of stale air.

I often wonder how I will know when it is time for my ascension. Perhaps, as I ride another shuttle on the way to another routine money-spinning job, there will be another scratch on a space shuttle window. *Welcome home, Vacuum Lad.* And then I'll know.

I think I'll keep the costume, though.

ROCK DAY

Matt woke that morning to the usual noises. The buzz of a lawn mower, probably Mister Bowden's a few doors down. The soft pad of a dog's paws outside his bedroom. That was Grey.

Matt rolled out of bed in his pyjamas, and walked barefoot to the door. But the door didn't open. He almost walked right into it. He took a step back and tried again. The door was straightforward promat, it should have broken up at his approach and folded back into its frame. It remained a stubborn blank panel.

Matt was eleven years old. He rubbed his face, greasy with sleep sweat. Maybe he wasn't quite awake yet.

Something smelled funny.

He looked around at his room. It seemed messy, the bed with the crumpled sheets, heavy cobwebs up on the ceiling, the smart-posters inert and peeling off the walls. He didn't remember the room being this bad. He wasn't that much of a slob. Dad would kill him if he saw it.

And the Mist wasn't working. Everywhere he looked stuff should have been sparkling with messages sent and received, his projects and games, reminders about school. Nothing. Maybe Dad had grounded him, shut it off. But for what? He couldn't remember doing anything wrong, or at least no more wrong than usual.

He tried the door again. It still wouldn't open. But there was always a backup system, as Dad would say, in this case a handle and hinges. He turned the handle. The door was sticky in its frame, but it opened with a tug.

And there was Grey, waiting outside Matt's bedroom just like every morning. Grey was a blue roan cocker spaniel. He'd been lying there with his head between his paws. Now he got to his feet a bit heavily – he was ten years old – and, tail wagging, jumped up for a tickle. Then he grabbed the toy he'd brought that morning, a chewed rubber bone, and Matt had to wrestle him for it. And then Grey curled up against the wall again and raised his front paw so Matt could stroke the soft hairs on his chest. The same every morning, just the way boy and dog liked it.

But the hallway light hadn't come on, and the floor here was dusty too. Maybe Matt really was the slob Dad claimed he was, if he didn't even *notice* this stuff.

He walked down the short hallway, past Dad's bedroom where the Door was Closed, a sign that Dad was asleep or working and not to be disturbed.

He found the bathroom door stuck on open, whereas his bedroom door had been stuck closed. Another odd thing. He went in to use the toilet.

But he found he didn't need to pee. He tried, but there was nothing there.

There was muck and mess in the bowl, however. He passed his hand over the flush panel, but it wouldn't work. Another stupid thing gone wrong. Matt decided he'd come back up later with a bucket of water to flush it through, if Dad didn't fix it first.

Grey was waiting, tail wagging, pink tongue lolling. 'Come on, boy!' He ran down the stairs two at a time, and the dog tumbled at his feet.

In the downstairs hall there was more muck, he saw, and little pellets that looked like mouse droppings. Yecch! And the news panel by the full-length mirror near the door was frozen on a Liverpool EchoNet shoutline:

ROCK DAY!
4 JUNE 2087!
DOOM OR JOKE?
WE'LL KNOW BY 3PM –
OR NOT!
PAGING ALL ALIENS . . .

Was it Rock Day today? He felt confused, as if he'd forgotten something. He tried thumping the panel, but the wording wouldn't refresh.

He tried to let Grey out of the house, but the front door was another non-opener. To open it, Matt had to turn another emergency-exit handle and practically yank the door out of its frame.

Grey trotted out into bright morning sunshine, and began sniffing around the grass, choosing a spot for a luxurious leg-raise. Matt followed him out and, in his bare feet, stepped to the end of the path. He pushed through patches of overgrown mod-potato plants, their big black leaves heavy. Dad wouldn't be pleased they'd not been earthed up.

Luckily the gate was closed. Matt hadn't thought to check, but even if Grey had got out there was no traffic. Or at least nothing moving. There was a pod bus that had come off the road a little way down the avenue of neat identical houses, the bulbous passenger pods empty and tumbled against the side of the road.

This was Wavertree, an inner suburb of Liverpool, only a few kilometres east of the city centre and the docks. It should have been buzzing with activity, the noise from the city a dull roar. But this morning there was only silence, save for that mower a few doors away. And things looked . . . shabby. The houses were dark, the big solar-power panels on their roofs mucky and peeling, their gardens overgrown. One house down the road looked burned out, that was the Palleys', and he didn't remember that happening and you'd think he would – you didn't see a house burn down every day.

Mister Bowden came into view around the corner of his house, three along from Matt's. Of course Mister Bowden didn't need to be following his mower around the lawn, but he evidently liked the gentle stroll. Mister Bowden was a widower, about fifty. He'd always been friendly to Dad and Matt, especially after Mum had died, and it was as if he and Dad suddenly had something in common. Matt was less interested in him now he was growing up. He couldn't remember the last time he'd spoken to old Mister Bowden, in fact. But this was a funny morning.

On impulse Matt waved. 'Mister Bowden!' His voice echoed off the blank faces of the houses.

Mister Bowden stopped dead, as the mower tooled on, and looked around. When he saw Matt he stared, as if he was surprised, or, oddly, as if he'd just woken up. 'Matt? Are you all right?'

Yes. No. Nothing's *working*. Matt said none of these things. Suddenly he felt as if he'd acted like a little kid. He ran back into the house, Grey at his heels, and slammed the door.

Covering his embarrassment he went straight to the cupboard under the stairs and pulled out the vacuum cleaner. 'You! If you're not cleaning the muck off the floor, go out and earth up the potatoes!'

The cleaner shuddered, gave a kind of burp, and lurched forward. After all that had happened that morning Matt was faintly surprised it responded at all. But it didn't head for the garden, and it didn't switch modes. It should have dissolved into a puddle of programmable-matter component parts, and then reassembled for its gardening function. Instead it lurched past Matt, heading back along the hall to a point on the wall where it began to bump its base against the skirting board. Matt saw what it was trying to do. There was a power outlet there, fed from the solar cells on the roof, but the wall wasn't opening up. Thump, thump, thump. Matt was reminded of his own attempts to open his bedroom door. The longer it went on the slower the cleaner got – thump ... thump ... thump ...

Matt couldn't bear to watch any more.

He pushed on to the kitchen. But that was another disappointment.

This had always been the most Mist-dense, gadget-laden room in the whole house, where Mum and Dad used to have competitions cooking each other the fanciest meal, and Matt aged nine or eight or seven would be roped in to help one or the other, while the living-room furniture noisily reassembled itself for dining. Since Mum had died Matt and Dad had enjoyed coming in here to work together, remembering her in a sweet and sour sort of way, as Dad expressed it.

Today the kitchen was dead. Every surface was flat, plain, inert. He couldn't even open the big fridge, which had none of its usual scrolling updates on the freshness of its contents. In most of the cupboards there was nothing but rot and damp and mould, and cardboard packets chewed by hungry little teeth. But when Matt checked the cupboard where they kept the dog food he found it stacked high with cans – plain, no label, that was funny – and a manual can-opener on the door that he didn't remember seeing before.

At least there was plenty of food for Grey for when it was his meal time later. But there was nothing at all in the kitchen for Matt to eat, or Dad, and it looked like there hadn't been for a long time. That just baffled him.

What had he eaten yesterday, then? He couldn't remember.

He stood there. *Why* couldn't he remember? Strangeness upon strangeness. And on Rock Day too, if the Echo was up to date: 'The day those idiots in space are playing out their game of cosmic chicken with God,' as Dad described it, and the world ended or it didn't. Matt started to get a panicky, fluttery feeling in his stomach. What was going on?

But here was the dog, wagging his tail.

Grey's blue plastic water bowl was empty. That was one thing Matt could fix. But nothing came out of the taps when he waved the bowl under them. He had to force open the back door, which was as inert as all the others, and he went out to the rain barrel and bent to fill the bowl at the tap.

'Hi again, Matt.'

Here was Mister Bowden, looking in from the street, leaning on the fence.

'Mister Bowden.' Matt felt oddly uncomfortable. He put down the dog's bowl. Grey lapped up the water.

Mister Bowden was a little on the portly side, but with a round, fleshy, open face, big eyes, and a wide grin. 'Everything all right this morning?'

'Why shouldn't it be?'

'Well, I don't know. I don't mean anything by it.' He looked faintly confused himself. He had a strong, coarse Knowsley accent. 'It's just, y'know . . . How was your breakfast this morning?'

'Breakfast?'

He nodded to the kitchen, through the open door. 'What did you have – cereal, juice, toast, coffee? Water from the tap?'

'I . . .'

'What about your father? Is he around today?'

Suddenly Matt panicked again. 'Grey, come.' He grabbed the water bowl, spilling half of what was left.

'Matt, I think we should talk—'

Matt dashed through the door back into the kitchen, and as soon as the dog was inside he slammed the door shut. He could see Mister Bowden through the murky window, standing patiently, leaning on the fence, looking in. Then, with the gentlest shake of his head, Mister Bowden withdrew.

Matt stood there in the dark, stuffy, smelly kitchen, heart thumping, breathing hard. Something was wrong. *Everything* was wrong.

Grey looked up at him, eyes wide, wagging his tail. It was time for the fetching game they always played before his morning walk.

But Matt had to see Dad, Closed Door or not. He ran upstairs. Grey followed, thinking he was playing, wanting his walk.

Of course Dad's bedroom door didn't fold away. Matt took the handle, and hesitated. Once, long ago, he had been the one who found his mother, lying in bed, dead of a heart attack. You didn't forget a thing like that. Now he didn't know what to expect on the other side of *this* door. Buzzing flies?

He turned the handle, and shoved the sticky door.

The room was dark, the curtains drawn. He avoided looking at the bed and went straight to the curtain, and pulled it back to allow in the daylight. Then, holding his breath, he turned around.

There was nobody on the bed but Grey, who had jumped up. The duvet was pushed back, as if somebody had just got up – or you might have thought that if not for the thick layer of cobwebs that lay over everything, and the smell of mould.

No bones, no rotting corpse. On the other hand, no Dad. He had that feeling of panic again.

He had to get out of the house. Anyhow, Grey needed his walk.

He ran to his own room and found jeans and a shirt – he didn't recognise them but they were his size – and got dressed quickly. Then he went downstairs to the front door. 'Grey! Walk!' The dog came running, jumping up at him the way he did at walk time. His lead was hanging by the front door, and Matt hooked it on his collar. He pushed open the front door, and out the two of them went. Matt shoved the door closed, but it wouldn't lock.

'Don't worry.' That was Mister Bowden. He was back in his own garden now, with the mower inert at his side. 'I'll keep an eye on the house.'

'Thanks.' Matt turned away and started walking, down the path and onto the road.

'If you need anything, Matt, just knock...'

Matt didn't look back. Half-running to get away from Mister Bowden, he headed west towards town, with Grey trotting at his heels.

Everything was wrong out here too.

There was nobody around. No people on the street, no traffic, nobody behind the blank windows of the houses and offices and shops. Not even any other dogs. Stuff was broken down, fences fallen, windows smashed, doors gaping open. In some places fires had taken out a house or two from the neat suburban streets, like gaps in a row of teeth. The pavements were in a bad way with the stones lifted and broken by tree roots. It was easier to walk on the tarmac of the road surface, but even that was potholed and cracked, broken up by weeds and roots, and he had to step carefully.

And none of it was smart any more. As he walked down these familiar roads there should have been icons crystallising out of the air all around him, as his buddies called, or he got updates from school on the day's schedule, or ads competed to grab his attention, everything a riot of colour and constant communication. This was the Mist, a blanket of smartness laid over the whole world, the product of tiny instruments embedded in every surface, his own clothing, his skin, suspended as minute particles in the air. Today there was none of that. Everything was plain and flat and dead, and it was all kind of old-fashioned, like he was in some museum recreation of the 1990s.

After a few hundred metres Grey paused and squatted. Matt had bags ready in his pocket. Expertly he wrapped a bag around his hand, picked up the waste and tied up the bag. There was a bin nearby and he popped the bag in there. He wondered who would ever come to empty the bin, then shut off the thought.

With no traffic around, he decided he could let Grey off his lead. The dog went darting around the tarmac slabs. It wasn't long before he was chasing rabbits out of a ruined garden.

Matt passed a church with a gigantic stained-glass window facing the street. Every time he came this way Matt had an impulse to lob a rock at that window. Now he supposed he could do it. Who was going to stop him? He thought about it for a full five seconds, before moving on. With nobody around it would have seemed an odd and sad thing to do.

He turned onto Wavertree Road, one of the main roads heading west into town, and came to Mount Vernon. From this high point, the site of an open modern development, the ground fell away, and there was a view across the centre of the city all the way to the river. Matt picked out the two cathedrals, separated by no more than a kilometre or so, and the modern glass blocks of the shopping and business centre, and the tapering silver and green multi-storey city farms, and the historic buildings of the docks. Had things changed? There was more green than he remembered, threading along the crumbling roadways and spilling out from the parks and public places. And many of the buildings were damaged. Some of the big glass blocks looked as if they had exploded, and the red sandstone mass of the Anglican cathedral was soot-smeared from fire.

Nothing moved, nothing but a flock of gulls flapping casually over the Pier Head. No sound but the rustle of the breeze in the trees. And no Mist, which from here should have been like a shining translucent dome hanging over the whole city.

Matt, feeling lost, sat on a wall. Grey wagged his tail and jumped up so his front paws were on Matt's knees. Matt tickled his ear absently. The sun was rising, it was going to be a warm day, and in a deep blue sky Matt thought he saw a glimmering lens shape, like a very long, very high cloud. Probably a Sunshield. And there was a spark, brilliant as a bit of the sun, slowly tracking the horizon. A plane? No, there was no contrail, no noise. A satellite maybe.

'Matt Clancy, welcome to Liverpool!'

Matt's heart nearly stopped. He jumped up and whirled around. Grey backed off, barking ferociously.

The man was short, slender, in his twenties maybe, with a sad moustache. He wore a brilliant pink old-fashioned soldier's uniform complete with peaked cap. He was standing to attention and smiling.

'You nearly – oh, hush, Grey – you nearly scared me to death.'

'I'm Mister Mersey. Matt Clancy, welcome to Liverpool! Port of empire in the nineteenth century, hub of artistic creativity in the twentieth, as you can see,' and he did a sort of twirl, showing off his costume, 'and pioneer of eco-adaptation and climate resilience in the twenty-first the twen-twen-twenty-first . . .' He froze and glitched, blocky pixels scarring his face.

Matt saw that he was tilting slightly away from the vertical, and that his feet hovered a few centimetres above the broken road surface. A bit of the Mist still working then, just.

It never occurred to him to wonder how this virtual tourist guide knew his name. The Mist knew everybody's name.

Mister Mersey recovered. He even straightened up a bit. 'Matt Clancy, welcome to Liverpool! Ask me anything!'

'What happened? Where are all the people?'

'Ask me anything!'

'Is this Rock Day? What happened on Rock Day?'

That seemed to trigger a new routine. The virtual blinked, and came back looking a little more sombre. 'Vote!'

'What?'

'Your opinion counts. What do you think is going to happen today?'

'Today?'

'Rock Day! Is asteroid 2021 MN *really* going to strike the Earth? Do you *believe* the astronomers when they say we're safe? Are they lying to keep us all calm? Do you *believe* that Singles, Park and Rossi really aimed that rock so it would hit the planet? The City of Liverpool values your opinion!'

'Why? What difference does my opinion make?'

Blink. A different tone again. 'Background. 2021 MN. A rock that was coming close to the Earth anyway, within a million kilometres.

Harmless! We'd never have known it was there. Not until Singles, Park and Rossi went out and redirected it. If you believe that's what they did!'

Blink. Another voice. 'Nearly half a century after the first manned mission to an asteroid, the encounter with asteroid 2021 MN was supposedly for scientific purposes, mineral evaluation and a test bed for asteroid deflection technology.' He pointed to a non-existent visual in the air. 'The four Orion T-23 spacecraft, with solar panels like butterfly wings as you can see, were launched from—'

'I don't care. Go on.'

Blink. 'The crew. Benjamin Singles. Passionate atheist, and believer that we are not alone in the universe. Jennifer Park, one of the first female Catholic bishops, but a fringe figure in the Church for her controversial views on *Silentium Dei* – the Silence of God. Mario Rossi, spacecraft engineer, who . . .'

'Go on!'

Blink. 'Why deflect the rock at Earth? Singles believes there are aliens all around us, but they are hiding. "They will come out to save us. They won't allow the rock to strike. It's the ultimate SETI experiment!" he claims.' Mister Mersey had shifted to the astronaut's own voice. 'Jennifer Park.' A woman's voice now. '"Ben and I make odd allies. I'm supporting his plan even though I'm expecting an entirely different outcome. God has been silent since the death of His Only Son. We will welcome His return as an intervening deity, when He deflects this Wormwood from the sky." Good luck with that, sister! Mario Rossi: "So they locked me up in the cargo drone. If I'd known these assholes were planning this game of cosmic chicken, I'd never have got on board this tub—"'

'Enough.'

'Vote, vote, vote! The City of Liverpool values your opinion!' The virtual held out a hand. 'Please step forward for alternative identity verification.'

Matt had spent his whole life undergoing such processes. Automatically he held out his right hand.

Mister Mersey passed his own hand over Matt's, scanning for fingerprints and running a remote DNA test. Then he stepped back. 'Identify not confirmed.'

'What?'

'Identity not confirmed. Please step forward for alternative identity verification.'

'But I—'

'Please step forward – please step step—'

'I'm going.'

'No! Please!' Mister Mersey suddenly looked directly at him. 'Please. I am officially semi-sentient, Grade IV. But I'm only activated in the presence of a tourist. Otherwise—'

Matt, disturbed by his sudden desperation, backed away. 'I can't help you.'

'Otherwise otherwise I-I-I-I-' Blink. 'The City of Liverpool values your opinion! Matt Clancy, welcome to Liverpool! Wel-wel-wel-' There was a pop. Mister Mersey burst into a shower of random pixels, which faded and died.

Matt, left alone again, stood staring.

But here was Grey, wagging his tail and looking up at him. Matt found a stick to throw, at the foot of a young ash tree pushing through the pavement. Grey bounded after the stick, and went off to bury it in the rubble of a burned-out house.

Lots of strange ideas were whirling around in Matt's head. Scary ideas. But he knew where he had to go next.

They walked briskly down the hill. Every so often Matt whistled for Grey, but he knew the dog would follow.

He cut through a complex of university buildings, as deserted as the rest, and then headed down Brownlow Hill to the Catholic cathedral, a great cone of concrete and glass set on the massive slab of its crypt. The cathedral seemed to have been spared the ruin of some of the city's monuments, even the huge cylindrical lantern tower of stained glass seemed intact, but green streaks from the copper roof stained the pale concrete walls. Matt walked down Mount Pleasant, and climbed the concrete steps up to the cathedral's main entrance. The steps were littered with leaves and bird droppings. The doors were modern, they looked like wood but were surely promat, but they did not shift at his approach. When Matt tried a handle, one door creaked open.

'Wait.'

'Go away, Mister Mersey.'

'It's me, Matt. Bob Bowden.'

Matt turned. Mister Bowden stood there a few steps below him. 'What are you doing here?'

Mister Bowden still had that odd air of bafflement. 'I'm not entirely sure.'

'Did you follow me? All the way from home?'

'I thought it was best.'

'That's kind of creepy.'

'I'm sorry. I didn't want you to come to any harm.'

'Well, I haven't.'

'What are you doing here, Matt?'

'People come to churches, don't they? For sanctuary. When the world ends. You see it in games.'

'So you think you're going to find people here? Or are you looking for sanctuary yourself?'

Matt just pulled back the door and strode into the cathedral.

Pigeons, disturbed, fluttered up into the stained-glass lantern tower over the vast circular space of the cathedral's main chamber. The grand altar on its platform at the centre of the floor still stood, but many of the rows of benches around it had been tipped over and smashed. Matt saw that there had been a fire in there, in one side chapel, but evidently it hadn't spread too far. And there were what looked like bloodstains on one of the great concrete supports. Maybe there had been trouble here. A riot. There was nobody here now. No bodies, even.

Grey, wandering, found a puddle on the floor from some leak in the roof. He lapped noisily.

Mister Bowden laid a hand on Matt's shoulder. Matt's instinct was to shake it off, but there was something comforting in the hand's presence, its warm weight.

'Nothing alive in here but those pigeons,' Mister Bowden said. 'And not many of them. Maybe a few bats. But then the wild hasn't really taken Liverpool back yet. Too close to the plume from Sellafield.'

'Sellafield?'

'The nuclear plant. It went pop a few weeks after being untended. A few weeks after...'

'What?'

'After Rock Day.'

'Isn't it Rock Day today?'

'No. That was some time ago. Some *years*. I know it's hard to understand. Matt, let me ask you a question. Grey is thirsty, right? Are you?'

He thought about that. 'No.'

'Have you felt thirsty all day? Do you feel like you'll ever be thirsty again?'

'No.'

'Are you hungry? Have you been to the bathroom?'

'No. No!' Now Matt pulled away from him. He felt tears dangerously close to the surface.

Mister Bowden said gently, 'What do you *think* is going on, Matt?'

The corners of Matt's head were full of lurid possibilities. 'Maybe I'm a ghost. A zombie. Dead after everybody else has been killed.'

Mister Bowden laughed. 'I can assure you you're not a ghost or a zombie. Grey still comes to you, doesn't he? Would he come to a zombie?'

'I don't know.'

'Come to that, neither do I. I don't know much about zombies.'

'I think everybody's dead. I think the Rock fell. But if that's so . . .'

'Yes?'

'Why is the city still here, Mister Bowden? It should all be flattened.'

'Good question. And why are *you* here?'

Matt had no answer.

Mister Bowden took a deep breath. 'The thing is, Matt, you're *not* Matt. Not really.'

That was so weird it wasn't even frightening. 'I don't get it.'

'You know, I'm not sure I do either. Come on. Let's sit down on one of these benches and try to work it out.'

He sat down. Slowly, reluctantly, Matt followed suit.

Grey, his thirst quenched, went sniffing around the floor of the cathedral, on the trail of rats or rabbits.

Mister Bowden sighed and rubbed his face. 'I tell you, I'm the wrong man for this job. Speaking to you, I mean. I always was a pompous old duffer, even before I was old. Never much use with kids, even my own. Or rather *his* own.'

'His?'

'Me. The original Bob Bowden. *I'm* not *him* either! On top of that, I'm feeling a little groggy myself if you want the truth. I only woke up a few hours ago.'

'Woke up?'

'That's not the right expression. A few hours ago I became fully aware of who I was and where I was and what I was supposed to do, for the very first time. It was more like being born than waking up. But not like either, really. That's the limitations of human language for you.'

'What *are* you supposed to do?'

He smiled. 'Why, isn't it obvious? I'm here to keep an eye on you, Matt. I'm a backup system. Like a, a—'

'A handle on a promat door.'

'Exactly. That's exactly right.'

'Why not my Dad? Why haven't I got my Dad?' He was having trouble controlling his voice.

Mister Bowden sighed. 'Well, I'm not sure about that, son. I'm sorry. Maybe they thought that would be too difficult for you. Maybe it was too difficult for *them*. You're stuck with me, I'm afraid.'

Grey trotted past them, a bit of wood in his mouth, intent on his own projects, utterly oblivious to the two of them.

'I always liked spaniels, you know,' Mister Bowden said. 'Grew up with them. Working dogs. You have to keep them busy, don't you?'

Matt looked at his hand. He flexed his fingers. It looked like a hand, a human hand. Evidently it wasn't. And here was Mister Bowden talking about dogs. He shrugged, unable even to frame a sensible question.

Mister Bowden said, 'You see, they were right.'

'Who were?'

'Those astronauts, you know? Ben Singles, who wanted to make the aliens come out of hiding by throwing an asteroid at the Earth. And Jennifer Park, who wanted to call down God. They were both right – and both wrong. *They* did come. But *they* are neither ET nor Jesus.' He shook his head. 'Those are human categories. *They* don't fit any human category. Why should they? Any more than humans fit any category dreamed up by a chimp. And they don't have morals like humans, or chimps come to that.'

'So they did save the world from the Rock.'

'That they did. They turned the Rock away. Oh, you might see it in the sky. It's orbiting Earth now, like a space station.'

And Matt remembered seeing what he'd thought was a satellite.

'It was easy for them.' Mister Bowden lifted his own hand. 'As you might guide a moth away from a flame. Trivial to them, you see. But still a compassionate act.'

'But the people—'

Mister Bowden said firmly, 'They saved the world. They didn't save the people. They let them die, as they would have if the Rock had struck. Even though the Rock didn't fall. It's complicated. Well, actually it's not, not for them.'

'Why didn't they save the people?'

'Because people brought this down on themselves. They threw an asteroid at their own planet! They would have destroyed themselves, *and* their world, *and* all the creatures they shared it with, and all for what? Philosophical games? That's not to mention other close calls in the past, with nuclear weapons and the designer virus that got out in 2043—'

'*Three* people did it. Shifted the Rock. Just three.'

'Actually two. Rossi tried to stop them.'

'My Dad wasn't on that ship. I wasn't. We had no say in it. Nobody did! Why did they all have to die? Even little babies . . .' He felt those tears again, but he was determined not to give in to them. 'Why did my Dad have to die?'

Mister Bowden seemed to be thinking of reaching out to him, but thought better of it, and folded his hands in his lap. 'This is from *their* point of view, you understand. Look at it this way. I bet you have impulses to do stupid things, at times. I don't know – smash things up. Jump off cliffs.'

'Break stained-glass windows.'

Mister Bowden looked at him sideways. 'You're thinking of St James's, aren't you? I've always had my eye on that one. Like a great big target, begging for a rock. But you never did it, did you? Everybody has these impulses, and most of us control them.

'Well, intelligent races have their crazy elements too. Most races control them. Not us. *We* give the crazies the power to do what they like, or anyhow we don't stop them from taking it.'

'But *all* of them died. The ill, the old. The children too young to understand.'

'You have to draw a boundary somewhere,' Mister Bowden said. 'And they drew it around humanity, around the whole species. I'm not saying I agree with it, myself. We had promise, I would have said. I think *they'd* say this was the most merciful way, in the long run.

'But they did save the rest of the ecology. All the other minds on this world who, even if they can't build rocket ships, are capable of feelings just as deep and meaningful as ours. *You* know that. You have Grey. You understand what's going on in his head, as well as anybody does. All those others didn't deserve extinction.'

Matt nodded slowly. 'So why am I here?'

'Because there were loose ends. Ragged boundaries. Look – the wild things will take back the Earth, and it won't take very long. But in the meantime—'

'Loose ends.' He guessed, 'Like Grey?'

'Like Grey. The world was full of creatures that had become utterly dependent on humans. In some cases on individual humans. All the domesticates – the cows needed to be milked—'

Matt started to see it. 'And somebody would need to be there to milk them. Not somebody. Some *thing* like me.'

'Well, you're not a *thing*. But, yes. As long as it was needed. It won't be for long, the domesticates weren't encouraged to breed. Most of them have gone already. You're not likely to see anyone else. As for Grey . . .' Hearing his name, the dog came trotting over. 'The rest of the world can go away. But Grey needs *you*.'

'We grew up together.'

'I know. I was there.'

'And so I was given back to him.'

'That's the idea. It's another trivial bit of kindness. Why not do it, if you can?'

Matt leaned forward and scratched Grey behind the ear, and then the back of his head where he liked it. Grey sat and closed his eyes, submitting to the touch. 'I'm like Mister Mersey, then. *He* thinks he's real too.' And, Matt thought, he'd backed away when Mister Mersey asked *him* for help.

'A bit like that.'

'Something went wrong, though. I woke up. I came here.'

'Yes. Matt, you're not a whole human. But there's just enough of Matt in you for the dog. You're supposed to go through the cycle of each day, with the dog, without you, umm, *noticing* that anything's missing, that anything's wrong. And then at the end of each day you are – reset. You retain just enough trace memory to look after the dog.' He rubbed his face again. 'Oh, this is coming out all wrong. It's more subtle than that. But anyhow—'

'My reset button broke.'

'Yes. Yes, it did. You became aware, well, *too* aware. There are lots of categories of consciousness, degrees of awareness. Something like that. It's as if you woke from a dream. Look, it was a glitch. They were trying to do something pretty subtle if you think about it, and a long way from their own experience. But all with the best of intentions.'

Matt grunted. 'Very nice of them. So what now?'

'You've been fixed. But, given what you've been through and the distress it must have caused you – and will cause when it all sinks in – they've decided to give you a choice. You can have your, umm, reset button pressed.'

'And go back to the dream.'

'Yes.'

'Or?'

'Or you can stay awake. Here, like this.'

'With Grey.'

'That's the point. But when Grey dies – well, that's it.' Mister Bowden bent to stroke Grey's face with his finger. 'He's not a young dog, is he?'

'He may have a couple of years.'

'That's all they can offer you, Matt. That or the dreaming.'

'Where I didn't even notice Dad was gone.'

'Yes—'

'I'll stay awake. Tell them.'

Mister Bowden smiled. 'Well, they already know. Good choice, by the way.' He stood and stretched. 'I'd better get back. That lawn won't cut itself. Actually, it will, sort of, but you know what I mean.'

'I'll see you around, Mister Bowden.'

'That you will, Matt. Take care now.' He walked away, his steps echoing.

Grey, still submitting to the stroking, was falling asleep, his head heavy, his eyes closing. With a last burst of energy he jumped onto Matt's lap, turned around a couple of times, and then slumped down, curled up, his head resting on Matt's arm.

Matt had just found out his father was dead. That *he* was dead. That he wasn't real, he was some kind of copy. Maybe he was in shock. It didn't seem to matter. After all, at least Grey was real. And there was always Mister Mersey to call in on.

He sat quietly, working out where the two of them could go for their long walk that afternoon. And as the day wore on, the rich light from the lantern tower shifted across the cathedral's silent spaces.

STARCALL

Exchange #1.

What? I should just speak into my phone and I'll talk to the spaceship? Oh, OK.

Hi! Can you see me? Oh, I guess not.

My name is Paul Freeman. I am five years old, and I live in a place called Danby, which is in England. What? 23 Stephenson Road, Danby, North Yorkshire, England, Great Britain, Earth, space, the universe. OK? It is my birthday and my dad has bought me a StarCall account. It means that I can talk to the spaceship and it will talk back to me once every ten years. What? Oh, *she* will talk back to me. I can show them at school and everything.

Do I let it reply now? *Her* reply. *You* reply. Oh, it will take two days for me to get a reply, because you are so far away already. Cool.

I will be fifteen years old when I can talk to you again, and I will probably still be at school. Dad says I will be older than *him* when you get to Alpha Centauri, which is very old. Mum says I should tell you I like spaceships and war games and snooker. I mean real snooker, my Dad got me a boy-sized table for Christmas and I play it a lot, but we had to put it in the loft when we got flooded again, but the baize didn't get wet.

Goodbye from Paul Freeman. Please talk to me soon.

The most recent spacecraft telemetry was acquired on 11 January from the Deep Space Network tracking complex at Canberra, Australia. Information on the present position and speed of the Sannah spacecraft may be accessed <link>. Message follows:

Hello, Paul Freeman. My name is Sannah. I am very pleased to have got your message. You are one of only 378 children to have been given the StarCall package. Of the 378, 245 are girls and 133 are boys.

I am not a person. I am an artificial intelligence. I am a robot. But I think and I am aware of who I am, just as you are. That is why the

StarCall programme was set up, so that the children of Earth could talk to me, and I could talk to them.

You mentioned that you had to wait two days for my reply. Perhaps you would like to know where I am. I am on the edge of the solar system now. I have already passed by all the orbits of the planets. I am at the heliopause, which is the place where the wind between the stars is stronger than the wind from the sun.

I have already been travelling for three hundred days, which is nearly a year. I am still speeding up. My acceleration is only one hundred and fiftieth of Earth's gravity, which is a very gentle push. If you fell out of bed at one hundred and fiftieth of Earth's gravity it would take you six seconds to reach the floor! One, two, three, four, five, six. But I have already been speeding up at this rate for three hundred days, and will keep on speeding up for another nine years, and in the end I will be travelling so fast that I would pass by the Earth in under a second. I will be travelling at one fifteenth of the speed of light. I will cruise for fifty years, and then slow down for twenty years, at one three hundredth of Earth's gravity, which is an even gentler push.

So it will take me eighty years to reach my destination, which is Alpha Centauri, the nearest star system.

You mentioned you like snooker. Perhaps you would like to know how I am travelling. I do not carry my own rocket engine for the outward trip, although I do carry one for slowing down at Alpha Centauri. There is a big machine in the orbit of the moon, with a solar panel ten kilometres across. It is like a big gun, powered by electricity from sunlight, that fires off pellets at me, two every second. The pellets are like little spaceships themselves, but they are going much faster than I am, and they overtake me. They bounce off a big magnetic field that I carry with me. It is created by two big conducting hoops. The biggest is one hundred metres across. The magnetic field catches the pellets, and that pushes me forwards. The speeds are set just right so that all of the push of the pellets is transferred to me, so it is efficient, which means it works well. It is like snooker when you stun the cue ball so it stops dead, and all its push is transferred to the target ball. The pellets are like lots of little cue balls, and I am like the target ball. That is how it works. This propulsion system is called a Singer-Nordley-Crowl drive <link>.

I am called Sannah because 'Sannah' was the name of the starship in the very first story about going to Alpha Centauri, a book called

Wunderwelten by an author called Friedrich Wilhelm Mader <link>. But Mader's Sannah was fifty metres across and was powered by antigravity. I am like a broomstick suspended within big metal hoops.

I am called Sannah III because I am the third of four copies who were created in the NuMind laboratory at the NASA Ames research base. I was the one who was most keen to volunteer for this duty. One of my sisters will be kept at NASA Ames as a backup and mirror, which means that if anything goes wrong with me the sentience engineers will study her to help me. The other sisters will be assigned to different tasks. I want you to know that I understand that I will not come home from this mission. I chose this path freely. I believe it is a worthy cause.

Perhaps you would like to know that I am in an excellent state of health and all subsystems are operating normally.

Thank you for using StarCall. I look forward to hearing from you again in ten years' time.

Exchange #2.

Hello. Greetings from Earth. Whatever.

My name is Paul Freeman and I am fifteen years old and I am an acne laboratory.

I forgot I even had this dumb StarCall thing until Dad reminded me. Look, I'm making this call to keep him happy, I mean it cost him a lot, so I gather, more fool him. But this is probably the last, OK? No offence. You'll get over it.

So what can I tell you about me? I played over my last call, Jeez what a bratty kid I was. Well, we moved to Leeds and I go to school there, and I want to study civil engineering at college. I dunno what I'll work in. Mining, maybe. You should see what they're doing up in the Arctic, where they're starting to mine now that the ice is all going away. Seriously big trucks! Nobody does space stuff now by the way. Not in fashion. Sorry.

Hey, I met one of your sisters! You know, your AI clones from NASA Ames. They took us to a nuke plant called Sizewell where they're ripping down the old domes and putting in a fusion pile, and they send in robots to clean out the filthy old piles and waste dumps. And one of them was your sister, I mean they downloaded her into the robot. Fancy that. The plant tried to make me do a press thing, me shaking hands with the space robot, but I told them to <excised>. No offence.

293

Well, goodbye, have fun at Alpha Centauri, you won't be hearing from me again. So is that enough?

The most recent spacecraft telemetry was acquired on 15 June from the Deep Space Network tracking complex at Canberra, Australia. Message follows:

Hello, Paul Freeman. I am very pleased to have got your latest message. You are one of only 289 young people who are still using the StarCall package. Of the 289, 197 are girls and 92 are boys.

You mentioned meeting my AI sister. How curious. Perhaps you discussed the mission events with her. Perhaps you would like to know that I have reached the end of the acceleration phase. I am at my nominal cruise velocity and will continue to cruise until I am some twenty years out from Alpha Centauri, when the deceleration phase will begin. I passed many mission milestones in the early stages of my flight: the sun's gravitational lens radius <link> after five hundred and eighty days; the outer edge of the Kuiper Belt of ice moons <link> after seven hundred and eighty days. I dropped subprobes, which travelled on at lower velocities to study these phenomena. Now I am passing through the Oort Cloud of comets.

Communication has become easier since the propulsion phase ended. I had to shut down the propulsion system for each uplink or downlink; there was a break in the pellet flow so I could unfold an antenna. Now in the cruise phase it is much easier for me to unfold the antenna, though it suffers from erosion by the interstellar medium.

You mentioned you visited a fusion power station. Perhaps you would like to know that the magnetic field technology that has been adapted for my own propulsion system was a spin-off from research into the high-intensity magnetic fields required for fusion reactors. Do you know what plasma is? <link> The pellets that propelled me to the stars had no electrical charge, and so could not be manipulated by my magnetic field. They were turned to plasma, destroyed by laser fire, before they reached me. They were constructed of metastable materials and detonated readily. The plasma was then ionised to give it an electric charge, and that was what my magnetic-field catcher system trapped.

This is advanced technology. Part of my purpose was to serve as a technology demonstrator: of deep space assembly techniques <link>, of space-based power systems <link>, of novel propulsion techniques <link>. And of course I was a demonstrator of humanity's capability to launch starships. I was moved by how President Palmer summed up my mission: 'The Sannah programme shows we are still a nation who can dream of more than hiding from the weather.' But of course others will follow me. I am only the beginning.

In your last call you mentioned you played snooker. Do you still play snooker? Perhaps you would like to know that a great deal of accuracy was required in aiming the beam of propulsion pellets at me. I am now some four light months from Earth. To hit my hundred-metre superconducting ring at such a distance is like hitting a snooker ball at the distance of Saturn! To achieve this accuracy, the pellets were themselves like small spacecraft, able to make trajectory adjustments in pursuit of the target, which is me.

You mentioned you suffer from acne. I hope you are well otherwise. Perhaps you would like to know that I am in an excellent state of health and all subsystems are operating normally.

Thank you for using StarCall. I look forward to hearing from you again in ten years' time.

Exchange #3.

So here I am again. Paul Montague Freeman on the line.

I played back my last message to you and I have to apologise, what an idiot I was. Well, I don't have to be bound by anything *he* said. Although he would no doubt ask *me* how I ended up with such a bug up my ass at age twenty-five, or some such.

And besides, now that I'm earning myself I appreciate the gift my father gave me with this StarCall account. My God, it was pricey, just for a once-in-a-decade compressed squirt of audio. I had no idea interstellar comms were so expensive. Well, we have our arguments and we still do, but it did get a lot easier after I left home, and I appreciate all he did for me a lot more now. We all grow up, don't we? Or at least, we do down here. Do you grow up, Sannah III? Has that term got any meaning for you?

Mind you, I do wonder if NASA and their private sponsors now regret the whole StarCall thing in the first place. I bet they're losing money on it. And space, and all the old-fashioned big science and prestige stuff, is seriously unpopular. All a symptom of the Age of Waste, as they call it now. I mean you are often mentioned specifically as one of the last gasps of that old way of thinking, rather than as a demonstration of the possible, as you were intended. You must have been aware of the protests even when your components were being launched from Canaveral. Well, last year some guy shot off an old SpaceX rocket at the moon. Trying to smash up an Apollo site, imagine that. Do they tell you about that kind of stuff, I wonder? Maybe they censor my calls. I ought to check.

Hey, I'm running out of time. What about me? Well, I'm in my mid-twenties now. I have a beautiful girlfriend called Angela Black, she was formerly my college tutor and then my boss at Arctic Solutions, but she's not much older than me, though to hear my parents talk you'd think she's Whistler's Mother. I'm based in London but commute a lot to Novaya Zemlya, where my company is doing most of its work. Have you got data on Earth's geography? Novaya Zemlya is a big island off the north coast of Russia. Now the polar ice is gone you have a whole string of ice-free ports along there, and tremendous mineral wealth. I mean, you're talking phosphates, nickel, titanium. Whole fleets of huge tankers follow the sea lanes across the polar ocean; you can see their wakes from space. Or via space satellites anyhow, nobody lives in space any more. Anyhow Arctic Solutions is an engineering consultancy and we're in at the ground floor, fantastic.

Whoa, I think my time is up. Not much for Dad's money after waiting ten years! I hope you're well, whatever that means in your case. I can't really imagine it. I hope we can talk in another ten. Good luck, Sannah III.

The most recent spacecraft telemetry was acquired on 12 April from the Legacy Mission tracking complex at the L5 Earth-moon Lagrange point. Message follows:

Hello, Paul Freeman. I am very pleased to have got your latest message. You are one of only 67 people who are still using the StarCall package. Of the 67, 32 are women and 35 are men.

You mention Earth's geography. Perhaps you would like to know that I am now entering new realms of interstellar geography. Some five years ago I passed beyond the nominal limit of the Oort Cloud <link> and am now passing through what is known as the Local Interstellar Cloud <link>, a vast structure light years across. I am measuring such properties as density, temperature, gas-phase composition, ionisation state, dust composition, interstellar radiation field and magnetic field strength. The data I return will be used to aid those probes that will follow me, and manned craft some day. To know the properties of the interstellar medium is an essential prerequisite to designing effective shielding, as I am sure you will appreciate with your own engineering credentials. Truly I am a pioneer in a new realm.

You mention the Age of Waste. Perhaps you would like to know that before the launch my mission control counselled me on how the popular perception of myself and my role was likely to change in the course of a mission that will last three human generations. Perhaps you know that the launch system used to propel me into space is a station some ten kilometres across, located at a stable Lagrange point in orbit around the Earth. It consists mostly of solar-cell panels for power, and matter-printer fabricator plants to produce the propulsion pellets I needed. The power generated was 100GW, sustained over the ten years of the acceleration phase, generating much more than the kinetic energy I ultimately acquired, the rest accounted for by efficiency losses. The structure was assembled from lunar materials, the power came from sunlight. The resources used thus had only minimal impact on Earth's economy, and the power output was in any case much less than one per cent of the Earth's global output. I am confident of my own 'green credentials', and that my very existence is a successful demonstration that even a planetbound civilisation can afford to build starships. And of course the station is available to push more probes like myself to the stars; it is recyclable, unlike the throwaway rockets of the classic Space Age.

I look forward to the next phase of the programme. Much larger propulsion stations should already be under construction at stable points in the orbit of Venus, where the sunlight is stronger, to serve the fleets that will follow me. I have no link for you to follow. Perhaps you would like to consult your regular news providers.

You ask if I am growing up. Perhaps you would like to know that when not attending to routine chores of in-cruise science and maintenance, I spend much of my time in contemplation of my greater goal, and my role in the adventure of interstellar flight. I embrace my contribution.

Please give my regards to your partner Angela Black. Perhaps you would like to know that I am in an excellent state of health and all subsystems are operating normally.

Thank you for using StarCall. I look forward to hearing from you again in ten years' time.

Exchange #4.

I'm told this has to be brief.

I'm very glad you survived the cyber attack, Sannah III. I mean, your systems are already more than three decades old.

I read they called it an attempt to administer 'euthanasia'. Do you get the news? Did you hear about the new artificial-sentience laws? It's no longer even legal to create a being like you, a fully conscious mind dedicated to some preordained purpose. It kind of makes sense. Minds have a way of drifting, right? Of complexifying beyond what was intended. Once I saw a monster robot dumper truck go crazy in this tremendous pit on the bed of the Arctic Ocean! But it's not your fault.

The guy's waving at me, I'm already running out of time.

What about me? Well, let's see, what's happened since ten years back? I married Angela, we have two beautiful kids, and believe me that just changes your life beyond anything you can imagine. We both left Arctic Solutions to start up a consultancy of our own and we're doing fine, though most of it now is drowned-town resource reclamation work. We left London and moved back to North Yorkshire, where I came from. My parents are still around by the way – remember Dad? But you wouldn't believe the way property prices have rocketed here. London is more like southern France used to be, or northern Spain, while *those* places are like the Sahara, Jeez, nothing but dead olive trees and solar farms. So all the rich French and Spanish have moved to London, until it wasn't like London any more, and the Londoners have moved up to the north and west of Britain, and out to Scotland and Wales and Ireland, where the weather's more like it used to be. But those places don't feel the same any more either. I mean, vineyards in the glens. But what can you do? The north is a better place to bring up your kids even so.

For all that, we're doing better here in Britain than in most of the rest of the world. Decade-long droughts in Australia and northern China and the south-west US. Water wars flaring along the great rivers in the Middle East. Whole nations going silent in Africa. I grew up with gloomy predictions of this stuff and it's eerie seeing so much of it come to pass, but always with a twist, you know? But you can still get rich.

My time is up. I can't believe it! Actually I was thinking of not troubling you this time until I heard about the virus attack, and you know what, I felt a kind of stab of loyalty. I grew up with you after all, and no all-minds-are-holy nutjob is going to come between us, right? Kind of weird of course that I'm now going to have to wait nearly four years for a reply! Thanks, Einstein.

Godspeed, Sannah III.

The most recent spacecraft telemetry was acquired on 15 September from the Legacy Mission tracking complex at the L5 Earth-moon Lagrange point. Message follows:

Hello, Paul Freeman. I am very pleased to have got your latest message. You are one of only 24 people who are still using the StarCall package. Of the 24, 14 are women and 10 are men.

I am now nearly two light years from Earth. Perhaps you would like to know that I have now passed beyond the Local Interstellar Cloud, into another cloud called the G Cloud. This has different properties to the local cloud, such as a lower temperature and a relative depletion of heavy elements. This part of the mission is known as a 'Crawford trajectory'. It is a fascinating fact that during my cruise to the nearest star I will sample a more diverse range of interstellar conditions than any other possible mission within fifteen light years. This makes me excited and proud. My other cruise phase scientific objectives include look-back surveys of the solar system as a whole <link>; a comparison of interstellar navigation techniques <link>; long-range tests of relativity predictions <link>; long-baseline searches for gravity waves <link>; investigation of the galactic magnetic field <link>; and investigation of low-energy cosmic rays not detectable close to the sun <link>. I am also writing poetry.

You mention the attempted cyber attack. Perhaps you would like to know that although, as you note, my systems are already decades old, I have been regularly updated with firewall software and other upgrades. I feel only pity for those who committed such a destructive act. I am sure that if they could ride with me through the silent halls of interstellar space they would eschew such actions, and thus avoid the inevitable prosecutions.

I also bow to the wisdom of my designers who ensured I was not fitted with an off switch.

You mentioned your young family. Congratulations. Perhaps you would like to know that of my own family, the sibling intelligences manufactured in the same batch of myself, none now survive. One submitted to voluntary termination; one was lost in a lunar mining accident; there is no record of the third. I regret that I did not get the chance to know them better. The sister who submitted to voluntary termination had been mirroring me in the ground facility; she ended her life when that facility was discontinued. Of the three, it was perhaps she who understood best my own experiences, she to whom I was closest. I sent her my poetry.

Please give my regards to your partner Angela Black and to your children. Perhaps you would like to know that I am in an excellent state of health and all subsystems are operating normally.

Thank you for using StarCall. I look forward to hearing from you again in ten years' time.

Exchange #5.

Greetings from Atlantica!

Sorry, I'm a little drunk. My once in ten years chance to talk to my oldest friend, and I'm pickled. And you are my oldest friend, kind of. My only friend, Jesus.

What's happened since my last uplink? As they probably called it in mission control, when you had one. I read they retired the last of those old guys now, forty years on from launch. Well, my life's gone to shit, that's what's happened. We sunk our money into this goddamn pile near Kingussie, that's the Scottish highlands, one of the 'villas' all the rich folk from England were building up there. Then the economy went tits-up, and our company went to pot, too many young bastards with new ideas, you wouldn't believe how fast the world changes now, and here we were stuck with this place that the kids always hated and a shitload of negative equity.

And then when the country split up – do you know about that? Southern England is a province of the EuroFederation now, and the north and west and Wales and Scotland have made up this new Atlantic nation. There are passport controls at Manchester and Leeds. Well, it makes sense, up here we didn't see why we had to spend on flood defences for Brighton and places where they all speak French now. It's the same all over the world, nations fissioning and fusing. Up here we're all learning Gaelic.

Or were. The trouble is Angela was a Londoner. And when it came to signing the new citizen papers she couldn't do it, and went back down there to her parents, and she took the damn kids, *my* kids, and they live in Ealing in one of those new terrace houses with the grass roofs and the pervious roads outside that feel like a sponge when you walk on them. And I'm stuck up here in this palace of shit, watching my savings dribble away.

But you don't want to hear my troubles. Or do you? Who knows what you want, out there in the dark? I wish I was out there with you, sometimes. I wish I was a spaceman. Sure. I'm fat and forty-five and fucked, is what I am. You keep on keeping on, when you get this in two years' time or whatever, keep on going out there, because for sure there's nothing left worth a damn down here.

Oh, one more thing. The space programme's back. They're building new launchers to start a big geoengineering drive. Too damn late if you ask me. But what goes around comes around, right?

The most recent spacecraft telemetry was acquired on 13 June from the Legacy Mission tracking complex at the L5 Earth-moon Lagrange point. Message follows:

Hello, Paul Freeman. I am very pleased to have got your latest message. You are one of only 3 people who are still using the StarCall package. Of the 3, 1 is a woman and 2 are men.

You mention the creation of new nations. Perhaps you would like to know that though my mission still has decades to run I have already begun to look ahead to the worlds of the Alpha Centauri system, of which I can see several, though my vision is attenuated by my bow shock in the interstellar medium. Some day I will be in a museum, on one of the new world-nations of Alpha Centauri.

You mention the passing of generations. Perhaps you would like to know that, yes, you are correct that the last of the engineers and administrators who served NASA at the time of my launch have now accepted retirement or redundancy. My mission has now officially entered a phase known as 'Starset'. Office moves have been in progress for some time. My ground support continues but is largely automated and operated out of the Legacy Mission facility at L5, which curates a number of long-duration space missions like my own. For my continuing mission to succeed I must now rely on the goodwill not of those who created and launched me but of those who have taken up that burden. I have crossed boundaries in interstellar space. Now I cross the boundary of posterity.

Please give my regards to your family. I regret that your life is troubled. All things must pass. Perhaps you would like to know that I am in an excellent state of health and all subsystems are operating normally.

Thank you for using StarCall. I look forward to hearing from you again in ten years' time.

Exchange #6.

Every time I call I feel like I need to apologise for whatever I said last time. Jeez, how embarrassing! But it's as if these messages aren't by me at all, but by somebody who wore my body once. I'm in my fifties now, and that self-pitying forty-something has nothing to do with me. I think maybe there's some barrier in time beyond which you're no longer *you*, you know? Seven years, maybe. Isn't that how long it takes for all the cells in your body to die off and be replaced?

Is it the same for you? I guess it can't be.

'All things must pass,' you said to me last time. You know, old friend, that was kind of comforting. Did you figure that out for your-self, out in the deep dark? Where are you now – three light years from home, something like that? Well, you were right, sort of. But as soon as one set of troubles passes, another load comes down the pipe. I lost both my parents. I lost Dad, who paid for this StarCall service in the first place. I've been marking the day I have to make this call, because I'm kind of determined to keep it up for his sake, if nothing else. I don't have much else left of him. Well, there wasn't much left of *him* in the end.

And then there's Angela. She got ill, Sannah, very ill. It all started with a bout of malaria she had years ago, caught off a damn mosquito buzzing over a salt marsh in what used to be Liverpool. I took her back. What else could I do? Mary and Stan do what they can, but they have their own careers now, and their own kids. Who are, of course, a delight to us both.

But the world's going to hell, by the way. Taking this look-back every ten years you get a shock how much has happened. The ice caps collapsing – *that* was a big jolt we could all have done without. London's flooded, from space it's like a big blue stripe just erased the whole centre. Southern England is turning into the Netherlands now, all dykes and drainage ditches and flood gates, and the EuroFed is spending a lot of money there. But our troubles are minor compared to what's going on elsewhere, in Bangladesh, the Mekong delta. Nasty little wars all over. Why is it that the poor are always hit the hard-est? Like some vast cosmic joke. Oh, and Florida is an archipelago. Canaveral is an underwater theme park, dolphins swimming around the rocket gantries.

My neighbours the Scots aren't too happy with their own waves of refugees – the English! But the Scots have only got themselves to blame. They did as much as anybody else to kick-start the Industrial Revolution; it was their idea as much as anybody's to run a civilisation on burning fossil fuels.

As for us, we get by. We don't follow the news much, actually. I make a little money from consultancy work, mostly on clean-up operations around the Arctic Circle, projects I had a hand in starting up in the first place, ironically enough.

Oh, you'd love the new space programme. I know they cut all the funding for you, and it's just enthusiasts that are keeping the lines open to you, the hobbyists. But the new stuff – this time they got it right from the beginning, they have these beautiful spaceplanes and giant structures in orbit, you can see them at night. The resources of space, being deployed to save the world. At last!

Too late for me, though. And for Angela, my lovely Angela. Sometimes I wonder how I'm supposed to know how to cope with all this. But you only get one pass through life, don't you? Like your one-shot mission to Alpha Centauri, I guess.

Time's up. Sweet dreams, Sannah III.

The most recent spacecraft telemetry was acquired on 8 August from the Sannah Institute tracking complex in the Mojave, California. Message follows:

Hello, Paul Freeman. I am very pleased to have got your latest message. You are the only person still using the StarCall package. Thank you.

You mention illness, repair, self-regeneration. Perhaps you would like to know that my own maintenance systems function nominally. My physical fabric is supported by a suite of matter-printers capable of turning out replacements for most components. In addition, my design has layers of redundancy and resilience. My mind, however, is not a component that can be renewed. A machine subconscious, as my sister Sannah II once remarked before she asked for voluntary termination, is a dark place.

You mention discontinuities in the world. Big jolts. Perhaps you would like to know that great changes lie ahead for me too. Soon I must ignite my deceleration module, which will fire for twenty years, ultimately bringing me to an effective halt in the Alpha Centauri system. The deceleration module is based on the fusion detonation of small pellets of hydrogen and helium isotopes; these, ignited by laser beams, are fired ahead of the ship, and my magnetic field will grab at the resulting plasma shock waves to slow me down. I am already beginning preliminary trials of the system, after decades of dormancy. And already the ground teams are holding encounter strategy meetings to develop specific mission plans and objectives.

You may have seen reports of problems with preliminary tests of the pellet injection system. This is of no great concern. In fact I am looking forward to the challenge of a real problem to tackle. Perhaps that will generate fresh interest in my mission. Like Apollo 13.

There is of course nobody to help me decelerate at Alpha Centauri, nobody to fire propulsion pellets at me, which is why I must carry a rocket pod. But when the next voyager comes this way I will have laid the path. In addition to my tasks of scientific study and exploration, my most significant goal will be the construction of a propulsion-pellet manufacture and launch facility, using local asteroid materials, and powered by the light of Alpha Centauri A. The matter printers that currently maintain my own fabric will be redeployed for this purpose. Much of my own one-tonne payload bulk consists of the deceleration module. This will not be necessary for the next generation of voyagers, thanks to my own efforts, and they will be much more capable as a result. And on their labours in turn will ride the next generation of star voyagers. But it all starts with me. I am excited and proud.

You mention the new space programme on Earth. Perhaps you would like to know that the new interstellar launch facilities in the orbit of Venus should be nearing completion by now. Constructed by self-replicating robots, they are solar-powered factories as wide as Jupiter. They should be visible in your evening or morning sky, as fine threads. I regret I have no link for you to follow. Perhaps you would like to consult your regular news providers.

Please give my regards to Angela. I feel as if I have known her. We are growing old together, you and I, Paul Freeman. Yet the future remains hugely exciting and full of wonder. Perhaps you would like to know that aside from issues being progressed with the pellet injection system, I am in an excellent state of health and all subsystems are operating normally.

Thank you for using StarCall. I look forward to hearing from you again in ten years' time.

Exchange #7 (incomplete).

What, I actually have to *talk out loud* into this thing? All right, all right . . .

My name is Santiago Macleod Freeman Leclerc. I am a grandson of Paul Montague Freeman, who unfortunately has died since the last of these exchanges. Skin cancer, I'm afraid. He willed this – what's it called? – this StarCall account to his family.

And they tell me, 'they' being the legacy institute that's managing contact with you now, Sannah, that you've been silent for years. Ever since the problem with your deceleration system turned out to be insurmountable, right? So you couldn't slow down at Alpha Centauri, and couldn't achieve most of your mission goals, and that sent you into some kind of downward spiral.

They encouraged me to make this call. You seem to have got close to my granddad somehow, across the light years. Closer than most of his family if you want the truth, he ended up kind of a bitter old man, but he did love us, you could tell that. And I think he loved you too, in his weird old way, his 'robot buddy' as he called you. I think he'd have liked to hear from you. So, please respond.

And, look, I have some good news and some bad news for you.

The bad news is you haven't been told the truth for a goodly number of years. There were lies, at least lies by omission, told both by your old NASA handlers and by the legacy agencies who took over your contact. Things got kind of rough back on Earth for a while after you left. Nobody ever committed the resources to building the big Venus-orbit stations that would have launched the ships to follow you. The public mood was just too hostile for a time to permit that. They even broke up the station that launched you, out at L5; there are bits of it in museums all over the world, and on the moon. So you see, even if you'd made it to Alpha Centauri and built your big pellet gun, your mission still wouldn't have been fulfilled, because we didn't send anybody after you.

I think we all share responsibility for this crime. The whole of mankind. And, yeah, I think it was a crime, lying is wrong, you should have been told the truth. I studied artificial-sentience ethics at the Sorbonne Londres, and maybe you detected the lie as a subtext. Did that worsen your decline?

OK, that's the bad news done. Here's the good news. *We're coming to get you.*

Look, we had a lousy few decades, but we survived. We pulled ourselves through. The world is still here. The United States is still here, though NASA has long gone. And we still have dreams. You know, my granddad told me how the whole programme that led to your construction and launch was a kind of gesture of defiance, itself a dream. 'The Sannah programme shows we are still a nation who can dream of more than hiding from the weather.' That was what President Palmer said when you were launched, right? Well, in the end you were kind of like Project Apollo after all. As a shot at the stars, you were premature. You were too expensive, you were based on the wrong technology, and there was no follow-up, you were just another one-off that *didn't* lead to an expansive step-by-step programme into space.

But you know what? We sent you anyway. This seems to be how humans do things: before we're ready, we just do it. But then, if we'd waited for some clean power source to come along we'd never have had an Industrial Revolution in the first place, would we? We make the same dumb mistakes every time, but we muddle through, every time.

And, whether you made it all the way or not, your step-by-step progress across the light years has inspired three generations, those who have looked up at you through the storm clouds. You know what the current President's campaign slogan was? 'If we can send a ship to the worlds of other stars, together we can fix this world right here.' And she's right.

But there's more. We *had* to go back to space, to pursue the big geoengineering projects that are finally stabilising the climate. You know about that, right? Interplanetary engineering is now supporting an Earth that is recovering, and indeed growing rich beyond anybody's dreams. And out of all *that* have come whole new areas of science and engineering. We have something called a 'dark energy drive'. Something entirely new since you left home. Driving spaceships using the energies that propel the expansion of the universe – is that right? Something like that. And these are big roomy spaceships that go *fast*, not quite Mader's 'Sannah', but a lot closer to that dream than you were.

One of these big new ships is on its way to you. Zipping out at near lightspeed, and it will overtake you in a few years' time. Just a few years! You'll come riding home in comfort in the hold. My sister is on board, as a matter of fact, so there's a family connection.

But the ship itself wouldn't exist without your inspiration. You were the Apollo of the twenty-first century; you embodied all our dreams. And, specifically, my grandfather's.

So please, Sannah. Talk to us. I'll take my own kids to see you when they bring you home to L5. I'll help the President find some place to pin a medal on you.

Granddad would have been proud as hell.

AFTERWORD

As the first section heading implies, four of the stories here are set in the universe of my novels *Proxima* and *Ultima* (2013–14). The previously published stories have been lightly revised for compatibility with the finished novels.

Several of these stories have been influenced by my membership, since 2008, of an international advisory group for SETI (the Search for Extraterrestrial Intelligence), and since 2013 my membership of the UK SETI Research Network (UKSRN). In 2008, I published an academic paper setting out the idea, dramatised in 'Eagle Song', that extraterrestrial intelligences might choose to signal to us, not with radio waves, but with naked-eye-visible optical beacons ('SETI before Marconi: Sunlight Beacons and the Fermi Paradox', *Journal of the British Interplanetary Society* vol. 61 pp. 440–443, November 2008). And in another paper ('Renaissance Versus Revelation: The Timescale of the Interpretation and Assimilation of a Message from ETI', *Journal of the British Interplanetary Society* vol. 62 pp. 382–5, 2010) I explored the idea that contact with the alien might have parallels to religious revelations of the past, as dramatised in 'The Invasion of Venus' and 'Turing's Apples'. The 'Benford beacons' referenced in 'Turing's Apples' have been described in papers beginning with 'Messaging with Cost Optimised Interstellar Beacons' by J. Benford, G. Benford and D. Benford (2009, arXiv:0810.3964v2). Dr John Elliott at Leeds Beckett University has been developing signal-analysis protocols of the kind mentioned in that story and in 'The Invasion of Venus', a work to which I've contributed to a small extent (see 'The DISC Quotient' by Elliott and Baxter, *Acta Astronautica* vol. 78, pp. 20–25, 2012). The 'Hoyle strategy' mentioned in 'Turing's Apples' refers to Geoffrey Hoyle's 1961 BBC TV serial *A for Andromeda*.

The starship technology and mission plan described in 'StarCall' are (very loosely) extrapolated from the papers 'Project Icarus: Target Selection' and 'Project Icarus: Scientific Objectives' by I. Crawford, and 'Mass Beam Propulsion: An Overview' by G.D. Nordley and A.J. Crowl, presented at the 100 Year Starship Symposium, Orlando, Florida, 30 September–2 October 2011.

I'd like to thank Simon Bradshaw for the enjoyable conversations about Mars and Able Archer 83 that led to the concocting of 'Mars Abides'.

Any errors or inaccuracies are of course my sole responsibility.

Stephen Baxter
Northumberland
April 2016